*Pride and Prejudice
and Zombies*

"A FEW OF THE GUESTS, WHO HAD THE MISFORTUNE OF BEING TOO
NEAR THE WINDOWS, WERE SEIZED AND FEASTED ON AT ONCE."

PRIDE AND PREJUDICE AND ZOMBIES

THE CLASSIC REGENCY ROMANCE—
NOW WITH ULTRAVIOLENT ZOMBIE MAYHEM

BY JANE AUSTEN AND SETH GRAHAME-SMITH

QUIRK BOOKS

PHILADELPHIA

Library of Congress Cataloging in Publication Number: 2008937609
ISBN: 978-1-59474-334-4
Printed in Canada
This book was printed on 100% post-consumer recycled paper
Typeset in Bembo

Cover zombification and design by Doogie Horner
Cover art courtesy the Bridgeman Art Library International Ltd.
Interior illustrations by Philip Smiley
Production management by John J. McGurk

Distributed in North America by Chronicle Books
680 Second Street
San Francisco, CA 94107

10 9 8

Quirk Books
215 Church Street
Philadelphia, PA 19106
www.quirkbooks.com

LIST OF ILLUSTRATIONS

CHAPTER 1

IT IS A TRUTH universally acknowledged that a zombie in possession of brains must be in want of more brains. Never was this truth more plain than during the recent attacks at Netherfield Park, in which a household of eighteen was slaughtered and consumed by a horde of the living dead.

"My dear Mr. Bennet," said his lady to him one day, "have you heard that Netherfield Park is occupied again?"

Mr. Bennet replied that he had not and went about his morning business of dagger sharpening and musket polishing—for attacks by the unmentionables had grown alarmingly frequent in recent weeks.

"But it is," returned she.

Mr. Bennet made no answer.

"Do you not want to know who has taken it?" cried his wife impatiently.

"Woman, I am attending to my musket. Prattle on if you must, but leave me to the defense of my estate!"

This was invitation enough.

"Why, my dear, Mrs. Long says that Netherfield is taken by a young man of large fortune; that he escaped London in a chaise and four just as the strange plague broke through the Manchester line."

"What is his name?"

"Bingley. A single man of four or five thousand a year. What a fine thing for our girls!"

"How so? Can he train them in the ways of swordsmanship and musketry?"

"How can you be so tiresome! You must know that I am thinking of his marrying one of them."

"Marriage? In times such as these? Surely this Bingley has no such designs."

"Designs! Nonsense, how can you talk so! It is very likely that he *may* fall in love with one of them, and therefore you must visit him as soon as he comes."

"I see no occasion for that. And besides, we mustn't busy the roads more than is absolutely necessary, lest we lose more horses and carriages to the unfortunate scourge that has so troubled our beloved Hertfordshire of late."

"But consider your daughters!"

"I am considering them, silly woman! I would much prefer their minds be engaged in the deadly arts than clouded with dreams of marriage and fortune, as your own so clearly is! Go and see this Bingley if you must, though I warn you that none of our girls has much to recommend them; they are all silly and ignorant like their mother, the exception being Lizzy, who has something more of the killer instinct than her sisters."

"Mr. Bennet, how can you abuse your own children in such a way? You take delight in vexing me. You have no compassion for my poor nerves."

"You mistake me, my dear. I have a high respect for your nerves. They are my old friends. I have heard of little else these last twenty years at least."

Mr. Bennet was so odd a mixture of quick parts, sarcastic humour, reserve, and self-discipline, that the experience of three-and-twenty years had been insufficient to make his wife understand his character. *Her* mind was less difficult to develop. She was a woman of mean understanding, little information, and uncertain temper. When she was discontented, she fancied herself nervous. And when she was nervous—as she was nearly all the time since the first outbreak of the strange plague in her youth—she sought solace in the comfort of the traditions which now seemed mere trifles to others.

The business of Mr. Bennet's life was to keep his daughters alive. The business of Mrs. Bennet's was to get them married.

CHAPTER 2

MR. BENNET WAS AMONG the earliest of those who waited on Mr. Bingley. He had always intended to visit him, though to the last always assuring his wife that he should not go; and till the evening after the visit was paid she had no knowledge of it. It was then disclosed in the following manner. Observing his second daughter employed in carving the Bennet crest in the handle of a new sword, he suddenly addressed her with:

"I hope Mr. Bingley will like it, Lizzy."

"We are not in a way to know *what* Mr. Bingley likes," said her mother resentfully, "since we are not to visit."

"But you forget, mamma," said Elizabeth, "that we shall meet him at the next ball."

Mrs. Bennet deigned not to make any reply, but, unable to contain herself, began scolding one of her daughters.

"Don't keep coughing so, Kitty, for Heaven's sake! You sound as if you have been stricken!"

"Mother! What a dreadful thing to say, with so many zombies about!" replied Kitty fretfully. "When is your next ball to be, Lizzy?"

"To-morrow fortnight."

"Aye, so it is," cried her mother, "and it will be impossible to introduce him, since we shall not know him ourselves. Oh, how I wish I had never heard the name Bingley!"

"I am sorry to hear *that*," said Mr. Bennet. "If I had known as much this morning I certainly would not have called on him. It is very unlucky; but as I have actually paid the visit, we cannot escape the acquaintance now."

The astonishment of the ladies was just what he wished; that of Mrs. Bennet perhaps surpassing the rest; though, when the first tumult of joy was over, she began to declare that it was what she had expected all the while.

"How good it was in you, my dear Mr. Bennet! But I knew I should persuade you at last. I was sure you loved your girls too well to neglect such an acquaintance. Well, how pleased I am! And it is such a good joke, too, that you should have gone this morning and never said a word about it till now."

"Do not mistake my indulgence for a relaxation in discipline," said Mr. Bennet. "The girls shall continue their training as ever—Bingley or no Bingley."

"Of course, of course!" cried Mrs. Bennet. "They shall be as deadly as they are fetching!"

"Now, Kitty, you may cough as much as you choose," said Mr. Bennet; and, as he spoke, he left the room, fatigued with the raptures of his wife.

"What an excellent father you have, girls!" said she, when the door was shut. "Such joys are scarce since the good Lord saw fit to shut the gates of Hell and doom the dead to walk amongst us. Lydia, my love, though you are the youngest, I dare say Mr. Bingley will dance with you at the next ball."

"Oh!" said Lydia stoutly, "I am not afraid; for though I *am* the youngest, I'm also the most proficient in the art of tempting the other sex."

The rest of the evening was spent in conjecturing how soon Mr. Bingley would return Mr. Bennet's visit, and determining when they should ask him to dinner.

CHAPTER 3

NOT ALL THAT Mrs. Bennet, however, with the assistance of her five daughters, could ask on the subject, was sufficient to draw from her husband any satisfactory description of Mr. Bingley. They attacked him in various ways—with barefaced questions, ingenious suppositions, and distant surmises; but he eluded the skill of them all, and they were at last obliged to accept the second-hand intelligence of their neighbour Lady Lucas. Her report was highly favourable. Sir William had been delighted with him. He was quite young, wonderfully handsome, and, to crown the whole, he meant to be at the next ball with a large party. Nothing could be more delightful!

"If I can but see one of my daughters happily settled at Netherfield," said Mrs. Bennet to her husband, "and all the others equally well married, I shall have nothing to wish for."

"And if I can see all five of them survive England's present difficulties, then neither shall I," he replied.

In a few days Mr. Bingley returned Mr. Bennet's visit, and sat about ten minutes with him in his library. He had entertained hopes of being admitted to a sight of the young ladies, of whose beauty and fighting skill he had heard much; but he saw only the father. The ladies were somewhat more fortunate, for they had the advantage of ascertaining from an upper window that he wore a blue coat, rode a black horse, and carried a French carbine rifle upon his back—quite an exotic weapon for an Englishman. However, from his clumsy wielding of it, Elizabeth was quite certain that he had little training in musketry or any of the deadly arts.

An invitation to dinner was soon afterwards dispatched; and already had Mrs. Bennet planned the courses that were to do credit to her housekeeping, when an answer arrived which deferred it all. Mr. Bingley was obliged to be in town the following day, and, consequently, unable to accept the honour of their invitation, etc. Mrs. Bennet was quite disconcerted. She could not imagine what business he could have in town so soon after his arrival in Hertfordshire. Lady Lucas quieted her fears a little by starting the idea of his being gone to London only to retrieve a large party for the ball; and a report soon followed that Mr. Bingley was to bring twelve ladies and seven gentlemen with him to the assembly. The girls grieved over such a number of ladies, but were comforted by hearing that instead of twelve he brought only six with him from London—his five sisters and a cousin. And when the party entered the ball, it consisted of only five altogether—Mr. Bingley, his two sisters, the husband of the eldest, and another young man.

Mr. Bingley was good-looking and gentlemanlike; he had a pleasant countenance, and easy, unaffected manners. His sisters were fine women, with an air of decided fashion, but little in the way of combat training. His brother-in-law, Mr. Hurst, merely looked the gentleman; but his friend Mr. Darcy soon drew the attention of the room by his fine, tall person, handsome features, noble mien—and the report which was in general circulation within five minutes after his entrance, of his having slaughtered more than a thousand unmentionables since the fall of Cambridge. The gentlemen pronounced him to be a fine figure of a man, the ladies declared he was much handsomer than Mr. Bingley, and he was looked at with great admiration, until his manners gave a disgust which turned the tide of his popularity; for he was discovered to be proud, to be above his company, and above being pleased.

Mr. Bingley had soon made himself acquainted with all the principal people in the room; he was lively and unreserved, danced every dance, was angry that the ball closed so early, and talked of giving one himself at Netherfield. And though he lacked Mr. Darcy's proficiency with both sword and musket, such amiable qualities must speak for themselves. What a contrast! Mr. Darcy was the proudest, most disagreeable man in the world, and everybody hoped that he would never come there again. Amongst the most violent against him was Mrs. Bennet, whose dislike of his general behaviour was sharpened into particular resentment by his having slighted one of her daughters.

Elizabeth Bennet had been obliged, by the scarcity of gentlemen, to sit down for two dances; and during part of that time, Mr. Darcy had been standing near enough for her to hear a conversation between him and Mr. Bingley, who came from the dance for a few minutes, to press his friend to join it.

"Come, Darcy," said he, "I must have you dance. I hate to see you standing about by yourself in this stupid manner."

"I certainly shall not. You know how I detest it, unless I am particularly acquainted with my partner. At such an assembly as this it would be insupportable. Your sisters are engaged, and there is not another woman in the room whom it would not be a punishment to me to stand up with."

"Upon my honour!" cried Mr. Bingley, "I never met with so many pleasant girls in my life as I have this evening; and there are several of them you see uncommonly pretty."

"*You* are dancing with the only handsome girl in the room," said Mr. Darcy, looking at the eldest Miss Bennet.

"Oh! She is the most beautiful creature I ever beheld! But there is one of her sisters sitting down just behind you, who is very pretty, and I dare say very agreeable."

"Which do you mean?" and turning round he looked for a moment at Elizabeth, till catching her eye, he withdrew his own and coldly said, "She is tolerable, but not handsome enough to tempt *me*; I am in no humour at present to give consequence to young ladies who are slighted by other men."

As Mr. Darcy walked off, Elizabeth felt her blood turn cold. She had never in her life been so insulted. The warrior code demanded she avenge her honour. Elizabeth reached down to her ankle, taking care not to draw attention. There, her hand met the dagger concealed beneath her dress. She meant to follow this proud Mr. Darcy outside and open his throat.

But no sooner had she grabbed the handle of her weapon than a chorus of screams filled the assembly hall, immediately joined by the shattering of window panes. Unmentionables poured in, their movements clumsy yet swift; their burial clothing in a range of untidiness. Some wore gowns so tattered as to render them scandalous; other wore suits so filthy that one would assume they were assembled from little more than dirt and dried blood. Their flesh was in varying degrees of putrefaction; the freshly stricken were slightly green and pliant, whereas the longer dead were grey and brittle—their eyes and tongues long since turned to dust, and their lips pulled back into everlasting skeletal smiles.

A few of the guests, who had the misfortune of being too near the windows, were seized and feasted on at once. When Elizabeth stood, she saw Mrs. Long struggle to free herself as two female dreadfuls bit into her head, cracking her skull like a walnut, and sending a shower of dark blood spouting as high as the chandeliers.

As guests fled in every direction, Mr. Bennet's voice cut through the commotion. "Girls! Pentagram of Death!"

Elizabeth immediately joined her four sisters, Jane, Mary, Catherine, and Lydia in the center of the dance floor. Each girl produced a dagger from her ankle and stood at the tip of an imaginary five-pointed star. From the center of the room, they began stepping outward in unison—each thrusting a razor-sharp dagger with one hand, the other hand modestly tucked into the small of her back.

From a corner of the room, Mr. Darcy watched Elizabeth and her sisters work their way outward, beheading zombie after zombie as they went. He knew of only one other woman in all of Great Britain who wielded a dagger with such skill, such grace, and deadly accuracy.

By the time the girls reached the walls of the assembly hall, the last of the unmentionables lay still.

"MR. DARCY WATCHED ELIZABETH AND HER SISTERS WORK THEIR WAY OUT-
WARD, BEHEADING ZOMBIE AFTER ZOMBIE AS THEY WENT."

Apart from the attack, the evening altogether passed off pleasantly for the whole family. Mrs. Bennet had seen her eldest daughter much admired by the Netherfield party. Mr. Bingley had danced with her twice, and she had been distinguished by his sisters. Jane was as much gratified by this as her mother could be, though in a quieter way. Elizabeth felt Jane's pleasure. Mary had heard herself mentioned to Miss Bingley as the most accomplished girl in the neighbourhood; and Catherine and Lydia had been fortunate enough never to be without partners, which was all that they had yet learnt to care for at a ball. They returned, therefore, in good spirits to Longbourn, the village where they lived, and of which they were the principal inhabitants.

CHAPTER 4

WHEN JANE AND ELIZABETH WERE ALONE, the former, who had been cautious in her praise of Mr. Bingley before, expressed to her sister just how very much she admired him.

"He is just what a young man ought to be," said she, "sensible, good-humoured, lively; and I never saw such happy manners! So much ease, with such perfect good breeding!"

"Yes," replied Elizabeth, "but in the heat of battle, neither he nor Mr. Darcy were to be found with blade or bludgeon."

"Well, I was very much flattered by his asking me to dance a second time. I did not expect such a compliment."

"He certainly is very agreeable, and I give you leave to like him, despite his lack of gallantry. You have liked many a stupider person."

"Dear Lizzy!"

"Oh! You are a great deal too apt, you know, to like people in general. You never see a fault in anybody. I never heard you speak ill of a human being in your life."

"I would not wish to be hasty in censuring anyone."

"With *your* good sense, to be so honestly blind to the follies and nonsense of others! You like this man's sisters, too, do you? Their manners are not equal to his."

They were in fact very fine ladies; not deficient in the power of making themselves agreeable when they chose it, but proud and conceited. They were rather handsome, had been educated in one of the first private seminaries in town, but knew little of the deadly arts in which she and her own sisters had been so thoroughly trained—both in England, and during their trips to the Orient.

As for Mr. Bingley himself, between him and Darcy there was a very steady friendship, in spite of great opposition of character. Bingley was by no means deficient, but Darcy was clever. He was at the same time haughty, reserved, and fastidious, and his manners, though well-bred, were not inviting. In that respect his friend had greatly the advantage. Bingley was sure of being liked wherever he appeared, Darcy was continually giving offense.

But what no one—not even Mr. Bingley—knew, was the reason behind Darcy's cold demeanor. For until recently, he had been the very picture of pleasantry; a young man of merry disposition and utmost attentiveness. But his nature had been forever altered by a betrayal he had not the stomache to speak of.

CHAPTER 5

WITHIN A SHORT THOUGH PERILOUS WALK of Longbourn lived a family with whom the Bennets were particularly intimate. Sir William Lucas had been formerly a maker of fine burial gowns of such stately beauty that the King had seen fit to knight him. He had made a tolerable fortune, until the strange plague had rendered his services unnecessary. Few thought it worth the expense to dress the dead in finery when they would only soil it upon crawling out of their graves. He had removed with his family to a house about a mile from Meryton.

Lady Lucas was a very good kind of woman, not too clever to be a valuable neighbour to Mrs. Bennet. They had several children. The eldest of them, a sensible, intelligent young woman, about twenty-seven, was Elizabeth's intimate friend.

"You began the evening well, Charlotte," said Mrs. Bennet with civil self-command to Miss Lucas. "You were Mr. Bingley's first choice."

"Yes; but he seemed to like his second better."

"Oh! You mean Jane, I suppose, because he danced with her twice, and because she fought so valiantly against the unmentionables."

"Did not I mention what I heard between him and Mr. Robinson? Mr. Robinson's asking Mr. Bingley how he liked our Meryton assemblies, and whether he did not think there were many pretty women in the room, and *which* he thought the prettiest? And his answering immediately to the last question, 'Oh! the eldest Miss Bennet, beyond a doubt; there cannot be two opinions on that point.'"

"Upon my word! Well, that is very decided indeed."

"Mr. Darcy is not so well worth listening to as his friend, is he," said Charlotte. "Poor Eliza! To be called only *tolerable*."

"I beg you would not put it into Lizzy's head to be vexed by his ill-treatment; for he is such a disagreeable man, that it would be quite a misfortune to be liked by him. Mrs. Long told me last night . . . " Mrs. Bennet's voice failed her at the thought of poor Mrs. Long, her skull crushed betwixt the teeth of those wretched creatures. The ladies sat in silent contemplation for a few moments.

"Miss Bingley told me," said Jane, finally, "that he never speaks much, unless among his intimate acquaintances. With *them* he is remarkably agreeable."

"His pride," said Miss Lucas, "does not offend *me* so much as pride often does, because there is an excuse for it. One cannot wonder that so very fine a young man, with family, fortune, everything in his favour, should think highly of himself. If I may so express it, he has a *right* to be proud."

"That is very true," replied Elizabeth, "and I could easily forgive *his* pride, if he had not mortified *mine*. I dare say I would've cut his throat had not the unmentionables distracted me from doing so."

"Pride," observed Mary, who piqued herself upon the solidity of her reflections, "is a very common failing, I believe. By all that I have ever read, I am convinced that it is very common indeed."

Elizabeth could not help but roll her eyes as Mary continued.

"Vanity and pride are different things, though the words are often used synonymously. A person may be proud without being vain. Pride relates more to our opinion of ourselves, vanity to what we would have others think of us."

At this point, Elizabeth let out a most palpable yawn. Though she admired Mary's bravery in battle, she had always found her a trifle dull in relaxed company.

CHAPTER 6

THE LADIES OF LONGBOURN soon waited on those of Netherfield. Jane's pleasing manners grew on the goodwill of Mrs. Hurst and Miss Bingley; and though the mother was found to be intolerable, and the younger sisters not worth speaking to, a wish of being better acquainted with *them* was expressed towards the two eldest. By Jane this attention was received with the greatest pleasure, but Elizabeth still saw superciliousness in their treatment of everybody. It was generally evident whenever they met, that Mr. Bingley *did* admire her and to *her* it was equally evident that Jane was in a way to be very much in love; but she considered with pleasure that it was not likely to be discovered by the world in general. Elizabeth mentioned this to her friend Miss Lucas.

"It may perhaps be pleasant," replied Charlotte, "but it is sometimes a disadvantage to be so very guarded. If a woman conceals her affection with the same skill from the object of it, she may lose the opportunity of fixing him. In nine cases out of ten a women had better show *more* affection than she feels. Bingley likes your sister undoubtedly; but he may never do more than like her, if she does not help him on."

"But she does help him on, as much as her nature will allow. Remember, Charlotte—she is a warrior first, and a woman second."

"Well," said Charlotte, "I wish Jane success with all my heart; and if she were married to him to-morrow, I should think she had as good a chance of happiness as if she were to be studying his character for a twelvemonth. Happiness in marriage is entirely a matter of chance, and it is better to know as little as possible of the defects of the person with whom you are to pass your life."

"You make me laugh, Charlotte; but it is not sound. You know it is not sound, and that you would never act in this way yourself."

"Remember, Elizabeth—I am not a warrior as you are. I am merely a silly girl of seven-and-twenty years, and that without a husband."

Occupied in observing Mr. Bingley's attentions to her sister, Elizabeth was far from suspecting that she was herself becoming an object of some interest in the eyes of his friend. Mr. Darcy had at first scarcely allowed her to be pretty; he had looked at her without admiration at the ball; and when they next met, he looked at her only to criticize. But no sooner had he made it clear to himself and his friends that she hardly had a good feature in her face, than he began to find it was rendered uncommonly intelligent by the beautiful expression of her dark eyes, and her uncommon skill with a blade. To this discovery succeeded some others equally mortifying. Though he had detected more than one failure of perfect symmetry in her form, he was forced to acknowledge her figure to be light and pleasing, and her arms surprisingly muscular, though not so much as to diminish her femininity.

He began to wish to know more of her, and as a step towards conversing with her himself, attended to her conversation with others. His doing so drew her notice. It was at Sir William Lucas's, where a large party were assembled.

"What does Mr. Darcy mean," said she to Charlotte, "by listening to my conversation with Colonel Forster?"

"That is a question which Mr. Darcy only can answer."

"Well if he does it any more I shall certainly let him know that I see what he is about. I have not yet forgiven him for insulting my honour, and may yet have his head upon my mantle."

Mr. Darcy approached them soon afterwards. Elizabeth turned to him and said, "Did you not think, Mr. Darcy, that I expressed myself uncommonly well just now, when I was teasing Colonel Forster to give us a ball at Meryton?"

"With great energy; but balls are always a subject which makes a lady energetic."

"It depends on who's throwing them, Mr. Darcy."

"Well," said Miss Lucas, her faced suddenly flushed, "I am going to open the instrument, Eliza, and you know what follows."

"You are a very strange creature by way of a friend! Always wanting me to play and sing before anybody and everybody!"

Elizabeth's performance was pleasing, though by no means capital. After a song or two, she was eagerly succeeded at the instrument by her sister Mary, who, at the end of a long concerto, joined eagerly in dancing with her younger sisters, some of the Lucases, and two or three officers at one end of the room.

Mr. Darcy stood near them in silent indignation at such a mode of passing the evening, to the exclusion of all conversation, and was too much engrossed by his thoughts to perceive that Sir William Lucas stood beside him, till Sir William thus began:

"What a charming amusement for young people this is, Mr. Darcy!"

"Certainly, sir; and it has the advantage also of being in vogue amongst the less polished societies of the world. Every savage can dance. Why, I imagine even zombies could do it with some degree of success."

Sir William only smiled, not sure of how to converse with so rude a gentleman. He was much relieved at the sight of Elizabeth approaching.

"My dear Miss Eliza, why are you not dancing? Mr. Darcy, you must allow me to present this young lady to you as a very desirable partner. You cannot refuse to dance, I am sure, when so much beauty is before you." He took Miss Bennet's hand and presented it to Mr. Darcy, who was not unwilling to receive it. But she instantly drew back, and said with some discomposure to Sir William, "Indeed, sir, I have not the least intention of dancing. I entreat you not to suppose that I moved this way in order to beg for a partner."

Mr. Darcy, with grave propriety, requested the honour of her hand, but in vain. Elizabeth was determined. She looked archly, and turned away. Her resistance had not injured her with Mr. Darcy, for indeed he was thinking of her with some complacency, when thus accosted by Miss Bingley:

"I can guess the subject of your reverie."

"I should imagine not."

"You are considering how insupportable it would be to pass many evenings in this manner—the insipidity, the noise, the nothingness, and yet the self-importance of all those people! What would I give to hear your strictures on them!"

"You conjecture is totally wrong, I assure you. My mind was more agreeably engaged. I have been meditating on the very great pleasure which a pair of fine eyes in the face of a pretty woman can bestow."

Miss Bingley immediately fixed her eyes on his face, and desired he would tell her what lady had the credit of inspiring such reflections. Mr. Darcy replied:

"Miss Elizabeth Bennet."

"Miss Elizabeth Bennet!" repeated Miss Bingley. "Defender of Longbourn? Heroine of Hertfordshire? I am all astonishment. You will be having a charming mother-in-law, indeed; and, of course, the two of you would fell many an unmentionable with your combined proficiencies in the deadly arts."

He listened to her with perfect indifference while she chose to entertain herself in this manner; and as his composure convinced her that all was safe, her wit flowed long.

CHAPTER 7

MR. BENNET'S PROPERTY consisted almost entirely in an estate of two thousand a year, which, unfortunately for his daughters, was entailed, in default of heirs male, on a distant relation; and unfortunately for all, was surrounded on all sides by high ground, making it troublesome to defend. Their mother's fortune, though ample for her situation in life, could but ill supply the deficiency of his. Her father had been an attorney in Meryton, and had left her four thousand pounds.

She had a sister married to a Mr. Philips, who had been a clerk to their father and succeeded him in the business, and a brother settled in London, where he had earned his letters in science, and where he now owned a pair of factories dedicated to the war effort.

The village of Longbourn was only one mile from Meryton; a most convenient distance for the young ladies, who were usually tempted thither three or four times a week, despite the unmentionables which frequently beset travelers along the road, to pay their duty to their aunt and to a milliner's shop just over the way. The two youngest of the family, Catherine and Lydia, were particularly frequent in these attentions; their minds were more vacant than their sisters', and when nothing better offered, a walk to Meryton was necessary to amuse their morning hours, and occasionally, practice their skills. At present, indeed, they were well supplied both with news and happiness by the recent arrival of a militia regiment in the neighbourhood; it was to remain the whole winter, wresting coffins from the hardened earth and setting fire to them. Meryton was to be the headquarters.

Their visits to Mrs. Philips were now productive of the most interesting intelligence. Every day added something to their knowledge of the officers' names and connections, and fresh news from the battlefields of Derbyshire, Cornwall, and Essex—where the fighting was at its fiercest. They could talk of nothing but officers; and Mr. Bingley's large fortune, the mention of which gave animation to their mother, was worthless in their eyes when opposed to the regimentals of an ensign, and the excited manner in which he spoke of beheading the stricken with a single touch of his sword.

After listening one morning to their effusions on this subject, Mr. Bennet coolly observed, "From all that I can collect by your manner of talking, you must be two of the silliest girls in the country. I have suspected it some time, but I am now convinced."

"I am astonished, my dear," said Mrs. Bennet, "that you should be so ready to think your own children silly."

"If my children are silly, I must hope to be always sensible of it."

"Yes—but as it happens, they are all of them very clever. You forget how quickly they became proficient in those Oriental tricks you insisted on bestowing them."

"Being practiced enough to kill a few of the sorry stricken does not make them sensible, particularly when their skills are most often applied for the amusement of handsome officers."

"Mamma," cried Lydia, "my aunt says that Colonel Forster and Captain Carter do not go so often to Miss Watson's as they did when they first came; she sees them now very often burning the crypts in Shepherd's Hill Cemetery."

Mrs. Bennet was prevented replying by the entrance of the footman with a note for Miss Bennet; it came from Netherfield, and the servant waited for an answer.

"Well, Jane, who is it from? What is it about?"

"It is from Miss Bingley," said Jane, and then read it aloud.

MY DEAR FRIEND,

If you are not so compassionate as to dine to-day with Louisa and me, we shall be in danger of hating each other for the rest of our lives, for a whole day's tête-à-tête between two women can never end without a quarrel. Come as soon as you can on receipt of this, provided the road is free of the unmentionable menace. My brother and the gentlemen are to dine with the officers.

Yours ever,

CAROLINE BINGLEY

"Dining out," said Mrs. Bennet, "that is very unlucky, given the troubles on the road to Netherfield."

"Can I have the carriage?" said Jane.

"No, my dear, you had better go on horseback, because it seems likely to rain; and they spring so easily from the wet earth. I should prefer you have speed at your disposal; besides, if it rains, you must stay all night."

"That would be a good scheme," said Elizabeth, "if you were sure that they would not offer to send her home."

"I had much rather go in the coach," said Jane, clearly troubled by the thought of riding alone.

"But, my dear, your father cannot spare the horses, I am sure. They are wanted in the farm, Mr. Bennet, are they not?"

"They are wanted in the farm much oftener than I can get them, and too many slaughtered upon the road already."

Jane was therefore obliged to go on horseback, and her mother attended her to the door with many cheerful prognostics of a bad day. Her hopes were answered; Jane had not been gone long before it rained hard, and the soft ground gave way to scores of the disagreeable creatures, still clad in their tattered finery, but possessing none of the good breeding that had served them so well in life.

Her sisters were uneasy for her, but her mother was delighted. The rain continued the whole evening without intermission; Jane certainly could not come back.

"This was a lucky idea of mine, indeed!" said Mrs. Bennet more than once, as if the credit of making it rain were all her own. Till the next morning, however, she was not aware of all the felicity of her contrivance. Breakfast was scarcely over when a servant from Netherfield brought the following note for Elizabeth:

> MY DEAREST LIZZY,
>
> I find myself very unwell this morning, which, I suppose, is to be imputed to my being set upon by several freshly unearthed unmentionables during my ride to Netherfield. My kind friends will not hear of my returning till I am better. They insist also on my seeing Mr. Jones—therefore do not be alarmed if you should hear of his having been to me—and, excepting a few bruises and a minor stab wound, there is not much the matter with me.
>
> YOURS, ETC.

"Well, my dear," said Mr. Bennet, when Elizabeth had read the note aloud, "if your daughter should die—or worse, succumb to the strange plague, it would be a comfort to know that it was all in pursuit of Mr. Bingley, and under your orders."

"Oh! I am not afraid of her dying. People do not die of cuts and bruises. She will be taken good care of."

Elizabeth, feeling really anxious, was determined to go to her, though the carriage was not to be had; and as she was no horsewoman, walking was her only alternative. She declared her resolution.

"How can you be so silly," cried her mother, "as to think of such a thing, with so many of them about, and in all this dirt! You will not be fit to be seen when you get there, assuming you make it alive!"

"You forget that I am student of Pei Liu of Shaolin, mother. Besides, for every unmentionable one meets upon the road, one meets three soldiers. I shall be back by dinner."

"We will go as far as Meryton with you," said Catherine and Lydia. Elizabeth accepted their company, and they set off together, armed only with their ankle daggers. Muskets and Katana swords were a more effective means of protecting one's self, but they were considered unladylike; and, having no saddle in which to conceal them, the three sisters yielded to modesty.

"If we make haste," said Lydia, as they walked cautiously along, "perhaps we may see something of Captain Carter before he goes."

In Meryton they parted; the two youngest repaired to the lodgings of one of the officers' wives, and Elizabeth continued her walk alone, crossing field after field at a quick pace, jumping over stiles and springing over puddles. During this impatient activity, a bootlace came undone. Not wanting to appear unkempt upon her arrival at Netherfield, she knelt down to tie it.

There was suddenly a terrible shriek, not unlike that which hogs make while being butchered. Elizabeth knew at once what it was, and reached for her ankle dagger most expeditiously. She turned, blade at the ready, and was met with the regrettable visage of three unmentionables, their arms outstretched and mouths agape. The closest seemed freshly dead, his burial suit not yet discolored and his eyes not yet dust. He lumbered toward Elizabeth at an impressive pace, and when he was but an arm's length from her, she plunged the dagger into his chest and pulled it skyward. The blade continued upward, cutting through his neck and face until it burst through the very top of his skull. He fell to the ground and was still.

The second unmentionable was a lady, and much longer dead than her companion. She rushed at Elizabeth, her clawed fingers swaying clumsily about. Elizabeth lifted her skirt, disregarding modesty, and delivered a swift kick to the creature's head, which exploded in a cloud of brittle skin and bone. She, too, fell and was no more.

The third was unusually tall, and though long dead, still possessed a great deal of strength and quickness. Elizabeth had not yet recovered from her kick when the creature seized her arm and forced the dagger from it. She pulled free before he could get his teeth on her, and took the crane position, which she thought appropriate for an opponent of such height. The creature advanced, and Elizabeth landed a devastating chop across its thighs. The limbs broke off, and the unmentionable fell to the ground, helpless. She retrieved her dagger and beheaded the last of her opponents, lifting its head by the hair and letting her battle cry be known for a mile in every direction.

Elizabeth found herself at last within view of the house, with weary ankles, dirty stockings, and a face glowing with the warmth of exercise.

She was shown into the breakfast-parlour, where all but Jane were assembled, and where her appearance created a great deal of surprise. That she should have walked three miles with so many unmentionables about, in such dirty weather, and by herself, was almost incredible to Mrs. Hurst and Miss Bingley; and Elizabeth was convinced that they held her in contempt for it. She was received, however, very politely by them; and in their brother's manners there was something better than politeness; there was good humour and kindness. Mr. Darcy said very little, and Mr. Hurst nothing at all. The former was divided between admiration of the brilliancy which exercise had given to her complexion, and doubt as to the occasion's justifying her to take the great risk of coming alone, with nothing but a dagger between her and death. The latter was thinking only of his breakfast.

"ELIZABETH LIFTED HER SKIRT, DISREGARDING MODESTY, AND DELIVERED A
SWIFT KICK TO THE CREATURE'S HEAD."

Her inquiries after her sister were not very favourably answered. Miss Bennet had slept ill, and though up, was very feverish and not well enough to leave her room. Elizabeth attended her, silently worrying that her beloved sister had caught the strange plague.

When breakfast was over, they were joined by the sisters; and Elizabeth began to like them herself, when she saw how much affection and solicitude they showed for Jane. The apothecary came, and having examined his patient, said, much to the relief of all, that she had caught not the strange plague, but a violent cold, no doubt from doing battle in the rain.

When the clock struck three, Elizabeth felt that she must go. Miss Bingley offered her the carriage. When Jane testified such concern in parting with her, Miss Bingley was obliged to convert the offer to an invitation to remain at Netherfield for the present. Elizabeth most thankfully consented, and a servant was dispatched to Longbourn to acquaint the family with her stay and bring back a supply of clothes, and at Elizabeth's request, her favourite musket.

CHAPTER 8

AT FIVE O'CLOCK Elizabeth retired to meditate and dress, and at half-past six she was summoned to dinner. Jane was by no means better. The sisters, on hearing this, repeated three or four times how much they were grieved, how shocking it was to have a bad cold, and how excessively they disliked being ill themselves; and then thought no more of the matter. Their indifference towards Jane when not immediately before them restored Elizabeth to her former dislike.

Their brother, Mr. Bingley, was the only one of the party whom she could regard with any complacency. His anxiety for Jane was evident, and his attentions to herself most pleasing, and they prevented her feeling herself so much an intruder as she believed she was considered by the others.

When dinner was over, Elizabeth returned directly to Jane, and Miss Bingley began abusing her as soon as she was out of the room. Her manners were pronounced to be very bad indeed, a mixture of pride and impertinence; she had no conversation, no style, no beauty. Mrs. Hurst thought the same, and added, "She has nothing, in short, to recommend her, but being well-schooled in the ways of combat. I shall never forget her appearance this morning. She really looked almost wild."

"She did, indeed, Louisa. Why must she be scampering about the country in such dangerous times, because her sister had a cold? Her hair, so untidy, so blowsy!"

"Yes, and her petticoat; I hope you saw her petticoat, six inches deep in mud, I am absolutely certain; and pieces of undead flesh upon her sleeve, no doubt from her attackers."

"Your picture may be very exact, Louisa," said Bingley; "but this was all lost upon me. I thought Miss Elizabeth Bennet looked remarkably well when she came into the room this morning. Her dirty petticoat quite escaped my notice."

"You observed it, Mr. Darcy, I am sure," said Miss Bingley; "and I am inclined to think that you would not wish to see your sister make such an exhibition."

"Certainly not."

"To walk three miles, or whatever it is, above her ankles in dirt, and alone, quite alone! With the unmentionable menace dragging poor souls off the road and to their doom day and night? What could she mean by it? It seems to me to show an abominable sort of conceited independence, a most country-town indifference to decorum."

"It shows an affection for her sister that is very pleasing," said Bingley.

"I am afraid, Mr. Darcy," observed Miss Bingley in a half whisper, "that this adventure has rather affected your admiration of her fine eyes."

"Not at all," he replied; "they were brightened by the exercise." A short pause followed this speech, and Mrs. Hurst began again:

"I have an excessive regard for Miss Jane Bennet, she is really a very sweet girl, and I wish with all my heart she were well settled. But with such a father and mother, and such low connections, I am afraid there is no chance of it."

"I think I have heard you say that their uncle is an attorney on Meryton."

"Yes; and they have another, who lives somewhere near Cheapside."

"That is capital," added her sister, and they both laughed heartily.

"If they had uncles enough to fill *all* Cheapside," cried Bingley, "it would not make them one jot less agreeable. Have you no regard for them as warriors? Indeed, I have never seen ladies so steady-handed in combat."

"But it must very materially lessen their chance of marrying men of any consideration in the world," replied Darcy. To this speech Bingley made no answer; but his sisters gave it their hearty assent.

With a renewal of tenderness, however, they returned to Jane's room on leaving the dining-parlour, and sat with her till summoned to coffee. She was still very poorly, and Elizabeth would not quit her at all, till late in the evening, when she had the comfort of seeing her sleep, and when it seemed to her rather right than pleasant that she should go downstairs herself. On entering the drawing-room she found the whole party at cards, and was immediately invited to join them; but suspecting them to be playing high she declined it, and making her sister the excuse, said she would amuse herself for the short time she could stay below, with a book. Mr. Hurst looked at her with astonishment.

"Do you prefer reading to cards?" said he; "that is rather singular."

"I prefer a great many things to cards, Mr. Hurst," said Elizabeth; "Not the least of which is the sensation of a newly sharpened blade as it punctures the round belly of a man."

Mr. Hurst was silent for the remainder of the evening.

"In nursing your sister I am sure you have pleasure," said Bingley; "and I hope it will be soon increased by seeing her quite well."

Elizabeth thanked him, and then walked towards the table where a few books were lying. He immediately offered to fetch her others—all that his library afforded.

"And I wish my collection were larger for your benefit and my own credit; but I am an idle fellow, and though I have not many, I have more than I ever looked into."

Elizabeth assured him that she could suit herself perfectly with those in the room.

"I am astonished," said Miss Bingley, "that my father should have left so small a collection of books. What a delightful library you have at Pemberley, Mr. Darcy!"

"It ought to be good," he replied, "it has been the work of many generations."

"And then you have added so much to it yourself, you are always buying books."

"I cannot comprehend the neglect of a family library in such days as these. What have we to do but stay indoors and read till the cure is at last discovered?"

Elizabeth turned her attention away from her book and drew near the card-table, and stationed herself between Mr. Bingley and his eldest sister, to observe the game.

"Is Miss Darcy much grown since the spring?" said Miss Bingley; "will she be as tall as I am?"

"I think she will. She is now about Miss Elizabeth Bennet's height, or rather taller."

"How I long to see her again! I never met with anybody who delighted me so much. Such a countenance, such manners! And so extremely accomplished for her age!"

"It is amazing to me," said Bingley, "how young ladies can have patience to be so very accomplished as they all are."

"All young ladies accomplished! My dear Charles, what do you mean?"

"They all paint tables, cover screens, and net purses. I scarcely know anyone who cannot do all this, and I am sure I never heard a young lady spoken of for the first time, without being informed that she was very accomplished."

"The word is applied," said Darcy, "to many a woman who deserves it no otherwise than by netting a purse or covering a screen. My sister Georgiana deserves the distinction, however, for she is not only master of the female arts, but the deadly as well. I cannot boast of knowing more than half a dozen, in the whole range of my acquaintance, that are thus accomplished."

"Nor I, I am sure," said Miss Bingley.

"Then, Mr. Darcy," observed Elizabeth, "you must comprehend a great deal in your idea of an accomplished woman."

"A woman must have a thorough knowledge of music, singing, drawing, dancing, and the modern languages; she must be well trained in the fighting styles of the Kyoto masters and the modern tactics and weaponry of Europe. And besides all this, she must possess a certain something in her air and manner of walking, the tone of her voice, her address and expressions, or the word will be but half-deserved. All this she must possess, and to all this she must yet add something more substantial, in the improvement of her mind by extensive reading."

"I am no longer surprised at your knowing only six accomplished women. I rather wonder now at your knowing any."

"Are you so severe upon your own sex as to doubt the possibility of all this?"

"I never saw such a woman. In my experience, a woman is either highly trained or highly refined. One cannot afford the luxury of both in such times. As for my sisters and I, our dear father thought it best that we give less of our time to books and music, and more to protecting ourselves from the sorry stricken."

Mrs. Hurst and Miss Bingley both cried out against the injustice of her implied doubt, and were both protesting that they knew many women who answered this description, when Mr. Hurst called them to order. All conversation was thereby at an end, Elizabeth soon afterwards left the room.

"Elizabeth Bennet," said Miss Bingley, when the door was closed on her, "is one of those young ladies who seek to recommend themselves to the other sex by undervaluing their own; and with many men, I dare say, it succeeds. But, in my opinion, it is a paltry device, a very mean art."

"Undoubtedly," replied Darcy, to whom this remark was chiefly addressed, "there is a meanness in all the arts which ladies sometimes condescend to employ for captivation. Whatever bears affinity to cunning is despicable."

Miss Bingley was not so entirely satisfied with this reply as to continue the subject.

Elizabeth joined them again only to say that her sister was worse, and that she could not leave her. Bingley urged Mr. Jones being sent for immediately; while his sisters, convinced that no country advice could be of any service, recommended an express to town for one of the most eminent physicians. This she would not hear of—it was too dangerous to dispatch a rider at night; but she was willing to comply with their brother's proposal; and it was settled that Mr. Jones should be sent for early in the morning, if Miss Bennet were not decidedly better. Bingley was quite uncomfortable; his sisters declared that they were miserable. They solaced their wretchedness, however, by duets after supper, while he could find no better relief to his feelings than by giving his housekeeper directions that every attention might be paid to the sick lady and her sister.

CHAPTER 9

ELIZABETH PASSED THE CHIEF of the night in her sister's room, and in the morning had the pleasure of being able to send a tolerable answer to the inquiries which she very early received from Mr. Bingley by a housemaid. She requested to have a note sent to Longbourn, desiring her mother to visit Jane, and form her own judgment of her situation. The note was immediately dispatched, but the rider was met with a group of freshly unearthed zombies on the road and dragged off to his presumable demise.

The note was dispatched a second time with more success, and its contents as quickly complied with. Mrs. Bennet, accompanied by her two youngest girls and their longbows, reached Netherfield soon after the family breakfast.

Had she found Jane in any apparent danger of having the strange plague, Mrs. Bennet would have been very miserable; but being satisfied on seeing her that her illness was not alarming, she had no wish of her recovering immediately, as her restoration to health would probably remove her from Netherfield. She would not listen, therefore, to her daughter's proposal of being carried home; neither did the apothecary, who arrived about the same time, think it at all advisable. Bingley met them with hopes that Mrs. Bennet had not found Miss Bennet worse than she expected.

"Indeed I have, sir," was her answer. "She is a great deal too ill to be moved. Mr. Jones says we must not think of moving her. We must trespass a little longer on your kindness."

"Removed!" cried Bingley. "It must not be thought of!"

Mrs. Bennet was profuse in her acknowledgments.

"I am sure," she added, "if it was not for such good friends I do not know what would become of her, for she is very ill indeed, and suffers a vast deal, though with the greatest patience in the world, no doubt due to her many months under the tutelage of Master Liu."

"Might I expect to meet this gentleman here in Hertfordshire?" asked Bingley.

"I rather think you shan't," she replied, "for he has never left the confines of the Shaolin Temple in Henan Province. It was there that our girls spent many a long day being trained to endure all manner of discomfort."

"May I inquire as to the nature of this discomfort?"

"You may inquire," said Elizabeth, "though I would much prefer to give you a demonstration."

"Lizzy," cried her mother, "remember where you are, and do not run on in the wild manner that you are suffered to do at home."

"I hardly knew you to possess such character," said Bingley.

"My own character is of little consequence," replied Elizabeth. "It is the character of others which concerns me. I devote a great many hours to the study of it."

"The country," said Darcy, "can in general supply but a few subjects for such a study. In a country neighbourhood you move in a very confined and unvarying society."

"Excepting, of course, when the country is overrun with the same unmentionables as town."

"Yes, indeed," cried Mrs. Bennet, offended by his manner of mentioning a country neighbourhood. "I assure you there is quite as much of *that* going on in the country as in town." Everybody was surprised, and Darcy, after looking at her for a moment, turned silently away. Mrs. Bennet, who fancied she had gained a complete victory over him, continued her triumph.

"I cannot see that London has any great advantage over the country, particularly since the wall was built. It may be a fortress replete with shops, but it is a fortress nonetheless—and hardly fit for the fragile nerves of a gentle lady. The country is a vast deal pleasanter, is it not, Mr. Bingley?"

"When I am in the country," he replied, "I never wish to leave it; and when I am in town it is pretty much the same. They have each their advantages, both in regards to the plague and otherwise. For while I sleep more soundly in the safety of town, I find my general disposition much improved by my present surroundings."

"Aye—that is because you have the right disposition. But that gentleman," looking at Darcy, "seemed to think the country was nothing at all."

"Indeed, Mamma, you are mistaken," said Elizabeth, blushing for her mother. "You quite mistook Mr. Darcy. He only meant that there was not such a variety of people to be met with in the country as in the town, which you must acknowledge to be true. Just as Mr. Darcy would surely acknowledge that the scarcity of graveyards makes the country altogether more agreeable in times such as these."

"Certainly, my dear; but as to not meeting with many people in this neighbourhood, I believe there are few neighbourhoods larger. I know we dine with four-and-twenty families. Well, three-and-twenty, I suppose—God rest poor Mrs. Long's soul."

Darcy only smiled; and the general pause which ensued made Elizabeth tremble. She longed to speak, but could think of nothing to say; and after a short silence Mrs. Bennet began repeating her thanks to Mr. Bingley for his kindness to Jane, with an apology for troubling him also with Lizzy. Mr. Bingley was unaffectedly civil in his answer, and forced his younger sister to be civil also, and say what the occasion required. She performed her part indeed without much graciousness, but Mrs. Bennet was satisfied, and soon afterwards ordered her carriage. Upon this signal, the youngest of her daughters put herself forward. The two girls had been whispering to each other during the whole visit, and the result of it was, that the youngest should tax Mr. Bingley with having promised on his first coming into the country to give a ball at Netherfield.

Lydia was a stout, well-grown girl of fifteen, with a fine complexion and good-humoured countenance. She had every bit of Lizzy's deadly nature, though little of her sense, and had vanquished her first unmentionable at the remarkable age of seven-and-one-half years. She was very equal, therefore, to address Mr. Bingley on the subject of the ball, and abruptly reminded him of his promise; adding, that it would be the most shameful thing in the world if he did not keep it. His answer to this sudden attack was delightful to their mother's ear.

"I am perfectly ready, I assure you, to keep my engagement; and when your sister is recovered, you shall, if you please, name the very day of the ball. But you would not wish to be dancing when she is ill."

Lydia declared herself satisfied. "Oh! Yes—it would be much better to wait till Jane was well, and by that time most likely Captain Carter would be at Meryton again. And when you have given *your* ball," she added, "I shall insist on their giving one also. I shall tell Colonel Forster it will be quite a shame if he does not."

Mrs. Bennet and her daughters then departed, and Elizabeth returned instantly to Jane, leaving her own and her relations' behaviour to the remarks of the two ladies and Mr. Darcy; the latter of whom, however, could not be prevailed on to join in their censure of *her*, in spite of all Miss Bingley's witticisms on *fine eyes*.

CHAPTER 10

THE DAY PASSED much as the day before had done. Mrs. Hurst and Miss Bingley had spent some hours of the morning with the invalid, who continued, though slowly, to mend; and in the evening Elizabeth joined their party in the drawing-room. The card table, however, did not appear. Mr. Darcy was writing, and Miss Bingley, seated near him, was watching the progress of his letter and repeatedly calling off his attention by messages to his sister. Mr. Hurst and Mr. Bingley were at piquet, and Mrs. Hurst was observing their game.

Elizabeth took up the oiling of her musket stock, and was sufficiently amused in attending to what passed between Darcy and his companion.

"How delighted Miss Darcy will be to receive such a letter!"

He made no answer.

"You write uncommonly fast."

"And you prattle uncommonly much."

"How many letters you must have occasion to write in the course of a year! Letters of business, too! How odious I should think them!"

"And how odious indeed that I should so often suffer to write them in your company."

"Pray tell your sister that I long to see her."

"I have already told her so once, by your desire."

"How can you contrive to write so even?"

He was silent.

"Tell your sister I am delighted to hear of her improvement on the harp; and pray let her know that I am quite in raptures with her beautiful little design for a table."

"Miss Bingley, the groans of a hundred unmentionables would be more pleasing to my ears than one more word from your mouth. Were you not otherwise agreeable, I should be forced to remove your tongue with my saber."

"Oh! It is of no consequence. I shall see her in January. But do you always write such charming long letters to her, Mr. Darcy?"

"They are generally long; but whether always charming it is not for me to determine."

"It is a rule with me that a person who can write a long letter with ease, cannot write ill."

"That will not do for a compliment to Darcy, Caroline," cried her brother, "because he does *not* write with ease. He studies too much for words of four syllables. Do not you, Darcy?"

Mr. Darcy continued to work on his letter in silence, though Elizabeth perceived him to be a great deal annoyed with his friends.

When that business was over, Mr. Darcy applied to Miss Bingley and Elizabeth for an indulgence of some music. Miss Bingley moved with some alacrity to the pianoforte; and, after a polite request that Elizabeth would lead the way, she seated herself.

Mrs. Hurst sang with her sister as Elizabeth played.

When once the earth was still and dead were silent,
And London-town was for but living men,
Came the plague upon us swift and violent,
And so our dearest England we defend.

While they were thus employed, Elizabeth could not help observing how frequently Mr. Darcy's eyes were fixed on her. She hardly knew how to suppose that she could be an object of admiration to so great a man; and yet that he should look at her because he disliked her, was still more strange. She could only imagine, however, that she drew his notice because there was something more wrong and reprehensible, according to his ideas of right, than in any other person present. The supposition did not pain her. She liked him too little to care for his approbation.

Miss Bingley played next, varying the charm by a lively Scotch air; and soon afterwards Mr. Darcy, drawing near Elizabeth, said to her:

"Do not you feel a great inclination, Miss Bennet, to seize such an opportunity of dancing a reel?"

She smiled, but made no answer. He repeated the question, with some surprise at her silence.

"Oh!" said she, "I heard you before, but I could not immediately determine what to say in reply. You wanted me, I know, to say 'Yes,' that you might have the pleasure of despising my taste; but I always delight in overthrowing those kind of schemes, and cheating a person of their premeditated contempt. I have, therefore, made up my mind to tell you, that

I do not want to dance a reel at all—and now despise me if you dare."

"Indeed I do not dare."

Elizabeth, having rather expected to affront him, was amazed at his gallantry; and Darcy had never been so bewitched by any woman as he was by her. He really believed, that were it not for the inferiority of her connections, he should be in some danger of falling in love, and were it not for his considerable skill in the deadly arts, that he should be in danger of being bested by hers—for never had he seen a lady more gifted in the ways of vanquishing the undead.

Miss Bingley saw, or suspected enough to be jealous; and her great anxiety for the recovery of her dear friend Jane received some assistance from her desire of getting rid of Elizabeth. She often tried to provoke Darcy into disliking her guest, by talking of their supposed marriage, and planning his happiness in such an alliance.

"I hope," said she, as they were walking together in the shrubbery the next day, "you will give your mother-in-law a few hints, when this desirable event takes place, as to the advantage of holding her tongue; and if you can compass it, do cure the younger girls of running after officers. And, if I may mention so delicate a subject, endeavour to check Miss Bennet's unladylike affinity for guns, and swords, and exercise, and all those silly things best left to men or ladies of low breeding."

"Have you anything else to propose for my domestic felicity?"

At that moment they were met from another walk by Mrs. Hurst and Elizabeth herself.

"I did not know that you intended to walk," said Miss Bingley, in some confusion, lest she had been overheard.

"You used us abominably ill," answered Mrs. Hurst, "running away without telling us that you were coming out."

Then taking the disengaged arm of Mr. Darcy, she left Elizabeth to walk by herself. The path just admitted three. Mr. Darcy felt their rudeness, and immediately said:

"This walk is not wide enough for our party. We had better go into the avenue."

But Elizabeth, who had not the least inclination to remain with them, laughingly answered:

"No, no; stay where you are. You are charmingly grouped, and appear to uncommon advantage. The picturesque would be spoilt by admitting a fourth. Besides, that path is most assuredly rife with zombies, and I have not the inclination to engage in fighting them off to-day. Good-bye."

She then ran gaily off, rejoicing as she rambled about, in the hope of being at home again in a day or two. Jane was already so much recovered as to intend leaving her room for a couple of hours that evening.

CHAPTER 11

WHEN THE LADIES REMOVED after dinner, Elizabeth ran up to her sister, and seeing her well, attended her into the drawing-room, where she was welcomed by Miss Bingley and Mrs. Hurst with many professions of pleasure. Elizabeth had never seen them so agreeable as they were during the hour which passed before the gentlemen appeared. Despite their lack of fighting skill, she had to admit that their powers of conversation were considerable. "If only words were capable of beheading a zombie," she thought, "I would presently find myself in the company of the world's two greatest warriors."

But when the gentlemen entered, Miss Bingley's eyes were instantly turned toward Darcy, and she had something to say to him before he had advanced many steps. He addressed himself to Jane, with a polite congratulation; Mr. Hurst also made her a slight bow, and said he was "very glad indeed that it had been but a cold, and not the strange plague." But the greatest warmth remained for Bingley's salutation. He was full of joy and attention. The first half-hour was spent in piling up the fire, lest she should suffer from the change of room. He then sat down by her, and talked scarcely to anyone else. Elizabeth took to the small grinding wheel in the corner of the room and watched it all with great delight whilst sharpening the gentlemen's swords—which she had found embarrassingly dull upon examination.

When tea was over, Mr. Hurst reminded his sister-in-law of the card-table—but in vain. She had obtained private intelligence that Mr. Darcy did not wish for cards; and Mr. Hurst soon found even his open petition rejected. She assured him that no one intended to play, and the silence of the whole party on the subject seemed to justify her. Mr. Hurst had there-fore nothing to do, but to stretch himself on one of the sofas and go to sleep. Darcy took up a book; Miss Bingley did the same; and Mrs. Hurst, principally occupied in playing with one of Elizabeth's throwing stars, joined now and then in her brother's conversation with Miss Bennet.

Miss Bingley's attention was quite as much engaged in watching Mr. Darcy's progress through his book, as in reading her own; and she was perpetually either making some inquiry, or looking at his page. She could not win him, however, to any conversation; he merely answered her question, and read on. At length, quite exhausted by the attempt to be amused with her own book, which she had only chosen because it was the second volume of his, she gave a great yawn and said, "How pleasant it is to spend an evening in this way! I declare after all there is no enjoyment like reading!"

"Spoken like one who has never known the ecstasy of holding a still-beating heart in her hand," said Darcy.

Miss Bingley—who was quite used to having her lack of combat training impugned—made no reply. She then yawned again, threw aside her book, and cast her eyes round the room in quest for some amuse-ment; when hearing her brother mentioning a ball to Miss Bennet, she turned suddenly towards him and said:

"By the bye, Charles, are you really serious in meditating a dance at Netherfield? I would advise you to consult the wishes of the present party; I am much mistaken if there are not some among us to whom a ball would be rather a punishment than a pleasure."

"If you mean Darcy," cried her brother, "he may go to bed, if he chooses, before it begins—but as for the ball, it is quite a settled thing; and as soon as the ground has sufficiently hardened and the present increase in unmentionables has passed, I shall send round my cards."

"I should like balls infinitely better," she replied, "if they were carried on in a different manner."

"You should like balls infinitely better," said Darcy, "if you knew the first thing about them."

Elizabeth blushed and suppressed a smile—slightly shocked by his flirtation with impropriety, and slightly impressed that he should endeavor to flirt with it at all. Miss Bingley, ignorant of his meaning, made no answer, and soon afterwards she got up and walked about the room. Her figure was elegant, and she walked well; but Darcy, at whom it was all aimed, was still inflexibly studious. In the desperation of her feelings, she resolved on one effort more, and, turning to Elizabeth, said:

"Miss Eliza Bennet, let me persuade you to follow my example, and take a turn about the room. I assure you it is very refreshing after sitting so long in one attitude."

Elizabeth needed no such refreshment—she had once been ordered to maintain a handstand for six days in the blistering Beijing sun—but agreed to it immediately. Miss Bingley succeeded no less in the real object of her civility; Mr. Darcy looked up and unconsciously closed his book. He was directly invited to join their party, but he declined it, observing that he could imagine but two motives for their choosing to walk up and down the room together, either of which his joining them would upset. "What could he mean?" She was dying to know what could be his meaning—and asked Elizabeth whether she could at all understand him?

"Not at all," was her answer; "but depend upon it, he means to be severe on us, and our surest way of disappointing him will be to ask nothing about it."

Miss Bingley, however, was incapable of such self-discipline, and persevered therefore in requiring an explanation of his two motives.

"I have not the smallest objection to explaining them," said he. "You either choose this method of passing the evening because you are incapable of sitting quietly, or because you are conscious that your figures appear to the greatest advantage in walking; if the first, you are but silly girls undeserving of my attention, and if the second, I can admire you much better from here. In fact, the glow of the fire casts quite a revealing silhouette against the fabric of your gowns."

"Oh! Shocking!" cried Miss Bingley, stepping away from the fireplace. "I never heard anything so abominable. How shall we punish him for such a speech?"

"I have several ideas on the subject," said Elizabeth, "but I'm afraid none would meet with the approval of the present party. Have you no insight into his weaknesses, you and he being so intimately acquainted?"

"Upon my honour, I do *not*. I do assure you that my intimacy has not yet taught me *that*. Mr. Darcy possesses calmness of manner, presence of mind, and bravery in battle."

"Yes, but does he not also possess vanity and pride?"

"Yes, vanity is a weakness indeed, said Miss Bingley, "but pride—where there is a real superiority of mind, pride will be always under good regulation."

Elizabeth turned away to hide a smile.

"Your examination of Mr. Darcy is over, I presume," said Miss Bingley, "and pray what is the result?"

"I am perfectly convinced by it that Mr. Darcy has no defect."

"No," said Darcy, "I have faults enough, but they are not, I hope, of understanding. My temper I dare not vouch for. I have taken many a life for offenses which would seem but trifles to other men."

"That is a failing indeed!" cried Elizabeth. "But you have chosen your fault well, for it is one which I share. I too live by the warrior code, and would gladly kill if my honour demanded it. You are safe from me."

"There is, I believe, in every disposition a tendency to some particular evil—a natural defect, which not even the best education can
overcome."

"And your defect, Mr. Darcy, is to hate everybody."

"And yours," he replied with a smile, "is willfully to misunderstand
them."

"Do let us have a little music," cried Miss Bingley, tired of a conversation in which she had no share. "Louisa, you will not mind my
waking Mr. Hurst?"

Her sister had not the smallest objection, and the pianoforte was
opened; and Darcy was not sorry for it. He began to feel the danger of
paying Elizabeth too much attention.

CHAPTER 12

IN CONSEQUENCE OF AN AGREEMENT between the sisters,
Elizabeth wrote the next morning to their mother, to beg that the
carriage might be sent for them in the course of the day. But Mrs.
Bennet, who had calculated on her daughters remaining at Netherfield
till the following Tuesday, which would exactly finish Jane's week, could
not bring herself to receive them with pleasure before. Her answer,
therefore, was disappointing. Mrs. Bennet sent them word that they
could not possibly have the carriage before Tuesday, for it had been badly
damaged by errant musket balls during a skirmish between soldiers and
a party of the sorry stricken near the encampment at Meryton.

This was at least partially true—for the carriage had indeed been
caught in a crossfire when Catherine and Lydia used it to visit with a
group of officers; but the damage was in fact less severe than Mrs. Bennet
suggested. In her postscript it was added that if Mr. Bingley and his sister
pressed them to stay longer, she could spare them. Against staying longer,

however, Elizabeth urged Jane to borrow Mr. Bingley's carriage immediately, and at length it was settled that their original design of leaving Netherfield that morning should be mentioned, and the request made.

The request excited many professions of concern; and enough was said of wishing them to stay at least till the following day to allow the ground to further harden; and till the morrow their going was deferred. Miss Bingley was then sorry that she had proposed the delay, for her jealousy and dislike of Elizabeth much exceeded her affection for Jane.

Mr. Bingley heard with real sorrow that they were to go so soon, and repeatedly tried to persuade Miss Bennet that it would not be safe for her—that she was not enough recovered to fight if the carriage should meet with trouble; but Jane reminded him that Elizabeth was as capable a bodyguard as there was in all of England.

To Mr. Darcy it was welcome intelligence—Elizabeth had been at Netherfield long enough. She attracted him more than he liked—and Miss Bingley was uncivil to *her*, and more teasing than usual to himself. He resolved that no sign of admiration should *now* escape him. Steady to his purpose, he scarcely spoke ten words to her through the whole of Saturday, and though they were at one time left by themselves for half an hour, he adhered most conscientiously to his book, and would not even look at her.

On Sunday, after morning service, the separation took place. Miss Bingley's civility to Elizabeth increased at last very rapidly, as well as her affection for Jane; and when they parted, after assuring the latter of the pleasure it would always give her to see her either at Longbourn or Netherfield and embracing her most tenderly, she even shook hands with the former. Elizabeth took leave of the whole party in the liveliest of spirits.

The ride to Longbourn was altogether agreeable, save for a brief encounter with a small herd of zombie children, no doubt from Mrs. Beechman's Home for Orphans, which had recently fallen along with the entire parish of St. Thomas. Mr. Bingley's coachman could not help

but vomit down the front of his cravat at the sight of the tiny devils grazing on sun-hardened corpses in a nearby field. Elizabeth kept her musket close, lest they advance. But luck was on their side, and the cursed
children took no notice of the carriage.

They were not welcomed home very cordially by their mother.
Mrs. Bennet thought them very wrong to give so much trouble, and was
sure Jane would have caught cold again. Her protests were inflamed by
the sight of vomit on the coachman's cravat—a sure sign that they had
encountered unmentionables en route. But their father was truly glad to
see them, for the evening sparring sessions had lost much of their animation by the absence of Jane and Elizabeth.

They found Mary, as usual, deep in the study of human nature;
Catherine and Lydia had information for them of a different sort. Much
had been done and much had been said in the regiment since the preceding Wednesday; several of the officers had dined lately with their
uncle, a private had been flogged for engaging in base acts with a head-
less corpse, and it had actually been hinted that Colonel Forster was
going to be married.

CHAPTER 13

I HOPE, MY DEAR," said Mr. Bennet to his wife, as they were at
breakfast the next morning, "that you have ordered a good dinner
to-day, because I have reason to expect an addition to our family party."

"Who do you mean, my dear? I know of nobody that is coming, I
am sure, unless Charlotte Lucas should happen to call in—and I am sure
my dinners are good enough for her, since she is an unmarried woman
of seven-and-twenty, and as such should expect little more than a crust
of bread washed down with a cup of loneliness."

"The person of whom I speak is a gentleman, and a stranger."

Mrs. Bennet's eyes sparkled. "A gentleman and a stranger! It is Mr. Bingley, I am sure! I shall be extremely glad to see Mr. Bingley. But—good Lord! How unlucky! There is not a bit of fish to be got to-day. Lydia, my love, ring the bell—I must speak to Hill this moment."

"It is *not* Mr. Bingley, you senseless old cur," said her husband; "it is a person whom I never saw in the whole course of my life."

After amusing himself some time with their curiosity, he thus explained:

"About a month ago I received this letter; and about a fortnight ago I answered it. It is from my cousin, Mr. Collins, who, when I am dead, may turn you all out of this house as soon as he pleases."

"Oh! My dear," cried his wife, "Pray do not talk of that odious man. I do think it is the hardest thing in the world that your estate should be entailed away from your own children!"

Jane and Elizabeth tried to explain that all five of them were capable of fending for themselves; that they could make tolerable fortunes as bodyguards, assassins, or mercenaries if need be. But it was a subject on which Mrs. Bennet was beyond the reach of reason, and she continued to rail bitterly against the cruelty of settling an estate away from a family of five daughters, in favour of a man whom nobody cared anything about.

"It certainly is a most iniquitous affair," said Mr. Bennet, "and nothing can clear Mr. Collins from the guilt of inheriting Longbourn. But if you will listen to his letter, you may perhaps be a little softened by his manner of expressing himself."

Hunsford, near Westerham, Kent,
15th October

DEAR SIR,

The disagreement subsisting between yourself and my late honoured father always gave me much uneasiness. He was a great warrior, as you once were, and I know he looked with fondness upon the days when both of you fought side by side—back when the strange plague was but an isolated inconvenience. Since his passing, I have frequently wished to heal the breach; but for some time I was kept back by my own doubts, fearing lest it might seem disrespectful to his memory for me to be on good terms with anyone with whom my father had once vowed to castrate. My mind, however, is now made up on the subject, for having entered the priesthood, I have been so fortunate as to be distinguished by the patronage of the Right Honourable Lady Catherine de Bourgh . . .

"Heavens!" cried Elizabeth, "He works for Lady Catherine!"
"Let me finish," said Mr. Bennet, sternly.

. . . whose skill with blade and musket are unmatched, and who has slain more unmentionables than any woman known. As a clergyman, I feel it my duty to promote and establish the blessing of peace in all families. If you should have no objection to receive me into your house, I propose myself the satisfaction of waiting on you and your family, Monday, November 18th, by four o'clock, and shall probably trespass on your hospitality till the Saturday following. I remain, dear sir, with respectful compliments to your lady and daughters, your well-wisher and friend,
    WILLIAM COLLINS

"At four o'clock, therefore, we may expect this peace-making gentleman," said Mr. Bennet, as he folded up the letter. "He seems to be a most conscientious and polite young man, and I doubt not will prove a valuable acquaintance, especially in light of his association with Lady Catherine.
    Mr. Collins was punctual to his time, and was received with great

politeness by the whole family. Mr. Bennet indeed said little; but the ladies were ready enough to talk, and Mr. Collins seemed neither in need of encouragement, nor inclined to be silent himself. He was a short, fat young man of five-and-twenty. His air was grave and stately, and his manners were very formal. He had not been long seated before he complimented Mrs. Bennet on having so fine a family of daughters; said he had heard much of their beauty, but that in this instance fame had fallen short of the truth; and added, that he could hardly wait to see a display of their legendary fighting skill.

"You are very kind, I am sure; but I should rather see them with husbands than muskets, for else they will be destitute enough. Things are settled so oddly."

"You allude, perhaps, to the entail of this estate."

"Ah! Sir, I do indeed. It is a grievous affair to my poor girls, you must confess."

"I am very sensible, madam, of the hardship to my fair cousins, and could say much on the subject, but that I am cautious of appearing forward and precipitate. But I can assure the young ladies that I come prepared to admire them. At present I will not say more; but, perhaps, when we are better acquainted—"

He was interrupted by a summons to dinner; and the girls smiled on each other. They were not the only objects of Mr. Collins's admiration. The hall, the dining-room, and all its furniture, were examined and praised; and his commendation of everything would have touched Mrs. Bennet's heart, but for the mortifying supposition of his viewing it all as his own future property. The dinner too was highly admired; and he begged to know to which of his fair cousins the excellency of its cookery was owing.

Briefly forgetting her manners, Mary grabbed her fork and leapt from her chair onto the table. Lydia, who was seated nearest her, grabbed her ankle before she could dive at Mr. Collins and, presumably, stab him about the head and neck for such an insult. Jane and Elizabeth turned away so Mr. Collins would not see them laughing.

He was set right by Mrs. Bennet, who assured him with some asperity that they were very well able to keep a good cook, and that her daughters were too busy training to be bothered with the kitchen. He begged pardon for having displeased Mary. In a softened tone she declared herself not at all offended; but he continued to apologise for about a quarter of an hour.

CHAPTER 14

DURING DINNER, Mr. Bennet scarcely spoke at all; but when the servants were withdrawn, he thought it time to have some conversation with his guest, and therefore started a subject in which he expected him to shine, by observing that he seemed very fortunate in his patroness. Lady Catherine de Bourgh was not only one of the King's richest servants, but also one of his deadliest. Mr. Bennet could not have chosen better. Mr. Collins was eloquent in her praise, offering that he had never in his life witnessed such self-discipline in a person of rank. Lady Catherine was reckoned proud by many people he knew, but *he* had never seen anything but a singular dedication to the art of killing zombies. She had always spoken to him as she would to any other gentleman; she made not the smallest objection to his watching her spar nor to his leaving the parish occasionally for a week or two, to visit his relations. She had even advised him to marry as soon as he could, provided he chose with discretion.

"I have oft dreamt of watching Lady Catherine spar," said Elizabeth. "Does she live near you, sir?"

"The garden in which stands my humble abode is separated only by a lane from Rosings Park, her ladyship's residence."

"I think you said she was a widow, sir? Has she any family?"

"She has only one daughter, the heiress of Rosings, and of very extensive property."

"Ah!" said Mrs. Bennet, shaking her head, "then she is better off than many girls. And what sort of young lady is she? Is she handsome?"

"She is a most charming young lady indeed. Lady Catherine herself says that, in point of true beauty, Miss de Bourgh is far superior to the handsomest of her sex, because there is that in her features which marks the young lady of distinguished birth. She is unfortunately of a sickly constitution, which has prevented her from following her mother's example in regards to the deadly arts. I fear can she hardly lift a saber, let alone wield one with such skill as Her Ladyship."

"Has she been presented? I do not remember her name among the ladies at court."

"Her indifferent state of health unhappily prevents her being in town; and by that means, as I told Lady Catherine one day, has deprived the British court of its brightest ornament. You may imagine that I am happy to offer these little delicate compliments which are always acceptable to ladies."

"You judge very properly," said Mr. Bennet. "May I ask whether these pleasing attentions proceed from the impulse of the moment, or are the result of previous study?"

"They arise chiefly from what is passing at the time, and though I sometimes amuse myself with suggesting and arranging such little elegant compliments as may be adapted to ordinary occasions, I always wish to give them as unstudied an air as possible."

Mr. Bennet's expectations were fully answered. His cousin was as absurd as he had hoped, and he listened to him with the keenest enjoyment, maintaining at the same time the most resolute composure of countenance.

When tea was over, Mr. Bennet was glad to invite him to read aloud to the ladies. Mr. Collins readily assented, and a book was produced; but, on beholding it (for everything announced it to be from a circulating library), he started back, and begging pardon, protested that he never read novels. Kitty stared at him, and Lydia exclaimed. Other books were produced, and after some deliberation he chose Fordyce's *Sermons*. Lydia gaped as he opened the volume, and before he had, with very monotonous solemnity, read three pages, she interrupted him with:

"Do you know, mamma, that my Uncle Philips talks of an additional battalion coming to join Colonel Forster's? My aunt told me so herself on Saturday. I shall walk to Meryton to-morrow to hear more about it, assuming one of my sisters is willing to join me."

Lydia was bid by her two eldest sisters to hold her tongue; but Mr. Collins, much offended, laid aside his book, and said:

"I have often observed how little young ladies are uninterested by books of a serious stamp. I will no longer importune my young cousin."

Then turning to Mr. Bennet, he offered himself as his antagonist at backgammon. Mr. Bennet accepted the challenge, observing that he acted wisely in leaving the girls to their own trifling amusements. Mrs. Bennet and her daughters apologised for Lydia's interruption, which, claimed Mrs. Bennet, would have earned her ten wet bamboo lashes had she still been under the tutelage of Master Liu. They promised that it should not occur again, if he would resume his book; but Mr. Collins, after assuring them that he bore his young cousin no ill-will, and should never resent her behaviour as any affront, seated himself at another table with Mr. Bennet, and prepared for backgammon.

CHAPTER 15

MR. COLLINS WAS NOT a sensible man, and the deficiency of nature had been but little assisted by education or society; the greatest part of his life having been spent under the guidance of a brave but illiterate father; and though he belonged to one of the universities, he had oft borne the condemnation of his peers for a perceived lack of bloodlust. The subjection in which his father had brought him up had given him much knowledge of the art of combat; but it was a good deal counteracted by his weak head, fleshy figure, and now, the ease of his current patronage. A fortunate chance had recommended him to Lady Catherine de Bourgh, who had been forced to behead her previous rector when he succumbed to the walking death.

Having now a good house and a very sufficient income, he intended to marry; and in seeking a reconciliation with the Longbourn family he had a wife in view, as he meant to choose one of the daughters, if he found them as handsome and amiable as they were represented by common report. This was his plan of amends—of atonement—for inheriting their father's estate; and he thought it an excellent one, full of eligibility and suitableness, and excessively generous on his own part.

His plan did not vary on seeing them. The eldest daughter's lovely face and striking muscle tone confirmed his views, and for the first evening she was his settled choice. The next morning, however, made an alteration; for in a quarter of an hour's tête-à-tête with Mrs. Bennet before breakfast, a conversation beginning with his parsonage-house, and leading naturally to the avowal of his hopes, that a mistress might be found for it at Longbourn, produced from her, amid very complaisant smiles and general encouragement, a caution against the very Jane he had fixed on. As to her *younger* daughters, she could not take upon her to say—she could not positively answer—but she did not know of any prepossession; her eldest daughter, she must just mention—she felt it incumbent on her to hint, was likely to be very soon engaged.

Elizabeth, equally next to Jane in birth and beauty, and perhaps surpassing her in skill, succeeded her of course. Mrs. Bennet treasured up the hint, and trusted that she might soon have two daughters married; and the man whom she could not bear to speak of the day before was now high in her good graces.

Lydia's intention of walking to Meryton was not forgotten; every sister except Mary agreed to go with her, determined that she survive the trip. Mr. Collins was to attend them, at the request of Mr. Bennet, who was most anxious to get rid of him, and have his library to himself.

Mr. Collins used the walk to Meryton to his advantage, spending most of it at the side of Elizabeth—who was watching the surrounding woods, prepared to meet to first sign of trouble with her Brown Bess. Jane and the others followed behind, their muskets also thus engaged. Mr. Collins, who fancied himself a man of peace, carried neither barrel nor blade; he happily puffed away on his ivory and chestnut pipe—"a gift from her ladyship," he boasted at every opportunity.

They were scarcely a quarter mile past the old croquet grounds, when Elizabeth first caught the scent of death. Seeing her body tense, the other girls raised their muskets and closed ranks, ready to meet an attack from any direction.

"Is . . . is there some sort of trouble?" asked Mr. Collins, who suddenly looked as if he might faint.

Elizabeth pressed a finger to her lips, and motioned for her sisters to follow. She led them along a set of carriage tracks, her footsteps so light as to leave even the smallest grain of sand undisturbed. The tracks continued for a few yards before suddenly veering toward the woods, where broken branches signaled the very spot it had left its wheels and plummeted into the ravine that paralleled one side of the road. Elizabeth peered over the side. Some twenty yards below, eight or nine blood-soaked zombies crawled over a shattered wagon and its leaking barrels. Most of them were busy picking at the innards of the carriage horse; but one happy dreadful was scooping the last morsels from the broken skull of the driver—a young girl the sisters recognized at once.

"Good Heavens!" whispered Jane. "Penny McGregor! Oh! Poor, miserable girl! How often we warned her not to ride alone!"

Penny McGregor had delivered lamp oil to Longbourn, and most of the estates within thirty miles of Meryton, since she was scarcely old enough to talk. The McGregors owned a modest home not far from town, where they daily received cartfuls of whale blubber, and processed it into lamp oil and fine perfumes. The smell was unbearable, especially during summer; but their goods were desperately needed, and the McGregors were known to be among the most pleasant people in all of Hertfordshire.

"God have mercy on that wretched girl," said Mr. Collins, who had joined them.

"Can't we just be on our way?" asked Lydia. "There's no helping her now. Besides, think of how dirty our dresses will get if we have to fight in that awful ravine." As Jane expressed her shock at such a senti- ment, and Kitty argued in favor of it, Elizabeth took the pipe from Mr. Collins' mouth, blew on the glowing tobacco, and threw it over the side.

"That was a gift from *her ladyship!*" he cried, loud enough to draw the attention of the zombies below. They looked up and let loose their terrible roars, which were cut short by a violent, fiery explosion as pipe and oil met. Suddenly engulfed, the zombies staggered about, flailing wildly and screaming as they cooked. Jane raised her Brown Bess, but Elizabeth pushed the barrel aside.

"Let them burn," she said. "Let them have a taste of eternity."

Turning to her cousin, who had averted his eyes, she added, "You see, Mr. Collins . . . God has no mercy. And neither must we."

Though angered by her blasphemy, he thought better of saying anything on the matter, for he saw in Elizabeth's eyes a kind of darkness; a kind of absence—as if her soul had taken leave, so that compassion and warmth could not interfere.

Upon entering Meryton, after stopping at the McGregors to deliver the unhappy news, the eyes of the younger ones were immedi- ately wandering up in the street in quest of the officers, and nothing less than a very smart bonnet indeed, or the wail of the undead, could recall them.

But the attention of every lady was soon caught by a young man, whom they had never seen before, of most gentlemanlike appearance, walking with another officer on the other side of the way. The other officer, Mr. Denny, was known to Lydia, and he bowed as they passed.

All were struck with the stranger's air, all wondered who he could be; and Kitty and Lydia, determined to find out, led the way across the street, under pretense of wanting something in an opposite shop, and fortunately had just gained the pavement when the two gentlemen, turning back, had reached the same spot. Mr. Denny addressed them directly, and entreated permission to introduce his friend, Mr. Wickham, who had returned with him the day before from town, and he was happy to say had accepted a commission in their corps. This was exactly as it should be; for the young man wanted only regimentals to make him completely charming. His appearance was greatly in his favour; he had all the best part of beauty, a fine countenance, a good figure, and very pleasing address. The introduction was followed up on his side by a happy readiness of conversation—a readiness at the same time perfectly correct and unassuming; and the whole party were still standing and talking together very agreeably, when the sound of horses drew their notice, and Darcy and Bingley were seen riding down the street. On distinguishing the ladies of the group, the two gentlemen came directly towards them, and began the usual civilities. Bingley was the principal spokesman, and Jane Bennet the principal object. He was then, he said, on his way to Longbourn on purpose to inquire after her. Mr. Darcy corroborated it with a bow, and was beginning to determine not to fix his eyes on Elizabeth, when they were suddenly arrested by the sight of the stranger.

Elizabeth happened to see the countenance of both as they looked at each other, so slight as to escape all but her highly trained eye. Both changed colour, one looked white, the other red. Mr. Wickham, after a few moments, touched his hat—a salutation which Mr. Darcy just deigned to return. Elizabeth could tell by the miniscule twitches of Darcy's sword hand that he had briefly flirted with the notion of drawing his blade. What could be the meaning of it?

In another minute, Mr. Bingley, without seeming to have noticed what passed, took leave and rode on with his friend.

Mr. Denny and Mr. Wickham walked with the young ladies to the door of Mr. Philips's house, and then made their bows, in spite of Miss Lydia's pressing entreaties that they should come in, and even in spite of Mrs. Philips's throwing up the parlour window and loudly seconding the invitation.

Mrs. Philips was always glad to see her nieces; and the two eldest, from their recent absence, were particularly welcome. Her civility was claimed towards Mr. Collins by Jane's introduction of him. She received him with her very best politeness, which he returned with as much more, apologising for his intrusion, without any previous acquaintance with her. Mrs. Philips was quite awed by such an excess of good breeding; but her contemplation of one stranger was soon put to an end by exclamations and inquiries about the other; of whom, however, she could only tell her nieces what they already knew, that Mr. Denny had brought him from London, and that he was to have a lieutenant's commission in the regiment which was presently engaged to the North. She had been watching him the last hour, she said, as he walked up and down the street, and had Mr. Wickham appeared, Kitty and Lydia would certainly have continued the occupation, but unluckily no one passed windows now except a few of the officers, who, in comparison with the stranger, were become "stupid, disagreeable fellows." Some of them were to dine with the Philipses the next day, and their aunt promised to make her husband call on Mr. Wickham, and give him an invitation also, if the family from Longbourn would come in the evening. This was agreed to, and Mrs. Philips protested that they would have a little bit of hot supper, and a nice comfortable noisy game of Crypt and Coffin. The prospect of such delights was very cheering, and they parted in mutual good spirits.

As they walked home, Elizabeth related to Jane what she had seen pass between the two gentlemen; but though Jane would have defended either or both, had they appeared to be in the wrong, she could no more explain such behaviour than her sister.

CHAPTER 16

A S NO OBJECTION was made to the young people's engagement with their aunt, the coach conveyed Mr. Collins and his
five cousins at a suitable hour to Meryton.

As they passed the croquet grounds and the scorched acre of woods
that marked Penny McGregor's final resting place, the idle chatter that
had engaged them thus far was suddenly ended; for all six could think
of nothing but the news which had only that morning reached them at
Longbourn. Penny's father, mad with grief, had thrown himself into a
vat of boiling perfume. By the time his apprentices pulled him out, he
had been badly disfigured and rendered blind. Doctors were unsure if he
would survive, or if the stench would ever leave him. All sat in reverent
silence until they reached the outskirts of Meryton.

Upon reaching their destination, Mr. Collins was at leisure to look
around him and admire, and he was so much struck with the size and
furniture of the apartment, that he declared he might almost have supposed himself in one of Lady Catherine's drawing-rooms. Mrs. Philips
felt all the force of the compliment, being herself quite aware of Lady
Catherine's proclivity for slaying the sorry stricken, which, she dare
thought, exceeded that of her own nieces'.

In describing to her all the grandeur of Lady Catherine and her
mansion, which had received considerable improvements, including a
grand dojo, and new quarters for her private guard of ninjas, Mr.
Collins was happily employed until the gentlemen joined them; and he
found in Mrs. Philips a very attentive listener, whose opinion of his
consequence increased with what she heard, and who was resolving to
retail it all among her neighbours as soon as she could. To the girls,
who could not listen to their cousin without taking a silent inventory

of the countless ways they could kill him, the interval of waiting appeared very long. It was over at last, however. The gentlemen did approach, and when Mr. Wickham walked into the room, Elizabeth felt as if she had just been stunned by a devastating roundhouse kick. Such was his effect on her—that those traits of her sex, despite all her training, remained susceptible to influence. The officers of the shire were in general a very creditable, gentlemanlike set; but Mr. Wickham was as far beyond them all in person, countenance, air, and walk, as *they* were superior to the broad-faced, stuffy Uncle Philips, breathing port wine, who followed them into the room.

Mr. Wickham was the happy man toward whom almost every female eye was turned, and Elizabeth was the happy woman by whom he finally seated himself; and the agreeable manner in which he immediately fell into conversation, though it was only on its being a wet night, made her feel that the commonest, dullest, most threadbare topic might be rendered interesting by the skill of the speaker.

With such rivals for the notice of the fair as Mr. Wickham and the officers, Mr. Collins seemed to sink into insignificance; to the young ladies he certainly was nothing; but he had still at intervals a kind listener in Mrs. Philips, and was by her watchfulness, most abundantly supplied with coffee and muffin. When the card-tables were placed, he had the opportunity of obliging her in turn, by sitting down to Crypt and Coffin.

Mr. Wickham did not play at Crypt and Coffin, and with ready delight was he received at the other table between Elizabeth and Lydia. At first there seemed danger of Lydia's engrossing him entirely, for she was a most determined talker; but being likewise extremely fond of cards, she soon grew too much interested in the game, too eager to know whether players would find their "crypts" eerily empty or their "coffins" happily full. Allowing for the common demands of the game, Mr. Wickham was therefore at leisure to talk to Elizabeth, and she was very willing to hear him, though what she chiefly wished to hear she could not hope to be told—the history of his acquaintance with Mr. Darcy. She dared not even mention that gentleman. Her curiosity, however, was unexpectedly relieved. Mr. Wickham began the subject himself. He inquired how far Netherfield was from Meryton; and, after receiving her answer, asked in a hesitating manner how long Mr. Darcy had been staying there.

"About a month," said Elizabeth. "He is a man of many kills, I understand."

"Yes," replied Mr. Wickham; "his talent as a warrior is above reproach. You could not have met with a person more capable of giving you certain information on that head than myself, for I have been connected with his family in a particular manner from my infancy."

Elizabeth could not but look surprised.

"You may well be surprised, Miss Bennet, at such an assertion, after seeing, as a lady of your training probably might, the very cold manner of our meeting yesterday. Are you much acquainted with Mr. Darcy?"

"As much as I ever wish to be," cried Elizabeth very warmly. "I have spent four days in the same house with him, and I think him very disagreeable."

"I have no right to give *my* opinion," said Wickham, "as to his being agreeable or otherwise. I am not qualified to form one. I have known him too long and too well to be a fair judge. It is impossible for *me* to be impartial. But I believe your opinion of him would in general astonish—and perhaps you would not express it quite so strongly anywhere else, other than here in your own family."

"Upon my word, I say no more *here* than I might say in any house in the neighbourhood, except Netherfield. He is not at all liked in Hertfordshire. Everybody is disgusted with his pride. I hope your plans in favour of the shire will not be affected by his being in the neighbourhood."

"Oh! No—it is not for *me* to be driven away by Mr. Darcy. If he wishes to avoid seeing me, he must go. We are not on friendly terms, and it always gives me pain to meet him, but I have no reason for avoiding *him.* We are, after all, both warriors—and it is beneath the honour of a warrior to shrink from the sight of any man. His father, Miss Bennet, the late Mr. Darcy, was one of the best zombie slayers that ever breathed, and the truest friend I ever had; and I can never be in company with this Mr. Darcy without being grieved by a thousand tender recollections. His behaviour to myself has been scandalous; but I believe I could forgive him anything, rather than his disappointing the hopes and disgracing the memory of his father."

Elizabeth found the interest of the subject increase, and listened with all her heart; but the delicacy of it prevented further inquiry.

Mr. Wickham began to speak on more general topics, Meryton, the neighbourhood, the society, appearing highly pleased with all that he had yet seen, excluding of course the ever-increasing number of unmentionables—no doubt a direct consequence of Manchester's collapse.

"A military life is not what I was intended for, but circumstances have now made it unavoidable, as they have for so many who intended otherwise with their lives. The church ought to have been my profession—I was brought up for the church, and I should at this time have been in possession of a most valuable living, had it pleased the gentleman we were speaking of just now."

"Indeed!"

"Yes—the late Mr. Darcy bequeathed me the next presentation of the best living in his gift. He was my godfather, and excessively attached to me. I cannot do justice to his kindness. He meant to provide for me amply, and thought he had done it; but when he was slain in the Second Battle of Kent, it was given elsewhere."

"Good heavens!" cried Elizabeth; "but how could that be? How could his will be disregarded? Why did you not seek legal redress?"

"There was just such an informality in the terms of the bequest as to give me no hope from law. A man of honour could not have doubted the intention, but Mr. Darcy chose to doubt it—or to treat it as a merely conditional recommendation, and to assert that I had

forfeited all claim to it by extravagance, imprudence—in short anything or nothing. But the fact is, that we are very different sort of
men, and that he hates me."

"This is quite shocking! He deserves to be felled at the end of a
Zatoichi Cane Sword!"

"Some time or other he *will* be—but it shall not be by *me*. Till I
can forget his father, I can never expose him or challenge him to duel."

Elizabeth honoured him for such feelings, and thought him handsomer than ever as he expressed them.

"But what," said she, after a pause, "can have been his motive? What
can have induced him to behave so cruelly?"

"A thorough, determined dislike of me—a dislike which I cannot
but attribute in some measure to jealousy. Had the late Mr. Darcy liked
me less, his son might have borne with me better; but his father's
uncommon attachment to me irritated him, I believe, very early in life.
He could find no fault with me, and I dare say it drove Darcy to resent
my very existence. And when his father passed, he saw his opportunity
to punish me for years of perceived injustice."

"I had not thought Mr. Darcy so bad as this—though I have never
liked him. I never suspected him of descending to such malicious
revenge, such injustice, such inhumanity as this."

Mr. Wickham related to Elizabeth a tale from his youth, which he
believed best illustrated the nature of that inhumanity. When he and
Darcy were both boys of no more than seven years, the elder Darcy had
taken a keen interest in their training. One day, during a daybreak spar,
the young Wickham landed a severe kick, which sent Darcy to the
ground. The elder Darcy implored Wickham to "finish" his son with a
blow to the throat. When the boy protested, the elder Darcy—rather
than punishing him for insolence, praised his generosity of spirit. The
young Darcy, embarrassed more by his father's preference than his own
defeat, attacked Wickham when his back was turned—sweeping his legs
with a quarterstaff, and shattering the bones of both. It was nearly a year

before he walked without the aid of a cane.

"Can such abominable pride as his have ever done him good?"

"Yes. It has often led him to be liberal and generous, to give his money freely, to display hospitality, to assist his tenants, and relieve the poor. He has also brotherly pride, which, with some brotherly affection, makes him a very kind and careful guardian of his sister."

"What sort of a girl is Miss Darcy?"

He shook his head. "I wish I could call her amiable. It gives me pain to speak ill of a Darcy. But she is too much like her brother—very, very proud. As a child, she was affectionate and pleasing, and extremely fond of me; and I have devoted hours and hours to her amusement. But she is nothing to me now. She is a handsome girl, about fifteen or sixteen, and, I understand, highly skilled in the deadly arts. Since her father's death, her home has been London, where a lady lives with her, and superintends her training."

After many pauses and many trials of other subjects, Elizabeth could not help reverting once more to the first, and saying:

"I am astonished at his intimacy with Mr. Bingley! How can Mr. Bingley, who seems good humour itself, and is, I really believe, truly amiable, be in friendship with such a man? How can they suit each other? Do you know Mr. Bingley?"

"Not at all."

"He is a sweet-tempered, amiable, charming man. He cannot know what Mr. Darcy is."

The Crypt and Coffin party soon afterwards breaking up, the players gathered round the other table and Mr. Collins took his station between his cousin Elizabeth and Mrs. Philips. The usual inquiries as to his success was made by the latter. It had not been very great; he had found the majority of his crypts quite full of zombies; but when Mrs. Philips began to express her concern thereupon, he assured her with much earnest gravity that it was not of the least importance, that he considered the money as a mere trifle, and begged that she would not make herself uneasy.

"I know very well, madam," said he, "that when persons sit down to a game of Crypt and Coffin, they must take their chances of these things, and happily I am not in such circumstances as to make five shillings any object. There are undoubtedly many who could not say the same, but thanks to Lady Catherine de Bourgh, I am removed far beyond the necessity of regarding little matters."

Mr. Wickham's attention was caught; and after observing Mr. Collins for a few moments, he asked Elizabeth in a low voice whether her relation was very intimately acquainted with the family of de Bourgh.

"Lady Catherine de Bourgh," she replied, "has very lately given him a living. I hardly know how Mr. Collins was first introduced to her notice, but he certainly has not known her long."

"You know of course that Lady Catherine de Bourgh and Lady Anne Darcy were sisters; consequently that she is aunt to the present Mr. Darcy."

"No, indeed, I did not. I knew only of Lady Catherine's claim to quieting more of Satan's servants than any woman in England."

"Her daughter, Miss de Bourgh, will have a very large fortune, and it is believed that she and her cousin will unite the two estates."

This information made Elizabeth smile, as she thought of poor Miss Bingley. Vain indeed must be all her attentions, vain and useless her affection for his sister and her praise of Mr. Darcy himself, unaware that he was already destined for another.

"Mr. Collins," said Elizabeth, "speaks highly both of Lady Catherine and her daughter; but I suspect his gratitude misleads him, and that in spite of her being his patroness and a great warrior, she is an arrogant, conceited woman."

"I believe her to be both in a great degree," replied Wickham; "I have not seen her for many years, but I very well remember that I never liked her, and that her manners were dictatorial and insolent. She has the reputation of being remarkably skilled; but I rather believe she derives part of her fame from her rank and fortune."

Elizabeth allowed that he had given a very rational account of it, and they continued talking together, with mutual satisfaction till supper put an end to cards, and gave the rest of the ladies their share of Mr. Wickham's attentions. There could be no conversation in the noise of Mrs. Philips's supper party, but his manners recommended him to everybody. Whatever he said, was said well; and whatever he did, done gracefully. Elizabeth went away with her head full of him. She could think of nothing but of Mr. Wickham, and of what he had told her, all the way home; but there was not time for her even to mention his name as they went, for she and her sisters could hear the groans of unmentionables echoing through the pitch black woods on either side of the carriage. They were distant enough so as not to arouse a fear of imminent attack, but close enough to necessitate a minimum of noise. They rode in silence, the girls with their firearms resting neatly on their laps. For once, Mr. Collins could not be persuaded to make a sound.

CHAPTER 17

ELIZABETH RELATED TO JANE the next day what had passed between Mr. Wickham and herself. Jane listened with astonishment and concern; she knew not how to believe that Mr. Darcy could be so unworthy of Mr. Bingley's regard; and yet, it was not in her nature to question the veracity of a young man of such amiable appearance as Wickham. The possibility of his having his legs shattered was enough to interest all her tender feelings; and nothing remained to be done, but to think well of them both, to defend the conduct of each, and throw into the account of accident or mistake whatever could not be otherwise explained.

"They have both," said she, "been deceived in some way or other.

Interested people have perhaps misrepresented each to the other. It is impossible for us to conjecture the causes which may have alienated them, without actual blame on either side."

"Very true, indeed; and now, my dear Jane, what have you got to say on behalf of the interested people who have probably been concerned in the business? Do clear *them* too, or we shall be obliged to think ill of somebody."

"Laugh as much as you choose, but you will not laugh me out of my opinion. My dearest Lizzy, do but consider in what a disgraceful light it places Mr. Darcy, to be treating his father's favourite in such a manner, one whom his father had trained in the deadly arts and promised to provide for. It is impossible."

"I can much more easily believe Mr. Bingley's being imposed on, than that Mr. Wickham should invent such a history of himself as he gave me last night; names, facts, everything mentioned without ceremony. If it be not so, let Mr. Darcy contradict it. Besides, there was truth in his looks."

"It is difficult indeed—it is distressing. One does not know what to think."

"I beg your pardon; one knows exactly what to think."

But Jane could think with certainty on only one point—that Mr. Bingley, if he *had been* imposed on, would have much to suffer when the affair became public, and may even feel a duel necessary to restore his honour. She could hardly bear the thought.

The two young ladies were summoned from the dojo, where this conversation passed, by the arrival of the very persons of whom they had been speaking; Mr. Bingley and his sisters came to give their personal invitation for the long-expected ball at Netherfield, which was fixed for the following Tuesday. Jane and Elizabeth were embarrassed to receive callers in their sparring gowns, but their unusual appearance did not deter the ladies from being delighted to see them—particularly, their dear friend Jane. The ladies called it an age since they had met, and repeatedly asked what she had been doing with herself since their separation. To the rest of the family they paid little attention; avoiding Mrs. Bennet as much as possible, saying not much to Elizabeth, and nothing at all to the others. They were soon gone again, rising from their seats with an activity which took their brother by surprise, and hurrying off as if eager to escape from Mrs. Bennet's civilities.

The prospect of the Netherfield ball was extremely agreeable to every female of the family. Mrs. Bennet chose to consider it as given in compliment to her eldest daughter, and was particularly flattered by receiving the invitation from Mr. Bingley himself, instead of a ceremonious card. Jane pictured to herself a happy evening in the society of her two friends, and the attentions of their brother; and Elizabeth thought with pleasure of dancing a great deal with Mr. Wickham, and of seeing a confirmation of everything in Mr. Darcy's look and behavior.

Elizabeth's spirits were so high on this occasion, that though she did not often speak unnecessarily to Mr. Collins, she could not help asking him whether he intended to accept Mr. Bingley's invitation, and if he did, whether he would think it proper to join in the evening's amusement; and she was rather surprised to find that he entertained no scruple whatever on that head, and was very far from dreading a rebuke either from the Archbishop, or Lady Catherine de Bourgh, by venturing to dance.

"I am by no means of the opinion," said he, "that a ball of this kind, given by a young man of character, can have any evil tendency; and I shall hope to be honoured with the hands of all my fair cousins in the course of the evening; and I take this opportunity of soliciting yours, Miss Elizabeth, for the two first dances especially, a preference which I trust my cousin Jane will attribute to the right cause, and not to any disrespect for her."

Elizabeth felt herself completely taken in. She had fully proposed being engaged by Mr. Wickham for those very dances; and to have Mr. Collins instead! Her liveliness had never been worse timed. There was no help for it, however. Mr. Wickham's happiness and her own were per-force delayed a little longer, and Mr. Collins's proposal accepted with as good a grace as she could. She was soon after afflicted with a most pal-pable urge to vomit, and politely cupped her hands lest the sight of her sick distress the present party. Thankfully, the urge subsided quickly, but the realization that invited it remained. Did this fat little priest mean to take her as a wife? She was horrified at the thought of marrying of man whose only skill with a blade was cutting slivers of gorgonzola.

If there had not been a Netherfield ball to prepare for, the younger Miss Bennets would have been in a very pitiable state, for from the day of the invitation, to the day of the ball, there was such a succession of rain as prevented their walking to Meryton once. The earth was again soft, and the dead numerous. No aunt, no officers, no news could be sought after. Even Elizabeth might have found some trial of her patience in weather which totally suspended the improvement of her acquain-tance with Mr. Wickham; and nothing less than a dance on Tuesday, could have made such a Friday, Saturday, Sunday, and Monday endurable to Kitty and Lydia.

CHAPTER 18

T ILL ELIZABETH ENTERED the drawing-room at Netherfield, and looked in vain for Mr. Wickham among the cluster of redcoats there assembled, a doubt of his being present had never occurred to her. She had dressed with more than usual care, and prepared in the highest spirits for the conquest of all that remained unsubdued of his heart, trusting that it was not more than might be won in the course of the evening. But in an instant arose the dreadful suspi-cion of his being purposely omitted for Mr. Darcy's pleasure in the Bingleys' invitation to the officers; and though this was not exactly the case, the absolute fact of his absence was pronounced by his friend Denny, who told them that Wickham had been obliged to go to town on business the day before, to attend a demonstration of a new carriage that boasted of being impervious to attacks by the manky dreadfuls. This assured Elizabeth that Darcy was not answerable for Wickham's absence, and her every feeling of displeasure against the former was sharpened by immediate disappointment. She was resolved against any sort of conversation with him.

Having told all her griefs to Charlotte Lucas, whom she had not seen for a week, Elizabeth was soon able to make a voluntary transition to the oddities of her cousin, and to point him out to her particular notice. The first two dances, however, brought a return of distress; they were dances of mortification. Mr. Collins, awkward and uncommonly round, gave her all the shame and misery which a disagreeable partner for a couple of dances can give. The moment of her release from him was ecstasy.

She danced next with an officer, and had the refreshment of talking of Wickham, and of hearing that he was universally liked. When those dances were over, she returned to Charlotte Lucas, and was in conversation with her, when she found herself suddenly addressed by Mr. Darcy, who took her so much by surprise in his application for her hand, that, without knowing what she did, she accepted him. He walked away again immediately, and she was left to fret over her own want of presence of mind. "If Master Liu had seen such a lapse of awareness! Twenty lashes at least, and another twenty trips up and down the thousand steps of Kwan Hsi!"

"I dare say you will find Mr. Darcy very agreeable," Charlotte tried to console her.

"Heaven forbid! *That* would be the greatest misfortune of all!"

When the dancing recommenced, however, and Darcy approached to claim her hand, Charlotte could not help cautioning her in a whisper not to be a simpleton and allow her fancy for Wickham to make her appear unpleasant in the eyes of a man ten times his consequence. Elizabeth made no answer, and took her place in the set. They stood for some time without speaking a word; and she began to imagine that their silence was to last through the two dances, and at first was resolved not to break it; till suddenly fancying that it would be the greater punishment to her partner to oblige him to talk, she made some slight observation on the dance. He replied, and was again silent. After a pause of some minutes, she addressed him a second time with:

"It is *your* turn to say something now, Mr. Darcy. I talked about the dance, and *you* ought to make some sort of remark on the size of the room, or the number of couples."

He smiled, and assured her that whatever she wished him to say should be said.

"Very well. That reply will do for the present. Perhaps by and by I may observe that private balls are much pleasanter than public ones."

"On the contrary, I find that balls are much more enjoyable when they cease to remain private." Elizabeth could not help but blush, but she was determined that her face betray not the slightest hint of amusement. Instead, she added archly; "I have always seen a great similarity in the turn of our minds. We are each of an unsocial, taciturn disposition, unwilling to speak, unless we expect to say something that will amaze the whole room, or be regarded as uncommonly clever."

"This is no very striking resemblance of your own character, I am sure," said he. "How near it may be to mine, I cannot pretend to say. You think it a faithful portrait undoubtedly."

"I must not decide on my own performance."

He made no answer, and they were again silent till they had gone down the dance, when he asked her if she and her sisters did not very often meet with zombies on their walks to Meryton. She answered in the affirmative, and, unable to resist the temptation, added, "When you met us there the other day, we had just been forming a new acquaintance."

The effect was immediate. A deeper shade of *hauteur* overspread his features, but he said not a word, and Elizabeth, though blaming herself for her own weakness, could not go on. At length Darcy spoke, and in a constrained manner said:

"Mr. Wickham is blessed with such happy manners as may ensure his *making* friends—whether he may be equally capable of *retaining* them, is less certain."

"He has been so unlucky as to lose *your* friendship," replied Elizabeth with emphasis, "and his ability to walk for a twelvemonth, I understand."

Darcy made no answer, and seemed desirous of changing the subject. At that moment, Sir William Lucas appeared close to them, meaning to pass through the set to the other side of the room; but on perceiving Mr. Darcy, he stopped with a bow of superior courtesy to compliment him on his dancing and his partner.

"I have been most highly gratified indeed, my dear sir. Such very superior dancing is not often seen. It is evident that you belong to the first circles. Allow me to say, however, that your fair partner does not disgrace you, for she is as ferocious as she is fetching! I must hope to have this pleasure often repeated, especially when a certain desirable event, my dear Eliza (glancing at her sister and Bingley) shall take place. What congratulations will then flow in! But let me not interrupt you, sir. You will not thank me for detaining you from the bewitching young lady. Oh! To think of the ways her many skills could be put to amorous employ!"

Darcy directioned his eyes with a very serious expression toward Bingley and Jane, who were dancing together. Recovering himself, however, he turned to his partner, and said, "Sir William's interruption has made me forget what we were talking of."

"I do not think we were speaking at all. Sir William could not have interrupted two people in the room who had less to say for themselves. We have tried two or three subjects already without success, and what we are to talk of next I cannot imagine."

"What think you of Orientals?" said he, smiling.

"Orientals—oh! No. I am sure we never met the same, or had the same feelings toward them."

"But if that be the case, we may compare our different opinions. I think them a strange lot—both in appearance and custom, though having studied solely in Japan, I admit that the opinion may be incomplete. I should be most interested to hear of your time in the company of Chinamen."

"No—I cannot talk of Orientals in a ball-room; my head is always full of something else."

"The *present* always occupies you in such scenes—does it?"

"Yes, always," she replied, without knowing what she said, for her thoughts had wandered far from the subject—to the pain of Master Liu's glowing brand searing her flesh; to sparring matches with her sisters atop a beam no wider than their swords, as pikes waited to punish an ill-placed foot below. Her mind returning to the present, she suddenly exclaimed, "I remember hearing you once say, Mr. Darcy, that you hardly ever forgave, that your resentment once created was unappeasable. You are very cautious, I suppose, as to its *being created*."

"I am," said he, with a firm voice.

"And never allow yourself to be blinded by prejudice?"

"I hope not."

"It is particularly incumbent on those who never change their opinion, to be secure of judging properly at first."

"May I ask to what these questions tend?"

"Merely to the illustration of *your* character," said she, endeavouring to shake off her gravity. "I am trying to make it out."

"And what is your success?"

She shook her head. "I do not get on at all. I hear such different accounts of you as puzzle me exceedingly."

"I can readily believe," answered he gravely, "that reports may vary greatly with respect to me; and I could wish, Miss Bennet, that you were not to sketch my character at the present moment."

"But if I do not take your likeness now, I may never have another opportunity."

"I would by no means suspend any pleasure of yours," he coldly replied. She said no more, and they went down the other dance and parted in silence; and on each side dissatisfied, though not to an equal degree, for in Darcy's breast there was a tolerable powerful feeling toward her, which soon procured her pardon, and directed all his anger against another.

Elizabeth then sought her eldest sister. "I want to know what you have learnt about Mr. Wickham. But perhaps you have been too pleasantly engaged to think of any third person; in which case you may be sure of my pardon."

"No," replied Jane, "I have not forgotten him; but I have nothing satisfactory to tell you. Mr. Bingley does not know the whole of his history, and is quite ignorant of the circumstances which have principally offended Mr. Darcy; but he will vouch for the good conduct, the probity, and honour of his friend. I am sorry to say by his account, Mr. Wickham is by no means a respectable young man."

"Mr. Bingley does not know Mr. Wickham himself?"

"No; he never saw him till the other morning at Meryton."

"I have not a doubt of Mr. Bingley's sincerity," said Elizabeth warmly; "but you must excuse my not being convinced by assurances only. Mr. Bingley's defense of his friend was a very able one, but since he is unacquainted with several parts of the story, I shall venture to still think of both gentlemen as I did before."

She then changed the discourse to one more gratifying to each. Elizabeth listened with delight to the happy, though modest hopes which Jane entertained of Mr. Bingley's regard, and said all in her power to heighten her confidence in it. On their being joined by Mr. Bingley himself, Elizabeth withdrew to Miss Lucas; to whose inquiry after the pleasantness of Darcy she had scarcely replied, before her fat cousin Mr. Collins came up to them, and told her with great exultation that he had just been so fortunate as to make a most important discovery.

"Ah! May I suppose, then, that you have discovered the location of the buffet?" said Elizabeth, rudely.

"No! I have found out," said he, "by a singular accident, that there is now in the room a near relation of my patroness. I happened to over-hear the gentleman himself mentioning to the young lady who does the honours of the house the names of his cousin Miss de Bourgh, and of her mother Lady Catherine. How wonderfully these sort of things occur! Who would have thought of my meeting with, perhaps, a nephew of Lady Catherine de Bourgh in this assembly! I am most thankful that the discovery is made in time for me to pay my respects to him, which I am now going to do."

"You are not going to introduce yourself to Mr. Darcy!"

"Indeed I am. I shall entreat his pardon for not having done it ear-lier. I believe him to be Lady Catherine's nephew."

Elizabeth tried hard to dissuade him from such a scheme, assuring him that Mr. Darcy would consider his addressing him without intro-duction as an impertinent freedom, rather than a compliment to his aunt; that it must belong to Mr. Darcy, the superior in consequence, to begin the acquaintance. When Elizabeth ceased speaking, Mr. Collins replied thus:

"My dear Miss Elizabeth, I have the highest opinion in the world in your excellent judgment in all matters within the scope of your understanding, particularly in the slaying of Satan's armies; but permit me to say, that there must be a wide difference between the estab-lished forms of ceremony amongst the laity, and those which regulate the clergy. After all, you may wield God's sword, but I wield His wis-dom. And it is wisdom, dear cousin, which will ultimately rid us of our present difficulties with the undead."

"You will excuse me for saying so, but I have never seen a zombie's head taken off by words—nor do I ever expect to."

"You must allow me to follow the dictates of my conscience on this occasion, which leads me to perform what I look on as a point of duty."

With a low bow he left her to attack Mr. Darcy, whose reception of his advances she eagerly watched, and whose astonishment at being so addressed was very evident. Her cousin prefaced his speech with a solemn bow, and though she could not hear a word of it, she felt as if hearing it all, and saw in the motion of his lips the words "apology," "Hunsford," and "Lady Catherine de Bourgh." It vexed her to see him expose himself to such a man. Mr. Darcy was eyeing him with unrestrained wonder, and when at last Mr. Collins allowed him time to speak, replied with an air of distant civility. Mr. Collins, however, was not discouraged from speaking again, and Mr. Darcy's contempt seemed abundantly increasing with the length of his second speech, and at the end of it he only made him a slight bow, and moved another way.

As Elizabeth had no longer any interest of her own to pursue, she turned her attention almost entirely on her sister and Mr. Bingley. She saw her in all the felicity which a marriage of true affection could bestow; and she felt capable, under such circumstances, of endeavouring even to like Bingley's two sisters. Her mother's thoughts were plainly bent the same way, and she determined not to venture near her, lest she suffer her endless prattling. When they sat down to supper, therefore, Elizabeth considered it a most unlucky perverseness which placed them within one of each other; and deeply was she vexed to find that her mother was talking to Lady Lucas freely, openly, and of nothing else but her expectation that Jane would soon be married to Mr. Bingley. It was an animating subject, and Mrs. Bennet seemed incapable of fatigue while enumerating the advantages of the match. His being such a charming young man, and so rich, and living but three miles from them, were the first points of self-gratulation; and then it was such a comfort to think how fond the two sisters were of Jane, and to be certain that they must desire the connection as much as she could do. It was, moreover, such a promising thing for her younger daughters, as Jane's marrying so greatly must throw them in the way of other rich men. "Oh!

What joy to see them all thus provided for! To see them entertaining at their own estates; raising their own children, instead of all this silly training and fighting." She concluded with many good wishes that Lady Lucas might soon be equally fortunate, though evidently and triumphantly believing there was no chance of it.

In vain did Elizabeth endeavour to check the rapidity of her mother's words, or persuade her to describe her felicity in a less audible whisper; for, to her inexpressible vexation, she could perceive that the chief of it was overheard by Mr. Darcy, who sat opposite to them. Her mother only scolded her for being nonsensical, her breath thick with meat and port.

"What is Mr. Darcy to me, pray, that I should be afraid of him? I am sure we owe him no such particular civility as to be obliged to say nothing *he* may not like to hear."

"For heaven's sake, madam, speak lower. What advantage can it be for you to offend Mr. Darcy? You will never recommend yourself to his friend by so doing!"

Nothing that she could say, however, had any influence. Elizabeth blushed and blushed again with shame and vexation. She could not help frequently glancing her eye at Mr. Darcy, though every glance convinced her of what she dreaded; for though he was not always looking at her mother, she was convinced that his attention was invariably fixed by her. The expression of his face changed gradually from indignant contempt to a composed and steady gravity.

At length, however, Mrs. Bennet had no more to say; and Lady Lucas, who had been long yawning at the repetition of delights which she saw no likelihood of sharing, was left to the comforts of cold ham and chicken. Elizabeth now began to revive. But not long was the interval of tranquillity; for, when supper was over, not a servant was to be found to attend to their empty plates. Seeing his guests grow restless, Mr. Bingley rose from his seat and excused himself—no doubt to scold his steward for the embarrassment.

Upon his return, Elizabeth promptly reached for her ankle dagger. Mr. Bingley's white face and troubled countenance were enough to solicit such a reaction.

"Mr. Darcy, if I may have the pleasure of your company in the kitchen," said Bingley. Darcy rose, taking care not to move too quickly, lest he alarm the guests. Elizabeth took it upon herself to follow him. When Darcy took notice of this, he turned to her and said, in a whisper, "Miss Bennet, I would much prefer you took your seat. I am quite capable of attending to Mr. Bingley myself."

"Of that I have no doubt, Mr. Darcy. Just as I have no doubt in my ability to form my own opinion on the matter. Now, do you wish to cause a stir, or shall we to the kitchen?"

Mr. Bingley led the two of them down a hidden staircase and into the cellar, which was divided into two halves by a long corridor—one side belonging to the servants' quarters and armory, the other to the exercise parlor and kitchen. It was in the latter that a most unfortunate sight awaited them. Two adult unmentionables—both of them male— busied themselves feasting upon the flesh of the household staff. How two zombies could have killed a dozen servants, four maids, two cooks, and a steward was beyond Elizabeth's comprehension, but she knew precisely how they had gotten in: The cellar door had been opened to let in the cool night air and relieve the oppression of the woodstoves.

"Well, I suppose we had ought to take all of their heads, lest they be born to darkness," she said.

Mr. Bingley observed the desserts his poor servants had been attending to at the time of their demise—a delightful array of tarts, exotic fruits, and pies, sadly soiled by blood and brains, and thus unusable.

"I don't suppose," said Darcy, "that you would give me the honour of dispensing of this unhappy business alone. I should never forgive myself if your gown were soiled."

"The honour is all yours, Mr. Darcy."

Elizabeth thought she detected the slightest smile on his face. She

"TWO ADULT UNMENTIONABLES—BOTH OF THEM MALE—BUSIED THEMSELVES
FEASTING UPON THE FLESH OF THE HOUSEHOLD STAFF."

watched as Darcy drew his blade and cut down the two zombies with savage yet dignified movements. He then made quick work of beheading the slaughtered staff, upon which Mr. Bingley politely vomited into his hands. There was no denying Darcy's talents as a warrior.

"If only," she thought, "his talents as a gentleman were their equal."

When they returned to the ball, they found the spirits of the others very much disturbed. Mary was entertaining them at the pianoforte, her shrill voice testing the patient ears of all present. Elizabeth looked at her father to entreat his interference, lest Mary should be singing all night. He took the hint, and when Mary had finished her second song, said aloud:

"That will do extremely well, child. You have delighted us long enough. Let the other young ladies have time to exhibit."

To Elizabeth it appeared that, had her family made an agreement to embarrass themselves as much as they could during the evening, it would have been impossible for them to play their parts with more success.

The rest of the evening brought her little amusement. She was teased by Mr. Collins, who continued most perseveringly by her side, and though he could not prevail on her to dance with him again, he put it out of her power to dance with others, by using his thick middle to hide her from view. In vain did she offer to introduce him to any young lady in the room. He assured her, that he was perfectly indifferent to it; that his chief object was by delicate attentions to recommend himself to her and that he should therefore make a point of remaining close to her the whole evening. There was no arguing upon such a project. She owed her greatest relief to her friend Miss Lucas, who often joined them, and good-naturedly engaged Mr. Collins's conversation to herself.

She was at least free from the offense of Mr. Darcy's further notice; though often standing within a very short distance of her, quite disengaged, he never came near enough to speak. She felt it to be the probable consequence of her allusions to Mr. Wickham, and rejoiced in it.

When at length they arose to take leave, Mrs. Bennet was most pressingly civil in her hope of seeing the whole family soon at Longbourn, and addressed herself especially to Mr. Bingley, to assure him how happy he would make them by eating a family dinner with them at any time, without the ceremony of a formal invitation. Bingley was all grateful pleasure, and he readily engaged for taking the earliest opportunity of waiting on her, after his return from London, whither he was obliged to go the next day for a meeting of the *Society of Gentlemen for a Peaceful Solution to Our Present Difficulties*, of which he was a member and patron.

Mrs. Bennet was perfectly satisfied, and quitted the house under the delightful persuasion that she should see her daughter settled at Netherfield, her weapons retired forever, in the course of three or four months. Of having another daughter married to Mr. Collins, she thought with equal certainty, and with considerable, though not equal, pleasure. Elizabeth was the least dear to her of all her children; and though the man and the match were quite good enough for her, the worth of each was eclipsed by Mr. Bingley and Netherfield.

CHAPTER 19

THE NEXT DAY opened a new scene at Longbourn. Mr. Collins made his declaration in form. On finding Mrs. Bennet, Elizabeth, and one of the younger girls together, soon after breakfast, he addressed the mother in these words:

"May I hope, madam, for your interest with your fair daughter Elizabeth, when I solicit for the honour of a private audience with her in the course of this morning?"

Before Elizabeth had time for anything but a blush of surprise, Mrs.

Bennet answered instantly, "Oh dear! Yes—certainly. I am sure Lizzy will be very happy—I am sure she can have no objection. Come, Kitty, I want you upstairs." And, gathering her work together, she was hastening away, when Elizabeth called out:

"Dear madam, do not go. I beg you will not go. Mr. Collins must excuse me. He can have nothing to say to me that anybody need not hear. I am going away myself."

"No, no, nonsense, Lizzy. I desire you to stay where you are." And upon Elizabeth's seeming really, with vexed and embarrassed looks, about to escape, she added: "Lizzy, I *insist* upon your staying and hearing Mr. Collins."

Mrs. Bennet and Kitty walked off, and as soon as they were gone, Mr. Collins began.

"Believe me, my dear Miss Elizabeth, that your modesty adds to your other perfections. You would have been less amiable in my eyes had there *not* been this little unwillingness; but allow me to assure you, that I have your respected mother's permission for this address. You can hardly doubt the purport of my discourse, for however preoccupied you might be with hastening the Devil's retreat—for which I earnestly applaud you—my attentions have been too marked to be mistaken. Almost as soon as I entered the house, I singled you out as the companion of my future life. But before I am run away with by my feelings on this subject, perhaps it would be advisable for me to state my reasons for marrying—and, moreover, for coming into Hertfordshire with the design of selecting a wife, as I certainly did."

The idea of Mr. Collins, with all his solemn composure, being run away with by his feelings, made Elizabeth so near laughing, that she could not use the short pause he allowed in any attempt to stop him further, and he continued:

"My reasons for marrying are, first, that I think it a right thing for every clergyman to set the example of matrimony in his parish. Secondly, that I am convinced it will add very greatly to my happiness;

and thirdly, that it is the particular advice and recommendation of the very noble lady whom I have the honour of calling patroness. It was but the very Saturday night before I left Hunsford that she said, 'Mr. Collins, you must marry. A clergyman like you must marry. Choose properly, choose a gentlewoman for *my* sake; and for your *own*, let her be an active, useful sort of person, not brought up high, but able to make a small income go a good way. This is my advice. Find such a woman as soon as you can, bring her to Hunsford, and I will visit her.' Allow me, by the way, to observe, my fair cousin, that I do not reckon the notice and kindness of Lady Catherine de Bourgh as among the least of the advantages in my power to offer. You will find her powers of combat beyond anything I can describe; and your own talents in slaying the stricken, I think, must be acceptable to her, though naturally, I will require you to retire them as part of your marital submission."

It was absolutely necessary to interrupt him now.

"You are too hasty, sir," she cried. "You forget that I have made no answer. Let me do it without further loss of time. Accept my thanks for the compliment you are paying me. I am very sensible of the honour of your proposals, but it is impossible for me to do otherwise than to decline them."

"I am not now to learn," replied Mr. Collins, "that it is usual with young ladies to reject the addresses of the man whom they secretly mean to accept, when he first applies for their favour; and that sometimes the refusal is repeated a second, or even a third time. I am therefore by no means discouraged by what you have just said, and shall hope to lead you to the altar ere long."

"You forget, sir, that I am a student of Shaolin! Master of the seven-starred fist! I am perfectly serious in my refusal. You could not make *me* happy, and I am convinced that I am the last woman in the world who could make *you* so. Nay, were your friend Lady Catherine to know me, I am persuaded she would find me in every respect ill qualified for the situation, for I am a warrior, sir, and shall be until my last breath is offered to God."

"Were it certain that Lady Catherine would think so," said Mr. Collins very gravely, "but I cannot imagine that her ladyship would at all disapprove of you. And you may be certain when I have the honour of seeing her again, I shall speak in the very highest terms of your modesty, economy, and other amiable qualification."

"Indeed, Mr. Collins, all praise of me will be unnecessary. You must give me leave to judge for myself, and pay me the compliment of believing what I say. I wish you very happy and very rich, and by refusing your hand, do all in my power to prevent your being otherwise." And rising as she thus spoke, she would have quitted the room, had Mr. Collins not thus addressed her:

"When I do myself the honour of speaking to you next on the subject, I shall hope to receive a more favourable answer than you have now given me. I know it to be the established custom of your sex to reject a man on the first application."

"Really, Mr. Collins," cried Elizabeth, "you puzzle me exceedingly. If what I have hitherto said can appear to you in the form of encouragement, I know not how to express my refusal in such a way as to convince you of its being one."

"You must give me leave to flatter myself, my dear cousin, that your refusal of my addresses is merely words of course."

To such perseverance in wilful self-deception Elizabeth would make no reply, and immediately and in silence withdrew; determined, if he persisted in considering her repeated refusals as flattering encouragement, to apply to her father, whose negative might be uttered in such a manner as to be decisive, and whose behavior at least could not be mistaken for the affectation and coquetry of an elegant female.

CHAPTER 20

MR. COLLINS WAS NOT left long to the silent contempla-tion of his successful love; for Mrs. Bennet, having dawdled about in the vestibule to watch for the end of the conference, no sooner saw Elizabeth open the door and with quick step pass her towards the staircase, than she entered the breakfast-room, and congratulated both him and herself in warm terms on the happy prospect of their nearer connection. Mr. Collins received and returned these felicitations with equal pleasure, and then proceeded to relate the particulars of their interview.

This information startled Mrs. Bennet; she would have been glad to be equally satisfied that her daughter had meant to encourage him by protesting against his proposals, but she dared not believe it, and could not help saying so.

"But, depend upon it, Mr. Collins," she added, "that Lizzy shall be brought to reason. I will speak to her about it directly. She is a very headstrong, foolish girl, and does not know her own interest—but I will *make* her know it."

Hurrying instantly to her husband, she called out as she entered the library, "Oh! Mr. Bennet, you are wanted immediately; we are all in an uproar. You must come and make Lizzy marry Mr. Collins, for she vows she will not have him."

Mr. Bennet raised his eyes from his book as she entered, and fixed them on her face with a calm unconcern.

"I have not the pleasure of understanding you," said he, when she had finished her speech. "Of what are you talking?"

"Of Mr. Collins and Lizzy. Lizzy declares she will not have Mr. Collins, and Mr. Collins begins to say that he will not have Lizzy."

"And what am I to do on the occasion? It seems a hopeless business."

"Speak to Lizzy about it yourself. Tell her that you insist upon her marrying him."

"Let her be called down. She shall hear my opinion."

Mrs. Bennet rang the bell, and Miss Elizabeth was summoned to the library.

"Come here, child," cried her father as she appeared. "I have sent for you on an affair of importance. I understand that Mr. Collins has made you an offer of marriage. Is it true?" Elizabeth replied that it was.

"Very well—and this offer of marriage you have refused?"

"I have, sir."

"Very well. We now come to the point. Your mother insists upon your accepting it. Is it not so, Mrs. Bennet?"

"Yes, or I will never see her again."

"An unhappy alternative is before you, Elizabeth. From this day you must be a stranger to one of your parents. Your mother will never see you again if you do *not* marry Mr. Collins, and I will never see you again if you *do*; for I shall not have my best warrior resigned to the service of a man who is fatter than Buddha and duller than the edge of a learning sword."

Elizabeth could not but smile at such a conclusion of such a beginning, but Mrs. Bennet, who had persuaded herself that her husband regarded the affair as she wished, was excessively disappointed.

"What do you mean, Mr. Bennet, in talking this way?"

"My dear," replied her husband, "I have two small favours to request. First, that you will spare me the expense of having your lips sewn shut; and secondly, that you will allow me the free use of my room. I shall be glad to have the library to myself as soon as may be."

Not yet, however, did Mrs. Bennet give up the point. She talked to Elizabeth again and again; coaxed and threatened her by turns. She endeavoured to secure Jane in her interest; but Jane, with all possible mildness, declined interfering; and Elizabeth, sometimes with real earnestness, and sometimes with playful gaiety, replied to her attacks. Though her manner varied, however, her determination never did.

While the family were in this confusion, Charlotte Lucas came to spend the day with them. She was met in the vestibule by Lydia, who cried in a half whisper, "I am glad you are come, for there is such fun here! What do you think has happened this morning? Mr. Collins has made an offer to Lizzy, and she will not have him."

Lydia noticed that Charlotte was flush with the warmth of exercise and had a rather disconcerted look on her face. "Charlotte? Are you ill?"

Charlotte hardly had time to answer, before they were joined by Kitty, who came to tell the same news; and no sooner had they entered the breakfast-room, where Mrs. Bennet was alone, than she likewise began on the subject, calling on Miss Lucas for her compassion, and entreating her to persuade her friend Lizzy to comply with the wishes of all her family. "Pray do, my dear Miss Lucas," she added in a melancholy tone, "for nobody is on my side, nobody takes part with me. I am cruelly used, nobody feels for my poor nerves."

Charlotte's reply was spared by the entrance of Jane and Elizabeth.

"Aye, there she comes," continued Mrs. Bennet, "looking as unconcerned as may be, and caring no more for us than if we were the very unmentionables she takes such pleasure in occupying her time with. But I tell you, Miss Lizzy—if you take it into your head to go on refusing every offer of marriage in this way, you will never get a husband at all—and I am sure I do not know who is to maintain you when your father is dead."

CHAPTER 21

THE DISCUSSION OF MR. COLLINS'S offer was now nearly at an end. The gentleman himself scarcely spoke to her, and his assiduous attentions were transferred for the rest of the day to

Miss Lucas, whose civility in listening to him was a seasonable relief to them all, and especially to her friend. Indeed, Charlotte seemed to flatter Mr. Collins with an almost unnatural attentiveness.

The morrow produced no abatement of Mrs. Bennet's ill-humour or ill health. Mr. Collins was also in the same state of angry pride. Elizabeth had hoped that his resentment might shorten his visit, but his plan did not appear in the least affected by it. He was always to have gone on Saturday, and to Saturday he meant to stay.

After breakfast, the girls retired to the dojo and attended to their mid-week musket disassembly and cleaning. With those very weapons on their person, they next set out for to Meryton to inquire if Mr. Wickham were returned, and to lament over his absence from the Netherfield ball.

They were less than a mile from Longbourn when Kitty, who had elected to take point, abruptly stopped, and signaled for the others to do so as well. She raised her musket, but at what, Elizabeth and the other girls knew not, for the road seemed free of trouble. After standing thus for a moment, a single chipmunk scurried out of the woods on their right. It darted across their path with considerable rapidity, before disappearing into the woods on the left. Lydia could not help but laugh at the sight. "My dear Kitty, how shall we ever thank you for sparing our toes a most unfortunate tickling!"

But Kitty kept her musket at the ready, and, after a moment, a second chipmunk scurried across the road with equal alacrity. It was followed in short order by a pair of weasels, then a skunk, then a fox and her pups. More creatures followed, and in ever-increasing numbers; as if Noah himself beckoned, offering refuge from some unseen flood. By the time deer began to leap across their path, the other girls had their muskets trained on the tree line, ready for the herd of zombies they suspected would appear at any moment.

The first was a young, freshly dead female in a white lace wedding gown, which, like her skin, was surprisingly white—almost shockingly so, save for the bright red rubies that dripped from her mouth and onto the lace covering her bosom. Kitty put the creature down with a shot to the face, upon which Lydia placed her barrel against its head and promptly dispatched it to Hell. So close was this shot, that the bride's hair was set alight by the powder flash. "Seems a shame," said Lydia, as acrid smoke began to rise. "Wasting perfectly good wedding clothes like tha . . . "

The wail of another zombie interrupted her; his flowing white beard and half-eaten face attached to a stout body, which was clad in a blood-crusted blacksmith's apron. Elizabeth and Jane aimed and discharged their muskets; Jane's ball finding one of the creature's eyes, and Elizabeth's striking its neck—cutting through the brittle flesh and separating head from body.

These zombies were followed by several more—each vanquished as quickly as the last, until the cracking of powder at last fell silent. Sensing the danger passed, the sisters lowered their barrels, and spoke of setting off again for Meryton. But these plans were belated by a most unusual noise from beyond the tree line. It was a shrill shrieking, neither human nor animal, and yet unlike any zombie wail the sisters had ever heard. It grew closer, and once again, all muskets were trained and readied. But when the source of this strange noise revealed itself, their barrels were lowered.

"Oh! *No* . . . " said Jane. "Oh! It simply cannot be!"

A long-dead female zombie stumbled out of the woods, her modest clothing slightly tattered; her brittle hair pulled back so tightly that it had begun to tear the skin of her forehead. In her arms, she held something exceedingly rare; something none of the sisters had ever seen, or ever wished to see—an unmentionable infant. It clawed at the female's flesh, emitting a most unpleasant series of shrieks. Elizabeth raised her musket, but Jane was quick to grab the barrel.

"You mustn't!"

"Have you forgotten your oath?"

"It's an infant, Lizzy!"

"A zombie infant—no more alive than the musket I mean to silence it with."

Elizabeth again raised her weapon and aimed. The female dreadful was now more than halfway across the road. She trained her sights on the elder's head; her finger caressing the trigger. She would put it down, reload, and dispense of them both. All she had to do was squeeze. And yet . . . she did not. There was a strange force at work, a feeling she faintly recalled from her earliest days, before she had first traveled to Shaolin. It was a curious feeling; something akin to shame, but without the dishonor of defeat—a shame that demanded no vengeance. "Could there be honor in mercy?" she wondered. It contradicted everything she had been taught, every warrior instinct she possessed. Why then could she not fire? Hopelessly bemused, Elizabeth lowered her musket, and the zombies continued into the woods until they were seen no more.

It was agreed that none of them would ever speak of it.

Wickham joined the sisters on their entering the town, and attended them to their aunt's, where his regret and vexation, and concern upon hearing of the regrettable fate of Mr. Bingley's household staff was well talked over. To Elizabeth, however, he voluntarily acknowledged that the necessity of his absence had been self-imposed.

"I found," said he, "as the time drew near that I had better not meet Mr. Darcy; that to be in the same room, with the very man who crippled me for a twelvemonth, might be more than I could bear, and that scenes might arise unpleasant to more than myself."

Elizabeth highly approved his forbearance, which was greater than her own, for she confessed that a duel would have almost certainly ensued, had she been in his place. Wickham and another officer walked back with them to Longbourn, and during the walk he particularly attended to her. His accompanying them was a triple advantage: the compliment of his attention, an occasion of introducing him to her father and mother, and the presence of an extra warrior, should they encounter trouble on the road.

Soon after their return, a letter was delivered to Miss Bennet; it came from Netherfield. The envelope contained a sheet of elegant, little, hot-pressed paper, well covered with a lady's fair, flowing hand; and Elizabeth saw her sister's countenance change as she read it, and saw her dwelling intently on some particular passages. "This is from Caroline Bingley; what it contains has surprised me a good deal. The whole party have left Netherfield by this time, and are on their way to town—and without any intention of coming back again. You shall hear what she says."

She then read the first sentence aloud, which comprised the information of their having just resolved to follow their brother to town directly, and of their meaning to dine in Grosvenor Street, where Mr. Hurst had a house. The next was in these words: "I do not pretend to regret anything I shall leave in the perilous, zombie-covered country, except your society, my dearest friend; but we will hope, at some future period, to enjoy many returns of that delightful intercourse we have known, and in the meanwhile may lessen the pain of separation by a very frequent and most unreserved correspondence. I depend on you for that." To these highflown expressions Elizabeth listened with all the insensibility of distrust; and though the suddenness of their removal surprised her, she saw nothing to lament.

"It is unlucky," said she, "that you should not be able to see your friends before they leave the country. But may we not hope that the period of future happiness to which Miss Bingley looks forward may arrive earlier than she is aware, and that the delightful intercourse you have known as friends will be renewed with yet greater satisfaction as sisters? Mr. Bingley will not be detained in London by them."

"Caroline decidedly says that none of the party will return into Hertfordshire this winter. I will read it to you: 'When my brother left us yesterday, he imagined that the business which took him to London might be concluded in three or four days; but we are certain it cannot be so. Many of my acquaintances are already there for the winter; I wish that I could hear that you, my dearest friend, had any intention of making one of the crowd—but of that I despair. I sincerely hope your Christmas in Hertfordshire may abound in the gaieties which that season generally brings, and be not the least bit similar to the Christmas of two years past, which resulted in so many unpleasantries.' It is evident by this," added Jane, "that he comes back no more this winter."

"It is only evident that Miss Bingley does not mean that he *should*," said Elizabeth.

"Mr. Bingley is his own master. Perhaps the sight of his bloodied staff was too much for his delicate character. But you do not know all. I will read you the passage which particularly hurts me: 'Mr. Darcy is impatient to see his sister and we are scarcely less eager to meet her again. I really do not think Georgiana Darcy has her equal for beauty, elegance, and skill in the deadly arts; and the affection she inspires in Louisa and myself is heightened from the hope we dare entertain of her being hereafter our sister. My brother admires her greatly already; he will have frequent opportunity now of seeing her on the most intimate footing. With all these circumstances to favour an attachment, and nothing to prevent it, am I wrong, my dearest Jane, in indulging the hope of an event which will secure the happiness of so many?'"

"What do you think of this sentence, my dear Lizzy?" said Jane as she finished it. "Is it not clear enough? Does it not expressly declare that Caroline neither expects nor wishes me to be her sister; that she is perfectly convinced of her brother's indifference; and that if she suspects the nature of my feelings for him, she means (most kindly!) to put me on my guard? Can there be any other opinion on the subject?"

"Yes, there can; for mine is totally different. Will you hear it?"

"Most willingly."

"You shall have it in a few words. Miss Bingley sees that her brother is in love with you, and wants him to marry Miss Darcy. I dare say she means to keep you from his attentions. Your honour demands she be slain."

Jane shook her head. "You forget yourself, Lizzy."

"Jane, no one who has ever seen you together can doubt his affection. Miss Bingley, I am sure, cannot. She may not be a warrior, but she has cunning enough. Dearest sister, I implore you—this unhappiness is best remedied by the hasty application of a cutlass to her throat."

"If we thought alike," replied Jane, "my honour would be restored at the expense of losing Mr. Bingley's affections forever. And what, pray, would be the purpose? Caroline is incapable of willfully deceiving anyone; and all that I can hope in this case is that she is deceiving herself."

"Is it she who is deceived, or you? You forget *yourself*, Jane—you have allowed your feelings for Mr. Bingley to soften the instincts bestowed by our Oriental masters."

Though they could not agree on a course of action, Jane and Elizabeth agreed that Mrs. Bennet should only hear of the departure of the family, but even this partial communication gave her a great deal of concern, and she bewailed it as exceedingly unlucky that the ladies should happen to go away just as they were all getting so intimate together. After lamenting it, however, at some length, she had the consolation that Mr. Bingley would be soon down again and soon dining at Longbourn, and the conclusion of all was the comfortable declaration, that though he had been invited only to a family dinner, she would take care to have two full courses.

CHAPTER 22

THE BENNETS WERE ENGAGED to dine with the Lucases, and again, during the chief of the day, was Miss Lucas so kind as to listen to Mr. Collins. Elizabeth took an opportunity of thanking her. "It keeps him in good humour," said she, "and I am more obliged to you than I can express."

This was very amiable, but Charlotte's kindness extended farther than Elizabeth had any conception of; its object was nothing else than to secure her from any return of Mr. Collins's proposals, by engaging them towards herself. Such was Miss Lucas's scheme; and appearances were so favourable, that when they parted at night, she would have felt almost secure of success if he had not been to leave Hertfordshire so very soon. But here she did injustice to the fire and independence of his character, for it led him to escape out of Longbourn House the next morning with admirable slyness, and hasten to Lucas Lodge to throw himself at her feet. He was anxious to avoid the notice of his cousins, from a conviction that if they saw him depart, they could not fail to conjecture his design, and he was not willing to have the attempt known till its success might be known likewise; for though feeling almost secure, and with reason, for Charlotte had been tolerably encouraging, he was comparatively diffident since the adventure of Elizabeth's rejection. His reception, however, was of the most flattering kind. Miss Lucas perceived him from an upper window as he walked towards the house, and instantly set out to meet him accidentally in the lane. But little had she dared to hope that so much love and eloquence awaited her there.

In as short a time as Mr. Collins's long speeches would allow, everything was settled between them to the satisfaction of both; and as they entered the house he earnestly entreated her to name the day that was to make him the happiest of men.

Sir William and Lady Lucas were speedily applied to for their consent; and it was bestowed with a most joyful alacrity. Mr. Collins's present circumstances made it a most eligible match for their daughter, to whom they could give little fortune; and his prospects of future wealth were exceedingly fair. Lady Lucas began directly to calculate, with more interest than the matter had ever excited before, how many years longer Mr. Bennet was likely to live; and Sir William gave it as his decided opinion, that whenever Mr. Collins should be in possession of the Longbourn estate, it would be highly expedient that both he and his wife should take up residence and dispense of the unsightly dojo post haste. The whole family, in short, were properly overjoyed on the occasion. The least agreeable circumstance in the business was the surprise it must occasion to Elizabeth Bennet, whose friendship Charlotte valued beyond that of any other person. Would she disapprove? Or worse, would she have no desire of further acquaintance? Charlotte resolved to give her the information herself, and therefore charged Mr. Collins, when he returned to Longbourn to dinner, to drop no hint of what had passed before any of the family. A promise of secrecy was of course very dutifully given, but it could not be kept without difficulty; for the curiosity excited by his long absence burst forth in such very direct questions on his return as required some ingenuity to evade.

As he was to begin his journey too early on the morrow to see any of the family, the ceremony of leave-taking was performed when the ladies moved for the night; and Mrs. Bennet, with great politeness and cordiality, said how happy they should be to see him at Longbourn again, whenever his engagements might allow him to visit them.

"My dear madam," he replied, "this invitation is particularly gratifying, because it is what I have been hoping to receive; and you may be very certain that I shall avail myself of it as soon as possible."

They were all astonished; and Mr. Bennet, who could by no means wish for so speedy a return, immediately said:

"But is there not danger of Lady Catherine's disapprobation here, my good sir? You had better neglect your relations than run the risk of offending your patroness."

"My dear sir," replied Mr. Collins, "I am particularly obliged to you for this friendly caution, and you may depend upon my not taking so material a step without her ladyship's concurrence."

"You cannot be too much upon your guard. Risk anything rather than her displeasure; and if you find it likely to be raised by your coming to us again, which I should think exceedingly probable, be satisfied that we shall take no offence."

"Believe me, my dear sir, my gratitude is warmly excited by such affectionate attention; and depend upon it, you will speedily receive from me a letter of thanks for this, and for every other mark of your regard during my stay in Hertfordshire. As for my fair cousins, I shall now take the liberty of wishing them health and happiness, not excepting my cousin Elizabeth."

Elizabeth had been expecting such a slight and determined to show not the least offense at it, lest he gain some measure of victory over her. She instead smiled, and said, "And I, Mr. Collins, wish you the safest of journeys—for there have been such an uncommon number of dreadfuls on the roads of late, that an encounter seems unavoidable. I am certain, however, that yours will be the exception."

With proper civilities the ladies then withdrew; all of them equally surprised that he meditated a quick return. Mrs. Bennet wished to understand by it that he thought of paying his addresses to one of her younger girls, and Mary might have been prevailed on to accept him. But on the following morning, every hope of this kind was done away. Miss Lucas called soon after breakfast, and in a private conference with Elizabeth related the event of the day before.

The possibility of Mr. Collins's fancying himself in love with her friend had once occurred to Elizabeth within the last day or two; but that Charlotte could encourage him seemed almost as far from possibility as she could encourage him herself.

"Engaged to Mr. Collins! My dear Charlotte—impossible!"

Miss Lucas calmly replied:

"Why should you be surprised, my dear Eliza? Do you think it incredible that Mr. Collins should be able to procure any woman's good opinion, because you thought him ill-suited to be the husband of so great a woman as yourself?"

Such an affront would have been met with fists had it come from any other person, but in this case, Elizabeth's affections were greater even than her honour. Seeing no hope of persuading her otherwise, she wished Charlotte all imaginable happiness.

"I see what you are feeling," replied Charlotte. "You must be surprised, very much surprised—so lately as Mr. Collins was wishing to
marry you. But when you have had time to think it over, I hope you
will be satisfied with what I have done. I am not romantic, you know; I
never was. I ask only a comfortable home; and considering Mr. Collins's
character, connection, and situation in life, I am convinced that my
chance of happiness with him is as fair as most people can boast on
entering the marriage state—especially since, oh! Elizabeth, I beg you
will not be angry with me or cut me down where I stand! But
Elizabeth, I can have no secrets from you—I have been *stricken*."

Elizabeth gasped. Her closest friend, stricken by the plague!
Condemned to serve Satan! Her instincts demanded she back away. She
listened as Charlotte recounted the unhappy event, which occurred during her Wednesday walk to Longbourn. Daring to make the trip alone
and unarmed, she had hastened upon the road undisturbed, until she
happened upon an overturned chaise and four. Seeing no unmentionables about, Charlotte approached and knelt—readying her eyes to meet
the gruesome visage of a crushed coachman. To her horror, she was
instead met by the grasp of a zombie who had been trapped beneath the
carriage. Her leg caught in its bony fingers, she screamed as the creature's
teeth broke her skin. She was able to free herself and continue to
Longbourn, but Hell's dark business had been carried out.

"I don't have long, Elizabeth. All I ask is that my final months be
happy ones, and that I be permitted a husband who will see to my
proper Christian beheading and burial."

CHAPTER 23

E LIZABETH WAS SITTING with her mother and sisters, reflecting on what she had heard, and resolving to speak of it to no one, when Sir William Lucas himself appeared, sent by his daughter, to announce her engagement to the family. With many compliments to them, he unfolded the matter—to an audience not merely wondering, but incredulous; for Mrs. Bennet, with more perseverance than politeness, protested he must be entirely mistaken; and Lydia, always unguarded and often uncivil, boisterously exclaimed:

"Good Lord! Sir William, how can you tell such a story? Do not you know that Mr. Collins wants to marry Lizzy?"

Thankfully, Sir William had been trained as a tailor and not a warrior, for nothing less than the patience of a man who had threaded ten-thousand needles could have borne such treatment without anger.

Elizabeth, feeling it incumbent on her to relieve him from so unpleasant a situation, now put herself forward to confirm his account, by mentioning her prior knowledge of it from Charlotte herself. Mrs. Bennet was too much overpowered to say a great deal while Sir William remained; but no sooner had he left them than her feelings found a rapid vent. In the first place, she persisted in disbelieving the whole of the matter; secondly, she was very sure that Mr. Collins had been taken in; thirdly, she trusted that they would never be happy together; and fourthly, that the match might be broken off. Two inferences, however, were plainly deduced from the whole: one, that Elizabeth was the real cause of the mischief; and the other that she herself had been barbarously misused by them all; and on these two points she principally dwelt during the rest of the day. Nothing could console and nothing could appease her. Nor did that day wear out her resentment.

Mr. Bennet's emotions were much more tranquil on the occasion; for it gratified him, he said, to discover that Charlotte Lucas, whom he had been used to think tolerably sensible, was as foolish as his wife, and more foolish than his daughter!

As for Elizabeth, she could hardly think on the matter without coming to tears, for she alone knew the sorrowful truth. She thought often of striking Charlotte down—of donning her Tabbi boots and slipping into her bedchamber under cover of darkness, where she would mercifully end her friend's misery with the Panther's Kiss. But she had given her word, and her word was sacred. She would not interfere with Charlotte's transformation.

Her grief for Charlotte made her turn with fonder regard to her sister, for whose happiness she grew daily more anxious, as Bingley had now been gone a week and nothing more was heard of his return.

Jane had sent Caroline an early answer to her letter, and was counting the days till she might reasonably hope to hear again. The promised letter of thanks from Mr. Collins (whose journey had been, against Elizabeth's hopes, unencumbered by zombies) arrived on Tuesday, addressed to their father, and written with all the solemnity of gratitude which a twelvemonth's abode in the family might have prompted. After discharging his conscience on that head, he proceeded to inform them of his happiness in having obtained the affection of their amiable neighbour, Miss Lucas, and then explained that it was merely with the view of enjoying her society that he had been so ready to close with their kind wish of seeing him again at Longbourn, whither he hoped to be able to return on Monday fortnight; for Lady Catherine, he added, so heartily approved his marriage, that she wished it to take place as soon as possible, which he trusted would be an unanswerable argument with his amiable Charlotte to name an early day for making him the happiest of men. Elizabeth could not help but feel for the poor fat fool; he had no idea what misery awaited.

Mr. Collins's return into Hertfordshire was no longer a matter of pleasure to Mrs. Bennet. On the contrary, she was as much disposed to complain of it as her husband. It was very strange that he should come to Longbourn instead of to Lucas Lodge; it was also very inconvenient and exceedingly troublesome. She hated having visitors in the house while her health was so indifferent, and lovers were of all people the most disagreeable. Such were the gentle murmurs of Mrs. Bennet, and they gave way only to the greater distress of Mr. Bingley's continued absence. An hour seldom passed in which she did not talk of Bingley, express her impatience for his arrival, or even require Jane to confess that if he did not come back she would think herself very ill used. It needed all Jane's training under Master Liu to bear these attacks with tolerable tranquillity.

Mr. Collins returned most punctually on Monday fortnight, but his reception at Longbourn was not quite so gracious as it had been on his first introduction. He was too happy, however, to need much attention; and luckily for the others, the business of love-making relieved them from a great deal of his company. The chief of every day was spent by him at Lucas Lodge, and he sometimes returned to Longbourn only in time to make an apology for his absence before the family went to bed.

Mrs. Bennet was really in a most pitiable state. The very mention of anything concerning the match threw her into an agony of ill-humour, and wherever she went she was sure of hearing it talked of. The sight of Miss Lucas was odious to her. As her successor in that house, she regarded her with jealous abhorrence. Whenever Charlotte came to see them, she concluded her to be anticipating the hour of possession; and whenever she spoke in a low voice to Mr. Collins, was convinced that they were talking of the Longbourn estate, and resolving to turn herself and her daughters out of the house, as soon as Mr. Bennet were dead. She complained bitterly of all this to her husband.

"Indeed, Mr. Bennet," said she, "it is very hard to think that Charlotte Lucas should ever be mistress of this house, that I should be forced to make way for her, and live to see her take her place in it!"

"My dear, do not give way to such gloomy thoughts. Let us hope for better things. Let us flatter ourselves that Mr. Collins, who seems always eager to talk of Heaven, may be dispatched there by a horde of zombies before I am dead."

CHAPTER 24

MISS BINGLEY'S LETTER ARRIVED, and put an end to doubt. The very first sentence conveyed the assurance of their being all settled in London for the winter, and concluded with her brother's regret at not having had time to pay his respects to his friends in Hertfordshire before he left the country.

Hope was over, entirely over; and when Jane could attend to the rest of the letter, she found little, except the professed affection of the writer, that could give her any comfort. Miss Darcy's praise occupied the chief of it. Her many attractions were again dwelt on, and Caroline boasted joyfully of their increasing intimacy.

Elizabeth, to whom Jane very soon communicated the chief of all this, heard it in silent indignation. Her heart was divided between concern for her sister, and thoughts of going immediately to town and dispensing of the lot of them.

"My dear Jane!" exclaimed Elizabeth, "you are too good. Your sweetness and disinterestedness are really angelic; you wish to think all the world respectable, and are hurt if I speak of killing anybody for any reason! Do not be afraid of my running into any excess, of my encroaching on your privilege of universal goodwill. You need not. There are few people whom I really love, and still fewer of whom I think well. The more I see of the world, the more am I dissatisfied with it; and every zombie confirms my belief that God has abandoned us as punishment for the evils of people such as Miss Bingley."

"My dear Lizzy, do not give way to such feelings as these. They will ruin your happiness. You do not make allowance enough for difference of situation and temper. For someone who so often speaks of our dear master, I fear you have forgotten much of his wisdom! Were we not taught to temper our feelings? We must not be so ready to fancy ourselves intentionally injured. It is very often nothing but our own vanity that deceives us."

"I am far from attributing any part of Mr. Bingley's conduct to design," said Elizabeth; "but without scheming to do wrong, or to make others unhappy, there may be error, and there may be misery. Thoughtlessness, want of attention to other people's feelings, and want of resolution—grave offenses to one's honour, all."

"And do you impute it to either of those?"

"Yes; to the last. But if I go on, I shall displease you by saying what I think of persons you esteem. Stop me whilst you can."

"You persist, then, in supposing his sisters influence him?"

"I believe it so ardently as to offer you my sword in their vanquishing."

"I cannot believe it. Why should they try to influence him? They can only wish his happiness; and if he is attached to me, no other woman can secure it."

"Your first position is false. They may wish many things besides his happiness; they may wish his increase of wealth and consequence; they may wish him to marry a girl who has all the importance of money, great connections, and pride."

"Beyond a doubt, they *do* wish him to choose Miss Darcy," replied Jane; "but this may be from better feelings than you are supposing. They have known her much longer than they have known me; no wonder if they love her better. But, whatever may be their own wishes, it is very unlikely they should have opposed their brother's. What sister would think herself at liberty to do it? If they believed him attached to me, they would not try to part us; if he were so, they could not succeed. By supposing such an affection, you make everybody acting unnaturally and wrong, and me most unhappy. Do not distress me by the idea. I am not ashamed of having been mistaken. Let me take it in the best light."

Elizabeth could scarcely contain her anger; still, Jane was her elder, and leader of the Sisters Bennet. She had no choice but to obey. From this time Mr. Bingley's name was scarcely ever mentioned between them.

Mrs. Bennet still continued to wonder and repine at his returning no more, and though a day seldom passed in which Elizabeth did not account for it clearly, there was little chance of her ever considering it with less perplexity. Mrs. Bennet's best comfort was that Mr. Bingley must be down again in the summer.

Mr. Bennet treated the matter differently. "So, Lizzy," said he one day, "your sister is crossed in love, I find. I congratulate her. Next to being married, a girl likes to be crossed a little in love now and then. It is something to think of, and it gives her a sort of distinction among her companions. When is your turn to come? You will hardly bear to be long outdone by Jane. Now is your time. Here are officers enough in Meryton to disappoint all the young ladies in the country. Let Wickham be your man. He is a pleasant fellow, and might teach you something of those wifely parts of life which you, above all your sisters, have forsaken."

"Thank you, sir, but I am perfectly content being the bride of death. We must not all expect Jane's good fortune."

"True," said Mr. Bennet, "but it is a comfort to think that whatever of that kind may befall you, you have an affectionate mother who will make the most of it."

CHAPTER 25

A FTER A WEEK SPENT in professions of love and schemes of felicity, Mr. Collins was called from his amiable Charlotte by the arrival of Saturday. He took leave of his relations at Longbourn with as much solemnity as before; wished his fair cousins health and happiness again, and promised their father another letter of thanks.

On the following Monday, Mrs. Bennet had the pleasure of receiving her brother and his wife, who came as usual to spend the Christmas at Longbourn. Mr. Gardiner was a sensible, gentlemanlike man, greatly superior to his sister, as well by nature as education. The Netherfield ladies would have had difficulty in believing that a man who lived by trade, and within view of his own warehouses, could have been so well bred and agreeable. Mrs. Gardiner, who was several years younger than Mrs. Bennet, was an amiable, intelligent, elegant woman, and a great favourite with all her Longbourn nieces. Between the two eldest and herself especially, there subsisted a particular regard. She had often provided encouragement to continue their training when it had become too severe, and provided refuge when their mother's derision of their "savage nature" became intolerable.

The first part of Mrs. Gardiner's business on her arrival was to distribute her presents and describe the goings on in town; she spoke of subjects as diverse as new fashions and recent victories against the sorry stricken. When this was done she had a less active part to play. It became her turn to listen. Mrs. Bennet had many grievances to relate, and much to complain of. They had all been very ill-used since she last saw her sister. Two of her girls had been upon the point of marriage, and after all there was nothing in it.

"I do not blame Jane," she continued, "for Jane would have got Mr.

Bingley if she could. But Lizzy! Oh, sister! It is very hard to think that she might have been Mr. Collins's wife by this time had it not been for her own perverseness. He made her an offer in this very room, and she refused him. The consequence of it is, that Lady Lucas will have a daughter married before I have, and that the Longbourn estate is just as much entailed as ever. The Lucases are very artful people indeed, sister. They are all for what they can get. I am sorry to say it of them, but so it is."

Mrs. Gardiner, to whom the chief of this news had been given before, in the course of Jane and Elizabeth's correspondence with her, made her sister a slight answer, and, in compassion to her nieces turned the conversation.

When alone with Elizabeth afterwards, she spoke more on the subject. "It seems likely to have been a desirable match for Jane," said she. "I am sorry it went off. But these things happen so often! A young man, such as you describe Mr. Bingley, so easily falls in love with a pretty girl for a few weeks, and when accident separates them, so easily forgets her."

"An excellent consolation in its way," said Elizabeth, "but it will not do for *us*. It does not often happen that the interference of friends will persuade a young man of independent fortune to think no more of a girl whom he was violently in love with only a few days before."

"Pray, how *violent was* Mr. Bingley's love?"

"As violent as the monks of Dragon Mountain. Every time they met, it was more decided and remarkable."

"Poor Jane! I am sorry for her, because, with her disposition, she may not get over it immediately. It had better have happened to you, Lizzy; you would have opened this Bingley's stomach and strangled him with his own bowels, I suspect. Do you think she would be prevailed upon to go back to town with us? Change of scene might be of service—and perhaps a little relief from home may be as useful as anything."

Elizabeth was exceedingly pleased with this proposal, and felt persuaded of her sister's ready acquiescence. It was too long since her eyes had been filled with the delights of London; which, though quarantined by towering walls, and divided into sections by the King's army, was still a city unrivaled in its ability to excite the senses.

"I hope," added Mrs. Gardiner, "that no consideration with regard to this young man will influence her. We go out so little, that it is very improbable that they should meet at all, unless he comes to see her."

"And that is quite impossible; for he is now in the custody of his friend, and Mr. Darcy would no more suffer him to call on Jane in Section Six East!"

"So much the better. I hope they will not meet at all."

The Gardiners stayed a week at Longbourn. Mrs. Bennet had so carefully provided for the entertainment of her brother and sister that they did not once sit down to a family dinner. When the engagement was for home, some of the officers always made part of it—of which Mr. Wickham was sure to be one; and on these occasions, Mrs. Gardiner, rendered suspicious by Elizabeth's warm commendation, narrowly observed them both. Their preference of each other was plain enough to make her a little uneasy; and she resolved to speak to Elizabeth on the subject before leaving Hertfordshire.

To Mrs. Gardiner, Wickham had one means of affording pleasure, unconnected with his general powers. About ten or a dozen years ago, before her marriage, she had spent a considerable time in that very part of Derbyshire to which he belonged. They had, therefore, many acquaintances in common; and though Wickham had been little there since the death of Darcy's father, it was yet in his power to give her fresher intelligence of her former friends than she had been in the way of procuring.

Mrs. Gardiner had seen Mr. Darcy's estate, Pemberley, and known the late Mr. Darcy by his reputation as a gentleman and powerful slayer of the undead. Here consequently was an inexhaustible subject of discourse. On being made acquainted with the present Mr. Darcy's treatment of him, she tried to remember some of that gentleman's reputed disposition, and was confident that she recollected having heard Mr. Fitzwilliam Darcy formerly spoken of as a very proud, ill-natured boy.

CHAPTER 26

MRS. GARDINER'S CAUTION to Elizabeth was punctually and kindly given on the first favourable opportunity of speaking to her alone; after honestly telling her what she thought, she thus went on:

"You are too sensible a girl, Lizzy, to fall in love merely because you are warned against it; and, therefore, I am not afraid of speaking openly. Seriously, I would have you be on your guard. I have nothing to say against *him*; he has felled many a zombie; and if he had the fortune he ought to have, I should think you could not do better. But as it is, you must not let your fancy run away with you."

"My dear aunt, this is being serious indeed."

"Yes, and I hope to engage you to be serious likewise."

"Well, then, you need not be under any alarm. I will take care of myself, and of Mr. Wickham too. He shall not be in love with me, if I can prevent it."

"Elizabeth, you are not serious now."

"I beg your pardon, I will try again. I am a warrior, madam: survivor of the thirty-six chambers of Shaolin, beholder of the scrolls of Gan Xian Tan. I do not seek love, and at present I am not in love with Mr. Wickham; though he is, beyond all comparison, the most agreeable man I ever saw—in form, character, and musketry. However, I see the imprudence of an attachment with one so deeply in want of fortune. I will not be in a hurry to believe myself his first object. When I am in company with him, I will not be wishing. In short, I will do my best."

"Perhaps it will be as well if you discourage his coming here so very often. At least, you should not *remind* your mother of inviting him."

"You know my mother's ideas as to the necessity of constant company for her friends. But really, and upon my honour, I will try to do what I think to be the wisest; and now I hope you are satisfied."

Her aunt assured her that she was, and Elizabeth having thanked her for the kindness of her hints, they parted; a wonderful instance of advice being given on such a point, without being resented.

Mr. Collins returned into Hertfordshire soon after it had been quitted by the Gardiners and Jane; but as he took up his abode with the Lucases, his arrival was no great inconvenience to Mrs. Bennet. His marriage was now fast approaching, and she was at length so far resigned as to think it inevitable, and even repeatedly to say, in an ill-natured tone, that she "wished they might be happy." Thursday was to be the wedding day, and on Wednesday Miss Lucas paid her farewell visit; and when she rose to take leave, Elizabeth, ashamed of her mother's ungracious and reluctant good wishes, and sincerely affected herself, accompanied her out of the room. As they went downstairs together, Charlotte said:

"I promise to write for as long as I am able. I shall depend on hearing from you very often, Eliza."

"*That* you certainly shall."

"We shall often meet, I hope, in Hertfordshire."

"I am not likely to leave Kent for some time. Promise me, therefore, to come to Hunsford." Elizabeth could not refuse, though she foresaw little pleasure in the visit. Charlotte was already showing the earliest signs of transformation, though she took great care to hide them from all but the trained eye. Her skin had taken on a slight pallor, and her speech seemed a trifle laboured.

"My father and Maria are coming to me in March," added Charlotte, "and I hope you will consent to be of the party. Indeed, Eliza, you will be as welcome as either of them."

The wedding took place, and no one other than Elizabeth seemed to suspect the bride's condition. Mr. Collins appeared happier than he ever had despite the fact that Charlotte had to be reminded to use her fork several times over the course of dinner. The bride and

"THE WEDDING TOOK PLACE, AND NO ONE OTHER THAN ELIZABETH SEEMED TO
SUSPECT THE BRIDE'S CONDITION."

bridegroom set off for Kent from the church door, and everybody had as much to say, or to hear, on the subject as usual. Elizabeth soon heard from her friend; and their correspondence was as regular and frequent as it had ever been; that it should be equally affectionate was impossible. Charlotte's first letters were received with a good deal of eagerness; there could not but be curiosity to know how she would speak of her new home, how she would like Lady Catherine, and how her transformation was proceeding. The house, furniture, neighbourhood, and roads, were all to her taste, and Lady Catherine's behaviour was most friendly and obliging. It was Mr. Collins's picture of Hunsford and Rosings rationally softened; and Elizabeth perceived that she must wait for her own visit there to know the rest. The only harbinger of Charlotte's unhappy fate was her ever-worsening penmanship.

Jane had already written a few lines to her sister to announce their safe arrival in London; and when she wrote again, Elizabeth hoped it would be in her power to say something of the Bingleys.

Her impatience for this second letter was as well rewarded as impatience generally is. Jane had been a week in town without either seeing or hearing from Caroline. She accounted for it, however, by supposing that her last letter to her friend from Longbourn had by some accident been lost.

"My aunt," she continued, "is going to-morrow into that part of the town, and I shall take the opportunity of calling in Section Four Central."

She wrote again when the visit was paid, and she had seen Miss Bingley. "I did not think Caroline in spirits," were her words, "but she was very glad to see me, and reproached me for giving her no notice of my coming to London. I was right, therefore, my last letter had never reached her. I inquired after their brother, of course. He was well, but so much engaged with Mr. Darcy that they scarcely ever saw him. I found that Miss Darcy was expected to dinner. I wish I could see her. My visit was not long, as Caroline and Mrs. Hurst were going out. I dare say I shall see them soon here."

Elizabeth shook her head over this letter. Jane was a fine killer, but a deficient judge of character. Indeed, her only weakness was her too-giving heart. Elizabeth was quite convinced that Caroline Bingley had no intentions of telling her brother about the visit, or even Jane's being in town. Once again, her thoughts turned to the satisfaction of seeing Miss Bingley's last rubies pour from her neck and down the front of her bodice.

As she predicted, four weeks passed away, and Jane saw nothing of him. She endeavoured to persuade herself that she did not regret it; but she could no longer be blind to Miss Bingley's inattention. After waiting at home every morning for a fortnight, the visitor did at last appear; but the shortness of her stay and the alteration of her manner would allow Jane to deceive herself no longer. The letter which she wrote to her sister will prove what she felt.

> MY DEAREST LIZZY,
>
> You will, I am sure, be incapable of triumphing in your better judgement, at my expense, when I confess myself to have been entirely deceived in Miss Bingley's regard for me. But, my dear sister, though the event has proved you right, do not think me obstinate if I still assert that my confidence was as natural as your suspicion. Caroline did not return my visit till yesterday; and not a note, not a line, did I receive in the meantime. When she did come, it was very evident that she had no pleasure in it; she made a slight, formal apology, for not calling before, said not a word of wishing to see me again, and was in every respect so altered a creature, that when she went away I was perfectly resolved to follow her into the street and confront her as you suggested, and, had I been appropriately dressed for an outing, I might have. He knows of my being in town, I am certain, from something she said herself; and yet it would seem, by her manner of talking, as if she wanted to persuade herself that he is really partial to Miss Darcy. I can-

not understand it. If I were not afraid of judging harshly, I should be almost tempted to demand satisfaction. But I will endeavour to banish every painful thought, and think only of what will make me happy—your affection, and the invariable kindness of my dear uncle and aunt. Let me hear from you very soon. Miss Bingley said something of his never returning to Netherfield again, of giving up the house, but not with any certainty. We had better not mention it. I am extremely glad that you have such pleasant accounts from our friends at Hunsford. Pray go to see them, with Sir William and Maria. I am sure you will be very comfortable there.

YOURS, ETC.

This letter gave Elizabeth some pain; but her spirits returned as she considered that Jane would no longer be duped, and that her focus might once again turn to combat. All expectation from the brother was now absolutely over. She would not even wish for a renewal of his attentions. His character sunk on every review of it; and as a punishment for him, as well as a possible advantage to Jane, she seriously hoped he might really soon marry Mr. Darcy's sister, as by Wickham's account, she would make him abundantly regret what he had thrown away.

Mrs. Gardiner about this time wrote and reminded Elizabeth of her promise concerning that gentleman, and required information; Elizabeth assured her that his apparent partiality had subsided, his attentions were over, he was the admirer of someone else. The sudden acquisition of ten thousand pounds was the most remarkable charm of the young lady to whom he was now rendering himself agreeable; but Elizabeth, less clear-sighted perhaps in this case than in Charlotte's, did not quarrel with him for his wish of independence. Nothing, on the contrary, could be more natural; and while able to suppose that it cost him a few struggles to relinquish her, she was ready to allow it a wise and desirable measure for both, and could very sincerely wish him happy.

All this was acknowledged to Mrs. Gardiner; and after relating the circumstances, she thus went on: "I am now convinced, my dear aunt, that I have never been much in love; for had I really experienced that pure and elevating passion, I should at present detest his very name, and wish him all manner of evil. But I find my thoughts returning to the protection of our beloved England, for truly there can be no higher purpose; indeed the feelings of one young lady seem rather insignificant in comparison. My talents and my times demand my service, and I believe the Crown more pleased to have me on the front lines than at the altar."

CHAPTER 27

WITH NO GREATER EVENTS than these in the Longbourn family, and otherwise diversified by little beyond the walks to Meryton (less often interrupted by zombies on account of the hardened earth of winter), did January and February pass away. March was to take Elizabeth to Hunsford. She had not at first thought very seriously of going thither; but Charlotte, she soon found, was struggling to keep the last of her senses, and Elizabeth thought it an appropriate tribute to their former friendship to see her one last time. She found that absence, as well as pity, had also weakened her disgust of Mr. Collins. The journey would moreover give her a peep at Jane; and, in short, as the time drew near, she would have been very sorry for any delay. Everything, however, went on smoothly, and was finally settled. She was to accompany Sir William and his second daughter. The improvement of spending a night in London was added in time, and the plan became perfect as a plan could be.

The farewell between herself and Mr. Wickham was perfectly friendly; on his side even more. His present pursuit could not make him forget that Elizabeth had been the first to excite and to deserve his attention, the first to listen and to pity, the first to be admired.

Her fellow-travellers the next day were not of a kind to make her think him less agreeable. Sir William Lucas, and his daughter Maria, a good-humoured girl, but as empty-headed and untrained as himself, had nothing to say that could be worth hearing, and were listened to with about as much delight as the rattle of the chaise. It was a journey of only twenty-four miles, and they began it so early as to be in Section Six East by noon. The coachman, as was the custom on trips to town, had employed two young men from Meryton to ride beside him with muskets. This was done in spite of the fact that Elizabeth was herself fully armed, and more than capable of defending them should they encounter any unpleasantness.

When they were but three miles from London, and Sir William was prattling on about the particulars of his knighthood for the second time in as many hours, the chaise lurched to a halt. The suddenness of this was enough to send Maria flying from one side of the carriage to the other, and was promptly followed by frightened shouts and the crack of powder outside. Had Elizabeth not been graced with steady nerves and the fortitude of years of combat, she might have gasped upon pulling back one of the curtains—for there were no less than one hundred unmentionables surrounding them on all sides. One of the young musket men had been dragged off the chaise and was being devoured, while the other two living men fired clumsily into the crowd as the hands of the dead pulled at their pant legs. Elizabeth grabbed her Brown Bess and Katana sword and told Sir William and Maria to remain as they were.

She kicked open the door and sprang atop the coach. From here Elizabeth could appreciate the full measure of their predicament, for rather than one hundred unmentionables, she now perceived no less than *twice* that number. The coachman's leg was in the possession of several zombies, who were quite close to getting their teeth on his ankle. Seeing no alternative, Elizabeth brought her sword down upon his thigh—amputating the leg, but saving the man. She picked him up with one arm and lowered him into the coach, where he fainted as blood poured forth from his new stump. Sadly, this action prevented her from saving the second musket man, who had been pulled from his perch. He screamed as the dreadfuls held him down and began to tear organs from his living belly and feast upon them. The zombies next turned their attention to the terrified horses. Elizabeth knew that she and the present party were all doomed to slow deaths if the horses should fall into Satan's hands, so she sprang skyward, firing her musket as she flew through the air, her bullets penetrating the heads of several unmentionables. She landed on her feet beside one of the horses, and with her sword, began cutting down the attackers with all the grace of Aphrodite, and all the ruthlessness of Herod.

Her feet, fists, and blade were too swift for the clumsy horde, and they began to retreat. Seeing her chance, Elizabeth sheathed her Katana, sprang into the driver's box, and grabbed the reins. The zombies had already begun to regroup as she cracked the coachman's whip, driving the horses forward and carrying them down the road at a rather unsafe speed, until she was satisfied that the danger had passed.

Shortly thereafter, they approached the southern face of London's wall. Though she had once walked upon China's Great Wall, Elizabeth was nonetheless impressed whenever she had occasion to lay eyes upon Britain's Barrier. Considered alone, each section offered little to boast of. The wall was similar in height and appearance to that of many older castles, and punctuated by the occasional gorge tower or cannon port. But considered as a whole, the wall was so massive as to defy the notions of what was possible with human hands. Elizabeth brought the carriage to a halt at the southern guard tower. A dozen or more chaises were stopped ahead of them—waiting as the guards searched for contraband and made certain that none of the passengers showed signs of the strange plague. Sir William poked his head out and informed Elizabeth that the coachman had died, and asked if she thought it appropriate to leave his body beside the road.

As they drove to Mr. Gardiner's door, Jane was at a drawing-room window watching their arrival; when they entered the passage she was there to welcome them, surprised by the sight of Elizabeth in the driver's box. Elizabeth's spirits lifted at the sight of her sister, who looked as healthful and lovely as ever. She relayed the details of their unhappy journey as swiftly as she could, and begged they speak no more of it, except to say that she had never seen such a number of unmentionables together in the country, and wonder why so many would attack a single chaise. The day passed most pleasantly away; the morning in bustle and shopping, and the evening at one of the theatres.

Elizabeth then contrived to sit by her aunt. Their first object was her sister; and she was more grieved than astonished to hear, in reply to her minute inquiries, that though Jane always struggled to support her spirits, there were periods of dejection. It was reasonable, however, to hope that they would not continue long. Mrs. Gardiner gave her the particulars also of Miss Bingley's visit in Section Six East, and repeated conversations occurring at different times between Jane and herself, which proved that the former had, from her heart, given up the acquaintance.

Mrs. Gardiner then rallied her niece on Wickham's desertion, and complimented her on bearing it so well.

"But my dear Elizabeth," she added, "what sort of girl is this new object of his affections? I should be sorry to think our friend mercenary."

"Pray, my dear aunt, what is the difference in matrimonial affairs, between the mercenary and the prudent motive? Last Christmas you were afraid of his marrying me, because it would be imprudent; and now, because he is trying to get a girl with only ten thousand pounds, you think him mercenary."

"If you will only tell me what sort of girl she is, I shall know what to think."

"She is a very good kind of girl, I believe. I know no harm of her."

Before they were separated by the conclusion of the play, Elizabeth had the unexpected happiness of an invitation to accompany her uncle and aunt in a tour of pleasure which they proposed taking in the summer.

"We have not determined how far it shall carry us," said Mrs. Gardiner, "but, perhaps, to the Lakes."

No scheme could have been more agreeable to Elizabeth, and her acceptance of the invitation was most ready and grateful. "My dear, dear aunt," she rapturously cried, "what delight! What felicity! You give me fresh life and vigour. Adieu to disappointment and spleen. What are young men to rocks and mountains? Oh! what hours of mountaintop sparring we shall spend! How many bucks we shall fell with nothing more than our daggers and swiftness of foot! Oh! How we will please Buddha by communing with the earth!"

CHAPTER 28

EVERY OBJECT in the next day's journey was new and interesting to Elizabeth. With a new coachman and twice their original number of musket men, they hastened to Hunsford. Once arrived (their journey happily uneventful), every eye was in search of the Parsonage, and every turning expected to bring it in view. Rosings Park was their boundary on one side. Elizabeth smiled at the recollection of all that she had heard of its inhabitants.

At length the Parsonage was discernible. The garden sloping to the road, the house standing in it, the green pales, and the laurel hedge, everything declared they were arriving. Elizabeth felt at once relaxed, for there had been no reports of zombies in Hunsford for years. Many attributed this to the presence of Lady Catherine—so great a slayer that the stricken dared not venture too close to her home.

Mr. Collins and Charlotte appeared at the door, and the carriage stopped at the small gate which led by a short gravel walk to the house, amidst the nods and smiles of the whole party. In a moment they were all out of the chaise, rejoicing at the sight of each other. But when Mrs. Collins welcomed Elizabeth, the latter was greatly distressed by the appearance of the former. It had been months since she had seen Charlotte, and kind months they had not been, for her friend's skin was now quite gray and marked with sores, and her speech appallingly laboured. That none of the others noticed this, Elizabeth attributed to their stupidity—particularly Mr. Collins, who apparently had no idea that his wife was three-quarters dead.

They were taken into the house; and as soon as they were in the parlour, Mr. Collins welcomed them a second time, with ostentatious formality to his humble abode, and punctually repeated all his wife's offers of refreshment.

Elizabeth was prepared to see him in his glory; and she could not help in fancying that in displaying the good proportion of the room, its aspect and its furniture, he addressed himself particularly to her, as if wishing to make her feel what she had lost in refusing him. But though everything seemed neat and comfortable, she was not able to gratify him by any sigh of repentance. After sitting long enough to admire every article of furniture in the room, Mr. Collins invited them to take a stroll in the garden. To work in this garden was one of his most respectable pleasures; and Elizabeth admired Charlotte's efforts to talk of the healthfulness of the exercise, even though it was quite difficult to understand her.

From his garden, Mr. Collins would have led them round his two meadows; but the ladies, not having shoes to encounter the remains of a white frost, turned back; and while Sir William accompanied him, Charlotte took her sister and friend over the house. It was rather small, but well built and convenient. Though she was pleased to see her friend comfortably settled, there was a grief about the whole affair, for Charlotte would not long be able to enjoy her happiness.

She had already learnt that Lady Catherine was still in the country.

It was spoken of again while they were at dinner, when Mr. Collins joining in, observed:

"Yes, Miss Elizabeth, you will have the honour of seeing Lady Catherine de Bourgh on the ensuing Sunday at church, and I need not say you will be delighted with her. Her behaviour to my dear Charlotte is charming. We dine at Rosings twice every week, and are never allowed to walk home. Her ladyship's carriage is regularly ordered for us. I *should* say, one of her ladyship's carriages, for she has several."

"Wady Caferine very respectable . . . sensible woman," groaned Charlotte, "and most attentive nay-bah."

"Very true, my dear, that is exactly what I say. She is the sort of woman whom one cannot regard with too much deference."

As dinner continued in this manner, Elizabeth's eye was continually drawn to Charlotte, who hovered over her plate, using a spoon to shovel goose meat and gravy in the general direction of her mouth, with limited success. As she did, one of the sores beneath her eye burst, sending a trickle of bloody pus down her cheek and into her mouth. Apparently, she found the added flavor agreeable, for it only increased the frequency of her spoonfuls. Elizabeth, however, could not help but vomit ever so slightly into her handkerchief.

The rest of the evening was spent chiefly in talking over Hertfordshire news, and telling again what had already been written; and when it closed, Elizabeth, in the solitude of her chamber, had to meditate upon Charlotte's worsening condition, and how no one—even Lady Catherine, supposed to be the greatest of all zombie slayers—had noticed it.

About the middle of the next day, as she was in her room getting ready for a walk, a sudden noise below seemed to speak the whole house in confusion; and, after listening a moment, she heard somebody running upstairs in a violent hurry, and calling loudly after her. Elizabeth grabbed her Katana, opened the door, and met Maria in the landing place, who cried out:

"Oh, my dear Eliza! Pray make haste and come into the dining-room, for there is such a sight to be seen! I will not tell you what it is. Make haste, and come down this moment."

Maria would tell her nothing more, and down they ran into the dining-room, which fronted the lane, in quest of this wonder. It was merely two ladies stopping in a low carriage at the garden gate.

"And is this all?" cried Elizabeth. "I expected at least a dozen unmentionables, and here is nothing but Lady Catherine and her daughter."

"La! My dear," said Maria, quite shocked at the mistake, "it is not Lady Catherine. The old lady is Mrs. Jenkinson, who lives with them; the other is Miss de Bourgh. Only look at her. She is quite a little creature. Who would have thought that she could be so thin and small?"

"She is abominably rude to keep Charlotte out of doors in all this wind. Why does she not come in?"

"Oh, Charlotte says she hardly ever does. It is the greatest of favours when Miss de Bourgh comes in."

"I like her appearance," said Elizabeth, struck with other ideas. "She looks sickly and cross. Yes, she will do for Mr. Darcy very well. She will make him a very proper wife."

Mr. Collins and Charlotte were both standing at the gate in conversation with the ladies; and Sir William, to Elizabeth's high diversion, was stationed in the doorway, in earnest contemplation of the greatness before him, and constantly bowing whenever Miss de Bourgh looked that way.

At length there was nothing more to be said; the ladies drove on, and the others returned into the house. Mr. Collins no sooner saw the two girls than he began to congratulate them on their good fortune, for he informed them that the whole party was asked to dine at Rosings the next day. Apparently overcome with excitement, Charlotte dropped to the ground and began stuffing handfuls of crisp autumn leaves in her mouth.

CHAPTER 29

"I CONFESS," said Mr. Collins, "that I should not have been at all surprised by her ladyship's asking us on Sunday to drink tea and spend the evening at Rosings. I rather expected, from my knowledge of her affability, that it would happen. But who could have foreseen such an attention as this? Who could have imagined that we should receive an invitation to dine there so immediately after your arrival!"

"I am the less surprised at what has happened," replied Sir William, "for her superior mastery of the deadly arts and high breeding are known throughout the courts of Europe."

Scarcely anything was talked of the whole day or next morning but their visit to Rosings. Mr. Collins was carefully instructing them in what they were to expect, that the sight of such rooms, so many servants, a personal guard of five-and-twenty ninjas, and so splendid a dinner, might not wholly overpower them.

When the ladies were separating for the toilette, he said to Elizabeth:

"Do not make yourself uneasy, my dear cousin, about your apparel. Lady Catherine is far from requiring that elegance of dress in us which becomes herself and her daughter. I would advise you merely to put on whatever of your clothes is superior to the rest—there is no occasion for anything more. Lady Catherine will not think the worse of you for being simply dressed, just as she will not think less of you for possessing combat skills so very beneath her own." Elizabeth's fists clenched at the insult, but out of affection for her three-quarters dead friend, she held her tongue and sword.

While they were dressing, he came two or three times to their different doors, to recommend their being quick, as Lady Catherine very much objected to be kept waiting for her dinner.

As the weather was fine, they had a pleasant walk of about half a mile across the park.

When they ascended the steps to the hall, Maria's alarm was every moment increasing, and even Sir William did not look perfectly calm. Elizabeth's courage did not fail her, even though she had been regaled with stories of Lady Catherine's accomplishments from the time she had been old enough to hold her first dagger. The mere stateliness of money or rank she could witness without trepidation, but the presence of a woman who had slain ninety dreadfuls with nothing more than a rain-soaked envelope was an intimidating prospect indeed.

They followed the servants through an ante-chamber to the room where Lady Catherine, her daughter, and Mrs. Jenkinson were sitting. Her ladyship, with great condescension, arose to receive them; and as Mrs. Collins had settled it with her husband that the office of introduction should be hers, it was performed with no shortage of difficulty as she struggled to speak in a manner comprehensible to others.

In spite of having been at St. James's, Sir William was so completely awed by the grandeur surrounding him, that he had but just courage enough to make a very low bow, and take his seat without saying a word; and his daughter, frightened almost out of her senses, sat on the edge of her chair, not knowing which way to look. Elizabeth found herself quite equal to the scene, and could observe the three ladies before her composedly. Lady Catherine was a tall, large woman, with strongly-marked features, which might once have been handsome. Her once-flawless figure had been softened by age, but her eyes no were less striking than Elizabeth had oft heard them described. They were they eyes of a woman who once held the wrath of God in her hands. Elizabeth wondered how much quickness those famed hands still possessed.

When, after examining the mother, in whose countenance and deportment she soon found some resemblance of Mr. Darcy, she turned her eyes on the daughter; she could almost have joined in Maria's astonishment at her being so thin and so small. There was neither in figure nor face any likeness between the ladies. Miss de Bourgh was pale and sickly; her features, though not plain, were insignificant; and she spoke very little, except in a low voice, to Mrs. Jenkinson, in whose appearance there was nothing remarkable, and who was entirely engaged in listening to what she said.

After sitting a few minutes, they were all sent to one of the windows to admire the view, Mr. Collins attending them to point out its beauties, and Lady Catherine kindly informing them that it was much better worth looking at in the summer.

The dinner was exceedingly handsome, and there were all the servants and all the articles of plate which Mr. Collins had promised; and, as he had likewise foretold, he took his seat at the bottom of the table, by her ladyship's desire, and looked as if he felt that life could furnish nothing greater. The party did not supply much conversation. Elizabeth was ready to speak whenever there was an opening, but she was seated between Charlotte and Miss de Bourgh—the former of whom had to be frequently reminded to use her silver, and the latter said not a word to her all dinner-time.

When the ladies returned to the drawing-room, there was little to be done but to hear Lady Catherine talk of her attempts to create a serum, which would slow—or even reverse—the effects of the strange plague. Elizabeth was surprised to learn that her ladyship was thus engaged, for trifling in plague cures was considered the last refuge of the naïve. The greatest minds in England had been vexed by the same pursuit for five-and-fifty years. She inquired into Charlotte's domestic concerns familiarly and minutely, and gave her a great deal of advice as to the management of them all; and told her how everything ought to be regulated in so small a family as hers. Elizabeth found that nothing was beneath this great lady's attention, which could furnish her with an occasion of dictating to others. In the intervals of her discourse with Mrs. Collins, she addressed a variety of questions to Maria and Elizabeth, but especially to the latter, of whose connections she knew the least.

"Mr. Collins tells me that you are schooled in the deadly arts, Miss Bennet."

"I am, though not to half the level of proficiency your Ladyship has attained."

"Oh! Then—some time or other I shall be happy to see you spar with one of my ninjas. Are your sisters likewise trained?"

"They are."

"I assume you were schooled in Japan?"

"No, your ladyship. In China."

"China? Are those monks still selling their clumsy kung fu to the English? I take it you mean Shaolin?"

"Yes, your ladyship; under Master Liu."

"Well, I suppose you had no opportunity. Had your father more means, he should have taken you to Kyoto."

"My mother would have had no objection, but my father hates Japan."

"Have your ninjas left you?"

"We never had any ninjas."

"No ninjas! How was that possible? Five daughters brought up at home without any ninjas! I never heard of such a thing. Your mother must have been quite a slave to your safety."

Elizabeth could hardly help smiling as she assured her that had not been the case.

"Then, who protected you when you saw your first combat? Without ninjas, you must have been quite a sorry spectacle indeed."

"Compared with some families, I believe we were; but such was our desire to prevail, and our affection for each other, that we had no trouble vanquishing even our earliest opponents."

"If I had known your mother, I should have advised her most strenuously to engage a team of ninjas. I always say that nothing is to be done in education without steady and regular instruction. Had my own daughter been blessed with a more suitable constitution, I should have sent her away the best dojos in Japan at the age of four. Are any of your younger sisters out, Miss Bennet?"

"Yes, ma'am, all."

"All! What, all five out at once? Very odd! And you only the second. The younger ones out before the elder ones are married! Your younger sisters must be very young?"

"Yes, my youngest is not sixteen. Perhaps *she* is full young to be much in company. But really, ma'am, I think it would be very hard upon younger sisters, that they should not have their share of society and amusement, because the elder may not have the means or inclination to marry early. The last-born has as good a right to the pleasures of youth at the first. And to be kept back on *such* a motive! I think it would not be very likely to promote sisterly affection or delicacy of mind."

"Upon my word," said her ladyship, "you give your opinion very decidedly for so young a person. Pray, what is your age?"

"With three younger sisters grown up," replied Elizabeth, smiling, "your ladyship can hardly expect me to own it."

Lady Catherine seemed quite astonished at not receiving a direct answer; and Elizabeth suspected herself to be the first creature who had ever dared to trifle with so much dignified impertinence.

"You cannot be more than twenty, I am sure, therefore you need not conceal your age."

"I am not one-and-twenty."

When the gentlemen had joined them, and tea was over, the card-tables were placed. Lady Catherine, Sir William, and Mr. and Mrs. Collins sat down to Crypt and Coffin; and as Miss de Bourgh chose to play Whip the Vicar, Elizabeth and Maria had the honour of assisting Mrs. Jenkinson to make up her party. Their table was superlatively stupid. Scarcely a syllable was uttered that did not relate to the game, except when Mrs. Jenkinson expressed her fears of Miss de Bourgh's being too hot or too cold, or having too much or too little light. A great deal more passed at the other table. Lady Catherine was generally speaking—stating the mistakes of the three others, or relating some anecdote of herself. Mr. Collins was employed in agreeing to everything her ladyship said, thanking her for every empty crypt he won, and apologising if he thought he won too many.

After drooling a third cup of tea onto her lap, Charlotte stood to excuse herself from the other table, clutching her stomach and wearing a rather pained expression. "I beg ya-oar pahdun, ya-oar wadyship." Lady Catherine gave no acknowledgment, and Mr. Collins and Sir William were too engrossed in their game to notice what happened next.

Elizabeth watched Charlotte bow slightly, and then limp to the furthest corner of the room, where she lifted the bottom of her gown and bent her knees into a squat. Elizabeth immediately excused herself, rose, and (taking care not to draw attention) grabbed Charlotte by the arm and escorted her to the toilette, where she watched her stricken friend suffer through a quarter-hour of a sickness so severe that decorum prevents its description in these pages.

The tables were shortly after broken up, the carriage was offered to Mrs. Collins, gratefully accepted, and immediately ordered. The party then gathered round the fire to hear Lady Catherine determine what weather they were to have on the morrow. From these instructions they were summoned by the arrival of the coach; and with many speeches of thankfulness on Mr. Collins's side and as many bows on Sir William's they departed. As soon as they had driven from the door, Elizabeth was called on by her cousin to give her opinion of all that she had seen at Rosings, which, for Charlotte's sake, she made more favourable than it really was. "Lady Catherine the Great" had been a disappointment in every sense, and Elizabeth could not forgive the slight against her temple and master.

CHAPTER 30

S IR WILLIAM STAYED only a week at Hunsford, but his visit was long enough to convince him of his daughter's being most comfortably settled. Mr. Collins devoted his mornings to driving Sir William out in his gig, and showing him the country; but when he went away, the whole family returned to their usual employments.

Now and then they were honoured with a call from Lady Catherine, and nothing escaped her observation during these visits. She examined into their employments, looked at their work, and advised them to do it differently; found fault with the arrangement of the furniture; or detected the housemaid in negligence; and if she accepted any refreshment, seemed to do it only for the sake of finding out that Mrs. Collins's joints of meat were too large for her family.

Elizabeth soon perceived, that though this great lady was no longer engaged in the daily defense of her country, she was a most active magistrate in her own parish, the minutest concerns of which were carried to her by Mr. Collins; and whenever any of the cottagers were disposed to be quarrelsome, discontented, or too poor, she sallied forth into the village to implore them to settle their differences, or failing that, wielding her still-mighty blade to settle them herself.

The entertainment of dining at Rosings was repeated about twice a week; and, allowing for the loss of Sir William, and there being only one card-table in the evening, every such entertainment was the counterpart of the first. On one such occasion, Elizabeth was solicited to spar with several of her ladyship's ninjas for the amusement of the party.

The demonstration took place in Lady Catherine's grand dojo, which she had paid to have carried from Kyoto, brick by brick, on the backs of peasants. The ninjas wore their traditional black clothing, masks, and Tabbi boots; Elizabeth wore her sparring gown, and her trusted Katana sword. As Lady Catherine rose to signal the beginning of the match, Elizabeth, in a show of defiance, blindfolded herself.

"My dear girl," said her ladyship, "I suggest you take this contest seriously. My ninjas will show you no mercy."

"Nor I they, your ladyship."

"Ms. Bennet, I remind you that you lack proper instruction in the deadly arts. Your master was a Chinese monk—these ninjas hail from the finest dojos in Japan."

"If my fighting is truly inferior, then your ladyship shall be spared the trouble of watching it for very long."

Elizabeth set her feet, and Lady Catherine, realising she would never convince such a stubborn, unusual girl, snapped her fingers. The first ninja drew his sword and let out a battle cry as he charged directly at Elizabeth. When his blade was only inches from her throat, she moved from her opponent's path and dragged her Katana across his belly. The ninja dropped to the floor—his innards spilling from the slit faster than he could stuff them back in. Elizabeth sheathed her sword, knelt behind him, and strangled him to death with his own large bowel.

Lady Catherine snapped her fingers a second time, and another ninja charged—this one unleashing throwing stars as he advanced. Elizabeth drew her Katana and shielded herself from the first three flying weapons, then snatched the fourth out of the air and threw it back at its originator—striking him in the thigh. The ninja cried out and grabbed the wound with both hands, and Elizabeth brought her blade down, taking off not only the hands, but the leg which they held firmly. The ninja fell to the floor and was promptly beheaded.

Though discontented with such a beginning, Lady Catherine held the greatest hopes for her third and final ninja, the deadliest of the three. But no sooner had she snapped her fingers, than Elizabeth flung her Katana across the dojo, piercing the ninja's chest and pinning him against a wooden column. Elizabeth removed her blindfold and confronted her

"'MY DEAR GIRL,' SAID HER LADYSHIP, 'I SUGGEST YOU TAKE THIS CONTEST SERIOUSLY. MY NINJAS WILL SHOW YOU NO MERCY.'"

opponent, who presently clutched the sword handle, gasping for breath. She delivered a vicious blow, penetrating his rib cage, and withdrew her hand—with the ninja's still-beating heart in it. As all but Lady Catherine turned away in disgust, Elizabeth took a bite, letting the blood run down her chin and onto her sparring gown.

"Curious," said Elizabeth, still chewing. "I have tasted many a heart, but I dare say, I find the Japanese ones a bit tender."

Her ladyship left the dojo without giving compliment to Elizabeth's skills.

Their other engagements were few, as the style of living in the neighbourhood was beyond Mr. Collins's reach. This, however, was no evil to Elizabeth, and upon the whole she spent her time comfortably enough; there were half-hours of pained, almost unintelligible conversation with Charlotte, and the weather was so fine for the time of year that she had often great enjoyment out of doors. Her favourite walk was along the open grove which edged that side of the park, where there was a nice sheltered path, which no one seemed to value but herself, and where she felt beyond the reach of Lady Catherine's curiosity.

In this quiet way, the first fortnight of her visit soon passed away. Easter was approaching, and the week preceding it was to bring an addition to the family at Rosings, which in so small a circle must be important. Elizabeth had heard soon after her arrival that Mr. Darcy was expected there in the course of a few weeks, and though there were not many of her acquaintances whom she did not prefer, his coming would furnish one comparatively new to look at in their Rosings parties, and she might be amused in seeing how hopeless Miss Bingley's designs on him were, by his behaviour to his cousin, for whom he was evidently destined by Lady Catherine, who talked of his coming with the greatest satisfaction, spoke of him in terms of the highest admiration, and seemed almost angry to find that he had already been frequently seen by Miss Lucas and herself.

His arrival was soon known at the Parsonage; for Mr. Collins was walking the whole morning within view of the lodges opening into

Hunsford Lane, in order to have the earliest assurance of it, and after making his bow as the carriage turned into the Park, hurried home with the great intelligence. On the following morning he hastened to Rosings to pay his respects. There were two nephews of Lady Catherine to require them, for Mr. Darcy had brought with him a Colonel Fitzwilliam, the younger son of his uncle, and, to the great surprise of all the party, when Mr. Collins returned, the gentleman accompanied him. Charlotte had seen them from her husband's room, crossing the road, and immediately running into the other, told the girls what an honour they might expect, adding:

"I fank you, Eliza, for dis piece of c-civiwity. Mr. Dah-cey would never have c-come so soon to w-w-w-wait upon me."

Elizabeth had scarcely time to disclaim all right to the compliment, before their approach was announced by the door-bell, and shortly afterwards the three gentlemen entered the room. Colonel Fitzwilliam, who led the way, was about thirty, not handsome, but in person and address most truly the gentleman. Mr. Darcy looked just as he had been used to look in Hertfordshire—paid his compliments, with his usual reserve, to Mrs. Collins, and whatever might be his feelings toward her friend, met her with every appearance of composure. Elizabeth merely curtseyed to him without saying a word.

Colonel Fitzwilliam entered into conversation directly with the readiness and ease of a well-bred man, and talked very pleasantly; but his cousin, after having addressed a slight observation on the house and garden to Mrs. Collins, sat for some time without speaking to anybody. At length, however, his civility was so far awakened as to inquire of Elizabeth after the health of her family. She answered him in the usual way, and after a moment's pause, added:

"My eldest sister has been in town these three months. Have you never happened to see her there?"

She was perfectly sensible that he never had; but she wished to see whether he would betray any consciousness of what had passed between the Bingleys and Jane, and she thought she perceived a slight twitch in his eye as he answered that he had never been so fortunate as to meet Miss Bennet. The subject was pursued no farther, and the gentlemen soon afterwards went away.

CHAPTER 31

COLONEL FITZWILLIAM'S MANNERS were very much admired at the Parsonage, and the ladies all felt that he must add considerably to the pleasures of their engagements at Rosings. It was some days, however, before they received any invitation thither—for while there were visitors in the house, they could not be necessary; and it was not till Easter-day, almost a week after the Colonel's arrival, that they were honoured by such an attention, and then they were merely asked on leaving church to come there in the evening.

The invitation was accepted of course, and at a proper hour they joined the party in Lady Catherine's drawing-room. Her ladyship received them civilly, but it was plain that their company was by no means so acceptable as when she could get nobody else.

Colonel Fitzwilliam seemed really glad to see them; anything was a welcome relief to him at Rosings; and Mrs. Collins's pretty friend had moreover caught his fancy very much. He now seated himself by her, and talked so agreeably of the engagements at Manchester, of the marvel of new mechanical weapons, of his favourite methods of slaying the sorry stricken, that Elizabeth had never been half so well entertained in that room before; and they conversed with so much spirit and flow, as to draw the attention of Lady Catherine herself, as well as of Mr. Darcy. His eyes had been repeatedly turned towards them with a look of curiosity; and that her ladyship, after a while, shared the feeling, was more openly acknowledged, for she did not scruple to call out:

"What is that you are saying, Fitzwilliam? What is it you are talk-ing of? What are you telling Miss Bennet? Let me hear what it is."

"We are speaking of the deadly arts, madam," said he, when no longer able to avoid a reply.

"Of the deadly arts! Then pray speak aloud. It is of all subjects my delight. I must have my share in the conversation if you are speaking of the deadly arts. There are few people in England, I suppose, who have more true enjoyment of them than myself, or a better natural ability. Had Anne's health allowed her to apply, I am confident that she would have become as great a slayer of zombies as I. How does Georgiana get on with her training, Darcy?"

Mr. Darcy spoke with affectionate praise of his sister's proficiency with blade, fist, and Brown Bess.

"I am very glad to hear such a good account of her," said Lady Catherine; "and pray tell her from me, that she cannot expect to excel if she does not practise a good deal."

"I assure you, madam," he replied, "that she does not need such advice. She practises very constantly."

"So much the better. It cannot be done too much; and when I next write to her, I shall charge her not to neglect it on any account. I often tell young ladies that no excellence in the deadly arts is to be acquired without constant practice. I have told Miss Bennet several times, that she will never be half my equal unless she practises more; and though Mrs. Collins has no dojo, she is very welcome, as I have often told her, to come to Rosings every day, and spar with my ninjas, provided she prom-ises to kill no more of them. She would be in nobody's way, you know, in that part of the house."

Mr. Darcy looked a little ashamed of his aunt's ill-breeding, and made no answer.

When coffee was over, Colonel Fitzwilliam reminded Elizabeth of having promised to give them a demonstration of her considerable finger strength; and she set about fastening a modesty string around her ankles. Lady Catherine and the others observed as Elizabeth placed her hands upon the floor and lifted her feet heavenward—her dress kept in place by the modesty string. Holding herself thus, she then lifted one of her palms off the floor, so that all of her weight rested on but one hand. Mr. Darcy presently stationed himself so as to command a full view of the fair performer's countenance. Elizabeth saw what he was doing, and at the first convenient pause, wore an arch smile, and said:

"You mean to frighten me, Mr. Darcy, by coming in all this state to see me? I will not be alarmed. There is a stubbornness about me that never can bear to be frightened at the will of others. My courage always rises at every attempt to intimidate me." To emphasise this point, she lifted her palm so that only one fingertip remained connected to the floor.

"I shall not say you are mistaken," he replied, "because you could not really believe me to entertain any design of alarming you; and I have had the pleasure of your acquaintance long enough to know that you find great enjoyment in occasionally professing opinions which in fact are not your own."

Elizabeth laughed heartily at this picture of herself, and said to Colonel Fitzwilliam, "Your cousin will give you a very pretty notion of me, and teach you not to believe a word I say. I am particularly unlucky in meeting with a person so able to expose my real character, in a part of the world where I had hoped to pass myself off with some degree of credit. Indeed, Mr. Darcy, it is very ungenerous in you to mention all that you knew to my disadvantage in Hertfordshire—for it is provoking me to retaliate, and such things may come out as will shock your relations to hear."

"I am not afraid of you," said he, smilingly.

"Pray let me hear what you have to accuse him of," cried Colonel Fitzwilliam. "I should like to know how he behaves among strangers."

"You shall hear then—but prepare yourself for something very dreadful." Elizabeth pushed off of the floor with her fingertip, landed gently on her feet, and unfastened her modesty string. "The first time of my ever seeing him in Hertfordshire, you must know, was at a ball—and at this ball, what do you think he did? He danced only four dances, though gentlemen were scarce; and, to my certain knowledge, more than one young lady was sitting down in want of a partner. Mr. Darcy, you cannot deny the fact."

"I had not at that time the honour of knowing any lady in the assembly beyond my own party."

"True; and nobody can ever be introduced in a ball-room. Well, Colonel Fitzwilliam, what shall I demonstrate next? My fingers wait your orders."

"Perhaps," said Darcy, "I should have judged better, had I sought an introduction; but I am ill-qualified to recommend myself to strangers."

"Shall we ask your cousin the reason of this?" said Elizabeth, still addressing Colonel Fitzwilliam. "Shall we ask him why a man of sense and education, and who has been sculpted into a killer of the highest order, is ill qualified to recommend himself to strangers?"

"I can answer your question," said Fitzwilliam, "without applying to him. It is because he will not give himself the trouble."

"I certainly have not the talent which some people possess," said Darcy, "of conversing easily with those I have never seen before. I cannot catch their tone of conversation, or appear interested in their concerns, as I often see done."

"My fingers," said Elizabeth, "do not possess the strength your aunt's do. They have not the same force or rapidity, and do not produce the same deadly results. But then I have always supposed it to be my own fault—because I will not take the trouble of practising. It is not that I do not believe my fingers as capable."

Darcy smiled and said, "You are perfectly right. You have employed your time much better."

Here they were interrupted by Lady Catherine, who called out to know what they were talking of. Elizabeth immediately fastened her modesty string and began walking about the room on her fingertips. Lady Catherine, after observing for a few minutes, said to Darcy:

"Miss Bennet would make a fine showing of Leopard's Claw if she practised more, and could have the advantage of a Japanese master. She has a very good notion of fingering."

"That she does," said Darcy, in a manner such as to make Elizabeth's face quite red.

Elizabeth looked at Darcy to see how cordially he attended to Miss de Bourgh; but neither at that moment nor at any other could she discern any symptom of love; and from the whole of his behaviour to her she derived this comfort for Miss Bingley, that he might have been just as likely to marry her, had she been his relation.

Lady Catherine continued her remarks on Elizabeth's performance, mixing with them many instructions on execution. Elizabeth received them with all the forbearance of civility, and, at the request of the gentlemen, remained on her fingertips till her ladyship's carriage was ready to take them all home.

CHAPTER 32

ELIZABETH WAS SITTING by herself the next morning, meditating while Mrs. Collins and Maria were gone on business into the village, when she was startled by a ring at the door. As she had heard no carriage, she thought it not unlikely to be Lady Catherine, and under that apprehension was extinguishing her incense, when the door opened, and, to her very great surprise, Mr. Darcy entered the room.

He seemed astonished too on finding her alone, and apologised for his intrusion by letting her know that he had understood all the ladies were to be within.

They then sat down, and when her inquiries after Rosings were made, seemed in danger of sinking into total silence. It was absolutely necessary, therefore, to think of something, and in this emergence recollecting *when* she had seen him last in Hertfordshire, and feeling curious to know what he would say on the subject of their hasty departure, she observed:

"How very suddenly you all quitted Netherfield last November, Mr. Darcy! It must have been a most agreeable surprise to Mr. Bingley to see you all after him so soon; for, if I recollect right, he went but the day before. He and his sisters were well, I hope, when you left London?"

"Perfectly so, I thank you."

She found that she was to receive no other answer, and, after a short pause, added:

"I think I have understood that Mr. Bingley has not much idea of ever returning to Netherfield again?"

"I have never heard him say so; but it is probable that he may spend very little of his time there in the future. He is rather afraid of zombies, and their numbers in that part of the country are continually increasing."

"If he means to be but little at Netherfield, it would be better for the neighbourhood that he should give up the place entirely, for then we might possibly get a settled family there—one with a keener interest in the deadly arts. But, perhaps, Mr. Bingley did not take the house so much for the convenience of the neighbourhood as for his own, and we must expect him to keep it or quit it on the same principle."

"I should not be surprised," said Darcy, "if he were to give it up as soon as any eligible purchase offers."

Elizabeth made no answer. She was afraid of talking longer of his friend; and, having nothing else to say, was now determined to leave the trouble of finding a subject to him.

He took the hint, and soon began with, "This seems a very comfortable house. Lady Catherine, I believe, did a great deal to it when Mr. Collins first came to Hunsford."

"I believe she did—and I am sure she could not have bestowed her kindness on a more grateful object."

"Mr. Collins appears to be very . . . fortunate in his choice of a wife."

Elizabeth detected hesitation in his compliment. Was he sensible of Charlotte's being stricken?

"Yes, indeed, his friends may well rejoice in his having met with one of the very few sensible women who would have accepted him, or have made him happy if they had. My friend has an excellent understanding—though I am not certain that I consider her marrying Mr. Collins as the wisest thing she ever did. She seems perfectly happy, however, and in a prudential light it is certainly a very good match for her."

"It must be very agreeable for her to be settled within so easy a distance of her own family and friends."

"An easy distance, do you call it? It is nearly fifty miles."

"And what is fifty miles of zombie-free road? Little more than half a day's journey. Yes, I call it a *very* easy distance."

"I should never have considered the distance as one of the *advantages* of the match," cried Elizabeth. "I should never have said Mrs. Collins was settled *near* her family."

"It is a proof of your own attachment to Hertfordshire. Anything beyond the very neighbourhood of Longbourn, I suppose, would appear far."

As he spoke he let slip a sort of smile which Elizabeth fancied she understood; he must be supposing her to be thinking of Jane and Netherfield, and she blushed as she answered:

"Sir, you forget that I have twice made the journey to the darkest reaches of the Orient—a journey you know to be frightfully long and fraught with bears. I assure you, my picture of the world is rather a bit bigger than Longbourn. However, Mr. and Mrs. Collins have never had a need of embarking on such adventures, so I suspect their ideas of distance are much like those of other ordinary people. I am likewise persuaded my friend would not call herself near her family under less than half the present distance."

Mr. Darcy drew his chair a little towards her.

Elizabeth looked surprised. The gentleman experienced some change of feeling; he drew back his chair, took a newspaper from the table, and glancing over it, said, in a colder voice:

"Are you pleased with the news from Sheffield?"

A short dialogue on the subject of the army's recent victory ensued, on either side calm and concise—and soon put an end to by the entrance of Charlotte and her sister, just returned from her walk. The tête-à-tête surprised them. Mr. Darcy related the mistake which had occasioned his intruding on Miss Bennet, and after sitting a few minutes longer without saying much to anybody, went away.

"Wah can be da meaning of dis?" howled Charlotte, as soon as he was gone. "Mah dear Ewiza, he muss be love you, aw he never wuh have called in dis famiwiar way."

But when Elizabeth told of his silence; it did not seem very likely, even to Charlotte's wishes, to be the case; and after various conjectures, they could at last only suppose his visit to proceed from the difficulty of finding anything to do, which was the more probable from the time of year. The ground was quite frozen, and neither fresh unmentionables nor field sports would be seen again till spring. Within doors there was Lady Catherine, books, and a billiard-table, but gentlemen cannot always be within doors; and in the nearness of the Parsonage, or the pleasantness of the walk to it, or of the people who lived in it, the two cousins found a temptation from this period of walking thither almost every day. They called at various times of the morning, sometimes separately, sometimes together, and now and then accompanied by their aunt. It was plain to them all that Colonel Fitzwilliam came because he had pleasure in their society, a persuasion which of course recommended him still more.

But why Mr. Darcy came so often to the Parsonage, it was more difficult to understand. It could not be for society, as he frequently sat there ten minutes together without opening his lips; and when he did speak, it seemed the effect of necessity rather than of choice. He seldom appeared really animated, even at the sight of Mrs. Collins gnawing upon her own hand. What remained of Charlotte would liked to have believed this change the effect of love, and the object of that love her friend Eliza. She watched him whenever they were at Rosings, and whenever he came to Hunsford; but without much success, for her thoughts often wandered to other subjects, such as the warm, succulent sensation of biting into a fresh brain. Mr. Darcy certainly looked at her friend a great deal, but the expression of that look was disputable. It was an earnest, steadfast gaze, but she often doubted whether there were much admiration in it, and sometimes it seemed nothing but absence of mind. And upon imagining Mr. Darcy's mind, her thoughts would again turn to the subject of chewing on his salty, cauliflower-like brain.

She had once or twice suggested to Elizabeth the possibility of his being partial to her, but Elizabeth always laughed at the idea; and Mrs. Collins did not think it right to press the subject, from the danger of raising expectations which might only end in disappointment.

In her kind schemes for Elizabeth, she sometimes planned her marrying Colonel Fitzwilliam. He was beyond comparison the most pleasant man; he certainly admired her, and his situation in life was most eligible; but, to counterbalance these advantages, Mr. Darcy had a considerably larger head, and thus, more brains to feast upon.

CHAPTER 33

MORE THAN ONCE did Elizabeth, in her ramble within the park, unexpectedly meet Mr. Darcy. She felt all the perverseness of the mischance that should bring him where no one else was brought, and, to prevent its ever happening again, took care to inform him at first that it was a favourite haunt of hers. How it could occur a second time, therefore, was very odd! Yet it did, and even a third. He never said a great deal, nor did she give herself the trouble of talking or of listening much; but it struck her in the course of their third rencontre that he was asking some odd unconnected questions—about her pleasure in being at Hunsford, which bones she had broken, and her opinion of the suitability of marriage for warriors such as they.

She was engaged one day as she walked, in perusing Jane's last letter, and dwelling on some passages which proved that Jane had not written in spirits, when, instead of being again surprised by Mr. Darcy, she saw on looking up that Colonel Fitzwilliam was meeting her. Putting away the letter immediately and forcing a smile, she said:

"I did not know before that you ever walked this way."

"I have been making the tour of the park," he replied, "as I generally do every year, and intend to close it with a call at the Parsonage. Are you going much farther?"

"No, I should have turned in a moment."

And accordingly she did turn, and they walked towards the Parsonage together.

"Do you certainly leave Kent on Saturday?" said she.

"Yes—if Darcy does not put it off again. But I am at his disposal. He arranges the business just as he pleases."

"And if not able to please himself in the arrangement, he has at least pleasure in the great power of choice. I do not know anybody who seems more to enjoy the power of doing what he likes than Mr. Darcy."

"He likes to have his own way very well," replied Colonel Fitzwilliam. "But so we all do. It is only that he has better means of having it than many others, because he is rich, and handsome, and highly skilled in the ways of death. I speak from experience. A younger son, you know, must be accustomed to self-denial and dependence."

"In my opinion, the younger son of an earl can know very little of either. Now seriously, what have you ever known of self-denial and dependence? When have you been prevented by want of money from going wherever you chose, or procuring anything you had a fancy for?"

"These are home questions—and perhaps I cannot say that I have experienced many hardships of that nature. But in matters of greater weight, I may suffer from want of money. Younger sons are required to serve in the King's army, as you know."

"Yes, though I imagine, as an earl's son, that you have seen little of the front lines."

"Quite the contrary, Miss Bennet."

The Colonel lifted one of his trouser legs and presented Elizabeth with the most unfortunate sight—for there was nothing but lead and hickory between his knee and the ground. Elizabeth had perceived a limp upon meeting him, but had presumed it the result of some slight injury or ill breeding. To interrupt a silence which might make him fancy her affected by the sight, she soon afterwards said:

"I imagine your cousin brought you down with him chiefly for the sake of having someone at his disposal. I wonder he does not marry, to secure a lasting convenience of that kind. But, perhaps, his sister does as well for the present, and, as she is under his sole care, he may do what he likes with her. I mean that in the most respectable way, naturally, and not as a suggestion that there exists any impropriety between them."

"If there did," said Colonel Fitzwilliam, "it would be an impropriety that I would be equally guilty of, for I am joined with him in the guardianship of Miss Darcy."

"Are you indeed? And pray what sort of guardians do you make? Does your charge give you much trouble?"

As she spoke she observed him looking at her earnestly; and the manner in which he immediately asked her why she supposed Miss Darcy likely to give them any uneasiness, convinced her that she had somehow or other got pretty near the truth. She directly replied:

"You need not be frightened. I never heard any harm of her; and I dare say she is one of the most tractable creatures in the world. She is a very great favourite with some ladies of my acquaintance, Mrs. Hurst and Miss Bingley. I think I have heard you say that you know them."

"I know them a little. Their brother is a pleasant gentlemanlike man—he is a great friend of Darcy's."

"Oh! Yes," said Elizabeth drily; "Mr. Darcy is uncommonly kind to Mr. Bingley, and takes a prodigious deal of care of him."

"Care of him! Yes, I really believe Darcy *does* take care of him in those points where he most wants care. From something that he told me in our journey hither, I have reason to think Bingley very much indebted to him. But I ought to beg his pardon, for I have no right to suppose that Bingley was the person meant. It was all conjecture."

"What is it you mean?"

"It is a circumstance which Darcy could not wish to be generally known, because if it were to get round to the lady's family, it would be an unpleasant thing."

"Sir, I have beheld the ancient secrets of the Orient, and shall take them to my grave. Surely I can be trusted with one of Mr. Darcy's dalliances."

"And remember that I have not much reason for supposing it to be Bingley. What he told me was merely this: that he congratulated himself on having lately saved a friend from the inconveniences of a most imprudent marriage, but without mentioning names or any other particulars, and I only suspected it to be Bingley from believing him the kind of young man to get into a scrape of that sort, and from knowing them to have been together the whole of last summer."

"Did Mr. Darcy give you reasons for this interference?"

"I understood that there were some very strong objections against the lady."

"And what arts did he use to separate them?"

"He did not talk to me of his own arts," said Fitzwilliam, smiling. "He only told me what I have now told you."

Elizabeth made no answer, and walked on, her thirst for vengeance growing mightier with every step. After watching her a little, Fitzwilliam asked her why she was so thoughtful.

"I am thinking of what you have been telling me," said she. "Your cousin's conduct does not suit my feelings. Why was he to be the judge?"

"You are rather disposed to call his interference officious?"

"I do not see what right Mr. Darcy had to decide on the propriety of his friend's inclination, or why, upon his own judgement alone, he was to determine and direct in what manner his friend was to be happy. But," she continued, recollecting herself, "as we know none of the particulars, it is not fair to condemn him. It is not to be supposed that there was much affection in the case."

"That is not an unnatural surmise," said Fitzwilliam, "but it is a lessening of the honour of my cousin's triumph very sadly."

This was spoken jestingly; but it appeared to her so just a picture of Mr. Darcy, that she would not trust herself with an answer, and therefore, abruptly changing the conversation talked on indifferent matters until they reached the Parsonage. There, shut into her own room, as soon as their visitor left them, she could think without interruption of all that she had heard. It was not to be supposed that any other people could be meant than those with whom she was connected. There could not exist in the world two men over whom Mr. Darcy could have such boundless influence. That he had been concerned in the measures taken to separate Bingley and Jane she had never doubted; but she had always attributed to Miss Bingley the principal design and arrangement of them. If his own vanity, however, did not mislead him, he was the cause, his pride and caprice were the cause, of all that Jane had suffered, and still continued to suffer. He had ruined for a while every hope of happiness for the most affectionate, generous heart in the world; and for that, Elizabeth was now resolved to hold Darcy's heart, still beating, in her hand before her time in Kent was concluded.

"There were some very strong objections against the lady," were Colonel Fitzwilliam's words; and those strong objections probably were, her having one uncle who was a country attorney, another who was in business in London, and possessing the power to crush Bingley's skull in the heat of a quarrel—for he was not trained as she.

"To Jane herself," she exclaimed, "there could be no possibility of objection; all loveliness and goodness as she is! Her understanding excellent, her musketry unmatched, and her manners captivating. Neither could anything be urged against my father, who, though with some peculiarities, has abilities Mr. Darcy himself need not disdain, and respectability which he will probably never reach." When she thought of her mother, her confidence gave way a little; but she would not allow that any objections there had material weight with Mr. Darcy, whose pride, she was convinced, would receive a deeper wound from the want of importance in his friend's connections, than from their want of sense; and she was quite decided, at last, that he had been partly governed by this worst kind of pride, and partly by the wish of retaining Mr. Bingley for his sister.

The agitation which the subject occasioned, brought on a headache; and it grew so much worse towards the evening, that, added to her unwillingness to kill Mr. Darcy in the company of his aunt (lest she interfere), it determined her not to attend her cousins to Rosings, where they were engaged to drink tea.

CHAPTER 34

WHEN THEY WERE GONE, Elizabeth, as if intending to exasperate herself as much as possible against Mr. Darcy, chose for her employment the examination of all the letters which Jane had written to her since her being in Kent. They contained no actual complaint, nor was there any revival of past occurrences, or any communication of present suffering. But in all, and in almost every line of each, there was a want of that cheerfulness which had been used to characterise her style. Elizabeth noticed every sentence conveying the idea of uneasiness, with an attention which it had hardly received on the first perusal. Mr. Darcy's shameful boast of what misery he had been able to inflict, gave her a keener sense of her sister's sufferings. It was some consolation to think that he would soon fall at the end of her blade—and that in less than a fortnight she should herself be with Jane again, and enabled to contribute to the recovery of her spirits, beginning with the presentation of Darcy's heart and head.

She could not think of Darcy without remembering his cousin; for agreeable as he was, Colonel Fitzwilliam was also the one man who could assign the guilt of Darcy's slaying to Elizabeth. He would have to be dispensed with as well.

While settling this point, she was suddenly roused by the sound of the door-bell, and her spirits were a little fluttered by the idea of its being Colonel Fitzwilliam himself. But this idea was soon banished, and her spirits were very differently affected, when, to her utter amazement, she saw Mr. Darcy walk into the room. In a hurried manner he immediately began an inquiry after her health, imputing his visit to a wish of hearing that she were better. She answered him with cold civility, scarcely able to believe her luck at his happening by so soon, and waiting for the first opportunity to excuse herself and retrieve her Katana. He sat down for a moment, and then getting up, walked about the room. After a brief silence, he came towards her in an agitated manner, and thus began:

"In vain I have struggled. It will not do. My feelings will not be repressed. You must allow me to tell you how ardently I admire and love you."

Elizabeth's astonishment was beyond expression. She stared, coloured, doubted, and was silent. This he considered sufficient encouragement; and the avowal of all that he felt, and had long felt for her, immediately followed. He spoke well; but there were feelings besides those of the heart to be detailed; and he was not more eloquent on the subject of tenderness than of pride. His sense of her inferiority—of its being a degradation—of the family obstacles which had always opposed to inclination, were dwelt on with a warmth which seemed due to the consequence he was wounding, but was very unlikely to recommend his suit.

In spite of her deeply rooted bloodlust, she could not be insensible to the compliment of such a man's affection, and though her intention of killing him did not vary for an instant, she was somewhat sorry for the pain he was to receive; till, roused to resentment by his subsequent language, she lost all compassion in anger. She tried, however, to compose herself to answer him with patience, lest her intentions be exposed. He concluded with representing to her the strength of that attachment which, in spite of all his endeavours, he had found impossible to conquer; and with expressing his hope that it would now be rewarded by her acceptance of his hand. As he said this, she could easily see that he had no doubt of a favourable answer. He *spoke* of apprehension and anxiety, but his countenance expressed real security. Such a circumstance could only exasperate farther, and, when he ceased, the colour rose into her cheeks, and she said:

"In such cases as this, it is, I believe, the established mode to express a sense of obligation for the sentiments avowed, however unequally they may be returned. It is natural that obligation should be felt, and if I could *feel* gratitude, I would now thank you. But I cannot—I have never desired your good opinion, and you have certainly bestowed it most unwillingly. I am sorry to have occasioned you pain, but only sorry because it has been most unconsciously done. Before you walked through that door, I had resolved to strike you down, sir. My honor—nay, the honor of my family, demands no lesser satisfaction."

Elizabeth presently lifted her dress above her ankles and struck a basic crane pose, which she thought well-suited for the cramped quarters. Mr. Darcy, who was leaning against the mantelpiece with his eyes fixed on her face, seemed to catch her words with no less resentment than surprise. His complexion became pale with anger, and the distur-

"ONE OF HER KICKS FOUND ITS MARK, AND DARCY WAS SENT INTO THE
MANTELPIECE WITH SUCH FORCE AS TO SHATTER ITS EDGE."

bance of his mind was visible in every feature. At length, with a voice of forced calmness, he said:

"And this is all the reply which I am to have the honour of expecting! I might, perhaps, wish to be informed why, with so little *endeavour* at civility, I am thus rejected and challenged?"

"I might as well inquire," replied she, "why with so evident a desire of offending and insulting me, you chose to tell me that you liked me against your will, against your reason, and even against your character? Do you think that any consideration would tempt me to accept the man who has been the means of ruining, perhaps forever, the happiness of a most beloved sister?"

As she pronounced these words, Mr. Darcy changed colour; but the emotion was short, for Elizabeth presently attacked with a series of kicks, forcing him to counter with the drunken washwoman defense. She spoke as they battled:

"I have every reason in the world to think ill of you. No motive can excuse the unjust and ungenerous part you acted *there*. You dare not, you cannot deny, that you have been the principal, if not the only means of dividing them from each other."

One of her kicks found its mark, and Darcy was sent into the mantelpiece with such force as to shatter its edge. Wiping the blood from his mouth, he looked at her with a smile of affected incredulity.

"Can you deny that you have done it?" she repeated.

With assumed tranquility he then replied, "I have no wish of denying that I did everything in my power to separate my friend from your sister, or that I rejoice in my success. Towards him I have been kinder than towards myself."

Elizabeth disdained the appearance of noticing this civil reflection, and grabbed the fire poker, which she pointed at Darcy's face.

"But it is not merely this affair," she continued, "on which my dislike is founded. Long before it had taken place my opinion of you was decided. Your character was unfolded in the recital which I received many months ago from Mr. Wickham. On this subject, what can you have to say? In what imaginary act of friendship can you here defend yourself?"

"You take an eager interest in that gentleman's concerns," said Darcy, in a less tranquil tone, and with a heightened colour.

"Who that knows what his misfortunes have been, can help feeling an interest in him?"

"His misfortunes!" repeated Darcy contemptuously; "yes, his misfortunes have been great indeed." With this, he swept her feet from beneath her and sprang to his own. Elizabeth was too quick to allow him the advantage, for she was soon upright and swinging the poker at him with renewed vigour.

"And of your infliction," cried Elizabeth with energy. "You have reduced him to his present state of poverty—comparative poverty. You have withheld the advantages which you must know to have been designed for him. You have deprived the best years of his life of that independence which was no less his due than his desert. You have done all this! And yet you can treat the mention of his misfortune with contempt and ridicule."

"And this," cried Darcy, as he grabbed the poker from her hand, "is your opinion of me! This is the estimation in which you hold me! I thank you for explaining it so fully. My faults, according to this calculation, are heavy indeed! But perhaps," added he, pressing the pointed end against her neck, "these offenses might have been overlooked, had not your pride been hurt by my honest confession of the scruples that had long prevented my forming any serious design. These bitter accusations might have been suppressed, had I, with greater policy, concealed my struggles, and flattered you into the belief of my being impelled by unqualified, unalloyed inclination; by reason, by reflection, by everything. But disguise of every sort is my abhorrence. Nor am I ashamed of the feelings I related. They were natural and just. Could you expect me to rejoice in the inferiority of your training? To congratulate myself on the hope of relations, whose condition in life is so decidedly beneath my own?"

Elizabeth felt herself growing more angry every moment; yet, as Darcy backed her against a wall, she tried to the utmost to speak with composure when she said:

"You are mistaken, Mr. Darcy, if you suppose that the mode of your declaration affected me in any other way, than as it spared the slightest grief which I might have felt in beheading you, had you behaved in a more gentlemanlike manner."

She saw him start at this, but he said nothing, and she continued:

"You could not have made the offer of your hand in any possible way that would have tempted me to accept it."

Again his astonishment was obvious; and he looked at her with an expression of mingled incredulity and mortification. She went on.

"From the very beginning—from the first moment, I may almost say—of my acquaintance with you, your manners, impressing me with the fullest belief of your arrogance, your conceit, and your selfish disdain of the feelings of others, were such as to form the groundwork of disapprobation on which succeeding events have built so immovable a dislike; and I had not known you a month before I felt that you were the last man in the world whom I could ever be prevailed on to marry."

"You have said quite enough, madam. I perfectly comprehend your feelings, and have now only to be ashamed of what my own have been. Forgive me for having taken up so much of your time, and accept my best wishes for your health and happiness."

And with these words he hastily left the room, throwing the poker in the fire as he did; and Elizabeth heard him the next moment open the front door and quit the house.

The tumult of her mind was now painfully great. She knew not how to support herself, and from the feminine weakness which she had so struggled to exercise from her nature, sat down and cried for half an hour. Her astonishment, as she reflected on what had passed, was increased by every review of it. That she should receive an offer of marriage from Mr. Darcy! That she should fail to kill him when her honor demanded it! That he should have been in love with her for so many months! So much in love as to wish to marry her in spite of all the objections which had made him prevent his friend's marrying her sister, and which must appear at least with equal force in his own case—was almost incredible! It was gratifying to have inspired unconsciously so strong an affection. But his pride, his abominable pride—his shameless avowal of what he had done with respect to Jane—his unpardonable assurance in acknowledging, though he could not justify it, and the unfeeling manner in which he had mentioned Mr. Wickham, his cruelty towards whom he had not attempted to deny, soon overcame the pity which the consideration of his attachment had for a moment excited. She continued in very agitated reflections till the sound of Lady Catherine's carriage made her feel how unequal she was to encounter Charlotte's observation, and hurried her away to her room.

CHAPTER 35

ELIZABETH AWOKE THE NEXT MORNING to the same thoughts and meditations which had at length closed her eyes. She could not yet recover from the surprise of what had happened; it was impossible to think of anything else; and, totally indisposed for employment, she resolved, soon after breakfast, to indulge herself in vigorous exercise. She was proceeding directly to her favourite walk, when the recollection of Mr. Darcy's sometimes coming there stopped her, and instead of entering the park, she turned up the lane, which led farther from the turnpike-road.

After walking two or three times along that part of the lane, she was tempted, by the pleasantness of the morning, to stop at the gates and look into the park. The five weeks which she had now passed in Kent had made a great difference in the country, and every day was adding to the verdure of the early trees. She was on the point of continuing her walk, when she caught a glimpse of a gentleman within the sort of grove which edged the park; he was moving that way; and, fearful of its being Mr. Darcy, she was directly retreating. Did he mean to strike her down? How could she have been so stupid as to leave the Parsonage without her Katana? With superior quickness of foot, Darcy was able to cut off her retreat at the gate, and, holding out a letter, which she instinctively took, said, with a look of haughty composure, "I have been walking in the grove some time in the hope of meeting you. Will you do me the honour of reading that letter?" And then, with a slight bow, turned again into the plantation, and was soon out of sight.

With no expectation of pleasure, but with the strongest curiosity, Elizabeth opened the letter, and, to her still increasing wonder, perceived an envelope containing two sheets of letter-paper, written quite through, in a very close hand. Pursuing her way along the lane, she then began it. It was dated from Rosings, at eight o'clock in the morning, and was as follows:

> Be not alarmed, madam, on receiving this letter, by the apprehension of its containing any repetition of those senti-ments or renewal of those offers which were last night so dis-gusting to you. I write without any intention of paining you, or humbling myself, by dwelling on wishes which, for the happiness of both, cannot be too soon forgotten.
>
> Two offenses of a very different nature, and by no means of equal magnitude, you last night laid to my charge. The first mentioned was, that, regardless of the sentiments of either, I had detached Mr. Bingley from your sister, and the other, that I had, in defiance of various claims, in defiance of honour and humanity, ruined the immediate prosperity and blasted the

prospects of Mr. Wickham. If, in the explanation of my actions and motives, I am under the necessity of relating feelings which may be offensive to yours, I can only say that I am sorry. The necessity must be obeyed, and further apology would be absurd.

I had not been long in Hertfordshire, before I saw, in common with others, that Bingley preferred your elder sister to any other young woman in the country. But it was not till she took ill and remained at Netherfield that I had any apprehension, for knowing of her occupation as a slayer of the undead, I was certain that she had been stricken with the strange plague. Not wishing to trouble you or any of the Netherfield party with my theory, I endeavoured to smother Bingley's affections, thus sparing him the agony of watching your sister succumb. Upon her recovery, which I expected to be temporary, I perceived that his partiality for Miss Bennet was beyond what I had ever witnessed in him. Your sister I also watched. Her look and manners were open, cheerful, and engaging as ever, but I remained convinced that she would soon begin the cheerless descent into Satan's service. As the weeks turned to months, I began to question my observations. Why had she not yet turned? Could I have been so wrong as to mistake a simple fever for the strange plague? By the time I realised my error, it was too late to affect any undoing of the scheme. Mr. Bingley had been quite separated from Miss Bennet, both in distance and affection. Though I did so without malice, my actions have surely pained your sister, and your resentment has not been unreasonable. But I shall not scruple to assert, that the severity of your sister's cold was such as might have given the most acute observer a conviction that, however amiable her temper, her heart was pledged to darkness. That I was desirous of believing her stricken is cer-

tain—but I will venture to say that my investigation and deci-
sions are not usually influenced by my hopes or fears. I did
not believe her to be afflicted because I wished it; I believed
it on impartial conviction, as truly as I wished it in reason. But
there were other causes of repugnance. These causes must be
stated, though briefly. The situation of your mother's family,
though objectionable, was nothing in comparison to that total
want of propriety so frequently betrayed by herself, your three
younger sisters, and even by your father. Pardon me. It pains
me to offend you. But amidst your concern for the defects of
your nearest relations, let it give you consolation to consider
that you and your elder sister are held in my highest esteem,
both in manners and skill as fellow warriors. I will only say
farther that from what passed that evening, that my opinion
of Miss Bennet being stricken was confirmed by her failure
to join us in the investigation of the unfortunate kitchen inci-
dent, and my will strengthened to preserve my friend from
what I esteemed a most unhappy connection. He left
Netherfield for London, on the day following, as you, I am
certain, remember, with the design of soon returning.

The part which I acted is now to be explained. His sisters' uneasiness had been equally excited with my own,
though for different reasons; our coincidence of feeling was
soon discovered, and, alike sensible that no time was to be lost
in detaching their brother, we shortly resolved on joining him
directly in London. We accordingly went—and there I readily engaged in the office of pointing out to my friend the
certain evils of such a choice. I described, and enforced them
earnestly. But, however this remonstrance might have staggered or delayed his determination, I do not suppose that it
would ultimately have prevented the marriage, had it not
been seconded by my assurance of your sister's indifference.

He had before believed her to return his affection with sincere, if not with equal regard. But Bingley has great natural modesty, with a stronger dependence on my judgment than on his own. To convince him, therefore, that he had deceived himself, was no very difficult point. To persuade him against returning into Hertfordshire, when that conviction had been given, was scarcely the work of a moment. I cannot blame myself for having done thus much. There is but one part of my conduct in the whole affair on which I do not reflect with satisfaction; it is that I condescended to adopt the measures of art so far as to conceal from him your sister's being in town. I knew it myself, as it was known to Miss Bingley; but her brother is even yet ignorant of it. That they might have met without ill consequence is perhaps probable; but his regard did not appear to me enough extinguished for him to see her without some danger. Perhaps this concealment, this disguise was beneath me; it is done, however, and it was done for the best. On this subject I have nothing more to say, no other apology to offer. If I have wounded your sister's feelings, it was done only as a consequence of affection for my friend, and the belief that Miss Bennet had been cursed to wander the earth in search of brains.

With respect to that other, more weighty accusation, of having injured Mr. Wickham, I can only refute it by laying before you the whole of his connection with my family. Of what he has particularly accused me I am ignorant; but of the truth of what I shall relate, I can summon more than one witness of undoubted veracity.

Mr. Wickham is the son of a very respectable man who had for many years the management of all the Pemberley estates, and whose good conduct in the discharge of his trust naturally inclined my father to be of service to him; and on

George Wickham, who was his godson, his kindness was therefore liberally bestowed. My father supported him at school, and afterwards at Kyoto—most important assistance, as his own father, always poor from the extravagance of his wife, would have been unable to give him a proper Oriental education. My father was not only fond of this young man's society, whose manner were always engaging; he had also the highest opinion of his fighting skill, and hoping the deadly arts would be his profession, intended to provide for him in it. As for myself, it is many, many years since I first began to think of him in a very different manner. The vicious propensities—the want of principle, which he was careful to guard from the knowledge of his benefactor, could not escape the observation of a young man of nearly the same age with himself, and who had opportunities of seeing him in unguarded moments, which Mr. Darcy could not have. During one such moment, Mr. Wickham happily boasted of his intention to practice his roundhouse kicks on our deaf stable boy, in the hopes that a broken neck would serve as punishment for a saddle polishing that hadn't met with his approval. My affection for the wretched servant required that I shatter both of Mr. Wickham's legs, lest he be able to carry out his dastardly plan. Here again I shall give you pain—to what degree you only can tell. But whatever may be the sentiments which Mr. Wickham has created, a suspicion of their nature shall not prevent me from unfolding his real character—it adds even another motive.

My excellent father died about five years ago; and his attachment to Mr. Wickham was to the last so steady, that in his will he particularly recommended it to me, to promote his advancement in the battle against the manky dreadfuls. There was also a legacy of one thousand pounds. His own father did not long survive mine, and within half a year from these events, Mr. Wickham wrote to inform me that he had some intention of studying advanced musketry, and I must be aware that the interest of one thousand pounds would be a very insufficient support therein. I rather wished, than believed him to be sincere; but, at any rate, was perfectly ready to accede to his proposal, and arranged for him to receive three thousand pounds. All connection between us seemed now dissolved. I thought too ill of him to invite him to Pemberley, or admit his society in town. In town I believe he chiefly lived, but his studying musketry was a mere pretence, and being now free from all restraint, his life was one of idleness and dissipation. For about three years I heard little of him; but on the termination of the funds which had been designed for him, he applied to me again by letter. His circumstances, he assured me, were exceedingly bad. He had found musketry a most unprofitable study, and was now absolutely resolved on entering the priesthood, if I would present him with a yearly allowance. You will hardly blame me for refusing to comply with this entreaty, or for resisting every repetition to it. His resentment was in proportion to the distress of his circum-stances—and he was doubtless as violent in his abuse of me to others as in his reproaches to myself. After this period every appearance of acquaintance was dropped. How he lived I know not. But last summer he was again most painfully obtruded on my notice.

I must now mention a circumstance which I would wish to forget myself, and which no obligation less than the pres-ent should induce me to unfold to any human being. Having said thus much, I feel no doubt of your secrecy. My sister, who is more than ten years my junior, was left to the guardianship of my mother's nephew, Colonel Fitzwilliam, and myself.

About a year ago, she was taken from school, and an establish-ment formed for her in London; and last summer she went with the lady who presided over it, Mrs. Younge, to Ramsgate; and thither also went Mr. Wickham, undoubtedly by design; for there proved to have been a prior acquaintance between him and Mrs. Younge, in whose character we were most unhappily deceived; and by her connivance and aid, he rec-ommended himself to Georgiana, whose affectionate heart retained a strong impression of his kindness to her as a child, that she was persuaded to believe herself in love, and to con-sent to an elopement. She was then but fifteen, which must be her excuse. I joined them unexpectedly a day or two before the intended elopement, and then Georgiana, unable to support the idea of grieving and offending a brother whom she almost looked up to as a father, acknowledged the whole to me. You may imagine what I felt and how I acted. Regard for my sister's credit and feelings prevented any public expo-sure; but my honor demanded a duel with Mr. Wickham, who left the place immediately. Mrs. Younge was of course savagely beaten in front of the other household staff. Mr. Wickham's chief object was unquestionably my sister's fortune, which is thirty thousand pounds; but I cannot help supposing that the hope of revenging himself on me was a strong inducement. His revenge would have been complete indeed.

This, madam, is a faithful narrative of every event in which we have been concerned together; and if you do not absolutely reject it as false, you will, I hope, acquit me hence-forth of cruelty towards Mr. Wickham. I know not in what manner, under what form of falsehood he had imposed on you; but his success is not perhaps to be wondered at. Ignorant as you previously were of everything concerning either, detection could not be in your power, and suspicion certainly not in your inclination.

You may possibly wonder why all this was not told you last night; but I was not then master enough of myself to know what could be revealed. For the truth of everything here related, I can appeal more particularly to the testimony of Colonel Fitzwilliam, who, from our near relationship and constant intimacy, and, still more, as one of the executors of my father's will, has been unavoidably acquainted with every particular of these transactions. If your abhorrence of me should make my assertions valueless, you cannot be prevented by the same cause from confiding in my cousin; and that there may be the possibility of consulting him, I shall endeavour to find some opportunity of putting this letter in your hands in the course of the morning. May God bless you, and save England from her present unhappiness.

FITZWILLIAM DARCY

CHAPTER 36

IF ELIZABETH, WHEN MR. DARCY gave her the letter, did not expect it to contain a renewal of his offers, she had formed no expectation at all of its contents. She read with an eagerness which hardly left her power of comprehension, and from impatience of knowing what the next sentence might bring, was incapable of attending to the sense of the one before her eyes. His belief of her sister's being stricken she instantly resolved to be false; and his account of the real, the worst objections to the match, made her too angry to have any wish of doing him justice.

But when this subject was succeeded by his account of Mr. Wickham—when she read with somewhat clearer attention a relation of events which, if true, must overthrow every cherished opinion of his worth, and which bore so alarming an affinity to his own history of himself—her feelings were yet more acutely painful and more difficult of definition. Astonishment, apprehension, and even horror, oppressed her. She wished to discredit it entirely, repeatedly exclaiming, "This must be false! This cannot be! This must be the grossest falsehood!"

In this perturbed state of mind, with thoughts that could rest on nothing, she walked on; but it would not do; in half a minute the letter was unfolded again, and collecting herself as well as she could, she again began the mortifying perusal of all that related to Wickham, and commanded herself so far as to examine the meaning of every sentence. The account of his connection with the Pemberley family was exactly what he had related himself; and the kindness of the late Mr. Darcy, though she had not before known its extent, agreed equally well with his own words. But the thought of so punishing a deaf stable boy! And for such a trifling offense! It was almost impossible to believe a man of Wickham's countenance capable of such cruelty. It was impossible not to feel that there was gross duplicity on one side or the other; and, for a few moments, she flattered herself that her wishes did not err. But when she read and re-read with the closest attention, the particulars immediately following of Wickham's resigning all of the elder Darcy's hopes that he would continue his training, of his receiving in lieu so considerable a sum as three thousand pounds, again was she forced to hesitate. She put down the letter, weighed every circumstance with what she meant to be impartiality—deliberated on the probability of each statement—but with little success. On both sides it was only assertion. Again she read on; but every line proved more clearly that the affair, which she had believed it impossible that any contrivance could so represent as to render Mr. Darcy's conduct in it less than infamous, was capable of a turn which must make him entirely blameless throughout the whole.

Of Wickham's former way of life nothing had been known in Hertfordshire but what he told himself. As to his real character, had information been in her power, she had never felt a wish of inquiring. His voice and manner had established him at once in the possession of every virtue. She tried to recollect some instance of goodness, some distinguished trait of integrity or benevolence, that might rescue him from the attacks of Mr. Darcy; or at least, by the predominance of virtue, atone for what Mr. Darcy had described as the idleness and vice of many years' continuance. But no such recollection befriended her.

She perfectly remembered everything that had passed in conversation between Wickham and herself, in their first evening at Mr. Philips's. Many of his expressions were still fresh in her memory. She was now struck with the impropriety of such communications to a stranger, and wondered it had escaped her before. She saw the indelicacy of putting himself forward as he had done, and the inconsistency of his professions with his conduct. She remembered that he had boasted of having no fear of seeing Mr. Darcy—that Mr. Darcy might leave the country, but that he should stand his ground; yet he had avoided the Netherfield ball the very next week. She remembered also that, till the Netherfield family had quitted the country, he had told his story to no one but herself; but that after their removal it had been everywhere discussed; that he had then no reserves, no scruples in sinking Mr. Darcy's character, though he had assured her that respect for the father would always prevent his exposing the son.

How differently did everything now appear in which he was concerned! His behaviour to herself could now have had no tolerable motive; he had either been deceived with regard to her fortune, or had been gratifying his vanity by encouraging the preference which she believed she had most incautiously shown. Every lingering struggle in his favour grew fainter and fainter; and in farther justification of Mr. Darcy, Jane had long ago asserted his blamelessness in the Wickham affair; that proud and repulsive as were his manners, she had never, in the whole course of their acquaintance, seen anything that betrayed him to be unprincipled or unjust.

She grew absolutely ashamed of herself. Of neither Darcy nor Wickham could she think without feeling she had been blind, partial, prejudiced, absurd. Had she her dagger, Elizabeth would have dropped to her knees and administered the seven cuts of dishonor without a moment's hesitation.

"How despicably I have acted!" she cried; "I, who have prided myself on my discernment! I, who have valued myself on my mastery of mind and body! Who have often disdained the generosity of my sister, and gratified my vanity in useless mistrust! How humiliating is this discovery! Oh! Were my master here to bloody my back with wet bamboo!"

From herself to Jane—from Jane to Bingley, her thoughts were in a line which soon brought to her recollection that Mr. Darcy's explanation *there* had appeared very insufficient, and she read it again. Widely different was the effect of a second perusal. How could she deny that credit to his assertions in one instance, which she had been obliged to give in the other? He declared himself to be suspicious of her sister's being stricken, and she could not deny the justice of this wariness; for Jane's cold had been severe indeed, and even Elizabeth had once or twice suspected the same.

When she came to that part of the letter in which her family were mentioned in terms of such mortifying, yet merited reproach, her sense of shame was severe.

The compliment to herself and her sister was not unfelt. It soothed, but it could not console her for the contempt which had thus been self-attracted by the rest of her family; and as she considered that Jane's disappointment had in fact been the work of her nearest relations, and reflected how materially the credit of both must be hurt by such impropriety of conduct, she felt depressed beyond anything she had ever known before.

After wandering along the lane for two hours, giving way to every variety of thought—reconsidering events, determining probabilities, and reconciling herself, as well as she could, to a change so sudden and so important, fatigue, and a recollection of her long absence, made her at length return home; and she entered the house with the wish of appearing cheerful as usual, and the resolution of repressing such reflections as must make her unfit for conversation.

She was immediately told that the two gentlemen from Rosings had each called during her absence; Mr. Darcy, only for a few minutes, to take leave—but that Colonel Fitzwilliam had been sitting with them at least an hour, hoping for her return, and almost resolving to walk after her till she could be found. Elizabeth could but just affect concern in missing him; she really rejoiced at it. Colonel Fitzwilliam was no longer an object; she could think only of her letter.

CHAPTER 37

THE TWO GENTLEMEN left Rosings the next morning, and Mr. Collins having been in waiting near the lodges, to make them his parting bow, was able to bring home the pleasing intelligence, of their appearing in very good health, and in as tolerable spirits as could be expected, after the melancholy scene so lately gone through at Rosings, due to the approaching departure of the gentlemen, and Elizabeth's killing of several of her ladyship's favourite ninjas. To Rosings he then hastened, to console Lady Catherine and her daughter for their loss of company; and on his return brought back, with great satisfaction, a message from her ladyship, importing that she felt herself so dull as to make her very desirous of having them all to dine with her.

Elizabeth could not see Lady Catherine without recollecting that, had she chosen it, she might by this time have been presented to her as her future niece; nor could she think, without a smile, of what her ladyship's indignation would have been. "What would she have said? How would she have behaved?" were questions with which she amused herself.

Their first subject was the shrinking of the Rosings party. "I assure you, I feel it exceedingly," said Lady Catherine; "I believe no one feels the loss of friends so much as I do. But I am particularly attached to these young men, and know them to be so much attached to me! They were excessively sorry to go! But so they always are. The dear Colonel rallied his spirits tolerably till just at last; but Darcy seemed to feel it most acutely, more, I think, than last year. His attachment to Rosings certainly increases."

Mrs. Collins had a compliment to throw in here, which was kindly smiled on by the mother and daughter, despite the fact that no one could discern what she was growling.

Lady Catherine observed, after dinner, that Miss Bennet seemed out of spirits, and immediately accounting for it by herself, by supposing that she did not like to go home again so soon, she added:

"But if that is the case, you must write to your mother and beg that you may stay a little longer. Mrs. Collins will be very glad of your company, I am sure."

"I am much obliged to your ladyship for your kind invitation," replied Elizabeth, "but it is not in my power to accept it. I must be in town next Saturday."

"Why, at that rate, you will have been here only six weeks. I expected you to stay two months. I told Mrs. Collins so before you came. There can be no occasion for your going so soon. Mrs. Bennet could certainly spare you for another fortnight."

"But my father cannot. He wrote last week to hurry my return, for the ground again softens, and Hertfordshire will soon be overrun with unmentionables."

"Oh! Your father of course may spare you. I have observed your skills in the deadly arts, my dear; and they are not of the level which would make any difference in the fate of Hertfordshire or anywhere else." Elizabeth could scarcely believe the insult. Had her affection for Mr. Darcy not been freshly restored, she might have challenged her ladyship to a duel for such an affront to her honor.

Lady Catherine continued, "And if you will stay another month complete, it will be in my power to take one of you as far as London, for I am going there early in June, to discuss strategy with His Majesty; and as my guard insists I travel in a barouche-box, there will be very good room for one of you—and indeed, if the weather should happen to be cool, I should not object to taking you both, as neither of you are fat like Mr. Collins."

"You are all kindness, madam; but I believe we must abide by our original plan."

Lady Catherine seemed resigned. "Mrs. Collins, you must send one of my ninjas with them. You know I always speak my mind, and I cannot bear the idea of two young women travelling by themselves. It is highly improper in times such as these. You must contrive to send somebody. Young women should always be properly guarded and attended, unless they are that rare sort of lady, like myself, who has been trained by the most respected masters in Japan—and not by those appalling Chinese peasants."

"My uncle is to send a servant for us, but I assure your ladyship that I am quite capable of—"

"Oh! Your uncle! He keeps a man-servant, does he? I am very glad you have somebody who thinks of these things. Where shall you change horses? Oh! Bromley, of course. If you mention my name at the Bell, you will be attended to."

Lady Catherine had many other questions to ask respecting their journey, and as she did not answer them all herself, attention was necessary, which Elizabeth believed to be lucky for her; or, with a mind so occupied, she might have forgotten where she was. Reflection must be reserved for solitary hours; whenever she was alone, she gave way to it as the greatest relief; and not a day went by without a solitary walk, in which she might indulge in all the delight of unpleasant recollections.

Mr. Darcy's letter she was in a fair way of soon knowing by heart.

She studied every sentence; and her feelings towards its writer were at times widely different. When she remembered the haughty style of his address, she dreamt of watching his eyes glaze over as she choked the life from his body; but when she considered how unjustly she had condemned and upbraided him, her anger was turned against herself; and she hastily applied her dagger to the seven cuts of shame, which had scarcely time to scab over. His attachment excited gratitude, his general character respect; but she could not approve him; nor could she for a moment repent her refusal, or feel the slightest inclination ever to see him again. In her own past behaviour, there was a constant source of vexation and regret; and in the unhappy defects of her family, a subject of yet heavier chagrin. They were hopeless of remedy. Her father, contented with laughing at them, would never exert himself to restrain the wild giddiness of his youngest daughters; and her mother, with manners so far from right herself, was entirely insensible of the evil. Elizabeth had frequently united with Jane in punishing the imprudence of Catherine and Lydia with wet bamboo; but while they were supported by their mother's indulgence, what chance could there be of improvement? Catherine, undisciplined, irritable, and completely under Lydia's guidance, had been always affronted by their attempts at correcting her; and Lydia, self-willed and dimwitted, would scarcely give them a hearing. They were ignorant, idle, and vain. While Meryton was within a walk of Longbourn, they would be going there forever, killing zombies only when it interfered with their chances of flirting with an officer.

Anxiety on Jane's behalf was another prevailing concern; and Mr. Darcy's explanation, by restoring Bingley to all her former good opinion, heightened the sense of what Jane had lost. His affection was proved to have been sincere, and his conduct cleared of all blame, unless any could attach to the implicitness of his confidence in his friend. How grievous then was the thought that, of a situation so desirable in every respect, so replete with advantage, so promising for happiness, Jane had been deprived, by the folly and indecorum of her own family! Oh!

Could she only bring herself to dispense with the lot of them!

When to these recollections was added the development of Wickham's character, it may be easily believed that the happy spirits which had seldom been depressed before, were now so much affected as to make it almost impossible for her to appear tolerably cheerful.

Their engagements at Rosings were as frequent during the last week of her stay as they had been at first. The very last evening was spent there; and her ladyship again demeaned the quality of Chinese combat training, gave them directions as to the best method of packing, and was so urgent on the necessity of placing gowns in the only right way, that Maria thought herself obliged, on her return, to undo all the work of the morning, and pack her trunk afresh.

When they parted, Lady Catherine, with great condescension, wished them a good journey, and invited them to come to Hunsford again next year; and Miss de Bourgh exerted herself so far as to curtsey and hold out her frail hand to both.

CHAPTER 38

ON SATURDAY MORNING Elizabeth and Mr. Collins met for breakfast a few minutes before the others appeared; and he took the opportunity of paying the parting civilities which he deemed indispensably necessary.

"I know not, Miss Elizabeth," said he, "whether Mrs. Collins has yet expressed her sense of your kindness in coming to us; but I am very certain you will not leave the house without receiving her thanks for it. The favor of your company has been much felt, I assure you. We know how little there is to tempt anyone to our humble abode. Our plain manner of living, our small rooms and few domestics, and the little we see of the world, must make Hunsford extremely dull to a young lady who has twice been to the Orient."

Elizabeth was eager with her thanks and assurances of happiness. She had spent six weeks with great enjoyment; and the pleasure of being with Charlotte, and the kind attentions she had received, must make *her* feel the obliged. Mr. Collins replied:

"My dear Charlotte and I have but one mind and one way of thinking. There is in everything a most remarkable resemblance of character and ideas between us. We seem to have been designed for each other."

Elizabeth might have said, given Charlotte's being stricken and Mr. Collins being himself so dreadfully unappealing in every way, that she agreed with his assessment. But she merely offered that she firmly believed and rejoiced in his domestic comforts. She was not sorry, however, to have the recital of them interrupted by the lady from whom they sprang. Poor Charlotte! It was melancholy to see her now almost entirely transformed! But she had chosen it with her eyes open. And though it wouldn't be long before even the daft Mr. Collins would discover her condition and be forced to behead her, she did not seem to ask for compassion. Her home and her housekeeping, her parish and her poultry, and her ever deepening lust for tender morsels of savory brains, had not yet lost their charms.

At length the chaise arrived, the trunks were fastened on, the parcels placed within, and it was pronounced to be ready. After an affectionate parting with Charlotte, who Elizabeth knew she would never see again, they were attended to the carriage by Mr. Collins, and as they walked down the garden he was commissioning her with his best respects to Elizabeth's family, not forgetting his thanks for the kindness he had received at Longbourn in the winter, and his compliments to Mr. and Mrs. Gardiner, though unknown. He then handed her in, Maria followed, and the door was on the point of being closed, when he suddenly reminded them, with some consternation, that they had hitherto forgotten to leave any message for the ladies at Rosings.

"But," he added, "you will of course wish to have your humble respects delivered to them, with your grateful thanks for their kindness to you while you have been here."

Elizabeth made no objection; the door was then allowed to be shut, and the carriage drove off.

"Good gracious!" cried Maria, after a few minutes' silence, "it seems but a day or two since we first came! And yet how many things have happened!"

"A great many indeed," said her companion with a sigh.

"We have dined nine times at Rosings, besides drinking tea there twice! How much I shall have to tell!"

Elizabeth added privately, "And how much I shall have to conceal!"

The first ten miles of their journey were performed without the slightest bit of conversation or alarm. But when they came upon the old white church in St. Ezra Parish, Elizabeth at once recognized the scent of death in the air, and ordered the coachman to stop.

It was a grand church for so small a village, built upon a frame of shaved tree trunks, and covered with hundreds of whitewashed planks. The denizens of St. Ezra were a notoriously pious lot, and they packed the pews every Saturday and Sunday to pray for deliverance from the legions of Satan. Stained glass windows ran the length of each side, which told the story of England's descent from peace into chaos; the last window portrayed a resurrected Christ returning to slay the last of the unmentionables, Excalibur in hand.

While the coachman and servant waited nervously with Maria, Elizabeth ascended the steps toward the church's splintered doors, sword at the ready. The scent of death was overwhelming, and several of the stained glass windows had been shattered. Something terrible had happened here, but how recently, she knew not.

Elizabeth entered the church ready to fight, but upon perceiving the inside, she sheathed her Katana, as it could do no good here. Not now. It seemed the whole of St. Ezra Parish had barricaded themselves in the church. Bodies lay everywhere: in pews; in aisles—the tops of their skulls cracked open; every last bite of their brains scraped out, like pumpkin seeds from a jack-o'-lantern. With their Parish under attack, these people had retreated to the only safe place they knew; but it hadn't been safe enough. The zombies had simply overwhelmed them with superior numbers and insatiable determination. Men still clutched their pitchforks. Ladies still huddled with their children. Elizabeth felt her eyes moisten as she imagined the horror of their final moments. The screams. The sight of others being torn to pieces before their eyes. The horror of being eaten alive by creatures of unspeakable evil.

A tear fell down Elizabeth's cheek. She was quick to wipe it away, feeling somewhat ashamed that it had escaped at all.

"A house of God so defiled!" said Maria, as their journey continued. "Have these unmentionables no sense of decency?"

"They know nothing of the sort," said Elizabeth, staring mindlessly out of the coach's window, "and neither must we."

With no further alarm, they reached Mr. Gardiner's house, where they were to remain for a few days. Jane looked well, and Elizabeth had little opportunity of studying her spirits, amidst the various engagements which the kindness of her aunt had reserved for them. But Jane was to go home with her, and at Longbourn there would be leisure enough for observation.

It was not without an effort, meanwhile, that she could wait even for Longbourn, before she told her sister of Mr. Darcy's proposals. To know that she had the power of revealing what would so exceedingly astonish Jane was such a temptation to openness as nothing could have conquered but the state of indecision in which she remained as to the extent of what she should communicate; and her fear, if she once entered on the subject, of being hurried into repeating something of Bingley which might only grieve her sister further.

CHAPTER 39

I T WAS THE SECOND WEEK in May, in which the three young ladies set out together from Section Six East for Hertfordshire; and, as they drew near the appointed inn where Mr. Bennet's carriage was to meet them, they quickly perceived, in token of the coachman's punctuality, both Kitty and Lydia looking out of a dining-room upstairs. These two girls had been above an hour in the place, happily employed in amusing the sentinel on guard with immodest displays of their proficiency with a throwing star, much to the consternation of the carriage horse which served as their unwilling target.

After welcoming their sisters, they triumphantly displayed a table set out with such cold meat as an inn larder usually affords, exclaiming, "Is not this nice? Is not this an agreeable surprise?"

"And we mean to treat you all," added Lydia, "but you must lend us the money, for we have just spent ours at the shop out there." Then, showing her purchases—"Look here, I have bought this bonnet."

And when her sisters abused it as ugly, she added, with perfect unconcern, "Oh! But there were two or three much uglier in the shop; and when I have bought some prettier-coloured satin to trim it with fresh, I think it will be very tolerable. Besides, it will not much signify what one wears this summer, after the soldiers have left Meryton, and they are going in a fortnight."

"Are they indeed!" cried Elizabeth, with the greatest satisfaction; for not only would her sisters have one less distraction from their training, but the very fact of the decampment meant that Hertfordshire had been much relieved of the unmentionable menace while she was away.

"They are going to be encamped near Brighton; and I do so want papa to take us all there for the summer! It would be such a delicious scheme; and I dare say would hardly cost anything at all. Mamma would like to go too of all things! Only think what a miserable summer else we shall have! With hardly any balls to be had in Meryton!"

"Yes," thought Elizabeth, "a summer with so few balls would be miserable indeed for a girl who thinks of little else."

"Now I have got some news for you," said Lydia, as they sat down at table. "What do you think? It is excellent news—capital news—and about a certain person we all like!"

Jane and Elizabeth looked at each other, and the waiter was told he need not stay. Lydia laughed, and said:

"Aye, that is just like your formality and discretion. You thought the waiter must not hear, as if he cared! I dare say he often hears worse things said than I am going to say. But he is an ugly fellow! I never saw such a long chin in my life. I nearly ran him through for thinking him a zombie. Well, but now for my news; it is about dear Wickham; too good for the waiter, is it not? There is no danger of Wickham's marrying Mary King. There's for you! She is gone down to her uncle at Liverpool: gone to stay. Wickham is safe."

"And Mary King is safe!" added Elizabeth; "safe from a connection imprudent as to fortune."

"She is a great fool for going away, if she liked him."

"But I hope there is no strong attachment on either side," said Jane.

"I am sure there is not on his. I will answer for it, he never cared three straws about her—who could about such a nasty little freckled thing, with not a skill to boast of?"

As soon as all had ate, and the elder ones paid, the carriage was ordered; and after some contrivance, the whole party, with all their boxes, weapons, and parcels, and the unwelcome addition of Kitty's and Lydia's purchases, were seated in it.

"How nicely we are all crammed in," cried Lydia. "I am glad I bought my bonnet, if it is only for the fun of having another hatbox! Well, now let us be quite comfortable and snug, and talk and laugh all the way home. And in the first place, let us hear what has happened to you all since you went away. Have you seen any pleasant men? Have you had any flirting? I was in great hopes that one of you would have got a husband before you came back. Jane will be quite an old maid soon, I declare. She is almost three-and-twenty! Lord, how ashamed I should be of not being married before three-and-twenty! My aunt Phillips wants you so to get husbands, you can't think. She says Lizzy had better have taken Mr. Collins; but I do not think there would have been any fun in it. Lord! How I should like to be married before any of you; and then I would chaperon you about to all the balls. Dear me! We had such a good piece of fun the other day at Colonel Forster's. Kitty and me were to spend the day there, and Mrs. Forster promised to have a little dance in the evening; (by the bye, Mrs. Forster and me are such friends!) and so she asked the two Harringtons to come, but Harriet was ill, and so Pen was forced to come by herself—"

Elizabeth presently drew her Katana and cut off Lydia's head, which fell into the open hatbox.

The others looked on in a state of silent shock as a torrent of blood sprang forth from Lydia's neck, staining their dresses. Elizabeth sheathed her blade, and in a most delicate tone, said "I beg you all forgive me, but I could stand her prattling no longer." However, when she spared another glance toward Lydia, she was surprised to see her head very much attached.

"Lord! How I laughed!" continued her younger sister. "And so did Mrs. Forster. I thought I should have died."

Elizabeth sighed. If only she could *really* cut off Lydia's head. With such tireless drivel did Lydia, assisted by Kitty's hints and additions, endeavour to amuse her companions all the way to Longbourn. Elizabeth listened as little as she could, but there was no escaping the frequent mention of Wickham's name.

Their reception at home was most kind. Mrs. Bennet rejoiced to see Jane in undiminished beauty; and more than once during dinner did

Mr. Bennet say voluntarily to Elizabeth:

"I am glad you are come back, Lizzy."

Their party in the dining-room was large, for almost all the Lucases came to meet Maria and hear the news; and various were the subjects that occupied them: Lady Lucas inquired after the welfare of her eldest daughter, who Maria reported in excellent health and spirits. "Has everyone gone mad?" thought Elizabeth. "Can no one see that she is nine-tenths dead from the plague?" Mrs. Bennet was doubly engaged, on one hand collecting an account of the present fashions from Jane, who sat some way below her, and, on the other, retailing them all to the younger Lucases; and Lydia, in a voice rather louder than any other person's, was enumerating the various pleasures of the morning to anybody who would hear her.

"Oh! Mary," said she, "I wish you had gone with us, for we had such fun! As we went along, Kitty and I opened the carriage windows and played at taunting the farmhands who were charged with burning the morning's body piles; and when we got to the George, I do think we behaved very handsomely, for we treated the other three with the nicest cold luncheon in the world, and if you would have gone, we would have treated you too. And then when we came away it was such fun! I thought we never should have got into the coach. I was ready to die of laughter. And then we were so merry all the way home! We talked and laughed so loud that zombies might have heard us ten miles off!"

To this Mary very gravely replied, "Far be it from me, my dear sister, to depreciate such pleasures! They would doubtless be congenial with the generality of female minds. But I confess they would have no charms for me—I should infinitely prefer a good spar."

But of this answer Lydia heard not a word. She seldom listened to anybody for more than half a minute, and never attended to Mary at all.

In the afternoon Lydia was urgent with the rest of the girls to walk to Meryton, and to see how everybody went on; but Elizabeth steadily opposed the scheme. It should not be said that the Miss

Bennets could not be at home half a day before they were in pursuit of the officers. There was another reason too for her opposition. She dreaded seeing Mr. Wickham again, and was resolved to bloody his mouth when she did. The comfort to her of the regiment's approaching removal was indeed beyond expression. In a fortnight they were to go—and once gone, she hoped there could be nothing more to plague her on his account.

She had not been many hours at home before she found that the Brighton scheme, of which Lydia had given them a hint at the inn, was under frequent discussion between her parents. Elizabeth saw directly that her father had not the smallest intention of yielding; but his answers were at the same time so vague and equivocal that her mother had never yet despaired of succeeding at last.

CHAPTER 40

ELIZABETH'S IMPATIENCE to acquaint Jane with what had happened could no longer be overcome; and at length, resolving to suppress every particular in which her sister was concerned, she related to her the next morning the chief of the scene between Mr. Darcy and herself.

Jane's astonishment was soon lessened by the strong sisterly partiality, which made any admiration of Elizabeth appear perfectly natural. She was sorry that Mr. Darcy should have delivered his sentiments in a manner so little suited to recommend them; but still more was she grieved to learn that they had resulted in combat, and the destruction of Mr. Collins's mantelpiece.

"His being so sure of succeeding was wrong," said she, "and certainly ought not to have appeared; but consider how much it must increase his disappointment!"

"Indeed," replied Elizabeth, "I am heartily sorry for him; but he has other feelings, which will probably soon drive away his regard for me. You do not blame me, however, for refusing him?"

"Blame you! Oh, no."

"But you blame me for having spoken so warmly of Wickham?"

"No—I do not know that you were wrong in saying what you did."

"But you *will* know it, when I tell you what happened the very next day."

She then spoke of the letter, repeating the whole of its contents as far as they concerned George Wickham—particularly his treatment of the deaf stable boy and Miss Darcy. What a stroke was this for poor Jane! She would willingly have gone through the world without believing that so much wickedness existed in the whole race of mankind, as was here collected in one individual. Nor was Darcy's vindication, though grateful to her feelings, capable of consoling her for such discovery. Most earnestly did she labour to prove the probability of error, and seek to clear the one without involving the other.

"This will not do," said Elizabeth; "you never will be able to make both of them good for anything. Take your choice, but you must be satisfied with only one. There is but such a quantity of merit between them; just enough to make one good sort of man; and of late it has been shifting about pretty much. For my part, I am inclined to believe it all Darcy's; but you shall do as you choose."

It was some time, however, before a smile could be extorted from Jane.

"I do not know when I have been more shocked by the living," said she. "Wickham so very bad! It is almost past belief. And poor Mr. Darcy! Dear Lizzy, only consider what he must have suffered. Such a disappointment! And with the knowledge of your ill opinion, too! And having to beat his sister's governess! It is really too distressing. I am sure you must feel it so."

"Certainly. But there is one point on which I want your advice. I want to be told whether I ought, or ought not, to make our acquaintances in general understand Wickham's character."

Miss Bennet replied, "Surely there can be no occasion for exposing him so dreadfully. What is your opinion?"

"That it ought not to be attempted. Mr. Darcy has not authorised me to make his communication public. On the contrary, every particular relative to his sister was meant to be kept as much as possible to myself; and if I endeavour to undeceive people as to the rest of his conduct, who will believe me? The general prejudice against Mr. Darcy is so violent, that it would be the death of half the good people in Meryton to attempt to place him in an amiable light. I am not equal to it. Wickham will soon be gone; and therefore it will not signify to anyone here what he really is. At present I will say nothing about it."

"You are quite right. To have his errors made public might force him to demand satisfaction from Mr. Darcy—and when two gentlemen duel, there is seldom a happy result. We must not make him desperate. In the words of our dear master, 'a caged tiger bites twice as hard.'"

The tumult of Elizabeth's mind was allayed by this conversation. She had got rid of two of the secrets which had weighed on her for a fortnight. But there was still something lurking behind, of which prudence forbade the disclosure. She dared not relate the other half of Mr. Darcy's letter, nor explain to her sister how sincerely she had been valued by Bingley.

She was now, on being settled at home, at leisure to observe the real state of her sister's spirits. Jane was not happy. She still cherished a very tender affection for Bingley. Having never even fancied herself in love before, her regard had all the warmth of first attachment, and, from her age and disposition, greater steadiness than most first attachments often boast; and so fervently did she value his remembrance, and prefer him to every other man, that all her good sense, and all her attention to the feelings of her friends, were requisite to check the indulgence of those regrets which must have been injurious to her own health and their tranquillity.

"Well, Lizzy," said Mrs. Bennet one day, "what is your opinion now of this sad business of Jane's? For my part, I am determined never to speak of it again to anybody. I told my sister Phillips so the other day. But I cannot find out that Jane saw anything of him in London. Well, he is a very undeserving young man—and I do not suppose there's the least chance in the world of her ever getting him now. There is no talk of his coming to Netherfield again in the summer; and I have inquired of everybody, too, who is likely to know."

"I do not believe he will ever live at Netherfield any more."

"Oh well! It is just as he chooses. Nobody wants him to come. My comfort is, I am sure Jane will die of a broken heart; and then he will be sorry for what he has done."

But as Elizabeth could not receive comfort from any such expectation, she made no answer.

"Well, Lizzy," continued her mother, soon afterwards, "and so the Collinses live very comfortable, do they? Well, well, I only hope it will last. And what sort of table do they keep? Charlotte is an excellent manager, I dare say. If she is half as sharp as her mother, she is saving enough. There is nothing extravagant in *their* housekeeping, I dare say."

"No, nothing at all." Elizabeth couldn't bring herself to tell her mother of Charlotte's doom. The poor woman was scarcely able to keep herself together as it was.

"I suppose they often talk of having Longbourn when your father is dead. They look upon it as quite their own, I dare say, whenever that happens."

"It was a subject which they could not mention before me."

"No; it would have been strange if they had; but I make no doubt they often talk of it between themselves. Well, if they can be easy with an estate that is not lawfully their own, so much the better. I should be ashamed of putting an old woman out of her home."

CHAPTER 41

THE FIRST WEEK of their return was soon gone. The second began. It was the last of the regiment's stay in Meryton, and all the young ladies in the neighbourhood were sick with melancholy. The dejection was almost universal. The elder Miss Bennets alone were still able to eat, drink, and sleep, and pursue their daily exercises, which at this time of year included games of "Kiss Me Deer"—a game their father had invented to better their softness of foot and arm strength. The rules were simple: Sneak up behind one of the large bucks grazing in the nearby woods, wrestle it to the ground, and kiss it on the nose before letting it go. Jane and Elizabeth laughed many an afternoon away in such a manner; very frequently were they reproached for this insensibility by Kitty and Lydia, whose own misery was extreme, and who could not comprehend such merrymaking in any of the family.

"Good Heaven! what is to become of us? What are we to do?" would they often exclaim in the bitterness of woe. "How can you be smiling so, Lizzy?"

Their affectionate mother shared all their grief; she remembered what she had herself endured on a similar occasion, five-and-twenty years ago.

"I am sure," said she, "I cried for two days together when Colonel Miller's regiment went away. I thought I should have broken my heart."

"I am sure I shall break mine," said Lydia.

"If one could but go to Brighton!" observed Mrs. Bennet.

"Oh, yes! If one could but go to Brighton! But papa is so disagreeable."

"A little sea-bathing would set me up forever."

"And my aunt Philips is sure it would do me a great deal of good," added Kitty.

THE RULES WERE SIMPLE: SNEAK UP BEHIND ONE OF THE LARGE BUCKS GRAZING IN THE NEARBY WOODS, WRESTLE IT TO THE GROUND, AND KISS IT ON THE NOSE BEFORE LETTING IT GO."

Such were the kind of lamentations resounding perpetually through Longbourn House. Elizabeth tried to be diverted by them; but all sense of pleasure was lost in shame. She felt anew the justice of Mr. Darcy's objections; and never had she been so happy to open the scabs of her seven cuts.

But the gloom of Lydia's prospect was shortly cleared away; for she received an invitation from Mrs. Forster, the wife of the colonel of the regiment, to accompany her to Brighton. This invaluable friend was a very young woman, and very lately married. A resemblance in good humour and good spirits had recommended her and Lydia to each other, and out of their three months' acquaintance they had been intimate two.

The rapture of Lydia on this occasion, her adoration of Mrs. Forster, the delight of Mrs. Bennet, and the mortification of Kitty, are scarcely to be described. Wholly inattentive to her sister's feelings, Lydia flew about the house in restless ecstasy, calling for everyone's congratulations, and laughing and talking with more violence than ever; whilst the luckless Kitty spent many an hour aiming her longbow at any deer, rabbit, or bird unfortunate enough to venture too close to the house.

"I cannot see why Mrs. Forster should not ask me as well as Lydia," said she, "though I am not her particular friend. I have just as much right to be asked as she has."

In vain did Elizabeth attempt to make her reasonable, and Jane to make her resigned. As for Elizabeth herself, this invitation was so far from exciting in her the same feelings as in her mother and Lydia, that she considered it as the death warrant of all possibility of common sense for the latter; and even though Lydia would think her detestable if it were known, Elizabeth could not help secretly advising her father not to let her go. She represented to him all the improprieties of Lydia's general behaviour, the little advantage she could derive from the friendship of such a woman as Mrs. Forster, and the probability of her being yet more imprudent with such a companion at Brighton, where the temptations must be greater than at home. He heard her attentively, and then said:

"Lydia will never be easy until she has exposed herself in some public place or other, and we can never expect her to do it with so little expense or inconvenience to her family as under the present circumstances."

"If you were aware," said Elizabeth, "of the very great disadvantage to us all which must arise from the public notice of Lydia's unguarded and imprudent manner—nay, which has already arisen from it, I am sure you would judge differently in the affair."

"Already arisen?" repeated Mr. Bennet. "What, has she frightened away some of your lovers? Poor little Lizzy! But do not be cast down. Such squeamish youths as cannot bear to be connected with a little absurdity are not worth a regret. Come, let me see the list of pitiful fellows who have been kept aloof by Lydia's folly."

"Indeed you are mistaken. I have no such injuries to resent. It is not of particular, but of general evils, which I am now complaining. Our importance, our respectability in the world must be affected by the wild volatility, the assurance and disdain of all restraint which mark Lydia's character. Excuse me, for I must speak plainly. If you, my dear father, will not take the trouble of checking her exuberant spirits, or reminding her of our blood oath to defend the Crown above all things, she will soon be beyond the reach of amendment. Her character will be fixed, and she will, at sixteen, be the most determined flirt that ever made herself or her family ridiculous, and a disgrace to the honour of our beloved master. In this danger Kitty also is comprehended. She will follow wherever Lydia leads. Vain, ignorant, idle, and absolutely uncontrolled! Oh! My dear father, can you suppose it possible that they will not be censured and despised wherever they are known, and that their sisters will not be often involved in the disgrace?"

Mr. Bennet saw that her whole heart was in the subject, and affectionately taking her hand said in reply:

"Do not make yourself uneasy, my love. Wherever you and Jane are known you must be respected and valued; and you will not appear to less advantage for having a couple of—or I may say, three—very silly sisters. We shall have no peace at Longbourn if Lydia does not go to Brighton. Let her go, then. Colonel Forster is a sensible man, and will keep her out of any real mischief; and she is luckily too poor to be an object of prey to anybody. At Brighton she will be of less importance even as a common flirt than she has been here. The officers will find women better worth their notice. Let us hope, therefore, that her being there may teach her her own insignificance. At any rate, she cannot grow many degrees worse, without authorizing us to have her head."

With this answer Elizabeth was forced to be content; but her own opinion continued the same, and she left him disappointed and sorry.

Had Lydia and her mother known the substance of her conference with her father, their indignation would hardly have warranted a moment of their tireless prattling. In Lydia's imagination, a visit to Brighton comprised every possibility of earthly happiness. She saw, with the creative eye of fancy, the streets of that gay bathing-place covered with officers. She saw herself the object of attention, to tens and to scores of them at present unknown. She saw herself seated beneath a tent, tenderly flirting with at least six officers at once as they pressed her for another demonstration of the deadly arts.

Had she known her sister sought to tear her from such prospects and such realities as these, what would have been her sensations? They could have been understood only by her mother, who might have felt nearly the same. Lydia's going to Brighton was all that consoled her for the sorrow of having not one of her five daughters married.

But they were entirely ignorant of what had passed; and their raptures continued, with little intermission, to the very day of Lydia's leaving home.

On the very last day of the regiment's remaining at Meryton, Mr. Wickham dined, with other of the officers, at Longbourn; and so little was Elizabeth disposed to part from him in good humour, that on his making some inquiry as to the manner in which her time had passed at

Hunsford, she mentioned Colonel Fitzwilliam's and Mr. Darcy's having both spent three weeks at Rosings, and asked him if he was acquainted with the former.

He looked surprised; but with a moment's recollection and a returning smile, replied, that he had formerly seen him often; and, after observing that he was a very gentlemanlike man, asked her how she had liked him. Her answer was warmly in his favour. With an air of indifference he soon afterwards added:

"How long did you say he was at Rosings?"

"Nearly three weeks."

"And you saw him frequently?"

"Yes, almost every day."

"His manners are very different from his cousin's."

"Yes, very different. But I think Mr. Darcy improves upon acquaintance."

"Indeed!" cried Mr. Wickham with a look which did not escape her. "And pray, may I ask—." But checking himself, he added, in a gayer tone, "Is it in address that he improves? For I dare not hope," he continued in a lower and more serious tone, "that he is improved in essentials."

"Oh, no!" said Elizabeth. "In essentials, I believe, he is very much what he ever was."

While she spoke, Wickham looked as if scarcely knowing whether to rejoice over her words, or to distrust their meaning. There was a something in her countenance which made him listen with an apprehensive and anxious attention, while she added:

"When I said that he improved on acquaintance, I did not mean that his mind or his manners were in a state of improvement, but that, from knowing him better, his disposition was better understood. Particularly in regard to his treatment of stable boys."

Wickham's alarm now appeared in a heightened complexion and agitated look; for a few minutes he was silent, till, shaking off his embarrassment, he turned to her again, and said in the gentlest of accents:

"You, who so well know my feeling towards Mr. Darcy, will readily comprehend how sincerely I must rejoice that he is wise enough to assume even the appearance of what is right. I only fear that the sort of cautiousness to which you, I imagine, have been alluding, is merely adopted on his visits to his aunt, of whose good opinion and judgment he stands much in awe. His fear of her has always operated, I know, when they were together; and a good deal is to be imputed to his wish of forwarding the match with Miss de Bourgh, which I am certain he has very much at heart."

Elizabeth could not repress a smile at this, but she answered only by a slight inclination of the head. She saw that he wanted to engage her on the old subject of his grievances, and she was in no humour to indulge him. The rest of the evening passed with the appearance, on his side, of usual cheerfulness, but with no further attempt to distinguish Elizabeth; and they parted at last with mutual civility, and possibly a mutual desire of never meeting again.

When the party broke up, Lydia returned with Mrs. Forster to Meryton, from whence they were to set out early the next morning. The separation between her and her family was rather noisy than pathetic. Kitty was the only one who shed tears; but they were tears of vexation and envy. Mrs. Bennet was diffuse in her good wishes for the felicity of her daughter, and impressive in her injunctions that she should not miss the opportunity of enjoying herself as much as possible—advice which there was every reason to believe would be well attended to; and in the clamorous happiness of Lydia herself in bidding farewell, the more gentle adieus of her sisters were uttered without being heard.

CHAPTER 42

H AD ELIZABETH'S OPINION been all drawn from her own family, she could not have formed a very pleasing opinion of conjugal felicity or domestic comfort. Her father, captivated by youth and beauty, and that appearance of good humour which youth and beauty generally give, had married a woman whose weak understanding and illiberal mind had very early in their marriage put an end to all real affection for her. Respect, esteem, and confidence had vanished for ever; and all his views of domestic happiness were overthrown. But Mr. Bennet was not of a disposition to seek comfort for the disappointment which his own imprudence had brought on. Instead, he sought to ensure that his daughters would not follow in their mother's silly, idle footsteps. In this regard, he had tried five times, and succeeded two. Other than the gift of Jane and Elizabeth, to Mrs. Bennet he was very little otherwise indebted. This is not the sort of happiness which a man would in general wish to owe to his wife.

Elizabeth, however, had never been blind to the impropriety of her father's behaviour as a husband. She had always seen it with pain; but respecting his abilities, and grateful for his affectionate treatment of herself, she endeavoured to forget what she could not overlook, and to banish from her thoughts that continual breach of conjugal obligation and decorum. This had been especially arduous during their trips to China, which Mr. Bennet had supervised without the company of his wife, and during which he had taken many a beautiful Oriental to his bedchamber. Master Liu had defended this as acquiescence to local custom, and Elizabeth had more than once felt the sting of wet bamboo on her back for daring to question her father's propriety. But she had never felt so strongly as now the disadvantages that must attend the children of so unsuitable a marriage.

When Lydia went away she promised to write very often and very minutely to her mother and Kitty; but her letters were always long expected, and always very short. Those to her mother contained little else than that they were just returned from the library, where such and such officers had attended them, and that she had a new gown, or a new parasol, which she would have described more fully, but was obliged to leave off in a violent hurry, as Mrs. Forster called her, and they were going off to the camp; and from her correspondence with her sister, there was still less to be learnt—for her letters to Kitty, though rather longer, were much too full of lines under the words to be made public.

After the first fortnight or three weeks of her absence, health, good humour, and cheerfulness began to reappear at Longbourn. Everything wore a happier aspect. The families who had fled the infestation came back again, and summer finery and summer engagements arose for the first time in memory. Mrs. Bennet was restored to her usual querulous serenity; and, by the middle of June, Kitty was so much recovered as to be able to enter Meryton without tears; an event of such happy promise as to make Elizabeth hope that by the following Christmas she might be so tolerably reasonable as not to mention an officer above once a day, unless, by some cruel and malicious arrangement at the War Office, another regiment should be quartered in Meryton.

The time fixed for the beginning of Elizabeth's northern tour was now fast approaching, and a fortnight only was wanting of it, when a letter arrived from Mrs. Gardiner, which at once delayed its commencement and curtailed its extent. Due to the recent troubles in Birmingham, and the army's want of more flints and powder, Mr. Gardiner would be prevented from setting out till a fortnight later in July, and must be in London again within a month, and as that left too short a period for them to go so far, and see so much as they had proposed, or at least to see it with the leisure and comfort they had built on, they were obliged to give up the Lakes, and substitute a more contracted tour, and, according to the present plan, were to go no farther northwards than Derbyshire. In that county there was enough to be seen to occupy the chief of their three weeks; and to Mrs. Gardiner it had a peculiarly strong attraction. The town where she had formerly passed some years of her life, and where they were now to spend a few days, was probably as great an object of her curiosity as all the celebrated beauties of Matlock, Chatsworth, Dovedale, or the Peak.

Elizabeth was excessively disappointed; she had set her heart on seeing the Lakes, and still thought there might have been time enough. But she was glad for the chance of being anywhere other than Hertfordshire, and all was soon right again.

Desperate to pass the time, Elizabeth set off to see the burning grounds of Oakham Mount one morning. It had been nearly two years since she had last visited, and it was only a few miles' walk to the top of the Mount—which was little more than a hill, with an ever-present column of smoke rising from its top. Such columns could be seen from one end of England to the other, no matter the season or weather. There was always burning to be done.

Elizabeth reached the grounds shortly after breakfast, and was somewhat surprised to see it so busy. Several wagons had already lined up outside the Paymaster's shack; each of them carrying large, box-shaped iron cages on their backs. Each cage held anywhere from one to four zombies (in rare cases, one might see a cage with five, or even six). Most of them belonged to farmers, who trapped unmentionables as a means of earning extra money. But a few belonged to professional zombie hunters, called *Reclaimers*, who traveled the countryside setting cages. Elizabeth knew that some of these so-called "Reclaimers" were nothing more than scoundrels, who made their living abducting innocents, infecting them with the plague, and selling them to burning grounds. But better to burn a few innocents than let the guilty run free.

Not far from the Paymaster's shack, the Fire Master stood beside his pit, only feet from flames which rose to twice his height. His bare chest was covered in exercise moisture, for he never stopped working—whether coating logs with tar, raking embers, or throwing bails of hay into the fire.

After haggling with the Paymaster and getting their pieces of silver, the men pulled their wagons to the Hook Master's station, where the cages were hoisted off with a large mechanical device, and swung over the flames. Elizabeth could not help but feel a sense of joy as she watched cage after cage of zombies burn—heard their terrible shrieks as the fire (which they feared above all else) licked at their feet, then ignited the whole of their putrid flesh and hastened them back to Hell. When the zombies were nothing more than bone and ash, the cages were lowered back onto their wagons, and carried away to be filled anew.

Apart from these sorts of excursions, the next four weeks passed slowly—but they did pass, and Mr. and Mrs. Gardiner, with their four children, did at length appear at Longbourn. The children, two girls of six and eight years old, and two younger boys, were to be left under the particular care of their cousin Jane, who was the general favourite, and whose steady sense and sweetness of temper exactly adapted her for attending to them in every way—teaching them, playing with them, and loving them.

The Gardiners stayed only one night at Longbourn, and set off the next morning with Elizabeth in pursuit of novelty and amusement. One enjoyment was certain—that of suitableness of companions; a suitableness which comprehended health and temper to bear inconveniences—cheerfulness to enhance every pleasure—and affection and intelligence, which might supply it among themselves if there were disappointments abroad.

It is not the object of this work to give a description of Derbyshire, nor of any of the remarkable places through which their route thither lay; Oxford, Blenheim, Warwick, Kenilworth, etc. are sufficiently known. Nor is it the object to describe the handful of zombie encounters which necessitated Elizabeth's intervention—for not one was sufficient to yield even a drop of sweat from her brow. A small part of Derbyshire is all the present concern. To the little town of Lambton, the scene of Mrs. Gardiner's former residence, and where she had lately learned some acquaintance still remained, they bent their steps, after having seen all the principal wonders of the country; and within five miles of Lambton, Elizabeth found from her aunt that Pemberley was situated. It was not in their direct road, nor more than a mile or two out of it. In talking over their route the evening before, Mrs. Gardiner expressed an inclination to see the place again. Mr. Gardiner declared his willingness, and Elizabeth was applied to for her approbation.

"My love, should not you like to see a place of which you have heard so much?" said her aunt; "a place, too, with which so many of your acquaintances are connected. Wickham passed all his youth there, you know."

Elizabeth was distressed. She felt that she had no business at Pemberley, and was obliged to assume a disinclination for seeing it. She must own that she was tired of seeing great houses; after going over so many, she really had no pleasure in fine carpets or satin curtains.

Mrs. Gardiner abused her stupidity. "If it were merely a fine house richly furnished," said she, "I should not care about it myself; but the grounds are delightful. They have some of the finest woods in the country."

Elizabeth said no more—but her mind could not acquiesce. The possibility of meeting Mr. Darcy, while viewing the place, instantly occurred. It would be dreadful!

Accordingly, when she retired at night, she asked the chamber-maid whether Pemberley were not a very fine place? What was the name of its proprietor? And, with no little alarm, whether the family were down for the summer? A most welcome negative followed the last question—Mr. Darcy was reported to be in town for a meeting of the *League of Gentlemen for the Encouragement of Continued Hostilities Against Our Most Unwelcome Enemy*. Her alarms now being removed, she was at leisure to feel a great deal of curiosity to see the house herself; and when the subject was revived the next morning, and she was again applied to, could readily answer, and with a proper air of indifference, that she had not really any dislike to the scheme. To Pemberley, therefore, they were to go.

CHAPTER 43

E LIZABETH, AS THEY DROVE ALONG, watched for the first appearance of Pemberley Woods with some perturbation; and when at length they turned in at the lodge, her spirits were in a high flutter.

The park was very large, and contained great variety of ground. They entered it in one of its lowest points, and drove for some time through a beautiful wood stretching over a wide extent—taking care to listen closely for moans or the snapping of twigs, for there was rumoured to be a large herd of freshly de-graved dreadfuls about.

Elizabeth's mind was too full to be of much use in this regard, but she saw and admired every remarkable spot and point of view. They gradually ascended for half a mile, and then found themselves at the top of a considerable eminence, where the wood ceased, and the eye was instantly caught by Pemberley House, situated on the opposite side of a valley, into which the road with some abruptness wound. It was a large, handsome stone building, made to resemble the grandest palaces of Kyoto, and backed by a ridge of high woody hills; and in front, a stream of some natural importance was swelled into a natural defense against frontal assault, but without any artificial appearance. Its banks were neither formal nor falsely adorned. Elizabeth was delighted. She had never seen a place for which nature had done more, or where the natural beauty of the Orient had been so little counteracted by English taste.

They were all of them warm in their admiration; and at that moment she felt that to be mistress of Pemberley might be something!

They descended the hill, crossed between the stone dragons on either side of the bridge, and drove to the solid jade door; and, while examining the nearer aspect of the house, all her apprehension of meeting its owner returned. She dreaded lest the chambermaid had been mistaken. On applying to see the place, they were admitted into the hall; and Elizabeth, as they waited for the housekeeper, had leisure to wonder at her being where she was.

The housekeeper came; a respectable-looking English woman, dressed in a kimono and shuffling about on bound feet. They followed her into the dining-parlour. It was a large, well proportioned room, handsomely fitted up with art and furniture from Darcy's beloved Japan. Elizabeth, after surveying it, went to a window to enjoy its prospect. The hill, crowned with wood, which they had descended, receiving increased abruptness from the distance, was a beautiful object. Every disposition of the ground was good; and she looked on the whole scene, the river, the trees scattered on its banks and the winding of the valley, as far as she could trace it, with delight. As they passed into other rooms these objects were taking different positions; but from every window there were beauties to be seen. The rooms were lofty and handsome, and their furniture suitable to the proprietor's taste for the East; but Elizabeth saw, with admiration of his taste, that it was neither gaudy nor uselessly fine; with less of splendour, and more real elegance, than the furniture of Rosings.

"And of this place," thought she, "I might have been mistress! With these rooms I might now have been familiarly acquainted! Instead of viewing them as a stranger, I might have rejoiced in them as my own, and welcomed to them as visitors my uncle and aunt. But no," recollecting herself, "that could never be; my uncle and aunt would have been lost to me; I should not have been allowed to invite them."

This was a lucky recollection—it saved her from something very like regret.

She longed to inquire of the housekeeper whether her master was really absent, but had not the courage for it. At length however, the question was asked by her uncle; and she turned away with alarm, while Mrs. Reynolds replied that he was, adding, "But we expect him to-morrow, with a large party of friends." How rejoiced was Elizabeth that their own journey had not by any circumstance been delayed a day!

Her aunt now called her to look at a picture. She approached and saw the likeness of Mr. Wickham, a crutch under each arm, amongst several other miniatures over the mantelpiece. Her aunt asked her, smilingly, how she liked it. The housekeeper came forward, and told them it was a picture of a young gentleman, the son of her late master's musket polisher, who had been brought up by him at his own expense. "He is now gone into the army," she added; "but I am afraid he has turned out very wild."

Mrs. Gardiner looked at her niece with a smile, but Elizabeth could not return it.

"And that," said Mrs. Reynolds, pointing to another of the miniatures, "is my master—and very like him. It was drawn at the same time as the other—about eight years ago."

"I have heard much of your master's fine person," said Mrs. Gardiner, looking at the picture; "it is a handsome face. But, Lizzy, you can tell us whether it is like or not."

Mrs. Reynolds respect for Elizabeth seemed to increase on this intimation of her knowing her master.

"Does that young lady know Mr. Darcy?"

Elizabeth coloured, and said—"A little."

"And do not you think him a very handsome gentleman, ma'am?"

"Yes, very handsome."

"I am sure I know none so handsome; but in the gallery upstairs you will see a finer, larger picture of him than this. This room was my late master's favourite room, and these miniatures are just as they used to be then. He was very fond of them."

This accounted to Elizabeth for Mr. Wickham's being among them.

Mrs. Reynolds then directed their attention to one of Miss Darcy, drawn when she was only eight years old.

"And is Miss Darcy as handsome as her brother?" said Mrs. Gardiner.

"Oh! Yes—the handsomest young lady that ever was seen; and so accomplished! She beheaded her first unmentionable not one month after her eleventh birthday! I grant you Mr. Darcy had chained the vile creature to a tree, but it was an impressive kill nonetheless. In the next room is a new Katana just come for her—a present from my master; she comes here to-morrow with him."

Mr. Gardiner, whose manners were very easy and pleasant, encouraged her communicativeness by his questions and remarks; Mrs. Reynolds, either by pride or attachment, had evidently great pleasure in talking of her master and his sister.

"Is your master much at Pemberley in the course of the year?"

"Not so much as I could wish, sir; but I dare say he may spend half his time here; and Miss Darcy is always down for the summer months."

"Except," thought Elizabeth, "when she goes to Ramsgate."

"If your master would marry, you might see more of him."

"Yes, sir; but I do not know when that will be. I do not know who is good enough for him."

Mr. and Mrs. Gardiner smiled. Elizabeth could not help saying, "It is very much to his credit, I am sure, that you should think so."

"I say no more than the truth, and everybody will say that knows him," replied the other. Elizabeth thought this was going pretty far; and she listened with increasing astonishment as the housekeeper added, "I have never known a cross word from him in my life, and I have known him ever since he was four years old. In that time, I have seen him savagely beat but one servant, and a most deserved beating it was. I dare say he is the gentlest man in all of Britain."

This was praise, of all others most extraordinary, most opposite to her ideas. That he was not a good-tempered man had been her firmest opinion. Her keenest attention was awakened; she longed to hear more, and was grateful to her uncle for saying:

"There are very few people of whom so much can be said. You are lucky in having such a master."

"Yes, sir, I know I am. If I were to go through the world, I could not meet with a better. But I have always observed, that they who are good-natured when children, are good-natured when they grow up; and he was always the sweetest-tempered, most generous-hearted boy in the world."

Elizabeth almost stared at her. "Can this be Mr. Darcy?" thought she.

"His father was an excellent man," said Mrs. Gardiner.

"Yes, ma'am, that he was indeed; and his son will be just like him— just as affable to the poor. Kind even to the wretched accidents of God—the lame and the deaf alike."

"In what an amiable light does this place him!" thought Elizabeth.

"This fine account of him," whispered her aunt as they walked, "is not quite consistent with his behaviour to our poor friend."

"Perhaps we might be deceived."

"That is not very likely; our authority was too good."

On reaching the spacious lobby above they were shown into a very pretty sitting-room, lately fitted up with greater elegance and lightness than the apartments below; and were informed that it was but just done to give pleasure to Miss Darcy, who had taken a liking to the room when last at Pemberley.

"He is certainly a good brother," said Elizabeth, as she walked towards one of the windows. Mrs. Reynolds anticipated Miss Darcy's delight, when she should enter the room. "And this is always the way with him," she added. "Whatever can give his sister any pleasure is sure to be done in a moment. There is nothing he would not do for her."

The battle-gallery, and two or three of the principal bedrooms, were all that remained to be shown. In the former were many good zombie heads and suits of Samurai armor; but Elizabeth cared little for such trophies, and turned to look at some drawings of Miss Darcy's, in crayons, whose subjects were almost exclusively the nude male form.

When all of the house that was open to general inspection had been seen, they returned downstairs, and, taking leave of the housekeeper, were consigned over to the gardener, who met them at the hall-door.

As the gardener led them along the river, stopping to point out the occasional coy pond or stone garden, Elizabeth turned back to appreciate the house from a greater distance, and was met with such a shock as to make her reach for the sword that she had neglected to bring—for behind them was a fast-approaching herd of unmentionables, no fewer than five-and-twenty in number. Elizabeth, her composure regained, alerted her party to this unhappy development, and ordered them to run and hide, which they did with no shortage of alacrity.

With the herd nearly upon her, she prepared for battle—ripping a branch from a nearby tree and placing her feet in the first position for the Windswept Peasant method. Pole fighting had never been her strongest discipline, but as she was otherwise unarmed, it seemed the most practical approach, given the large number of opponents. The zombies let forth a most unpleasant roar as they came within biting distance, and Elizabeth returned it in kind as she began her counterattack. But no sooner had she struck down the first five or six, than the cracking of gunpowder scattered the score that remained. Elizabeth held a defensive pose as the zombies limped hurriedly for the safety of the woods, and then, upon being assured of their retreat, turned her gaze in the direction of the musket fire. On this she was again met with shock, though of a decidedly different nature—for upon a steed, holding a still-smoking Brown Bess, was none other than the owner of the grounds on which she stood. The smoke from Darcy's musket hung in the air around him, wafting Heavenward through his thick mane of chestnut hair. His steed let forth a mighty neigh and reared upon its hind legs—high enough to throw a lesser horseman clear. But Darcy's free hand held

"THE SMOKE FROM DARCY'S MUSKET HUNG IN THE AIR AROUND HIM, WAFTING HEAVENWARD THROUGH HIS THICK MANE OF CHESTNUT HAIR."

true, and he coaxed the spooked beast back to earth.

It was impossible to avoid his sight. Their eyes instantly met, and the cheeks of both were overspread with the deepest blush. He absolutely started, and for a moment seemed immovable from surprise; but shortly recovering himself, advanced towards her, dismounted, and spoke to Elizabeth, if not in terms of perfect composure, at least of perfect civility, as the rest of her party came out of hiding and joined them.

Amazed at the alteration of his manner since they last parted, every sentence that he uttered was increasing her embarrassment; and every idea of the impropriety of her being found there recurring to her mind, the few minutes in which they continued were some of the most uncomfortable in her life. Nor did he seem much more at ease; when he spoke, his accent had none of its usual sedateness; and he repeated his inquiries as to the well being of her aunt and uncle, so often, and in so hurried a way, as plainly spoke the distraction of his thoughts.

At length every idea seemed to fail him; and, after standing a few moments without saying a word, he suddenly handed Elizabeth his Brown Bess, mounted his steed, and took leave.

The others then joined her, and expressed admiration of his figure; but Elizabeth heard not a word, and wholly engrossed by her own feelings, followed them in silence. She was overpowered by shame and vexation. Her coming there was the most unfortunate, the most ill-judged thing in the world! How strange it must appear to him! In what a disgraceful light might it not strike so vain a man! It might seem as if she had purposely thrown herself in his way again! Oh! Why did she come? Or, why did he thus come a day before he was expected? Had they been only ten minutes sooner, they should have been beyond the reach of his discrimination; for it was plain that he was that moment arrived. She blushed again and again over the perverseness of the meeting. And his behaviour, so strikingly altered—what could it mean? That he should even come to her aid was amazing! But to speak to her, and with such civility, to inquire after her well being! Never in her life had she seen his manners so little dignified, never had he spoken with such gentleness as on this unexpected meeting. What a contrast did it offer to his last address in Rosings Park, when he put his letter into her hand! She knew not what to think, or how to account for it.

They entered the woods and ascended some of the higher grounds, where the zombies, with their dry muscles and brittle bones, were less likely to bother them. Mr. Gardiner expressed a wish of going round the whole park, but feared it might be too dangerous given the propinquity of the herd. A nearby roar from one of Satan's soldiers settled the matter; and they pursued the accustomed circuit; which brought them again, after some time, in a descent among hanging woods, to the edge of the water, and one of its narrowest parts. They crossed it by a simple bridge, which they were informed was assembled from the violated headstones of Pemberley. It was a spot less adorned than any they had yet visited; and the valley, here contracted into a glen, allowed room only for the stream, and a narrow walk amidst the rough coppice-wood which bordered it. Elizabeth longed to explore its windings, but when they had crossed the bridge and perceived their distance from the house, Mrs. Gardiner, who was still frightened by what had transpired, begged they go no farther, and thought only of returning to the carriage as quickly as possible. Her niece was, therefore, obliged to submit, and they took their way towards the house on the opposite side of the river, in the nearest direction. Their progress was slow, for Mr. Gardiner, though seldom able to indulge the taste, was very fond of fishing, and was so much engaged in watching the occasional appearance of some trout in the water, and talking to the man about them, that he advanced but little.

Whilst wandering on in this slow manner, they were again surprised by the sight of Mr. Darcy approaching them, and at no great distance. The walk here being less sheltered than on the other side, allowed them to see him before they met. Elizabeth, however astonished, was at least more prepared for an interview than before, and resolved to appear and to speak with calmness, if he really intended to meet them. For a few moments, indeed, she felt that he would probably strike into some other path. Perhaps he had merely returned to hunt the scattered unmentionables. The idea lasted while a turning in the walk concealed him from their view; the turning past, he was immediately before them. With a glance, she saw that he had lost none of his recent civility; and, to imitate his politeness, she began, as they met, to admire the beauty of the place; but she had not got beyond the words "delightful," and "charming," when some unlucky recollections obtruded, and she fancied that praise of Pemberley from her might be mischievously construed. Her colour changed, and she said no more.

Mrs. Gardiner was standing a little behind; and on her pausing, he asked her if she would do him the honour of introducing him to her friends. This was a stroke of civility for which she was quite unprepared; and she could hardly suppress a smile at his being now seeking the acquaintance of some of those very people against whom his pride had revolted in his offer to herself. "What will be his surprise," thought she, "when he knows who they are? He takes them now for people of fashion."

The introduction, however, was immediately made; and as she named their relationship to herself, she stole a sly look at him, to see how he bore it, and was not without the expectation of his decamping as fast as he could from such disgraceful companions. That he was surprised by the connection was evident; he sustained it, however, with fortitude, and so far from going away, turned back with them, and entered into conversation with Mr. Gardiner. Elizabeth could not but be pleased, could not but triumph. It was consoling that he should know she had some relations for whom there was no need to blush. She listened most attentively to all that passed between them, and gloried in every expression, every sentence of her uncle, which marked his intelligence, his taste, or his good manners.

The conversation soon turned upon musket fishing; and she heard Mr. Darcy invite him, with the greatest civility, to shoot fish there as often as he chose while he continued in the neighbourhood, offering at the same time to supply him with a fishing musket, and pointing out those parts of the stream where there was usually most sport. Mrs. Gardiner, who was walking arm-in-arm with Elizabeth, gave her a look expressive of wonder. Elizabeth said nothing, but it gratified her exceedingly; the compliment must be all for herself. Her astonishment, however, was extreme, and continually was she repeating, "Why is he so altered? From what can it proceed? It cannot be for *me*—it cannot be for *my* sake that his manners are thus softened. It is impossible that he should still love me, unless, by kicking him into the mantelpiece during our battle at Hunsford, I affected some severe change in his countenance."

After walking some time in this way, the two ladies in front, the two gentlemen behind, on resuming their places, after descending to the brink of the river for the better inspection of some zombie droppings, there chanced to be a little alteration. It originated in Mrs. Gardiner, who, fatigued by the exercise of the morning, found Elizabeth's arm inadequate to her support, and consequently preferred her husband's. Mr. Darcy took her place by her niece, and they walked on together. After a short silence, the lady first spoke. She wished him to know that she had been assured of his absence before she came to the place, and accordingly began by observing, that his arrival had been very unexpected—"for your housekeeper," she added, "informed us that you would certainly not be here till to-morrow; and indeed, before we left Bakewell, we understood that you were not immediately expected in the country." He acknowledged the truth of it all, and said that business with his steward had occasioned his coming forward a few hours before the rest of the party with whom he had been travelling. "They will join me early to-morrow," he continued, "and among them are some who will claim an acquaintance with you—Mr. Bingley and his sisters."

Elizabeth answered only by a slight bow. Her thoughts were instantly driven back to the time when Mr. Bingley's name had been the

last mentioned between them; and, if she might judge by his complexion, his mind was not very differently engaged.

"There is also one other person in the party," he continued after a
pause, "who more particularly wishes to be known to you. Will you
allow me, or do I ask too much, to introduce my sister to your acquaintance during your stay at Lambton?"

The surprise of such an application was great indeed; it was too
great for her to know in what manner she acceded to it. She immediately felt that whatever desire Miss Darcy might have of being
acquainted with her must be the work of her brother, and, without
looking farther, it was satisfactory; it was gratifying to know that his
resentment had not made him think really ill of her.

They now walked on in silence, each of them deep in thought.
Elizabeth was not comfortable; that was impossible; but she was flattered
and pleased. His wish of introducing his sister to her was a compliment
of the highest kind. They soon outstripped the others, and when they
had reached the carriage, Mr. and Mrs. Gardiner were half a quarter of
a mile behind.

He then asked her to walk into the house—but she declared herself not tired, and they stood together on the lawn. At such a time much
might have been said, but nothing was. Elizabeth and Darcy merely
looked at one another in awkward silence, until the latter reached both
arms around her. She was frozen—"What does he mean to do?" she
thought. But his intentions were respectable, for Darcy merely meant to
retrieve his Brown Bess, which Elizabeth had affixed to her back during
her walk. She remembered the lead ammunition in her pocket and
offered it to him. "Your balls, Mr. Darcy?" He reached out and closed
her hand around them, and offered, "They belong to you, Miss Bennet."
Upon this, their colour changed, and they were forced to look away
from one another, lest they laugh. On Mr. and Mrs. Gardiner's coming
up they were all pressed to go into the house and take some refreshment;
but this was declined, and they parted on each side with utmost

politeness. Mr. Darcy handed the ladies into the carriage; and when it drove off, Elizabeth saw him walking slowly towards the house.

The observations of her uncle and aunt now began; and each of them pronounced him to be infinitely superior to anything they had expected. "He is perfectly well behaved, polite, and unassuming," said her uncle.

"There is something a little stately in him, to be sure," replied her aunt, "but it is confined to his air, and is not unbecoming. I can now say with the housekeeper, that though some people may call him proud, I have seen nothing of it. Such horsemanship! Such musketry!"

"I was never more surprised than by his behaviour to us. It was more than civil; it was really attentive; and there was no necessity for such attention. His acquaintance with Elizabeth was very trifling."

"To be sure, Lizzy," said her aunt, "he is not so handsome as Wickham; or, rather, he has not Wickham's countenance, for his features are perfectly good. But how came you to tell me that he was so disagreeable?"

Elizabeth excused herself as well as she could; said that she had liked him better when they had met in Kent than before, and that she had never seen him so pleasant as this morning.

"But perhaps he may be a little whimsical in his civilities," replied her uncle. "Your great men often are; and therefore I shall not take him at his word, as he might change his mind another day, and bludgeon me with his musket for taking trout from his stock."

Elizabeth felt that they had entirely misunderstood his character, but said nothing.

"From what we have seen of him," continued Mrs. Gardiner, "I really should not have thought that he could have behaved in so cruel a way by anybody as he has done by poor Wickham. He has not an ill-natured look. On the contrary, there is something pleasing about his mouth when he speaks. And there is something of dignity in the way his trousers cling to those most English parts of him. But, to be sure, the good lady who showed us his house did give him a most congratulatory appraisal! I could hardly help laughing aloud sometimes. But he is a liberal master, I suppose, and servants are often too complimentary out of a desire to keep their heads."

Elizabeth here felt herself called on to say something in vindication of his behaviour to Wickham; and therefore gave them to understand, in as guarded a manner as she could, that by what she had heard from his relations in Kent, his actions were capable of a very different construction; and that his character was by no means so faulty, nor Wickham's so amiable, as they had been considered in Hertfordshire. In confirmation of this, she related the particulars of the stable boy business, without actually naming her authority, but stating it to be such as might be relied on.

Mrs. Gardiner was surprised and concerned; but as they were now approaching the scene of her former pleasures, every idea gave way to the charm of recollection; and she was too much engaged in pointing out to her husband all the interesting spots where she and her former lover had frittered away many a summer afternoon, before circumstances required the affair to be broken off. Fatigued as she had been by the morning's attack, they had no sooner dined than she set off in quest of her former acquaintance, and (unbeknownst to the sleeping Mr. Gardiner) her evening was spent in the satisfactions of intercourse renewed after many years' discontinuance.

The occurrences of the day were too full of interest to leave Elizabeth much attention for her aunt's dalliances; and she could do nothing but think, and think with wonder, of Mr. Darcy's civility, and, above all, of his wishing her to be acquainted with his sister.

CHAPTER 44

E LIZABETH HAD SETTLED IT that Mr. Darcy would bring his sister to visit her the very day after her reaching Pemberley; and was consequently resolved not to be out of sight of the inn the whole of that morning. But her conclusion was false; for on the very morning after their arrival at Lambton, these visitors came. Much to Mr. Gardiner's displeasure, they had been walking about the place with Mrs. Gardiner's old "friend," a Polish-born gentleman who went only by "Sylak," and were just returning to the inn to dress themselves for dining with the same, when the sound of a carriage drew them to a window, and they saw a gentleman and a lady in a curricle driving up the street. Elizabeth immediately recognizing the livery, guessed what it meant, and imparted no small degree of her surprise to her relations by acquainting them with the honour which she expected. Her uncle and aunt were all amazement; and the embarrassment of her manner as she spoke, joined to the circumstance itself, and many of the circumstances of the preceding day, opened to them a new idea on the business. Nothing had ever suggested it before, but they felt that there was no other way of accounting for such attentions from such a quarter than by supposing a partiality for their niece. While these newly-born notions were passing in their heads, the perturbation of Elizabeth's feelings was at every moment increasing. Given her battle-tested nerves, she was quite amazed at her own discomposure; but amongst other causes of disquiet, she dreaded lest the partiality of the brother should have said too much in her favour; and, more than commonly anxious to please, she naturally suspected that every power of pleasing would fail her.

She retreated from the window, fearful of being seen; and as she walked up and down the room, endeavouring to compose herself, saw such looks of inquiring surprise in her uncle and aunt as made everything worse.

Miss Darcy and her brother appeared, and this formidable introduction took place. With astonishment did Elizabeth see that her new acquaintance was at least as much embarrassed as herself. Since her being at Lambton, she had heard that Miss Darcy was exceedingly proud; but the observation of a very few minutes convinced her that she was only exceedingly shy. She found it difficult to obtain even a word from her beyond a monosyllable.

Miss Darcy was tall, and on a larger scale than Elizabeth; and, though little more than sixteen, her figure was formed, and her appearance womanly and soft. There was something of a natural grace to her movements, and though she clearly had much to learn in the ways of delivering death, she was far from the distracting clumsiness of most girls her age. Her legs and fingers were uncommonly long, and Elizabeth could not help but think what a fine apprentice she would make, were she only inclined to follow her brother's example with greater enthusiasm. She was less handsome than her brother; but there was sense and good humour in her face, and her manners were perfectly unassuming and gentle.

They had not long been together before Mr. Darcy told her that Bingley was also coming to wait on her; and she had barely time to express her satisfaction, and prepare for such a visitor, when Bingley's clumsy, untrained steps were heard on the stairs, and in a moment he entered the room. All Elizabeth's anger against him had been long done away; but had she still felt any, it could hardly have stood its ground against the unaffected cordiality with which he expressed himself on seeing her again. He inquired in a friendly, though general way, after her family, and looked and spoke with the same good-humoured ease that he had ever done.

In seeing Bingley, her thoughts naturally flew to Jane; and, oh! How ardently did she long to know whether any of his were directed in a like manner. Sometimes she could fancy that he talked less than on former occasions, and once or twice pleased herself with the notion that, as he looked at her, he was trying to trace a resemblance. But, though this might be imaginary, she could not be deceived as to his behaviour to Miss Darcy, who had been set up as a rival to Jane. No look appeared on either side that spoke to an attraction. Nothing occurred between them that could justify the hopes of Bingley's sister. On this point she was soon satisfied; and two or three little circumstances occurred before they parted, which, in her anxious interpretation, denoted a recollection of Jane touched by tenderness, and a wish of saying more that might lead to the mention of her, had he dared. He observed to her, at a moment when the others were talking together, and in a tone which had something of real regret, that it "was a very long time since he had had the pleasure of seeing her"; and, before she could reply, he added:

"It is above eight months. We have not met since the 26th of November, when my staff at Netherfield was so unhappily visited upon."

Elizabeth was pleased to find his memory so exact; and he afterwards took occasion to ask her, when unattended to by any of the rest, whether all her sisters were at Longbourn. There was not much in the question, nor in the preceding remark; but there was a look and a manner which gave them meaning.

It was not often that she could turn her eyes on Mr. Darcy himself; but, whenever she did catch a glimpse, she felt an excitement greater even than the thrill of confronting the Devil's legions, and in all that he said she heard an accent so removed from hauteur or disdain of his companions, as convinced her that the improvement of manners which she had yesterday witnessed had at least outlived one day. When she saw him thus courting the good opinion of people with whom any intercourse a few months ago would have been a disgrace—when she saw him thus civil, not only to herself, but to the very relations whom he had openly disdained—the difference, the change was so great, and struck so forcibly on her mind, that she could hardly believe herself unaffected by a cup of dragon's milk tea. Never, even in the company of his dear friends at Netherfield, or his dignified relations at Rosings, had she seen him so desirous to please as now, when no importance could result from the success of his endeavours, and when even the acquaintance of those to whom his attentions were addressed would draw down the ridicule and censure of the ladies both of Netherfield and Rosings.

Their visitors stayed with them above half-an-hour; and when they arose to depart, Mr. Darcy called on his sister to join him in expressing their wish of seeing Mr. and Mrs. Gardiner, and Miss Bennet, to dinner at Pemberley, before they left the country. Miss Darcy, though with a timidity which marked her little in the habit of giving invitations, readily obeyed. Mrs. Gardiner looked at her niece, desirous of knowing how she, whom the invitation most concerned, felt disposed as to its acceptance, but Elizabeth had turned away her head. Presuming however, that this studied avoidance spoke rather a momentary embarrassment than any dislike of the proposal, and seeing in her husband, who was fond of society, a perfect willingness to accept it, she ventured to engage for her attendance, and the day after the next was fixed on.

Bingley expressed great pleasure in the certainty of seeing Elizabeth again, having still a great deal to say to her, and many inquiries to make after all their Hertfordshire friends. Elizabeth, construing all this into a wish of hearing her speak of her sister, was pleased, and on this account, as well as some others, found herself, when their visitors left them, capable of considering the last half-hour as one of the happiest she had ever spent without spilling a drop of blood. Eager to be alone, and fearful of inquiries or hints from her uncle and aunt, she stayed with them only long enough to hear their favourable opinion of Bingley, and then hurried away to dress.

But she had no reason to fear Mr. and Mrs. Gardiner's curiosity; for unlike her meddling mother, it was not their wish to force her communication. It was evident that she was much better acquainted with Mr. Darcy than they had before any idea of; it was evident that he was very much in love with her. They saw much to interest, but nothing to justify inquiry.

Of Mr. Darcy it was now a matter of anxiety to think well; and, as far as their acquaintance reached, there was no fault to find. They could not be untouched by his coming to their rescue at Pemberley, or his politeness thereafter; and had they drawn his character from their own feelings and his servant's report, the circle in Hertfordshire to which he was known would not have recognized it for Mr. Darcy.

With respect to Wickham, the travellers soon found that he was not held there in much estimation; for though the chief of his concerns with the son of his patron were imperfectly understood, it was yet a well-known fact that, on his quitting Derbyshire, he had left many debts behind him, which Mr. Darcy afterwards discharged. It was also widely rumoured that he had engaged in improprieties with two local girls, both of whom, sadly, fell victim to the plague and had to be burned before charges could be brought.

As for Elizabeth, her thoughts were at Pemberley this evening more than the last; and the evening, though as it passed it seemed long, was not long enough to determine her feelings towards one in that mansion; and she lay awake two whole hours endeavouring to make them out. She certainly did not hate him. No; hatred had vanished long ago, and she had almost as long been ashamed of ever wishing to drink the blood from his severed head. The respect created by the conviction of his valuable qualities, though at first unwillingly admitted, had for some time ceased to be repugnant to her feeling; and it was now heightened into somewhat of a friendlier nature, by the testimony so highly in his favour, and bringing forward his disposition in so amiable a light, which yesterday had produced. But above all, above respect and esteem, there was a motive within her of goodwill which could not be overlooked. It was gratitude; gratitude, not merely for having once loved her, but for loving her still well enough to forgive all the petulance and acrimony of her manner in rejecting his offer with a kick to the face, and all the unjust accusations accompanying her rejection. He who, she had been persuaded, would avoid her as his greatest enemy, seemed, on this accidental meeting, most eager to preserve the acquaintance, and without any indelicate display of regard, or any peculiarity of manner, where their two selves only were concerned, was soliciting the good opinion of her friends, and bent on making her known to his sister. Such a change in a man of so much pride exciting not only astonishment but gratitude—for to love, ardent love, it must be attributed; and as such its impression on her was by no means unpleasing, though it could not be exactly defined. She respected, she esteemed, she was grateful to him, she felt a real interest in his welfare; where she had been taught to ignore all feeling, all excitement—she now found herself with an excess of both. How strange! For the more she dwelled on the subject, the more powerful she felt; not for her mastery of the deadly arts, but for her power over the heart of another. What a power it was! But how to wield it? Of all the weapons she had commanded, Elizabeth knew the least of love; and of all the weapons in the world, love was the most dangerous.

It had been settled in the evening between the aunt and the niece, that such a striking civility as Miss Darcy's in coming to see them on the very day of her arrival at Pemberley ought to be imitated, though it could not be equalled, by some exertion of politeness on their side; and, consequently, that it would be highly expedient to wait on her at Pemberley the following morning. They were, therefore, to go. Elizabeth was pleased; though when she asked herself the reason, she had very little to say in reply.

Mr. Gardiner left them soon after breakfast. The fishing scheme had been renewed the day before, and a positive engagement made of his meeting some of the gentlemen at Pemberley before noon.

CHAPTER 45

C ONVINCED AS ELIZABETH now was that Miss Bingley's dislike of her had originated in jealousy, she could not help feeling how unwelcome her appearance at Pemberley must be to her, and was curious to know with how much civility on that lady's side the acquaintance would now be renewed.

On reaching the house, they were shown through the hall into the Shinto shrine, whose northern aspect rendered it delightful for summer. Its windows opening to the ground, the shrine admitted a most refreshing view of the high woody hills behind the house, and its many sacred mirrors honored the gods while creating a most pleasing abundance of light.

In this shrine they were received by Miss Darcy, who was sitting there with Mrs. Hurst and Miss Bingley, and the lady with whom she lived in London. Georgiana's reception of them was very civil, but attended with all the embarrassment which, though proceeding from shyness and the fear of doing wrong, would easily give to those who felt themselves inferior the belief of her being proud and reserved. Mrs. Gardiner and her niece, however, did her justice, and pitied her.

By Mrs. Hurst and Miss Bingley they were noticed only by a curtsey; and, on their being seated, a pause, awkward as such pauses must always be, succeeded for a few moments. It was first broken by Mrs. Annesley, a genteel, agreeable-looking woman, whose endeavour to introduce some kind of discourse proved her to be more truly well-bred than either of the others; and between her and Mrs. Gardiner, with occasional help from Elizabeth, the conversation was carried on. Miss Darcy looked as if she wished for courage enough to join in it; and sometimes did venture a short sentence when there was least danger of its being heard.

Elizabeth saw that she was herself closely watched by Miss Bingley, and that she could not speak a word, especially to Miss Darcy, without calling her attention. "Oh! How she must long to strike at me with her clumsy, untrained fists," thought Elizabeth. "What fun it would be to see her lose her composure so!"

The next variation which their visit afforded was produced by the entrance of servants with cold meat, cake, and a variety of Japanese delicacies. There was now employment for the whole party—for though they could not all talk, they could all eat; and the beautiful pyramids of ham, frosting, and zarezushi soon collected them round the table.

While thus engaged, Elizabeth had a fair opportunity of deciding whether she most feared or wished for the appearance of Mr. Darcy, by the feelings which prevailed on his entering the room; and then, though but a moment before she had believed her wishes to predominate, she began to regret that he came—for she realized that her breath must tang of sweets and raw eel.

He had been some time with Mr. Gardiner, who, with two or three other gentlemen from the house, was musket fishing in the river, and had left him only on learning that the ladies of the family intended a visit to Georgiana that morning. No sooner did he appear than Elizabeth wisely resolved to be perfectly easy and unembarrassed, because she saw that the suspicions of the whole party were awakened against them, and that there was scarcely an eye which did not watch his behaviour when he first came into the room. In no countenance was attentive curiosity so strongly marked as in Miss Bingley's, in spite of the smiles which overspread her face whenever she spoke to one of its objects; for jealousy had not yet made her desperate, and her attentions to Mr. Darcy were by no means over. Miss Darcy, on her brother's entrance, exerted herself much more to talk, and Elizabeth saw that he was anxious for his sister and herself to get acquainted, and forwarded as much as possible, every attempt at conversation on either side. Miss Bingley saw all this likewise;

and, in the imprudence of anger, took the first opportunity of saying, with sneering civility:

"Pray, Miss Eliza, are not the Militia removed from Meryton? They must be a great loss to your family."

In Darcy's presence she dared not mention Wickham's name; but Elizabeth instantly comprehended that he was uppermost in her thoughts; and she had to forcefully repress the desire to blacken Miss Bingley's eyes for such insolence. Exerting her tongue rather than her fists to repel the ill-natured attack, she presently answered the question in a tolerably detached tone. While she spoke, an involuntary glance showed her Darcy, with a heightened complexion, his sword hand twitching ever so slightly, and his sister overcome with confusion, and unable to lift up her eyes. Had Miss Bingley known what pain she was then giving her beloved friend, she undoubtedly would have refrained from the hint; but she had merely intended to discompose Elizabeth by bringing forward the idea of a man to whom she believed her partial, to make her betray a sensibility which might injure her in Darcy's opinion, and, perhaps, to remind the latter of all the follies and absurdities by which some part of her family were connected with that corps. Not a syllable had ever reached her of Miss Darcy's meditated elopement.

Elizabeth's collected behaviour, however, soon quieted Mr. Darcy's emotion; and as Miss Bingley, vexed and disappointed, dared not approach nearer to Wickham, Georgiana also recovered in time, though not enough to be able to speak any more. Her brother, whose eye she feared to meet, scarcely recollected her interest in the affair, and the very circumstance which had been designed to turn his thoughts from Elizabeth seemed to have fixed them on her more and more cheerfully. Not since the Battle of Tumu Fortress had an assault been so poorly conceived.

Their visit did not continue long after the above mentioned; and while Mr. Darcy was attending them to their carriage Miss Bingley was venting her feelings in criticisms on Elizabeth's person, behaviour, and dress. But Georgiana would not join her. Her brother's recommendation was enough to ensure her favour; his judgement could not err. And he had spoken in such terms of Elizabeth as to leave Georgiana without the power of finding her otherwise than lovely and amiable. When Darcy returned to the shrine, Miss Bingley could not help repeating to him some part of what she had been saying to his sister.

"How very ill Miss Eliza Bennet looks this morning, Mr. Darcy," she cried; "I never in my life saw anyone so much altered as she is since the winter. She is grown so brown and coarse! Louisa and I were agreeing that we should not have known her again."

However little Mr. Darcy might have liked such an address, he contented himself with coolly replying that he perceived no other alteration than her being rather tanned, no miraculous consequence of traveling in the summer.

"For my own part," she rejoined, "I must confess that I never could see any beauty in her. Her midriff is too firm; her arms too free of loose flesh; and her legs too long and flexible. Her nose wants character—it is unbearably petite. Her teeth are tolerable, but not out of the common way; and as for her eyes, which have sometimes been called so fine, I could never see anything extraordinary in them. They have a sharp, knowing look, which I do not like at all; and in her air altogether there is a self sufficiency and composure, which is intolerable."

Persuaded as Miss Bingley was that Darcy admired Elizabeth, this was not the best method of recommending herself; but angry people are not always wise; and in seeing him at last look somewhat nettled, she had all the success she expected. He was resolutely silent, however, and, from a determination of making him speak, she continued:

"I remember, when we first knew her in Hertfordshire, how amazed we all were to find that she was a reputed beauty; and I particularly recollect your saying one night, after they had been dining at Netherfield, 'She a beauty! I should as soon call her mother a wit.' But afterwards she seemed to improve on you, and I believe you thought her rather pretty at one time."

"Yes," replied Darcy, who could contain himself no longer, "but that was only when I first saw her, for I now consider her as one of the handsomest women of my acquaintance."

He then went away, and Miss Bingley was left to all the satisfaction of having forced him to say what gave no one any pain but herself.

Mrs. Gardiner and Elizabeth talked of all that had occurred during their visit, as they returned, except what had particularly interested them both. The look and behaviour of everybody they had seen were discussed, except of the person who had mostly engaged their attention. They talked of his sister, his friends, his shrine, his zarezushi—of everything but himself; yet Elizabeth was longing to know what Mrs. Gardiner thought of him, and Mrs. Gardiner would have been highly gratified by her niece's beginning the subject.

CHAPTER 46

ELIZABETH HAD BEEN a good deal disappointed in not finding a letter from Jane on their first arrival at Lambton; and this disappointment had been renewed on each of the mornings that had now been spent there; but on the third her repining was over, and her sister justified, by the receipt of two letters from her at once, on one of which was marked that it had been aboard a post carriage that had been overrun by zombies, thus the delay in its delivery.

They had just been preparing to walk as the letters came in; and her uncle and aunt, leaving her to enjoy them in quiet, set off by themselves. The one delayed must first be attended to; it had been written five days ago. The beginning contained an account of all their little parties and engagements, with such news as the country afforded; but the latter half, which was dated a day later, and written in evident agitation, gave more important intelligence. It was to this effect:

Since writing the above, dearest Lizzy, something has occurred of a most unexpected and serious nature. What I have to say relates to poor Lydia. An express came at twelve last night, just as we were all gone to bed, from Colonel Forster, to inform us that she was gone off to Scotland with one of his officers; to own the truth, with Wickham! Imagine our surprise. I am very, very sorry. So imprudent a match on both sides! But I am willing to hope the best, and that his character has been misunderstood. Thoughtless and indiscreet I can easily believe him, but this step (and let us rejoice over it) marks nothing bad at heart. His choice is disinterested at least, for he must know my father can give her nothing. Our poor mother is sadly grieved. My father bears it better. How thankful am I that we never let them know of his falling out with Mr. Darcy, or of his treatment of the deaf; we must forget it ourselves.

On finishing this letter Elizabeth instantly seized the other, and opening it with the utmost impatience, read as follows: it had been written a day later than the conclusion of the first.

DEAREST LIZZY,

I hardly know what I would write, but I have bad news for you, and it cannot be delayed. Imprudent as the marriage between Mr. Wickham and our poor Lydia would be, we are now anxious to be assured it has taken place, for there is now reason to believe that Lydia may have been taken against her will! Colonel Forster came yesterday, having left Brighton the day before, not many hours after the express. Though Lydia's short letter to Mrs. F. gave them to understand that they intended to elope, something was dropped by another officer that Wickham had no such intentions, which was repeated to

Colonel F., who, instantly taking the alarm, set off from B. intending to trace their route. He did trace them easily to Clapham, but no further; for on entering that place, he was met with a hail of musket balls, and forced to seek cover while Wickham and Lydia removed into a hackney coach and sped away. All that is known after this is, that they were seen to continue the London road. I know not what to think. After making every possible inquiry on that side of London, Colonel F. came on to Longbourn, and broke his apprehensions to us in a manner most creditable to his heart. I am sincerely grieved for him and Mrs. F., but no one can throw any blame on them. Our distress, my dear Lizzy, is very great. My father and mother believe the worst, that she will be stripped of her clothes, her honour, and her head in quick succession—but I cannot think so ill of him. Many circumstances might make it more eligible for them to be married privately in town than to pursue their first plan; and even if he could carry out such a scheme against a young woman of Lydia's training, which is not likely, can I suppose his character so misjudged by us? Impossible! My father is going to London with Colonel Forster instantly, to try to discover her. What he means to do I am sure I know not; but his excessive distress will not allow him to pursue any measure in the best and safest way, and Colonel Forster is obliged to be at Brighton again to-morrow evening. In such distress, my uncle's advice and assistance would be everything in the world; he will immediately comprehend what I must feel, and I rely upon his goodness.

"Oh! Where, where is my uncle?" cried Elizabeth, darting from her seat as she finished the letter, without losing a moment of the time so precious; but as she reached the door it was opened by a servant, and Mr. Darcy appeared. Her pale face and impetuous manner made him start, and before he could recover himself to speak, she hastily exclaimed, "I beg your pardon, but I must leave you. I must find Mr. Gardiner this moment, on business that cannot be delayed; I have not an instant to lose."

"Good God! What is the matter?" cried he, "I will not detain you a minute; but let me, or let the servant go after Mr. and Mrs. Gardiner. You are not well enough; you cannot go yourself."

Elizabeth hesitated, but her knees trembled under her and she felt how little would be gained by her attempting to pursue them. Calling back the servant, therefore, she commissioned him, though in so breathless an accent as made her almost unintelligible, to fetch his master and mistress home instantly.

On his quitting the room she sat down, unable to support herself, and looking so miserably ill, that it was impossible for Darcy to leave her, or to refrain from saying, in a tone of gentleness and commiseration, "Let me call your maid. Is there nothing you could take to give you present relief? Kampo herbs; shall I get you some? You are very ill."

"No, I thank you," she replied, endeavouring to recover herself. "There is nothing the matter with me. I am only distressed by some dreadful news which I have just received from Longbourn."

She burst into tears and for a few minutes could not speak another word. Darcy, in wretched suspense, could only say something indistinctly of his concern, and observe her in compassionate silence. At length she spoke again. "I have just had a letter from Jane, with such dreadful news. It cannot be concealed from anyone. My younger sister is in the power of—of Mr. Wickham. They are gone off together from Brighton. You know him too well to doubt the rest. She has no money, no connections, nothing that can tempt him to marriage—she is lost for ever."

Darcy was fixed in astonishment. "When I consider," she added in a yet more agitated voice, "that I might have prevented it! I, who knew what he was. Had I but explained some part of it only—some part of what I learnt, to my own family! Had his character been known, this could not have happened. But it is all—all too late now."

"I am grieved indeed," cried Darcy; "grieved—shocked. But is it certain—absolutely certain?"

"Oh, yes! They left Brighton together on Sunday night, and were traced almost to London, but not beyond; Colonel Foster has reason to doubt their elopement, and suspects that Lydia was taken against her will."

"And what has been done, what has been attempted, to recover her?"

"My father is gone to London, and Jane has written to beg my uncle's immediate assistance; and we shall be off, I hope, in half-an-hour. But nothing can be done. How are they even to be discovered? I have not the smallest hope."

Darcy shook his head in silent acquiescence.

"When my eyes were opened to his real character—Oh! Had I known what I ought, what I dared to do! But I knew not—I was afraid of doing too much. Wretched, wretched mistake!"

Darcy made no answer. He seemed scarcely to hear her, and was walking up and down the room in earnest meditation, his brow contracted, his air gloomy. Elizabeth soon observed, and instantly understood it. His opinion of her was sinking; everything must sink under such a proof of family weakness, such an assurance of the deepest disgrace. Never had she so honestly felt that she could have loved him, as now, when all love must be vain.

Covering her face with her handkerchief, Elizabeth was soon lost to everything else; and was only recalled to a sense of her situation by the voice of her companion. "Would to Heaven that anything could be either said or done on my part that might offer consolation to such distress! But I will not torment you with vain wishes, which may seem purposely to ask for your thanks. This unfortunate affair will, I fear, prevent my sister's having the pleasure of seeing you at Pemberley to-day."

"Oh, yes. Be so kind as to apologise for us to Miss Darcy. Say that urgent business calls us home immediately. Conceal the unhappy truth as long as it is possible, I know it cannot be long."

He readily assured her of his secrecy; again expressed his sorrow for her distress, wished it a happier conclusion than there was at present reason to hope, and leaving his compliments for her relations, with only one serious, parting look, went away.

As he quitted the room, Elizabeth felt how improbable it was that they should ever see each other again on such terms of cordiality again; and as she threw a retrospective glance over the whole of their acquaintance, so full of contradictions and varieties, sighed at the perverseness of those feelings which would now have promoted its continuance, and would formerly have rejoiced in its termination.

She saw him go with regret; and in this early example of the shame which Lydia's imminent violation and murder must produce, found additional anguish as she reflected on that wretched business. Never, since reading Jane's second letter, had she entertained a hope of Wickham's meaning to marry her. No one but Jane, she thought, could flatter herself with such an expectation. Surprise was the least of her feelings on this development. While the contents of the first letter remained in her mind, she was all surprise—all astonishment that Wickham should have captured a student of Shaolin—even one so careless as Lydia. But now it was all too natural. For such was her eagerness for the company of handsome officers, that her guard would have been sufficiently lowered to allow such a disgrace.

Elizabeth was wild to be at home—to hear, to see, to be upon the spot to share with Jane in the cares that must now fall wholly upon her, in a family so deranged, a father absent, a mother surely vomiting by now, and requiring constant attendance; and though almost persuaded that nothing could be done for Lydia, her uncle's interference seemed of the utmost importance, and till he entered the room her impatience was severe. Mr. and Mrs. Gardiner had hurried back in alarm, supposing by the servant's account that their niece was slain by some unknown enemy; but satisfying them instantly on that head, she eagerly communicated the cause of their summons, reading the two letters aloud. Mr. and Mrs. Gardiner could not but be deeply afflicted. Not Lydia only, but all were concerned in it; and after the first exclamations of surprise and horror, Mr. Gardiner promised every assistance in his power. Elizabeth, though expecting no less, thanked him with tears of gratitude; and all three being actuated by one spirit, everything relating to their journey was speedily settled. They were to be off as soon as possible. "But what is to be done about Pemberley?" cried Mrs. Gardiner. "John told us Mr. Darcy was here when you sent for us; was it so?"

"Yes; and I told him we should not be able to keep our engagement. That is all settled."

"What shall we tell our other friends?" said the other, as she ran into her room to prepare. "Oh, how I wish there were time to see Sylak once more!"

But wishes were vain, or at least could only serve to amuse her in the hurry and confusion of the following hour. Had Elizabeth been at leisure to be idle, she would have remained certain that all employment was impossible to one so wretched as herself; but she had her share of business as well as her aunt, and amongst the rest there were notes to be written to all their friends at Lambton, with false excuses for their sudden departure. An hour, however, saw the whole completed; and Mr. Gardiner meanwhile having settled his account at the inn, nothing remained to be done but to go; and Elizabeth, after all the misery of the morning, found herself, in a shorter space of time than she could have supposed, seated in the carriage, and on the road to Longbourn.

CHAPTER 47

"I HAVE BEEN THINKING it over again, Elizabeth," said her uncle, as they drove from the town; "and really, upon serious consideration, I am much more inclined than I was to judge as your eldest sister does on the matter. It appears to me so very unlikely that any young man should form such a design against a girl who is by no means unprotected or friendless, and who was actually staying in his colonel's family, that I am strongly inclined to hope the best. Could he expect that her friends would not step forward? Could he expect that her sisters would not pursue him to the ends of the earth with their swords? Could he expect to be noticed again by the regiment, after such an affront to Colonel Forster? His temptation is not adequate to the risk!"

"Do you really think so?" cried Elizabeth.

"Upon my word," said Mrs. Gardiner, "I begin to be of your uncle's opinion. It is really too great a violation of decency, honour, and interest, for him to be guilty of. I cannot think so very ill of Wickham. Can you yourself, Lizzy, so wholly give him up, as to believe him capable of it?"

"Not, perhaps, of neglecting his own interest; but of every other neglect I can believe him capable. If, indeed, it should be so! But I dare not hope it. Why should he fire upon the Colonel if that had been the case?"

"In the first place," replied Mr. Gardiner, "there is no absolute proof that they do not intend to marry."

"But why all this secrecy? Why any fear of detection? Why must their marriage be private? Oh, no, no—this is not likely. His fellow officer, you see by Jane's account, was persuaded of his never intending to marry her. Wickham will never marry a woman without some money. He cannot afford it. And what claims has Lydia—what attraction has she beyond youth and good length of bone that could make him, for her sake, forego every chance of benefiting himself by marrying well? As to your other objection, I am afraid it will hardly hold good. My sisters and I cannot spend any substantial time searching for Wickham, as we are each commanded by His Majesty to defend Hertfordshire from all enemies until such time as we are dead, rendered lame, or married."

"But can you think that Lydia is so helpless as to allow herself—nay, her family to be so dishonoured?"

"It does seem, and it is most shocking indeed," replied Elizabeth, with tears in her eyes, "that a Bennet sister's mastery of the deadly arts should admit of doubt. But, really, I know not what to say. Perhaps I am not doing her justice. But she is very young; and for the last half-year, nay, for a twelvemonth—she has been given up to nothing but amusement and vanity. She has been allowed to dispose of her time in the most idle and frivolous manner, and to neglect her daily sparring, meditation, or even the simplest game of Kiss Me Deer. Since the Militia were first quartered in Meryton, nothing but love, flirtation, and officers have been in her head. And we all know that Wickham has every charm of person and address that can captivate a woman."

"But you see that Jane," said her aunt, "does not think so very ill of Wickham as to believe him capable of the attempt."

"Of whom does Jane ever think ill? I have seen her cradle unmentionables in her arms, apologising for taking their limbs, even as they tried to bite her with their last. But Jane knows, as well as I do, what Wickham really is. We both know that he has been profligate in every sense of the word; that he has neither integrity nor honour."

"And do you really know all this?" cried Mrs. Gardiner.

"I do indeed," replied Elizabeth, colouring. "I told you, the other day, of his infamous behaviour to Mr. Darcy; and you yourself, when last at Longbourn, heard in what manner he spoke of the man who had behaved with such forbearance and liberality towards him. And there are other circumstances which I am not at liberty—which it is not worth while to relate; but his lies about the whole Pemberley family are endless."

"But does Lydia know nothing of this? Can she be ignorant of what you and Jane seem so well to understand?"

"Oh, yes! That is the worst of all. Till I was in Kent, and saw so much both of Mr. Darcy and his relation Colonel Fitzwilliam, I was ignorant of the truth myself—so ignorant that my honour required the seven cuts. And when I returned home, the Militia was to leave Meryton in a week or fortnight's time. As that was the case, neither Jane, to whom I related the whole, nor I, thought it necessary to make our knowledge public; for of what use could it apparently be to any one, that the good opinion which all the neighbourhood had of him should then be overthrown? And even when it was settled that Lydia should go with Mrs. Forster, the necessity of opening her eyes to his character never occurred to me."

"When they all removed to Brighton, therefore, you had no reason, I suppose, to believe them fond of each other?"

"Not the slightest. I can remember no symptom of affection on either side, other than her carving his name into her midriff with a dagger; but this was customary with Lydia. When first he entered the corps, she was ready enough to admire him; but so we all were. Every girl in or near Meryton was out of her senses about him for the first two months; but he never distinguished her by any particular attention; and, consequently, after a moderate period of extravagant and wild admiration, her fancy gave way, and others of the regiment, who treated her with more distinction, again became her favourites."

However little of novelty could be added to their fears, hopes, and conjectures, on this interesting subject, by its repeated discussion, no other could detain them from it long, during the whole of the journey. From Elizabeth's thoughts it was never absent. Fixed there by the keenest of all anguish, self-reproach, she could find no interval.

They travelled as expeditiously as possible, until they neared the village of Lowe, where there had lately been a skirmish between the King's army and a southerly herd. Here, the road became so littered with bodies (human and unmentionable alike), that it was rendered almost impassable. As the bodies were unsafe to touch, the coachman was forced to lift the iron beak from the undercarriage and affix it to the horses—hanging it with leather straps from their necks, so that it rested front of their feet, forming a plow, which pushed the bodies aside as they continued.

Determined that they should lose no more time, Elizabeth sat next to the coachman with her Brown Bess, ready to meet the slightest sign of trouble with the crack of powder. She ordered him to stop for nothing; even that most personal business would have to be attended to from where they sat. They drove through the night, and reached Longbourn by dinner time the next day. It was a comfort to Elizabeth to consider that Jane could not have been wearied by long expectations.

The little Gardiners, attracted by the sight of a chaise, were standing on the steps of the house as they entered the paddock; and, when the carriage drove up to the door, the joyful surprise that lighted up their faces was the first pleasing earnest of their welcome.

Elizabeth jumped out; and, after giving each of them a hasty kiss, hurried into the vestibule, where Jane immediately met her.

Elizabeth, as she affectionately embraced her, whilst tears filled the eyes of both, lost not a moment in asking whether anything had been heard of the fugitives.

"Not yet," replied Jane. "But now that my dear uncle is come, I hope everything will be well. Oh! Lizzy! Our sister abducted and repeatedly dishonoured, even as we stand here helpless!"

"Is my father in town?"

"Yes, he went on Tuesday, as I wrote you word."

"And have you heard from him often?"

"We have heard only twice. He wrote me a few lines on Wednesday to say that he had arrived in safety, and to give me his directions, which I particularly begged him to do. He merely added that he should not write again till he had something of importance to mention."

"And my mother—how is she? How are you all?"

"Mother is tolerably well, I trust; though she vomits often, and quite copiously, as you no doubt expected. She is upstairs and will have great satisfaction in seeing you all. She does not yet leave her dressing-room. Mary and Kitty, thank Heaven, are quite well, and have both sworn blood-oaths against Mr. Wickham, bless their hearts."

"But you—how are you?" cried Elizabeth. "You look pale. How much you must have gone through!"

Her sister, however, assured her of her being perfectly well; and their conversation, which had been passing while Mr. and Mrs. Gardiner were engaged with their children, was now put an end to by the approach of the whole party. Jane ran to her uncle and aunt, and welcomed and thanked them both, with alternate smiles and tears.

When they were all in the drawing-room, the questions which Elizabeth had already asked were of course repeated by the others, and they soon found that Jane had no intelligence to give. She still clung to the sanguine hope that it would all end well, and that every morning would bring some letter, either from Lydia or her father, to explain their proceedings, and, perhaps, announce their marriage.

Mrs. Bennet, to whose apartment they all repaired, after a few minutes' conversation together, received them exactly as might be expected; with tears and lamentations of regret, invectives against the villainous conduct of Wickham, and half a bucket's worth of vomit; blaming everybody but the person to whose ill-judging indulgence the errors of her daughter must principally be owing.

"If I had been able," said she, "to carry my point in going to Brighton, with all my family, this would not have happened; but poor dear Lydia had nobody to take care of her. Why did the Forsters ever let her go out of their sight? I am sure there was some great neglect or other on their side, for she is not the kind of girl to do such a thing if she had been well looked after. I always thought they were very unfit to have the charge of her; but I was overruled, as I always am. Poor dear child! And now here's Mr. Bennet gone away, and I know he will fight Wickham wherever he meets him, and then he will be killed—for no matter how full his mind of Oriental trickery, his frail old body possesses none of its former grace. And then what is to become of us all? The Collinses will turn us out before he is cold in his grave, and if you are not kind to us, brother, I do not know what we shall do."

They all exclaimed against such terrific ideas; and Mr. Gardiner, after general assurances of his affection for her and all her family, told her that he meant to be in London the very next day, and would assist Mr. Bennet in every endeavour for recovering Lydia.

"Do not give way to useless alarm," added he. "Till we know that they are not married, and have no design of marrying, do not let us give her honour over as lost. As soon as I get to town I shall go to my brother, and make him come home with me to Section Six East; and then we may consult together as to what is to be done."

"Oh! My dear brother," replied Mrs. Bennet, "that is exactly what I could most wish for. When you get to town, find them out; and if they are not married already, make them marry. And as for wedding clothes, do not let them wait for that, but tell Lydia she shall have as much money as she chooses to buy them, after they are married. And, above all, keep Mr. Bennet from fighting. Tell him what a dreadful state I am in, that I am frighted out of my wits—and have such tremblings, such flutterings, all over me—such spasms in my side and pains in my head, and such a ceaseless torrent of sick into my bucket, that I can get no rest by night nor by day."

Mr. Gardiner assured her again of his earnest endeavours in the cause, and after talking with her in this manner till dinner was on the table, they all left her to vomit in the company of the housekeeper, who attended in the absence of her daughters.

Though her brother and sister were persuaded that there was no real occasion for such a seclusion from the family, they did not attempt to oppose it. In the dining-room they were soon joined by Mary and

Kitty, who had been too busily engaged in their sparring to make their appearance before. They had been busy at little else since swearing their blood oaths. Soon after they were seated at the table, Mary whispered to Elizabeth:

"This is a most unfortunate affair, and will probably be much talked of. But we must stem the tide of idle chatter, and pour into our wounded bosoms the soothing balm of vengeance."

Then, perceiving in Elizabeth no inclination of replying, she added, "Unhappy as the event must be for Lydia, we may draw from it this useful lesson: that virtue in a female is as easily removed as a piece of clothing; that one false step can cause endless ruin; that the only remedy for wounded honour is the blood of he who hath defiled it."

Elizabeth lifted up her eyes in amazement, but was too much oppressed to make any reply. Mary, however, continued to console herself with such kind of moral extractions from the evil before them.

In the afternoon, the two elder Miss Bennets were able to be for half-an-hour by themselves; after joining in general lamentations over the dreadful dishonouring of their sister, which Elizabeth considered as all but certain, and Jane could not assert to be wholly impossible, the former continued the subject, by saying, "But tell me all and everything about it which I have not already heard. Give me further particulars. What did Colonel Forster say? Had they no apprehension of anything before the abduction took place?"

"Colonel Forster did own that he had often suspected some partiality, especially on Lydia's side, but nothing to give him any alarm. I am so grieved for him! His behaviour was attentive and kind to the utmost. He was coming to us, in order to assure us of his concern, before he had any idea of Wickham's having no intention of marrying: when that apprehension first got abroad, it hastened his journey."

"And was the officer convinced that Wickham would not marry? Did he know of their intending to go off?"

"Yes; but, when questioned by him, the officer denied knowing anything of their plans, and would not give his real opinion about it, even after the Colonel threatened to feed his most English parts to the unmentionables. He did not repeat his persuasion of their not marrying—and from that, I am inclined to hope, he might have been misunderstood before."

"And till Colonel Forster came himself, not one of you doubted that they would be hastily married?"

"How was it possible that such an idea should enter our brains? I felt a little uneasy—a little fearful of my sister's happiness with him in marriage, because I knew that his conduct had not been always quite right. My father and mother knew nothing of that; they only felt how imprudent a match it must be. Kitty then owned, with a very natural triumph on knowing more than the rest of us, that in Lydia's last letter she had prepared her for such a step. She had known, it seems, of their being in love with each other, many weeks."

"But not before they went to Brighton?"

"No, I believe not."

"And did Colonel Forster appear to think well of Wickham himself? Does he know his real character?"

"I must confess that he did not speak so well of Wickham as he formerly did. He believed him to be imprudent and extravagant. And since this sad affair has taken place, it is said that he left Meryton greatly in debt, and left at least one poor milkmaid in a delicate condition; but I hope this may be false."

"Oh, Jane, had we told what we knew of him, this could not have happened!"

"Perhaps it would have been better," replied her sister. "But to expose the former faults of any person without knowing what their present feelings were, seemed unjustifiable. We acted with the best intentions."

"Could Colonel Forster repeat the particulars of Lydia's note to his wife?"

"He brought it with him for us to see."

Jane then took it from her pocket-book, and gave it to Elizabeth.

These were the contents:

> MY DEAR HARRIET,
>
> You will laugh when you know where I am gone, and I cannot help laughing myself at your surprise to-morrow morning, as soon as I am missed. I am going to Gretna Green, and if you cannot guess with who, I shall think your brains in a zombie's teeth, for there is but one man in the world I love, and he is an angel. I should never be happy without him, so think it no harm to be off. You need not send them word at Longbourn of my going, if you do not like it, for it will make the surprise the greater, when I write to them and sign my name "Lydia Wickham." What a good joke it will be! I can hardly write for laughing.
>
> I shall send for my clothes and weapons when I get to Longbourn; but I wish you would tell Sally to mend a great claw mark in my worked muslin gown before they are packed up. Good-bye. Give my love to Colonel Forster. I hope you will drink to our good journey.
>
> Your affectionate friend,
>
> LYDIA BENNET.

"Oh! Thoughtless, thoughtless Lydia!" cried Elizabeth when she had finished it. "What a letter is this, to be written at such a moment! But at least it shows that she was serious on the subject of their journey. Whatever he might afterwards force her into, it was not on her side a scheme of infamy. My poor father! How he must have felt it!"

"I never saw anyone so shocked. He could not speak a word for full ten minutes. My mother was taken ill immediately, and the whole house in such confusion!"

"Oh! Jane," cried Elizabeth, "you do not look well. Oh that I had been with you! You have had every care and anxiety upon yourself alone."

"Mary and Kitty have been very kind, and would have shared in every fatigue, I am sure, had they not been engaged in crafting Mr. Wickham's doom. My aunt Philips came to Longbourn on Tuesday, after my father went away; and was so good as to stay till Thursday with me. She was of great use and comfort to us all. And Lady Lucas has been very kind; she walked here on Wednesday morning to condole with us, and offered her services, or any of her daughters', if they should be of use to us."

Upon hearing Lady Lucas mentioned, Elizabeth's thoughts turned to Hunsford. She wondered if there were any of the old Charlotte left, or if Mr. Collins had yet perceived her affliction. It had, after all, been some time since she had received a letter from the parsonage. Was her friend still living? It was too frightful a subject to long dwell upon. She then proceeded to inquire into the measures which her father had intended to pursue, while in town, for the recovery of his daughter.

"He meant I believe," replied Jane, "to go to Epsom, the place where they last changed horses. His principal object must be to discover the number of the hackney coach which took them from Clapham after Mr. Wickham tried to kill the Colonel. It had come with a fare from London; and as he thought that the circumstance of a gentleman and lady's removing from one carriage into another in a hail of musket fire might be remembered, he meant to make inquiries at Clapham."

CHAPTER 48

THE WHOLE PARTY were in hopes of a letter from Mr. Bennet the next morning, but the post came in without bringing a single line from him. His family knew him to be a most negligent and dilatory correspondent; but at such a time they had hoped for exertion. They were forced to conclude that he had no pleasing intelligence to send; but even of that they would have been glad to be certain. Mr. Gardiner had waited only for the letters before he set off, with three hired men and their guns as his companions and guarantors of expeditious passage.

Mrs. Gardiner and the children were to remain in Hertfordshire a few days longer, as the former thought her presence might be serviceable to her nieces. She shared in their attendance on Mrs. Bennet, and was a great comfort to them in their hours of freedom. Their other aunt also visited them frequently, and always, as she said, with the design of cheering and heartening them up—though, as she never came without reporting some fresh instance of Wickham's leaving this bill or that bastard child, she seldom went away without leaving them more dispirited than she found them.

All Meryton seemed striving to blacken the man who, but three months before, had been hailed as "more praiseworthy than Christ himself." He was declared to be in debt to every tradesman in the place, and his intrigues, all honoured with the title of seduction, had been extended into every tradesman's family. Everybody declared that he was the wickedest young man in the world; and everybody began to find out that they had always distrusted the appearance of his goodness. Elizabeth, though she did not credit above half of what was said, believed enough to make her former assurance of her sister's ruin more certain; and even Jane, who believed still less of it, became almost hopeless, more especially as the time was now come when, if they had been married, they must in all probability have gained some news of it.

Mr. Gardiner left Longbourn on Sunday; on Tuesday his wife received a letter from him; it told them that, on his arrival, he had immediately found out his brother, and persuaded him to come to Section Six East; that Mr. Bennet had been to Epsom and Clapham, before his arrival, but without gaining any satisfactory information; and that he was now determined to inquire at all the principal hotels in town. There was also a postscript to this effect:

> I have written to Colonel Forster to desire him to find
> out, if possible, from some of the young man's intimates in the
> regiment, whether Wickham has any relations or connections
> who would be likely to know in what part of town he has
> now concealed himself. If there were anyone that one could
> apply to with a probability of gaining such a clue as that, it
> might be of essential consequence. At present we have noth-
> ing to guide us. Colonel Forster will, I dare say, do everything
> in his power to satisfy us on this head. But, on second
> thoughts, perhaps, Lizzy could tell us what relations he has
> now living, better than any other person.

Elizabeth had never heard of his having had any relations, except
a father and mother, both of whom had been dead many years. It was
possible, however, that some of his companions in the Militia might be
able to give more information, though she was not very sanguine in
expecting it.

Elizabeth and Jane could find no solace in their deer wrestling, nor
could they depend on their younger sisters for company, as both were
forever engaged in crafting some new method of disembowelment for
Mr. Wickham. Every day at Longbourn was now a day of anxiety; but
the most anxious part of each was when the post was expected. The
arrival of letters was the grand object of every morning's impatience.
Through letters, whatever of good or bad was to be told would be communicated, and every succeeding day was expected to bring some news
of importance.

But before they heard again from Mr. Gardiner, a letter arrived for
their father, from a different quarter, from Mr. Collins; which, as Jane had
received directions to open all that came for him in his absence, she
accordingly read; and Elizabeth, who knew what curiosities his letters

always were, looked over her, and read it likewise. It was as follows:

MY DEAR SIR,

I feel myself called upon, by our relationship, and my situation in life, to condole with you on the grievous affliction you are now suffering under, and likewise inform you of my own suffering, due to a tragedy that has befallen one of your dearest acquaintances, my beloved wife, Charlotte. It is my sad duty to report that she is no more with us upon this earth; that she was somehow stricken with the strange plague—an affliction we were all blind to until Lady Catherine de Bourgh condescended to bring it to my attention in a most graceful manner. Her ladyship, I might add, was kind enough to offer her hand in carrying out the customary beheading and burning; but I felt it my husbandly duty to perform them with my own hand—trembling though it was. Be assured, my dear sir, that despite my own crippling grief, I sincerely sympathise with you and all your respectable family, in your present distress, which must be of the bitterest kind. The death of your daughter would have been a blessing in comparison of this, just as the beheading and burning of my bride was a fate preferable to seeing her join the ranks of Lucifer's brigade. You are grievously to be pitied; in which opinion I am joined Lady Catherine and her daughter, to whom I have related the affair. They agree with me in apprehending that this dishonouring of one's daughter will be injurious to the fortunes of all the others; for "who," as Lady Catherine herself condescendingly says, "will connect themselves with such a family?" And this consideration leads me moreover to reflect, with augmented satisfaction, on my offer to Elizabeth last November; for had she replied otherwise, I must have been involved in your disgrace, instead of the mere sorrow which I am presently condemned to. Let me then advise you, dear sir, to throw off your unworthy child from your affection for ever, and leave her to reap the fruits of her own heinous offense. And let me conclude by congratulating you, for I shall no longer be requiring Longbourn upon your death, as I shall myself be dead by the time this post reaches you— hanging from a branch of Charlotte's favourite tree, in the garden which her ladyship was so magnanimous in granting us stewardship over.

      I AM, DEAR SIR, ETC., ETC.

Mr. Gardiner did not write again till he had received an answer from Colonel Forster; and then he had nothing of a pleasant nature to send. It was not known that Wickham had a single relationship with whom he kept up any connection, and it was certain that he had no near one living. His former acquaintances had been numerous; but since he had been in the militia, it did not appear that he was on terms of particular friendship with any of them. There was no one, therefore, who could be pointed out as likely to give any news of him. And in the wretched state of his own finances, there was a very powerful motive for secrecy, in addition to his fear of discovery by Lydia's relations, for it had just transpired that he had left bastards and gaming debts behind him to a very considerable amount. Colonel Forster believed that more than a thousand pounds would be necessary to clear his expenses at Brighton, and another thousand to provide for those sorry girls he had left with the stains of shame. Mr. Gardiner did not attempt to conceal these particulars from the Longbourn family. Jane heard them with horror. "A gamester! A bastard maker!" she cried. "This is wholly unexpected. I had not an idea of it."

Mr. Gardiner added in his letter, that they might expect to see their father at home on the following day, which was Saturday.

Rendered spiritless by the ill-success of all their endeavours, he had yielded to his brother-in-law's entreaty that he would return to his family. When Mrs. Bennet was told of this, she did not express so much satisfaction as her children expected, considering what her anxiety for his life had been before.

"What, is he coming home? And without poor Lydia?" she cried. "Sure he will not leave London before he has found them. Who is to fight Wickham, and make him marry her, if he comes away?"

As Mrs. Gardiner began to wish to be at home, it was settled that she and the children should go to London, at the same time that Mr. Bennet came from it. The coach, therefore, took them the first stage of their journey, and brought its master back to Longbourn.

Mrs. Gardiner went away in all the perplexity about Elizabeth and Mr. Darcy that had attended her from that part of the world. His name had never been voluntarily mentioned before them by her niece; and Elizabeth had received no letters since her return that could come from Pemberley.

The present unhappy state of the family rendered any other excuse for the lowness of her spirits unnecessary. Elizabeth, who was by this time tolerably well acquainted with her own feelings, was perfectly aware that, had she known nothing of Darcy, she could have borne the dread of Lydia's infamy somewhat better. It would have spared her, she thought, one sleepless night out of two.

When Mr. Bennet arrived, he had all the appearance of his usual philosophic composure. He said as little as he had ever been in the habit of saying; made no mention of the business that had taken him away, and it was some time before his daughters had courage to speak of it.

It was not till the afternoon, when he had joined them at tea, that Elizabeth ventured to introduce the subject; and then, on her briefly expressing her sorrow for what he must have endured, he replied, "Say nothing of that. Who should suffer but myself? 'For every rod of wet bamboo upon the student's back, the teacher deserves two.' Did not

Master Liu say as much?"

"You must not be too severe upon yourself," replied Elizabeth.

"You may well warn me against such an evil. Human nature is so prone to fall into it! No, Lizzy, let me once in my life feel how much I have been to blame. For it was I who resolved that you should be warriors, and not ladies. It is I who saw to your instruction in the ways of death, while neglecting to teach you anything of life. Grant me my shame, for it is most deserved."

"Do you suppose them to be in London?"

"Yes; where else can they be so well concealed?"

"And Lydia used to want to go to London," added Kitty.

"She is happy then," said her father drily; "and her residence there will probably be of some duration."

Then after a short silence he continued:

"Lizzy, I bear you no ill-will for being justified in your advice to me last May, which, considering the event, shows some greatness of mind."

They were interrupted by Kitty, who came to fetch her mother's tea.

"This is a parade!" he cried. "Can I have not a moment's peace in which to suffer my misfortune? Tomorrow I will sit in my library, in my nightcap and robes of silk, and remain there till Kitty runs away."

"I am not going to run away, papa," said Kitty fretfully. "If I should ever go to Brighton, I would behave better than Lydia."

"You go to Brighton. I would not trust you so near it as Eastbourne for fifty pounds! No, Kitty, I have at last learnt to be cautious, and you will feel the effects of it. No officer is ever to enter into my house again, nor even to pass through the village. Balls will be absolutely prohibited, unless you stand up with one of your sisters. And you are never to stir out of doors till you can prove that you have spent ten hours of every day in pursuit of your studies."

Kitty, who took all these threats in a serious light, began to cry.

"Well, well," said he, "do not make yourself unhappy. If you are a good girl for the next ten years, I will take you to a review at the end of them."

CHAPTER 49

TWO DAYS AFTER Mr. Bennet's return, as Jane and Elizabeth were tracking a buck through the shrubbery behind the house, they saw the housekeeper coming towards them, and, concluding that she came to report their mother's latest fit of vomiting, went forward to meet her; but, instead of the expected news, when they approached her, she said to Miss Bennet, "I beg your pardon, madam, for interrupting you, but I was in hopes you might have got some good news from town, so I took the liberty of coming to ask."

"What do you mean, Hill? We have heard nothing from town."

"Dear madam," cried Mrs. Hill, in great astonishment, "don't you know there is an express come for master from Mr. Gardiner? He has been here this half-hour, and master has had a letter."

Away ran the girls, too eager to get in to have time for speech. They ran through the vestibule into the breakfast-room; from thence to the library; their father was in neither; and they were on the point of seeking him upstairs with their mother, when they were met by the butler, who said:

"If you are looking for my master, ma'am, he is walking towards the dojo."

Upon this information, they instantly passed through the hall once more, and ran across the lawn after their father, who was deliberately pursuing his way toward the modest building.

Elizabeth came up with him, and eagerly cried out:

"Oh, papa, what news—what news? Have you heard from my uncle?"

"Yes I have had a letter from him by express."

"Well, and what news does it bring—good or bad?"

"What is there of good to be expected?" said he, taking the letter from his pocket. "But perhaps you would like to read it."

Elizabeth impatiently caught it from his hand. Jane now came up.

"Read it aloud," said their father, "for I hardly know myself what it is about."

> Section Six East, Monday,
> August 2.

MY DEAR BROTHER,

At last I am able to send you some tidings of my niece, and such as, upon the whole, I hope it will give you satisfaction. Soon after you left me on Saturday, I was fortunate enough to find out in what part of London they were. The particulars I reserve till we meet; it is enough to know they are discovered. I have seen them both—

"Then it is as I always hoped," cried Jane; "they are married!" Elizabeth read on:

I have seen them both. They are not married, nor can I find there was any intention of being so; but I can happily report that Mr. Wickham has lately undergone a most remarkable change of heart on the subject, and wishes they be wed with the utmost expediency. He is in a most dreadful state, however, for a carriage accident has left him bedridden and unable to move his limbs, or control his personal business. I am afraid his doctors are of the opinion that he shall remain thus for the whole course of his life; but imagine their relief to know that he shall have a devoted wife to attend to his every need till death do they part. He wishes no share of your daughter's five thousand pounds, nor does he require more than five pounds per annum to offset the cost of his linens.

These are conditions which, considering everything, I had no hesitation in complying with, as far as I thought myself privileged, for you. I shall send this by express, that no time may be lost in bringing me your answer. If, as I conclude will be the case, you send me full powers to act in your name throughout the whole of this business, there will not be the smallest occasion for your coming to town again; therefore stay quiet at Longbourn, and depend on my diligence and care. Send back your answer as fast as you can, and be careful to write explicitly. We have judged it best that my niece should be married at Wickham's bedside, of which I hope you will approve, as there is little chance of his being moved. She comes to us to-day. I shall write again as soon as anything more is determined on.

> Yours, etc.,
> EDW. GARDINER.

"Is it possible?" cried Elizabeth, when she had finished. "Can it be possible that he will marry her?"

"Wickham is not so undeserving, then, as we thought him. Oh! Rendered lame by a carriage! Cruel fate!" said her sister. "My dear father, I congratulate you."

"And have you answered the letter?" cried Elizabeth.

"No; but it must be done soon."

"Oh! My dear father," she cried, "come back and write immediately. Consider how important every moment is in such a case."

"Let me write for you," said Jane, "if you dislike the trouble yourself."

"I dislike it very much," he replied; "but it must be done."

And so saying, he turned back with them, and walked towards the house.

"And may I ask," said Elizabeth; "but the terms, I suppose, must be complied with."

"Complied with! I am only ashamed of his asking so little."

"Oh! Wretched Lydia! To be a nurse for the rest of her days! And they must marry! Yet he is a cripple!"

"Yes, yes, they must marry. There is nothing else to be done. But there are two things that I want very much to know; one is, how much money your uncle has laid down to bring it about; and the other, how am I ever to pay him."

"Money! My uncle!" cried Jane, "what do you mean, sir?"

"I mean, that no man in his senses would marry Lydia on so slight a temptation as five pounds a year during my life, and nothing after I am gone."

"That is very true," said Elizabeth; "though it had not occurred to me before. His debts to be discharged, and something still to remain! Oh! It must be my uncle's doings! Generous, good man, I am afraid he has distressed himself. A small sum could not do all this."

"No," said her father; "Wickham's a fool if he takes her with a farthing less than ten thousand pounds, especially since he will now have little opportunity of earning and fortune of his own. I should be sorry to think so ill of him, in the very beginning of our relationship."

"Ten thousand pounds! Heaven forbid! How is half such a sum to be repaid?"

Mr. Bennet made no answer, and each of them, deep in thought, continued silent till they reached the house. Their father then went on to the library to write, and the girls walked into the breakfast-room.

"And they are really to be married!" cried Elizabeth, as soon as they were by themselves. "How strange this is! And for this we are to be thankful. That they should marry, small as is their chance of happiness, and wretched as is his broken body, we are forced to rejoice. Oh, Lydia!"

"I comfort myself with thinking," replied Jane, "that he certainly would not marry Lydia if he had not a real regard for her. Though our kind uncle has done something towards clearing him, I cannot believe that ten thousand pounds, or anything like it, has been advanced. He has children of his own, and may have more. How could he spare half ten thousand pounds?"

"If he were ever able to learn what Wickham's debts have been," said Elizabeth, "and how much is settled on his side on our sister, we shall exactly know what Mr. Gardiner has done for them, because Wickham has not sixpence of his own. The kindness of my uncle and aunt can never be requited. Their affording her their personal protection and countenance, is such a sacrifice to her advantage as years of gratitude cannot enough acknowledge. If such goodness does not make her miserable now, she will never deserve to be happy! What a meeting for her, when she first sees my aunt!"

"We must endeavour to forget all that has passed on either side," said Jane, "I hope and trust they will yet be happy. His consenting to marry her is a proof, I will believe, that he is come to a right way of thinking. Their mutual affection will steady them; and I flatter myself they will settle so quietly—he in his bed, and she at his side, as may in time make their past imprudence forgotten."

"Their conduct has been such," replied Elizabeth, "as neither you, nor I, nor anybody can ever forget. It is useless to talk of it, except to persuade our younger sisters that they must renounce their blood oath post haste."

It now occurred to the girls that their mother was in all likelihood perfectly ignorant of what had happened. They went to the library, therefore, and asked their father whether he would not wish them to make it known to her. He was writing and, without raising his head, coolly replied:

"Just as you please."

"May we take my uncle's letter to read to her?"

"Take whatever you like, and get away."

Elizabeth took the letter from his writing-table, and they went upstairs together. Mary and Kitty were both with Mrs. Bennet: one communication would, therefore, do for all. After a slight preparation for good news, the letter was read aloud. Mrs. Bennet could hardly contain herself. As soon as Jane had read Mr. Gardiner's hope of Lydia's being soon married, her joy burst forth, and every following sentence added to its exuberance. She was now in an irritation as violent from delight, as she had ever been fidgety from alarm and vexation. To know that her daughter would be married was enough. She was disturbed by no fear for her happiness as the eternal nurse to a lame, fortuneless husband, nor humbled by any remembrance of her misconduct.

"My dear, dear Lydia!" she cried. "This is delightful indeed! She will be married! I shall see her again! She will be married at sixteen! My good, kind brother! I knew how it would be. I knew he would manage everything! How I long to see her! And to see dear Wickham too! Dear, crippled Wickham! What a husband he shall make! In a short time I shall have a daughter married. *Mrs. Wickham!* How well it sounds! And she was only sixteen last June. My dear Jane, I am in such a flutter, that I am sure I can't write; so I will dictate, and you write for me. We will settle with your father about the money afterwards; but the things should be ordered immediately."

She was then proceeding to all the particulars of calico, muslin, and silver bedpans, and would shortly have dictated some very plentiful orders, had not Jane, though with some difficulty, persuaded her to wait till her father was at leisure to be consulted. One day's delay, she observed, would be of small importance; and her mother was too happy to be quite so obstinate as usual. Other schemes, too, came into her head.

"I will go to Meryton," said she, "as soon as I am dressed, and tell the good, good news to my sister Philips. And as I come back, I can call on Lady Lucas. Her grief for dear Charlotte will be much assuaged by this joyous development! Kitty, run down and order the carriage. An airing would do me a great deal of good, I am sure. Girls, can I do anything for you in Meryton? Oh! Here comes Hill! My dear Hill, have you heard the good news? Miss Lydia is going to be married; and you shall all have a bowl of punch to make merry at her wedding."

CHAPTER 50

M R. BENNET HAD VERY OFTEN wished before this period of his life that, instead of spending his whole income every year, he had set aside an annual sum for the better provision of his children, and of his wife, if she survived him. He now wished it more than ever. Had he done his duty in that respect, Lydia need not have been indebted to her uncle for whatever of honour or credit could now be purchased for her. The satisfaction of prevailing on one of the most worthless young men in Great Britain might have been a trifle less disappointing than it now was.

He was seriously concerned that a cause of so little advantage to anyone should be forwarded at the sole expense of his brother-in-law, and he was determined, if possible, to find out the extent of his assistance, and to discharge the obligation as soon as he could.

When first Mr. Bennet had married, economy was held to be perfectly useless, for, of course, they were to have a son. The son was to join in cutting off the entail, as soon as he should be of age, and the widow and younger children would by that means be provided for. Five daughters successively entered the world, but yet the son was to come; and Mrs. Bennet, for many years after Lydia's birth, had been certain that he would. This event had at last been despaired of, but it was then too late to be saving. Mrs. Bennet had no turn for economy, and her husband's love of independence had alone prevented their exceeding their income.

Five thousand pounds was settled by marriage articles on Mrs. Bennet and the children. But in what proportions it should be divided amongst the latter depended on the will of the parents. This was one point, with regard to Lydia, at least, which was now to be settled, for Mr.

Bennet felt no obligation to leave her a single sixpence. In terms of grateful acknowledgment for the kindness of his brother, though expressed most concisely, he then delivered on paper his perfect approbation of all that was done, and his willingness to fulfill the engagements that had been made for him. He had never before supposed that, could Wickham be prevailed on to marry his daughter, it would be done with so little inconvenience to himself as by the present arrangement.

That it would be done with such trifling exertion on his side, too, was another very welcome surprise; for his wish at present was to have as little trouble in the business as possible. When the first transports of rage which had produced his activity in seeking her were over, he naturally returned to all his former lethargy. His letter was soon dispatched; for, though dilatory in undertaking business, he was quick in its execution. He begged to know further particulars of what he was indebted to his brother, but was too angry with Lydia to send any message to her.

The good news spread quickly through the house, and with proportionate speed through the neighbourhood. It was borne in the latter with decent philosophy. To be sure, it would have been more for the advantage of conversation had Miss Lydia Bennet come upon the town; or, as the happiest alternative, been secluded from the world, in some distant Eastern land. But there was much to be talked of in marrying her; and the good-natured wishes for her well-doing which had proceeded before from all the spiteful old ladies in Meryton lost but a little of their spirit in this change of circumstances, because with such a lame, indebted husband her misery was considered certain.

It was a fortnight since Mrs. Bennet had been downstairs; but on this happy day she again took her seat at the head of her table, and in spirits oppressively high. No sentiment of shame gave a damp to her triumph. The marriage of a daughter, which had been the first object of her wishes since Jane was sixteen, was now on the point of accomplishment, and her thoughts and her words ran wholly on those attendants of elegant nuptials, fine muslins, new muskets, and servants. She was busily searching through the neighbourhood for a proper house for her daughter, and, without knowing or considering what their income might be, rejected many as deficient in size and importance.

"Haye Park might do," said she, "if the Gouldings could quit it— or the great house at Stoke, if the drawing-room were larger; but Ashworth is too far off! I could not bear to have her ten miles from me; and as for Pulvis Lodge, the attics are dreadful."

Her husband allowed her to talk on without interruption while the servants remained. But when they had withdrawn, he said to her:

"Mrs. Bennet, before you take any or all of these houses for your son and daughter, let us come to a right understanding. Into one house in this neighbourhood they shall never have admittance. I will not encourage the impudence of either, by receiving them at Longbourn."

A long dispute followed this declaration; but Mr. Bennet was firm. It soon led to another; and Mrs. Bennet found, with amazement and horror, that her husband would not advance a guinea to buy clothes for his daughter. He protested that she should receive from him no mark of affection whatever on the occasion. Mrs. Bennet could hardly comprehend it. That his anger could be carried to such a point of inconceivable resentment as to refuse his daughter a privilege with-out which her marriage would scarcely seem valid, exceeded all she could believe possible. She was more alive to the disgrace which her want of new clothes must reflect on her daughter's nuptials, than to any sense of shame at her future son's having abducted her daughter a fortnight before they took place.

Elizabeth was now most heartily sorry that she had, from the dis-tress of the moment, been led to make Mr. Darcy acquainted with their fears for her sister; for since her marriage would so shortly give the proper termination to the elopement, they might hope to conceal its unfavourable beginning from all those who were not immediately on the spot.

She had no fear of its spreading farther through his means. There were few people on whose secrecy she would have more confidently depended; but, at the same time, there was no one whose knowledge of a sister's frailty would have mortified her so much—not, however, from any fear of disadvantage to herself, for she expected there would be no more civilities between them. Had Lydia's marriage been concluded on the most honourable terms, it was not to be supposed that Mr. Darcy would connect himself with a family where, to every other objection, would now be added an alliance with a man whom he so justly scorned.

"What a triumph for him," she often thought, "could he know that the proposals which she had proudly spurned only four months ago, would now have been most gladly and gratefully received!" He was as generous, she doubted not, as the most generous of his sex; but while he was mortal, there must be a triumph.

She began now to comprehend that he was exactly the man who, in disposition and talents, would most suit her. His understanding and temper, though unlike her own, would have answered all her wishes. It was an union that must have been to the advantage of both; by her aggression and liveliness, his introversion might have been softened, his manners improved; and from his judgement, information, and knowledge of the world, she must have received benefit of greater importance. What a pair of warriors they would make! Sparring by the river at Pemberley; crossing the Altai Mountains in a fine coach on their way to Kyoto or Shanghai—their children eager to master death as their mother and father had before them.

But no such happy marriage could now teach the admiring multitude what connubial felicity really was. An union of a different tendency, and precluding the possibility of the other, was soon to be formed in their family. How Wickham and Lydia were to be supported in tolerable independence, she could not imagine. But how little of permanent happiness could belong to a couple who were only brought together by an abduction, an attempted murder, and a carriage accident, she could easily conjecture.

Mr. Gardiner soon wrote again to his brother. The principal purport of his letter was to inform them that Mr. Wickham had resolved on quitting the militia.

> It was greatly my wish that he should do so, as soon as his marriage was fixed on. And I think you will agree with me, in considering that he can do little good in the fight against the zombies given his present condition. It is Mr. Wickham's intention to enter the priesthood; and among his former friends, there are still some who are able and willing to assist him in this endeavour. He has the promise of joining a special seminary for the lame in northernmost Ireland. It is an advantage to have it so far from this part of the kingdom. He promises fairly; and I hope among different people, where they may each have a character to preserve, they will both be more prudent. I have written to Colonel Forster, to inform him of our present arrangements, and to request that he will satisfy the various creditors of Mr. Wickham in and near Brighton, with assurances of speedy payment, for which I have pledged myself. And will you give yourself the trouble of carrying similar assurances to his creditors in Meryton, of whom I shall subjoin a list according to his information? He has given in all his debts; I hope at least he has not deceived us. I understand from Mrs. Gardiner, that my niece is very desirous of seeing you all before she leaves for Ireland. She is well, and begs to be dutifully remembered to you and your mother.
> Yours, etc.,
> E. GARDINER.

Mr. Bennet and his daughters saw all the advantages of Wickham's removal from England as clearly as Mr. Gardiner could do. But Mrs.

Bennet was not so well pleased with it. Lydia's being settled in the north, just when she had expected most pleasure and pride in her company, was a severe disappointment; and, besides, it was such a pity that Lydia should be taken from a regiment where she was acquainted with everybody, and could instruct soldiers in new methods of annihilating the walking dead.

"She is so fond of Mrs. Forster," said she, "it will be quite shocking to send her away! And there are several of the young men, too, that she likes very much."

His daughter's request, for such it might be considered, of being admitted into her family again before she set off for the North, received at first an absolute negative. But Jane and Elizabeth, who agreed in wishing, for the sake of their sister's feelings and consequence, that she should be noticed on her marriage by her parents, urged him so earnestly yet so rationally and so mildly, to receive her and her husband at Longbourn, as soon as they were married, that he was prevailed on to think as they thought, and act as they wished. And their mother had the satisfaction of knowing that she would be able to show her married daughter in the neighbourhood before she was banished to St. Lazarus Seminary for the Lame at Kilkenny. When Mr. Bennet wrote again to his brother, therefore, he sent his permission for them to come; and it was settled, that as soon as the ceremony was over, they should proceed to Longbourn. Elizabeth was surprised, however, that Wickham should consent to such a scheme, considering what a dreadful visage he must present in his sorry condition.

CHAPTER 51

THEIR SISTER'S WEDDING DAY arrived; and Jane and Elizabeth felt for her probably more than Lydia felt for herself.

The carriage was sent to meet them, and they were to return in it by dinner-time. Their arrival was dreaded by the elder Miss Bennets, and Jane more especially, who imagined the feelings which would have attended herself, had she been forced to marry her crippled abductor, and was wretched in the thought of what her sister must endure for the rest of her miserable life.

They came. The family were assembled in the breakfast room to receive them. Smiles decked the face of Mrs. Bennet as the carriage drove up to the door; her husband looked impenetrably grave; her daughters, alarmed, anxious, uneasy.

Lydia's voice was heard in the vestibule; the door was thrown open, and she ran into the room. Her mother stepped forwards, embraced her, and welcomed her with rapture; gave her hand, with an affectionate smile, to Wickham, who was carried through the door by servants. Leather straps kept him fastened to his traveling bed, which was redolent of stale piss; and Elizabeth, who had been expecting as much, was nevertheless shocked at the severity of his injuries. His face remained bruised—his eyes half closed with swelling. His legs were broken and bent beyond hope, and his speech much affected. "Dear, sweet Wickham!" cried Mrs. Bennet. "What a fine priest you shall make! What a delightful husband!" Wickham replied with a polite moan.

Their reception from Mr. Bennet, to whom they then turned, was not quite so cordial. His countenance rather gained in austerity; and he scarcely opened his lips. The stench of Wickham's bed, indeed, was enough to provoke him. Elizabeth was disgusted, and even Miss Bennet was shocked. Lydia was Lydia still; untamed, unabashed, wild, noisy, and fearless. She turned from sister to sister, demanding their congratulations; and when at length they all sat down—save Wickham, who was placed by the fire—looked eagerly round the room, took notice of some little alteration in it, and observed, with a laugh, that it was a great while since she had been there.

There was no want of discourse. The bride and her mother could neither of them talk fast enough. They seemed each of them to have the happiest memories in the world. Nothing of the past was recollected with pain; and Lydia led voluntarily to subjects which her sisters would not have alluded to for the world.

"Only think of its being three months," she cried, "since I went away; it seems but a fortnight I declare; and yet there have been things enough happened in the time. Good gracious! When I went away, I am sure I had no more idea of being married till I came back again! Though I thought it would be very good fun if I was."

Her father lifted up his eyes. Jane was distressed. Elizabeth looked expressively at Lydia; but she, who never heard nor saw anything of which she chose to be insensible, gaily continued, "Oh! Mamma, do the people hereabouts know I am married to-day? I was afraid they might not; and we passed William Goulding, whose curricle had been over-turned and horses devoured, so I was determined he should know it, and so I let down the side-glass next to him, and took off my glove, and let my hand just rest upon the window frame, so that he might see the ring, and then I bowed and smiled like anything. He yelled after us—something about his son being trapped; but oh! Mamma, I am sure he saw the ring. Oh! Think of how the news will spread!"

Elizabeth could bear it no longer. She got up, and ran out of the room; and returned no more, till she heard them passing through the hall to the dining parlour. She then joined them soon enough to see Lydia, with anxious parade, walk up to her mother's right hand, and hear her say to her eldest sister, "Ah! Jane, I take your place now, and you must go lower, because I am a married woman."

It was not to be supposed that time or the odor of stale piss would give Lydia that embarrassment from which she had been so wholly free at first. Her ease and good spirits increased. She longed to see Mrs. Philips, the Lucases, and all their other neighbours, and to hear herself called "Mrs. Wickham" by each of them; and in the mean time, she went after dinner to show her ring, and boast of being married, to Mrs. Hill and the two housemaids.

"Well, mamma," said she, when they were all returned to the breakfast room, "and what do you think of my husband? Is not he a charming man? I am sure my sisters must all envy me. I only hope they may have half my good luck. They must all go to Brighton. That is the place to get husbands. What a pity it is, mamma, we did not all go."

"Very true; and if I had my will, we should. But my dear Lydia, I don't at all like your going such a way off. Must it be so?"

"Oh, Lord! Yes—there is nothing in that. I shall like it of all things. You and papa, and my sisters, must come to the seminary and see us. We shall be at Kilkerry these next three years, and I will take care to get good husbands for them all."

"I should like it beyond anything!" said her mother.

"Oh! So many young priests! And each of them in dire need of a loving, caring wife! I dare say I shall see each of my sisters married before winter!"

"I thank you for my share of the favour," said Elizabeth; "but I do not particularly desire the rest of my life spent emptying piss pots."

Their visitors were not to remain above ten days with them. Mr. Wickham had received his letter of acceptance to Kilkerry, and given his condition, the journey North would be frightfully slow.

No one but Mrs. Bennet regretted that their stay would be so short; and she made the most of the time by visiting about with her daughter, and having very frequent parties at home, so that their neighbors might congratulate Mr. Wickham, who remained by the fire during the whole of their stay.

Lydia was exceedingly fond of him. He was her dear Wickham on every occasion. He did every thing best in the world; and she was sure he would kill more zombies this season, than any body else in the country, in spite of the fact that he had no use of his arms. One morning, soon after their arrival, as she was sitting with her two elder sisters, she said to Elizabeth:

"Lizzy, I never gave you an account of my wedding. Are not you curious to hear how it was managed?"

"No really," replied Elizabeth; "I think there cannot be too little said on the subject."

"La! You are so strange! But I must tell you how it went off. We were married, you know, at St. Clement's, because it had the fewest steps to carry my beloved up. And it was settled that we should all be there by eleven o'clock. My uncle and aunt and I were to go together; and the others were to meet us at the church. Well, Monday morning came, and I was in such a fuss! I was so afraid, you know, that something would happen to put it off, for there had lately been some trouble on the east wall, and everywhere one heard talk of relinquishing the neighborhood for safety. And there was my aunt, all the time I was dressing, preaching and talking away just as if she was reading a sermon. However, I did not hear above one word in ten, for I was thinking, you may suppose, of my dear Wickham. I longed to know whether he would be married in his blue coat, or if he had soiled it like the others."

"Well, and so we breakfasted at ten as usual; I thought it would never be over; for, by the bye, you are to understand, that my uncle and aunt were horrid unpleasant all the time I was with them. If you'll believe me, I did not once put my foot out of doors, though I was there a fortnight. Not one party, or scheme, or anything. To be sure London was rather thin because of the attacks, but, however, the Little Theatre was open. Well, and so just as the carriage came to the door, my uncle was called away upon business to that horrid powder factory. Well, I was so frightened I did not know what to do, for my uncle was to give me away; and if we were beyond the hour, we could not be married all day. But, luckily, he came back again in ten minutes' time, and then we all set out. However, I recollected afterwards that if he had been prevented going, the wedding need not be put off, for Mr. Darcy might have done as well."

"Mr. Darcy!" repeated Elizabeth, in utter amazement.

"Oh, yes! He was to come there with Wickham, you know. But gracious me! I quite forgot! I ought not to have said a word about it. I promised them so faithfully! What will Wickham say? It was to be such a secret!"

"If it was to be secret," said Jane, "say not another word on the subject. You may depend upon my seeking no further."

"Oh! Certainly," said Elizabeth, though burning with curiosity; "we will ask you no questions."

"Thank you," said Lydia, "for if you did, I should certainly tell you all, and then Wickham would surely punish me with an ill-timed soiling."

On such encouragement to ask, Elizabeth was forced to put it out of her power by running away.

But to live in ignorance on such a point was impossible; or at least it was impossible not to try for information. Mr. Darcy had been at her sister's wedding. What possible motive could he have had? Conjectures, rapid and wild, hurried into her brain; but she was satisfied with none. Those that best pleased her, as placing his conduct in the noblest light, seemed most improbable. She could not bear such suspense; and hastily seizing a sheet of paper, wrote a short letter to her aunt, to request an explanation of what Lydia had dropt.

"You may readily comprehend," she added, "what my curiosity must be to know how a person unconnected with any of us, and (comparatively speaking) a stranger to our family, should have been amongst you at such a time. Pray write instantly, and let me understand it—unless it is, for very cogent reasons, to remain in the secrecy which Lydia seems to think necessary; and then I must endeavour to be satisfied with ignorance."

"And my dear aunt," she added to herself, as she finished the letter; "if you do not tell me in an honourable manner, I shall certainly be reduced to tricks and stratagems to find it out."

CHAPTER 52

ELIZABETH HAD THE SATISFACTION of receiving an answer to her letter as soon as she possibly could. She was no sooner in possession of it than, hurrying into the dojo, where she was least likely to be interrupted, she sat down and prepared to be happy; for the length of the letter convinced her that it did not contain a denial.

Section Six East, Sept. 6.

MY DEAR NIECE,

I have just received your letter, and shall devote this whole morning to answering it, as I foresee that a little writing will not comprise what I have to tell you.

On the very day of my coming home from Longbourn, your uncle had a most unexpected visitor. Mr. Darcy called, and was shut up with him several hours. It was all over before I arrived; so my curiosity was not so dreadfully racked as yours seems to have been. He came to tell Mr. Gardiner that he had found out where your sister and Mr. Wickham were. From what I can collect, he left Derbyshire only one day after ourselves, and came to town with the resolution of hunting for them. Mr. Darcy felt himself to blame for not making Wickham's worthlessness more known—for if he had, no young woman of character would have dared love or confide in him. He generously imputed the whole to his mistaken pride, and confessed that he had before thought it beneath him to lay his private actions open to the world. He called it, therefore, his duty to step forward, and endeavour to remedy an evil which had been brought on by himself.

There is a lady, it seems, a Mrs. Younge, who was some time ago governess to Miss Darcy, and was dismissed from her charge on some cause of disapprobation, though he did not say what. She then took a large house in Edward Street, and has since maintained herself by letting lodgings. This Mrs. Younge was, he knew, intimately acquainted with Wickham; and he went to her for intelligence of him as soon as he got to town. But it was two or three minutes of savage beating before he could get from her what he wanted. She would not betray her trust, I suppose, without an application of severe blows about the head and neck. At length, however, our kind friend procured the wished-for direction. They were in Hen's Quarry Street. Mr. Darcy saw Wickham, and with no want of force, insisted on seeing Lydia. His first object with her, he acknowledged, had been to persuade her to quit her present disgraceful situation, and return to her friends as soon as they could be prevailed on to receive her, offering his assistance, as far as it would go. But he found Lydia absolutely resolved on remaining where she was. She cared for none of her friends; she wanted no help of his; she would not hear of leaving Wickham, who, in spite of his abducting her, she claimed to love more than anything on earth. Since such were her feelings, Mr. Darcy had but one choice to restore her honour—to secure and expedite a marriage between she and Wickham. But the latter had no intentions of marrying, and as to his future situation, he could conjecture very little about it. He must go somewhere, but he did not know where, and he knew he should have nothing to live on.

Mr. Darcy asked him why he did not marry your sister at once. Though Mr. Bennet was not imagined to be very rich, he would be able to do something for him, and his situation would be benefited by marriage. But he found, in reply to this question, that Wickham still cherished the hope of more effectually making his fortune by marriage into a family of greater means.

Mr. Darcy saw an opportunity here, and met with Wickham again to propose a solution beneficial to all parties. Mr. Wickham, after a great deal of consideration, agreed.

Every thing being settled between them, Mr. Darcy's next step was to make your uncle acquainted with the arrangement, and he first called in Section Six East the evening before I came home, and they had a great deal of talk together.

They met again on Sunday, and then *I* saw him too. It was not all settled before Monday: as soon as it was, the express was sent off to Longbourn. The terms were as follows: Wickham's debts were to be paid, amounting, I believe, to considerably more than a thousand pounds, plus another thousand per annum to sustain him. In return, he would marry Lydia, thus restoring her honour, and that of the Bennet family. Second, he would allow Mr. Darcy to render him lame, as punishment for a lifetime of vice and betrayal, and to ensure that he would never lay another hand in anger, nor leave another bastard behind. To spare what little of his reputation remained, the injuries would be attributed to a carriage accident. Finally, he would pursue the priesthood, in hopes that the teachings of Christ would improve his general character. Darcy personally saw to it that all of this was attended to with the greatest expedience. (I dare say he took particular pleasure in beating Mr. Wickham lame.)

I fancy, Lizzy, that stubbornness is the real defect of his character, after all. He has been accused of many faults at different times, but this is the true one. He insisted on shouldering the entire burden himself; though I am sure (and I do not speak it to be thanked, therefore say nothing about it), your uncle would most readily have settled the whole.

He and your uncle battled it together for a long time, which was more than either the gentleman or lady concerned in it deserved. But at last your uncle was forced to yield, and instead of being allowed to be of use to his niece, was forced to put up with only having the probable credit of it, which went sorely against the grain; and I really believe your letter this morning gave him great pleasure, because it required an explanation that would rob him of his borrowed feathers, and give the praise where it was due. But, Lizzy, this must go no farther than yourself, or Jane at most.

The reason why all this was to be done by him alone, was such as I have given above. It was owing to him, to his reserve, that Wickham's character had been so misunderstood. Perhaps there was some truth in this; though I doubt whether *his* reserve, or *anybody's* reserve, can be answerable to anything so scandalous. But in spite of all this fine talking, my dear Lizzy, you may rest perfectly assured that your uncle would never have yielded, if we had not been convinced of Mr. Darcy's having *another interest* in the affair.

When all this was resolved on, he returned again to his friends, who were still staying at Pemberley; but it was agreed that he should be in London once more when the wedding took place, and all money matters were then to receive the last finish.

I believe I have now told you every thing. It is a relation which you tell me is to give you great surprise; I hope at least it will not afford you any displeasure. Lydia came to us; and Wickham, newly lame, was carried to the house to recover, and to be fitted for his traveling bed, which Mr. Darcy generously paid for. I would not tell you how little I was satisfied with your sister's behaviour while she remained with us, if I had not perceived, by Jane's letter last Wednesday, that her conduct on coming home was exactly as reprehensible, and therefore what I now tell you can give you no fresh pain.

Mr. Darcy was punctual in his return, and as Lydia informed you, attended the wedding. He dined with us the next day, gave his congratulations to the new couple, and took leave. Will you be very angry with me, my dear Lizzy, if I take this opportunity of saying how much I like him. His behaviour to us has, in every respect, been as pleasing as when we were in Derbyshire. His understanding and opinions all please me; he wants nothing but a little more liveliness, and that, if he marry prudently, his wife may teach him. I thought him very sly—he hardly ever mentioned your name. But slyness seems the fashion.

Pray forgive me if I have been very presuming, or at least do not punish me so far as to exclude me from Pemberley. I shall never be quite happy till I have been all round the park. A low phaeton, pulled by a pair of captured zombies, would be the very thing.

But I must write no more. There is some commotion on the street, and I fear the east gate has fallen again.

Yours, very sincerely,

M. GARDINER.

The contents of this letter threw Elizabeth into a flutter of spirits, in which it was difficult to determine whether pleasure or pain bore the greatest share. The vague and unsettled suspicions of what Mr. Darcy might have been doing to forward her sister's match, which she had feared too great to be probable, and at the same time wished for more than anything, were proved beyond their greatest extent to be true! He had followed them purposely to town, he had taken on himself to defile his hands with the blood of a woman whom he surely never wished to see again, and he was reduced to meet, reason with, persuade, and finally bribe, the man whom he always most wished to avoid, and whose very name it was punishment to him to pronounce. He had done all this for Lydia—a girl whom he could neither regard nor esteem. Brother-in-law of Wickham! Every kind of pride must revolt from the connection. He had, to be sure, done much. She was ashamed to think how much. Oh! How she longed to see her seven scabs opened and bleeding once more! True, Darcy had given a reason for his interference, which asked no extraordinary stretch of belief. It was reasonable that he should feel he had been wrong; and though she would not place herself as his principal inducement, she could, perhaps, believe that remaining partiality for her might assist his endeavours in a cause where her peace of mind must be materially concerned. It was painful, exceedingly painful, to know that Elizabeth and her family were under obligations to a person who could never receive a return. They owed the restoration of Lydia, her character, every thing, to him. Oh! How heartily did she grieve over every ungracious sensation she had ever encouraged, every saucy speech she had ever directed towards him. For herself she was humbled; but she was proud of him. Proud that in a cause of compassion and honour, he had been able to get the better of himself. She read over her aunt's commendation of him again and again. It was hardly enough; but it pleased her. She was even sensible of some pleasure, though mixed with regret, on finding how steadfastly both she and her uncle had been persuaded that affection and confidence subsisted between Mr. Darcy and herself.

She was roused from her reflections by some one's approach. She scarcely had time to fold the letter and remove it from sight before a pair of servants entered the dojo carrying Mr. Wickham on his traveling bed. They set him down on the floor beside her and took their leave.

"I am afraid I interrupt your solitary ramble, my dear sister?" mumbled he through a shattered jaw.

"You certainly do," she replied with a smile; "but it does not follow that the interruption must be unwelcome."

"I should be sorry indeed, if it were. I thought the peace of the dojo a most refreshing change from my little corner of the breakfast parlor."

"Are the others coming out?"

"I do not know. Mrs. Bennet and Lydia are going in the carriage to Meryton. And so, my dear sister, I find, from our uncle and aunt, that you have actually seen Pemberley."

She replied in the affirmative.

"I almost envy you the pleasure, and yet I believe it would be too much for me in my sorry state. And you saw the old housekeeper, I suppose? Poor Reynolds, she was always very fond of me—to see me thus affected would be quite a shock to her. But of course she did not mention my name to you."

"Yes, she did."

"And what did she say?"

"That you were gone into the army, and she was afraid that—that you had not turned out well. At such a distance as that, you know, things are strangely misrepresented."

"Certainly," he replied, biting his lips. Elizabeth hoped she had silenced him; but he soon afterwards said:

"Did you see Darcy while you were there? I thought I understood from the Gardiners that you had."

"Yes; he introduced us to his sister."

"And do you like her?"

"Very much."

"I have heard, indeed, that she is uncommonly improved within this year or two. When I last saw her, she was not very promising. I am very glad you liked her. I hope she will turn out well."

"I dare say she will; she has got over some rather extraordinary challenges."

"Did you go by the village of Kympton?"

"I do not recollect that we did."

"I mention it, because it is the living which I ought to have had. A most delightful place! Excellent house! It would have suited me in every respect."

"I have heard from authority, which I thought as good, that it was left you conditionally only, and at the will of the present patron."

"You have. Yes, there was something in that; I told you so from the first, you may remember."

"I did hear, too, that you were a most disagreeable child, exceedingly cruel to the elder Darcy's servants, and disrespectful of his wishes. As to your more recent behaviour, I have heard nothing that would persuade me of your having improved; whether it be your debts of honour, or the countless bastards strewn about His Majesty's empire."

To this, Wickham could find no reply other than a fresh, aromatic soiling. Elizabeth stood and grabbed one end of his traveling bed, lifting it to her waist. Then, with a good-humoured smile, she said:

"Come, Mr. Wickham, we are brother and sister, you know. Do not let us quarrel about the past. In future, I hope we shall be always of one mind."

She dragged his bed across the dojo floor, through the grass, and towards the house.

CHAPTER 53

MR. WICKHAM WAS SO PERFECTLY DISMAYED by this conversation that he never again provoked his dear sister Elizabeth by introducing the subject of it; and she was pleased to find that she had said enough to keep him quiet.

The day of his and Lydia's departure soon came, and Mrs. Bennet was forced to submit to a separation, which, as her husband by no means entered into her scheme of their all going to Ireland, was likely to continue at least a twelvemonth.

"Oh! My dear Lydia," she cried, "when shall we meet again?"

"Oh, Lord! I don't know. Not these two or three years, perhaps."

"Write to me very often, my dear."

"As often as I can. But you know married women have never much time for writing. My sisters may write to me. They will have nothing else to do."

Mr. Wickham's adieus were no more affectionate than his wife's. He said little as his traveling bed was hoisted into the carriage, accompanied by spare linens and feeding jars.

"He is as fine a fellow," said Mr. Bennet, as soon as they were out of the house, "as ever I saw. I dare say I much prefer him in this relaxed state."

The loss of her daughter made Mrs. Bennet very dull for several days.

"I often think," said she, "that there is nothing so bad as parting with one's friends. One seems so forlorn without them."

"This is the consequence of marrying a daughter," said Elizabeth. "It must make you better satisfied that your other four are single."

"It is no such thing. Lydia does not leave me because she is married, but only because St. Lazarus happens to be so far off. If it had been nearer, she would not have gone so soon."

But the spiritless condition which this event threw her into was shortly relieved, and her mind opened again to the agitation of hope, by an article of news which then began to be in circulation. The housekeeper at Netherfield had received orders to prepare for the arrival of her master, who was coming down in a day or two to inspect his new staff, and the reinforcements made to the kitchen. Mrs. Bennet was quite in the fidgets. She looked at Jane, and smiled, and shook her head by turns.

"Well, well, and so Mr. Bingley is coming down. Not that I care about it, though. He is nothing to us, you know, and I am sure I never want to see him again. But, however, he is very welcome to come to

Netherfield, if he likes it. Is it quite certain he is coming?"

"You may depend on it," replied the other, "for Mrs. Nicholls was in Meryton last night; I saw her passing by, and went out myself on purpose to know the truth of it; and she told me that it was certain true. He comes down on Thursday at the latest, very likely on Wednesday. She was going to the butcher's, she told me, on purpose to order in some meat on Wednesday, and she has got three couple of ducks just fit to be killed."

Jane Bennet had not been able to hear of his coming without changing colour. It was many months since she had mentioned his name to Elizabeth; but now, as soon as they were alone together, she said:

"I saw you look at me to-day, Lizzy, when my aunt told us of the present report; and I know I appeared distressed. But don't imagine it was from any silly cause. I was only confused for the moment, because I felt that I should be looked at. I do assure you that the news does not affect me either with pleasure or pain. I am glad of one thing, that he comes alone; because we shall see the less of him."

Elizabeth did not know what to make of it. Had she not seen Mr. Bingley in Derbyshire, she might have supposed him capable of coming there with no other view than what was acknowledged; but she still thought him partial to Jane, and she wavered as to the greater probability of his coming there with his friend's permission, or being bold enough to come without it.

"Yet it is hard," she sometimes thought, "that this poor man cannot come to a house which he has legally hired, without raising all this speculation! I will leave him to himself."

In spite of what her sister declared, and really believed to be her feelings in the expectation of his arrival, Elizabeth could easily perceive that her spirits were affected by it. They were more disturbed, more unequal, than she had often seen them. No longer did she suggest morning games of Kiss Me Deer or evening games of Crypt and Coffin. So occupied were her thoughts that Mary was able to pin her during afternoon grappling for the first time.

The subject which had been so warmly canvassed between their parents, about a twelvemonth ago, was now brought forward again.

"As soon as ever Mr. Bingley comes, my dear," said Mrs. Bennet, "you will wait on him of course."

"No, no. You forced me into visiting him last year, and promised, if I went to see him, he should marry one of my daughters. But it ended in nothing, and I will not be sent on a fool's errand again. Not by a fool such as yourself, anyhow."

His wife represented to him how absolutely necessary such an attention would be from all the neighbouring gentlemen, on his returning to Netherfield.

"'Tis an etiquette I despise," said he. "If he wants our society, let him seek it. He knows where we live. I will not spend my hours in running after my neighbours every time they go away and come back again."

"Well, all I know is, that it will be abominably rude if you do not wait on him. But, however, that shan't prevent my asking him to dine here, I am determined."

Mr. Bingley arrived. Mrs. Bennet, through the assistance of servants, contrived to have the earliest tidings of it, that the period of anxiety and fretfulness on her side might be as long as it could. She counted the days that must intervene before their invitation could be sent; hopeless of seeing him before. But on the third morning after his arrival in Hertfordshire, she saw him, from her dressing-room window, enter the paddock and ride towards the house with his French musket.

Her daughters were eagerly called to partake of her joy. Jane resolutely kept her place at the table; but Elizabeth, to satisfy her mother, went to the window—she looked, she saw Mr. Darcy with him, and sat down again by her sister, suddenly alarmed beyond the capacity for rational thought.

"There is a gentleman with him, mamma," said Kitty; "who can it be?"

"Some acquaintance or other, my dear, I suppose; I am sure I do not know."

"La!" replied Kitty, "it looks just like that man that used to be with him before. Mr. What's-his-name. That tall, proud man."

"Good gracious! Mr. Darcy! And so it does, I vow. Well, any friend of Mr. Bingley's will always be welcome here, to be sure; but else I must say that I hate the very sight of him."

Jane looked at Elizabeth with surprise and concern. She knew but little of their meeting in Derbyshire, and therefore felt for the awkwardness which must attend her sister, in seeing him almost for the first time after receiving his explanatory letter. Both sisters were uncomfortable enough. Each felt for the other, and of course for themselves; and their mother talked on, of her dislike of Mr. Darcy, and her resolution to be civil to him only as Mr. Bingley's friend, without being heard by either of them. But Elizabeth had sources of uneasiness which could not be suspected by Jane, to whom she had never yet had courage to reveal her aunt's letter, or to relate her own change of sentiment towards him. To Jane, he could be only a man whose proposals she had refused, and whose head she had sent crashing into a mantle; but to her own more extensive information, he was the person to whom the whole family were indebted, and whom she regarded herself with an interest, if not quite so tender, at least as reasonable and just as what Jane felt for Bingley. Her astonishment at his coming—at his coming to Netherfield, to Longbourn, and voluntarily seeking her again, was almost equal to what she had known on first witnessing his altered behaviour in Derbyshire.

The colour which had been driven from her face, returned for half a minute with an additional glow, and a smile of delight added lustre to her eyes, as she thought for that space of time that his affection and wishes must still be unshaken. But she would not be secure.

"Let me first see how he behaves," said she.

She sat intently at work whittling blowgun darts, striving to be composed, and without daring to lift up her eyes, till anxious curiosity carried them to the face of her sister as the servant was approaching the door. Jane looked a little paler than usual, but more sedate than Elizabeth had expected. On the gentlemen's appearing, her colour increased; yet she received them with tolerable ease, and with a propriety of behaviour equally free from any symptom of resentment or any unnecessary complaisance.

Elizabeth said as little to either as civility would allow, and sat down again to her work, with an eagerness which it did not often command. She had ventured only one glance at Darcy. He looked serious, as usual; and, she thought, more as he had used to look in Hertfordshire, than as she had seen him at Pemberley. But, perhaps he could not in her mother's presence be what he was before her uncle and aunt. It was a painful, but not an improbable, conjecture.

Bingley, she had likewise seen for an instant, and in that short period saw him looking both pleased and embarrassed. He was received by Mrs. Bennet with a degree of civility which made her two daughters ashamed, especially when contrasted with the cold and ceremonious politeness of her curtsey and address to his friend.

Elizabeth, particularly, who knew that her mother owed to the latter the preservation of her favourite daughter from irremediable infamy, was hurt and distressed to a most painful degree by a distinction so ill applied.

Darcy, after inquiring of her how Mr. and Mrs. Gardiner fared in the collapse of the east gate, a question which she could not answer, said scarcely anything. She was in no humour for conversation with anyone but himself; and to him she had hardly courage to speak. "Me!" she thought. "Who fears no man! Who fears not death itself! And yet unable am I to summon but a single word."

"It is a long time, Mr. Bingley, since you went away," said Mrs. Bennet. He readily agreed to it.

"I began to be afraid you would never come back again. People did say you meant to quit the place entirely; but, however, I hope it is not true. A great many changes have happened in the neighbourhood, since you went away. The number of unmentionables has been happily reduced to but a fraction of what it was when first you came. Miss Lucas is sent to her grave by the plague. And one of my own daughters is newly married. I suppose you have heard of it; indeed, you must have seen it in the papers. It was in the *Times* and the *Courier*, I know; though it was not put in as it ought to be. It was only said, 'Lately, George Wickham, Esq. to Miss Lydia Bennet,' without there being a syllable said of her father, or her service to His Majesty, or anything. Did you see it?"

Bingley replied that he did, and made his congratulations. Elizabeth dared not lift up her eyes. How Mr. Darcy looked, therefore, she could not tell.

"It is a delightful thing, to be sure, to have a daughter well married," continued her mother, "but at the same time, Mr. Bingley, it is very hard to have her taken such a way from me. They are gone down to Kilkenny, a place in Ireland, it seems, and there they are to stay I do not know how long. The St. Lazarus Seminary for the Lame is there; for I suppose you have heard of his being crippled in a carriage accident, and of his intention to enter the priesthood. Oh! My poor Wickham! If only he had as many friends as he deserves."

Elizabeth, who knew this to be levelled at Mr. Darcy, was in such misery of shame, that she could hardly keep her seat. Her misery received soon afterwards material relief, from observing how much the beauty of her sister rekindled the admiration of her former lover. When first he came in, he had spoken to her but little; but every five minutes seemed to be giving her more of his attention. He found her as handsome as she had been last year; as good natured, and as unaffected, though not quite so chatty. Jane was anxious that no difference should be perceived in her at all, and was really persuaded that she talked as much as ever. But her mind was so busily engaged, that she did not always know when she was silent.

When the gentlemen rose to go away, Mrs. Bennet was mindful of her intended civility, and they were invited and engaged to dine at Longbourn in a few days time.

"You are quite a visit in my debt, Mr. Bingley," she added, "for when you went to town last winter, you promised to take a family dinner with us, as soon as you returned. I have not forgot, you see; and I assure you, I was very much disappointed that you did not come back and keep your engagement."

Bingley looked a little silly at this reflection, and said something of his concern at having been prevented by business. They then went away.

Mrs. Bennet had been strongly inclined to ask them to stay and dine there that day; but, though she always kept a very good table, she did not think anything less than two courses could be good enough for a man on whom she had such anxious designs, or satisfy the appetite and pride of one who had ten thousand a year.

CHAPTER 54

AS SOON AS THEY WERE GONE, Elizabeth walked out to recover her spirits. Mr. Darcy's behaviour astonished and vexed her.

"Why, if he came only to be silent, grave, and indifferent," said she, "did he come at all?"

She could settle it in no way that gave her pleasure.

"He could be still amiable, still pleasing, to my uncle and aunt, when he was in town; and why not to me? If he fears me, why come hither? If he no longer cares for me, why silent? Teasing, teasing, man! I will think no more about him. I am Death's betrothed, after all. Sworn to honour and obey only the warrior code and my beloved Master Liu."

Her resolution was for a short time involuntarily kept by the approach of her sister, who joined her with a cheerful look. "Now," said she, "that this first meeting is over, I feel perfectly easy. I know my own strength, and I shall never be embarrassed again by his coming. I am glad he dines here on Tuesday. It will then be publicly seen that, on both sides, we meet only as common and indifferent acquaintance."

"Yes, very indifferent indeed," said Elizabeth, laughing. "Oh, Jane, take care."

"My dear Lizzy, you cannot think me so weak."

"Weak? Not in the slightest. Rather I think you more powerful than ever, in making him fall very much in love with you."

They did not see the gentlemen again till Tuesday; and Mrs. Bennet, in the meanwhile, was giving way to all the happy schemes, which the good humour and common politeness of Bingley, in half an hour's visit, had revived.

On Tuesday there was a large party assembled at Longbourn; and the two who were most anxiously expected were in very good time. When they repaired to the dining-room, Elizabeth eagerly watched to see whether Bingley would take the place, which, in all their former parties, had belonged to him, by her sister. Her prudent mother, occupied by the same ideas, forbore to invite him to sit by herself. On entering the room, he seemed to hesitate; but Jane happened to look round, and happened to smile: It was decided. He placed himself by her.

Elizabeth, with a triumphant sensation, looked towards Mr. Darcy, who bore his friend's choice of seat with noble indifference. She would have imagined that Bingley had received his permission to pursue Jane, had she not seen his eyes likewise turned towards Mr. Darcy, with an expression of half-laughing alarm.

His behaviour to her sister was such, during dinner time, as showed an admiration of her, which persuaded Elizabeth, that if left wholly to himself, Jane's happiness, and his own, would be speedily secured. Though she dared not depend upon the consequence, she yet received pleasure from observing his behaviour. It gave her all the animation that her spirits could boast; for she was in no cheerful humour. Mr. Darcy was almost as far from her as the table could divide them. He was on one side of her mother. She knew how little such a situation would give pleasure to either. She was not near enough to hear any of their discourse, but she could see how seldom they spoke to each other, and how formal and cold was their manner whenever they did. Her mother's ungraciousness, made the sense of what they owed him more painful to Elizabeth's mind; and she would, at times, have given anything to leap onto the table and administer the seven cuts of shame in front of Mr. Darcy—to see her pitiful blood drip onto his plate; atonement for her many prejudices against him.

She was in hopes that the evening would afford some opportunity of bringing them together; that the whole of the visit would not pass away without enabling them to enter into something more of conversation than the mere ceremonious salutation attending his entrance. Anxious and uneasy, the period which passed in the drawing-room, before the gentlemen came, was wearisome and dull to a degree that almost made her uncivil. She looked forward to their entrance as the point on which all her chance of pleasure for the evening must depend.

"If he does not come to me, then," said she, "I shall give him up for ever, and shall never again divert my eyes from the end of my blade."

The gentlemen came; and she thought he looked as if he would have answered her hopes; but, alas! The ladies had crowded round the table, where Miss Bennet was making tea, and Elizabeth pouring out the coffee, in so close a confederacy that there was not a single vacancy near her which would admit of a chair.

Darcy walked away to another part of the room. She followed him with her eyes, envied everyone to whom he spoke, had scarcely patience enough to help anybody to coffee; and then was enraged against herself for being so silly!

"A man who has been refused with foot and fist! How could I ever be foolish enough to expect a renewal of his love? Is there one among the sex who would not protest against such a weakness as a second proposal to the same woman? He should sooner make an offer to a zombie!"

She was a little revived, however, by his bringing back his coffee cup himself; and she seized the opportunity of saying:

"Is your sister at Pemberley still?"

"Yes, she will remain there till Christmas."

"And quite alone? Have all her friends left her?"

"All but the servants and her personal guard."

She could think of nothing more to say; but if he wished to converse with her, he might have better success. He stood by her, however, for some minutes, in silence; and, at last, walked away.

When the tea-things were removed, and the card-tables placed, the ladies all rose, and Elizabeth was then hoping to be soon joined by Mr. Darcy, when all her hopes were overthrown by seeing him fall a victim to her mother's voracious recruitment of Crypt and Coffin players. She now lost every expectation of pleasure. They were confined for the evening at different tables, and she had nothing to hope, but that his eyes were so often turned towards her side of the room, as to make him play as unsuccessfully as herself.

Mrs. Bennet had designed to keep the two Netherfield gentlemen to supper; but their carriage was unluckily ordered before any of the others, and she had no opportunity of detaining them.

"Well girls," said she, as soon as they were left to themselves, "What say you to the day? I think every thing has passed off uncommonly well, I assure you. The dinner was as well dressed as any I ever saw. The venison was roasted to a turn—and everybody said they never saw so fat a haunch. Thank you, Lizzy, for wrestling us so fine a buck. The soup was fifty times better than what we had at the Lucases' last week; and even Mr. Darcy acknowledged, that the partridges were remarkably well done; and I suppose he has two or three French cooks at least. And, my dear Jane, I never saw you look in greater beauty."

Mrs. Bennet, in short, was in very great spirits; she had seen enough of Bingley's behaviour to Jane, to be convinced that she would get him at last; and her expectations of advantage to her family, when in a happy humour, were so far beyond reason, that she was quite disappointed at not seeing him there again the next day, to make his proposals.

"It has been a very agreeable day," said Jane to Elizabeth. "The party seemed so well selected, so suitable one with the other. I hope we may often meet again."

Elizabeth smiled.

"Lizzy, you must not do so. You must not suspect me. It mortifies me. I assure you that I have now learnt to enjoy his conversation as an agreeable and sensible young man, without having a wish beyond it. I am perfectly satisfied, from what his manners now are, that he never had any design of engaging my affection. It is only that he is blessed with greater sweetness of address, and a stronger desire of generally pleasing, than any other man."

"You are very cruel," said her sister, "you will not let me smile, and are provoking me to it every moment. I have half a mind to force a profession of love from you."

"How hard it is in some cases to be believed!"

"And how impossible in others!"

"But why should you wish to persuade me that I feel more than I acknowledge?"

"Oh! You are more obstinate than a Hunan mule! If you persist in indifference, do not make me your confidante."

CHAPTER 55

A FEW DAYS AFTER this visit, Mr. Bingley called again, and alone. His friend had left him that morning for London, but was to return home in ten days time. He sat with them above an hour, and was in remarkably good spirits. Mrs. Bennet invited him to dine with them; but he confessed himself engaged elsewhere.

"Next time you call," said she, "I hope we shall be more lucky."

He should be particularly happy at any time, etc. etc.; and if she would give him leave, would take an early opportunity of waiting on them.

"Can you come to-morrow?"

Yes, he had no engagement at all for to-morrow; and her invitation was accepted with alacrity.

He came, and in such very good time that the ladies were still in their sparring gowns, and none of them without considerable beads of exercise moisture on their skin. In ran Mrs. Bennet to her daughter's room, in her dressing gown, and with her hair half finished, crying out:

"My dear Jane, make haste and hurry down. He is come—Mr. Bingley is come. He is, indeed. Make haste, make haste. Here, Sarah, come to Miss Bennet this moment, wash away her exercise moisture, and help her on with her gown. Never mind Lizzy's hair."

"We will be down as soon as we can," said Jane; "but I dare say Kitty is forwarder than either of us, for she went up stairs half an hour ago."

"Oh! Hang Kitty! What has she to do with it? Come be quick, be quick! Where is your sash, my dear?"

But Jane would not be prevailed on to go down without one of her sisters.

The same anxiety to get them by themselves was visible again in the evening. After tea, Mr. Bennet retired to the library, as was his custom, and Mary went up stairs to her weights. Two obstacles of the five being thus removed, Mrs. Bennet sat looking and winking at Elizabeth and Kitty for a considerable time, without making any impression on them. Elizabeth would not observe her; and when at last Kitty did, she very innocently said, "What is the matter, mamma? What do you keep winking at me for? What am I to do?"

"Nothing child, nothing. I did not wink at you." She then sat still five minutes longer; but unable to waste such a precious occasion, she suddenly got up, and saying to Kitty, "Come here, my love, I want to speak to you," took her out of the room. Jane instantly gave a look at Elizabeth which spoke her distress at such premeditation, and her entreaty that she would not give in to it. In a few minutes, Mrs. Bennet half-opened the door and called out:

"Lizzy, my dear, I want to speak with you."

Elizabeth was forced to go.

"We may as well leave them by themselves you know," said her mother, as soon as she was in the hall. "Kitty and I are going upstairs to sit in my dressing-room."

Elizabeth made no attempt to reason with her mother, but remained quietly in the hall, till she and Kitty were out of sight, then returned into the drawing-room.

Mrs. Bennet's schemes for this day were ineffectual. Bingley was every thing that was charming, except the professed lover of her daughter. His ease and cheerfulness rendered him a most agreeable addition to their evening party; and he bore with the ill-judged officiousness of the mother, and heard all her silly remarks with a forbearance and command of countenance particularly grateful to the daughter.

He scarcely needed an invitation to stay for supper; and before he went away, an engagement was formed, chiefly through his own and Mrs. Bennet's means, for his coming next morning to shoot the first autumn zombies with her husband.

After this day, Jane said no more of her indifference. Not a word passed between the sisters concerning Bingley; but Elizabeth went to bed in the happy belief that all must speedily be concluded, unless Mr. Darcy returned within the stated time. However, she felt tolerably persuaded that Bingley's attentiveness to Jane had met with that gentleman's concurrence.

Bingley was punctual to his appointment; and he and Mr. Bennet spent the morning together hunting the first unmentionables to wander south in search of soft earth. Mr. Bennet lead his companion to Longbourn's northernmost field, where they spent the better part of an hour setting several hand traps (of Mr. Bennet's own design), which they baited with heads of cauliflower. Every so often, a zombie would stagger out of the woods and into the field, where Mr. Bennet and Mr. Bingley were concealed beneath a bundle of branches. The living would watch as the dead discovered the cauliflower, and, thinking it was a soft, succulent brain, reach down to grab it. Upon this, the trap would clamp shut around its arm, and the men would advance—beating the creature with their musket stocks, shooting it, and setting it alight.

Bingely was much more agreeable than Mr. Bennet expected. There was nothing of presumption or folly in the young man that could provoke his ridicule, or disgust him into silence; and for his part, Mr. Bennet was more communicative, and less eccentric, than Mr. Bingley had ever seen him. Bingley of course returned with him to dinner; and in the evening Mrs. Bennet's invention was again at work to get every body away from him and her daughter. Elizabeth, who had a letter to write, went into the breakfast room for that purpose soon after tea.

On returning to the drawing-room, when her letter was finished, she saw her sister and Bingley standing together over the hearth, as if engaged in earnest conversation; and had this led to no suspicion, the faces of both, as they hastily turned round and moved away from each other, would have told it all. *Their* situation was awkward enough; but *hers* she thought was still worse. Not a syllable was uttered by either; and Elizabeth was on the point of going away again, when Bingley, who as well as the other had sat down, suddenly rose, and whispering a few words to her sister, ran out of the room.

Jane could have no reserves from Elizabeth, where confidence would give pleasure; and instantly embracing her, acknowledged, with the liveliest emotion, that she was the happiest creature in the world.

"'Tis too much!" she added, "by far too much. I do not deserve it. Oh! why is not everybody as happy?"

Elizabeth's congratulations were given with a sincerity which words could but poorly express. Every sentence of kindness was a fresh source of happiness to Jane. But she would not allow herself to stay with her sister, or say half that remained to be said for the present.

"I must go instantly to my mother," she cried. "I would not on any account allow her to hear it from anyone but myself. He is gone to my father already. Oh! Lizzy, to know that what I have to relate will give such pleasure to all my dear family! How shall I bear so much happiness!"

She then hastened away to her mother, who was sitting upstairs with Kitty.

Elizabeth, who was left by herself, now smiled at the rapidity and ease with which an affair was finally settled, that had given them so many previous months of suspense and vexation.

For the moment, it mattered little to Elizabeth that she would be losing her most trusted companion on the battlefield; her closest confidant, and the only sister she never feared the slightest silliness from. She was overcome by a feeling of complete victory; for after all of Darcy's anxious circumspection, all of Miss Bingley's falsehood and contrivance, the affair had reached the happiest, wisest, most reasonable end.

In a few minutes she was joined by Bingley, whose conference with her father had been short and to the purpose.

"Where is your sister?" said he.

"With my mother upstairs. She will be down in a moment, I dare say."

He then shut the door, and, coming up to her, claimed the good wishes and affection of a sister. Elizabeth honestly and heartily expressed her delight in the prospect of their relationship. They shook hands with great cordiality; and then, till her sister came down, she listened to all he had to say of his own happiness, and of Jane's perfections; and in spite of his being little trained in the deadly arts, Elizabeth really believed all his expectations of felicity to be rationally founded, because he and Jane were so alike in every other imaginable way.

It was an evening of no common delight to them all; the satisfaction of Miss Bennet's mind gave a glow of such sweet animation to her face, as made her look handsomer than ever. Kitty simpered and smiled, and hoped her turn was coming soon. Mrs. Bennet could not give her consent or speak her approbation in terms warm enough to satisfy her feelings; and when Mr. Bennet joined them at supper, his voice and manner plainly showed how really happy he was.

Not a word, however, passed his lips in allusion to it, till their visitor took his leave for the night; but as soon as he was gone, he turned to his daughter, and said:

"Jane, I congratulate you. You will be a very happy woman."

Jane went to him instantly, kissed him, and thanked him for his goodness.

"You are a good girl," he replied, "and I have great pleasure in thinking you will be so happily settled. I have not a doubt of your doing very well together. Your tempers are by no means unlike. You are each of you so complying, that nothing will ever be resolved on; so easy, that every servant will cheat you; and so generous, that you will always exceed your income."

"I hope not so. Imprudence or thoughtlessness in money matters would be unpardonable in *me*."

"Exceed their income! My dear Mr. Bennet," cried his wife, "what are you talking of? Why, he has four or five thousand a year, and very likely more." Then addressing her daughter, "Oh! My dear, dear Jane, I am so happy! I was sure you could not be so beautiful for nothing! I remember, as soon as ever I saw him, when he first came into Hertfordshire last year, I thought how likely it was that you should come together. Oh! He is the handsomest young man that ever was seen!"

Wickham, Lydia, all were forgotten. Jane was beyond competition her favourite child. At that moment, she cared for no other. Her younger sisters soon began to make interest with her for objects of happiness which she might in future be able to dispense.

Mary petitioned for the use of the library at Netherfield; and Kitty begged very hard for a few balls there every winter.

Bingley, from this time, was of course a daily visitor at Longbourn; coming frequently before breakfast, and always remaining till after supper; unless when some barbarous neighbour, who could not be enough detested, had given him an invitation to dinner which he thought himself obliged to accept.

As the days grew shorter, the number of zombies in Hertfordshire grew greater. The herds now came in droves, chased south by hardening earth and His Majesty's muskets. Elizabeth had now but little time for conversation with her sister; for she, Kitty, and Mary were every day needed to dispense of this trouble or that; and Jane could bestow no attention on anyone else while Bingley was present. In the absence of Jane, he always attached himself to Elizabeth, for the pleasure of talking of her; and when Bingley was gone, Jane constantly sought the same means of relief.

"He has made me so happy," said she, one evening, "by telling me that he was totally ignorant of my being in town last spring! I had not believed it possible."

"I suspected as much," replied Elizabeth. "But how did he account for it?"

"It must have been his sister's doing. They were certainly no friends to his acquaintance with me, which I cannot wonder at, since he might have chosen so much more advantageously in many respects. But when they see, as I trust they will, that their brother is happy with me, they will learn to be contented, and we shall be on good terms again; though we can never be what we once were to each other."

"That is the most unforgiving speech," said Elizabeth, "that I ever heard you utter. Good girl! It would vex me, indeed, to see you again the dupe of Miss Bingley's pretended regard."

"Would you believe it, Lizzy, that when he went to town last November, he really loved me, and nothing but a persuasion of *my* being indifferent or another siege of London would have prevented his coming to the country again!"

Elizabeth was pleased to find that he had not betrayed the interference of his friend; for, though Jane had the most generous and forgiving heart in the world, she knew it was a circumstance which must prejudice her against him.

"I am certainly the most fortunate creature that ever existed!" cried Jane. "Oh! Lizzy, why am I thus singled from my family, and blessed above them all! If I could but see *you* as happy! If there *were* but such another man for you!"

"If you were to give me forty such men, I never could be so happy as you. Till I have your disposition, your goodness, I never can have your happiness. No, no, let me find comfort in cutting down dreadfuls; and, perhaps, if I have very good luck, I may meet with another Mr. Collins in time."

The situation of affairs in the Longbourn family could not be long a secret. Mrs. Bennet was privileged to whisper it to Mrs. Philips, and *she* ventured, without any permission, to do the same by all her neighbours in Meryton.

The Bennets were speedily pronounced to be the luckiest family in the world, though only a few weeks before, when Lydia had first run away, they had been generally proved to be marked out for misfortune.

CHAPTER 56

ONE MORNING, about a week after Bingley's engagement with Jane had been formed, as he and the females of the family were sitting together in the dining-room, their attention was suddenly drawn to the window, by the sound of a carriage; and they perceived a chaise and four driving up the lawn. The horses were post; and neither the carriage, nor the livery of the servant who preceded it, were familiar to them. As it was certain, however, that somebody was coming, Bingley instantly prevailed on Jane to avoid the confinement of such an intrusion, and walk away with him into the shrubbery, where she had promised to instruct him in buck wrestling. They both set off, and the conjectures of the remaining three continued, though with little satisfaction, till the door was thrown open and their visitor entered, accompanied by a pair of ninjas.

It was Lady Catherine de Bourgh.

They were of course all intending to be surprised; but their astonishment was beyond their expectation.

She entered the room with an air more than usually ungracious, made no other reply to Elizabeth's salutation than a slight inclination of the head, dismissed her guard, and sat down without saying a word. Elizabeth had mentioned her name to her mother on her ladyship's entrance, though no request of introduction had been made.

Mrs. Bennet, all amazement, though flattered by having a guest of such high importance, received her with the utmost politeness. After sitting for a moment in silence, she said very stiffly to Elizabeth:

"I hope you are well, Miss Bennet. That lady, I suppose, is your mother."

Elizabeth replied very concisely that she was.

"And *that* I suppose is one of your sisters."

"Yes, madam," said Mrs. Bennet, delighted to speak to a Lady Catherine. "She is my youngest girl but one. My youngest of all is lately married, and my eldest is somewhere about the grounds, walking with a young man who, I believe, will soon become a part of the family."

"You have a very small park here," returned Lady Catherine after a short silence.

"It is nothing in comparison of Rosings, my lady, I dare say."

Elizabeth now expected that she would bestow her condolences on the passing of Charlotte and Mr. Collins, as it seemed the only probable motive for her calling. But none were offered, and she was completely puzzled.

Mrs. Bennet, with great civility, begged her ladyship to take some refreshment; but Lady Catherine very resolutely, and not very politely, declined eating anything; and then, rising up, said to Elizabeth:

"Miss Bennet, there seemed to be a prettyish little dojo on one side of your lawn. I should be glad to examine it, if you will favour me with your company."

"Go, my dear," cried her mother, "and show her ladyship about. I think she will be pleased with the artifacts."

Elizabeth obeyed, and running into her own room for her parasol, attended her noble guest downstairs. As they passed through the hall, Lady Catherine opened the doors into the dining-parlour and drawing-room, and pronouncing them, after a short survey, to be decent looking rooms, walked on.

Her carriage remained at the door, and Elizabeth saw that her waiting-geisha was in it. They proceeded in silence to the dojo; Elizabeth was determined to make no effort for conversation with a woman who was now more than usually insolent and disagreeable.

"How could I ever think her like her nephew?" said she, as she looked in her face.

As soon as they entered, Lady Catherine began in the following manner:

"You can be at no loss, Miss Bennet, to understand the reason of my journey hither. Your own heart, your own conscience, must tell you why I come."

Elizabeth looked with unaffected astonishment.

"Indeed, you are mistaken, Madam. I have not been able to account for the honour of seeing you here."

"Miss Bennet," replied her ladyship, in an angry tone, "you ought to know, that I am not to be trifled with. But however insincere you may choose to be, you shall not find *me* so. My character has ever been celebrated for its sincerity and frankness, just as my killing powers have been celebrated as having no equal. A report of a most alarming nature reached me two days ago. I was told that not only was your sister on the point of being most advantageously married, but that *you*, that Miss Elizabeth Bennet, would, in all likelihood, be soon afterwards united to my nephew, my own nephew, Mr. Darcy. Though I *know* it must be a scandalous falsehood, though I would not injure him so much as to suppose him to take any interest in a girl of your low birth, I instantly resolved on setting off for this place, that I might make my sentiments known to you."

"If you believed it impossible to be true," said Elizabeth, colouring with astonishment and disdain, "I wonder you took the trouble of coming so far. What could your ladyship propose by it?"

"To insist upon having such a report universally contradicted."

"Your coming to Longbourn, to see me and my family," said Elizabeth coolly, "will be rather a confirmation of it; if, indeed, such a report is in existence."

"If! Do you then pretend to be ignorant of it? Has it not been industriously circulated by yourselves? Do you not know that such a report is spread abroad?"

"I never heard that it was."

"And can you likewise declare, that there is no *foundation* for it?"

"I do not pretend to possess equal frankness with your ladyship. *You* may ask questions which *I* shall not choose to answer."

"This is not to be borne. Miss Bennet, I insist on being satisfied. Has he, has my nephew, made you an offer of marriage?"

"Your ladyship has declared it to be impossible."

"It ought to be so; it must be so, while he retains the use of his reason. But *your* arts and allurements may, in a moment of infatuation, have made him forget what he owes to himself and to all his family. You may have drawn him in with your cheap Chinese parlour tricks."

"If I have, I shall be the last person to confess it."

"Miss Bennet, do you know who I am? Have you not heard the songs of my victories over legions of Satan's slaves? Have you not read of my unmatched skill? I am almost Mr. Darcy's nearest relation in the world, and entitled to know all his dearest concerns."

"Such great skills! Such a slayer of zombies! And yet, when one was in your home, you had not perception enough to see her."

"Are you so daft as to suppose that I did not know Charlotte for what she was? Are you incapable of understanding my generous motives? That my new priest might know some measure of happiness? Tell me, why do you suppose she changed so slowly? Why did I invite her to tea so often—for the pleasure of her company? No! It was my serum which kept her alive those few happy months. A few drops at a time, unnoticed, into her cup."

"Such an experiment can hardly be called 'generous.' You did nothing but prolong her suffering!"

"Let me be rightly understood. This match, to which you have the presumption to aspire, can never take place. Never! Mr. Darcy is engaged to *my daughter*. Now what have you to say?"

"Only this; that if he is so, you can have no reason to suppose he will make an offer to me."

Lady Catherine hesitated for a moment, and then replied:

"The engagement between them is of a peculiar kind. From their infancy, they have been intended for each other. It was the favourite wish of his mother, as well as of hers. While in their cradles, we planned the union: and now, at the moment when the wishes of both sisters would be accomplished in their marriage, to be prevented by a young woman of inferior birth, of no importance in the world, and trained in China of all places! Are you lost to every feeling of propriety and delicacy? Have you not heard me say that from his earliest hours he was destined for his cousin?"

"Yes, and I had heard it before. But what is that to me? If there is no other objection to my marrying your nephew, I shall certainly not be kept from it by knowing that his mother and aunt wished him to marry Miss de Bourgh. If Mr. Darcy is neither by honour nor inclination confined to his cousin, why is not he to make another choice? And if I am that choice, why may not I accept him?"

"Because honour, decorum, prudence, nay, interest, forbid it. Yes, Miss Bennet, interest; for do not expect to be noticed by his family or friends, if you wilfully act against the inclinations of all. You will be censured, slighted, and despised, by everyone connected with him. Your alliance will be a disgrace; your name will never even be mentioned by any of us."

"These are heavy misfortunes," replied Elizabeth. "But the wife of Mr. Darcy must have such extraordinary sources of happiness necessarily attached to her situation, that she could, upon the whole, have no cause to repine."

"Obstinate, headstrong girl! I am ashamed of you! Is this your gratitude for my attentions to you last spring? Is nothing due to me on that score? I am not in the habit of being refused!"

"Nor am I in the habit of being intimidated."

"I will not be interrupted! Hear me in silence! My daughter and my nephew are formed for each other. Their fortune on both sides is splendid. They are destined for each other by the voice of every member of their respective houses; and what is to divide them? The upstart pretensions of a young woman whose sister was lately concerned in a scandalous elopement with the son of the elder Darcy's musket-polisher? A woman without family, connections, or fortune?"

"Your daughter's fortune is indeed splendid. But pray tell, what other qualities does she possess? Is she fetching? Is she trained in the deadly arts? Has she even strength enough to lift a Katana?"

"How dare you! Tell me once for all, are you engaged to him?"

Though Elizabeth would not, for the mere purpose of obliging Lady Catherine, have answered this question, she could not but say, after a moment's deliberation:

"I am not."

Lady Catherine seemed pleased.

"And will you promise me, never to enter into such an engagement?"

"I would sooner die than see my honour so defiled."

"Then Miss Bennet," said Lady Catherine, setting down her parasol and removing her coat, "die you shall." Upon this, she set her feet for combat.

"Do you mean to challenge me to a duel, your ladyship? Here, in my family dojo?"

"I mean only to rid the world of an insolent little girl, and preserve the dignity of a superior man, lest Pemberley be forever polluted by your stench."

"If that be the case," said Elizabeth, dropping her parasol, "then let this be our first and final battle." Elizabeth set her feet in return.

The two ladies—separated by more than fifty years, yet hardly at all in abilities—remained thus for a moment, until Lady Catherine, her plan of attack fully formed, leapt skyward with a strength quite striking for a woman of her advanced age. She flipped through the air, over Elizabeth's head, and landed a blow on the top of her skull, the force of which brought the younger to her knees. Had Elizabeth been anything less than perfectly fit, the blow would have most assuredly splintered her spine.

Lady Catherine landed gently on her feet, and seeing her opponent attempt to rise, sent her flying the length of the dojo with a ruinous kick to the back. Unable to gain her wind, Elizabeth struggled to stand as the aged warrior again approached.

"You have no regard for the honour and credit of my nephew! Unfeeling, selfish girl! Do you not consider that a connection with you must disgrace him in the eyes of everybody?"

Her ladyship grabbed Elizabeth's gown and lifted her to her feet. "Well? Have you anything to say before I remit you to Satan?"

"Just . . . one thing, your ladyship . . . "

Lady Catherine's eyes widened as she felt a sharp pain in her belly. She let go and stumbled backward, the handle of Elizabeth's dagger protruding from her gown. The younger took full advantage of this confusion, striking her ladyship about the head, neck, and bosom with a severe combination of blows, and a final kick which drove her so high as to shatter two of the wooden rafters overhead.

Outside, Lady Catherine's ninjas turned towards the dojo, alarmed by this tumult.

Inside, her ladyship lay motionless on the floor. Elizabeth stood over her, waiting for any sign of life—but none appeared. "Dear Lord," she thought. "What have I done? How shall Darcy ever forgive me for killing his beloved aunt?"

The thought was no sooner in her head than Elizabeth felt herself fall to the ground, brought down by Lady Catherine's legs. The latter leapt to her feet, and with a hearty laugh, pulled the dagger from her belly, and flung it into Elizabeth's hand—pinning her to the floor.

"It would take skills far exceeding your own to draw but a single bead of exercise moisture from my skin. Weak, silly girl! So long as there is life in this old body, you shall never again be in the company of my nephew!"

Lady Catherine's ninjas entered, throwing stars at the ready, but were quickly put at ease by their master, who had the duel well in hand. "Remain thus, dear ninjas. When I have removed her head, you may do with the body as you please."

As Elizabeth struggled to free herself, her ladyship removed one of the swords from the wall. She unsheathed it and examined its glistening blade. "Remarkable. As fine a Katana as ever I saw in Kyoto. Pity it should have spent these many years in the charge of so unworthy a family." Lady Catherine looked up from the blade, expecting to see her opponent. Instead, she saw nothing—nothing but an empty dojo, and a pair of broken, lifeless ninjas. She met this, too, with a hearty laugh.

"What good fun! I must admit, had you been vanquished with so little effort, I should have been rather disappointed."

"'WEAK, SILLY GIRL! SO LONG AS THERE IS LIFE IN THIS OLD BODY, YOU SHALL NEVER AGAIN BE IN THE COMPANY OF MY NEPHEW!'"

Lady Catherine walked to the center of the dojo, sword in hand. She turned herself round, expecting an attack—but none came. "Such cowardice!" she cried. "Have you not courage enough to face me? Did your master teach you nothing more than retreat?"

"My master," said Elizabeth, "taught me that the shortest path to ruin was underestimating one's opponent." Her ladyship looked skyward and saw Elizabeth atop a rafter—sword in hand. The younger dove toward the floor as the elder leapt toward the ceiling; and their swords met in the air that separated the two. A ferocious contest of blades filled the dojo with the clanging of steel upon steel. The two women were evenly matched, but Elizabeth's youth bestowed to her the advantage of vigor, and she tired more slowly than her ladyship.

After several minutes of flying about, attacking one another with force that would have sent legions of lesser warriors to their graves, Lady Catherine's sword was dispatched with a well-aimed butterfly kick. Defenseless, her ladyship retreated to the wall of weaponry, where she hastily procured a pair of nunchucks; but these were promptly cut in two by Elizabeth's Katana.

Elizabeth backed Lady Catherine against a wall, and held the tip of her sword to her wrinkled throat. "Well?" said Catherine, "Take my head then, but be quick about it."

Elizabeth lowered her blade, and with a voice much affected by exercise, said, "To what end, your ladyship? That I might procure the condemnation of a man for whom I care so much? No. No, your ladyship—whether you shall live to see him married to your daughter, or married to me, I know not. But you shall live. And for the rest of your days, you shall know that you have been bested by a girl for whom you have no regard, and whose family and master you have insulted in the harshest possible manner. Now, I beg you take your leave."

Upon being walked to her carriage, Lady Catherine turned hastily round, and added, "My position remains unchanged. I send no compliments to your mother. You deserve no such attention. I am most seriously displeased."

"Her ladyship would be wise to climb into her carriage, lest I change my mind about taking her head."

With the deepest disgust, the elder did as she was told. Offering not so much as a slight bow, Elizabeth turned and walked toward the house.

She heard the carriage drive away as she proceeded up stairs, taking care to conceal her injuries. Her mother impatiently followed her, to ask why Lady Catherine would not come in again and rest herself.

"She did not choose it," said her daughter.

"She is a very fine-looking woman! And her calling here was prodigiously civil! For she only came, I suppose, to offer her condolences for the passing of Mr. Collins and his wife. She is on her road somewhere, I dare say, and so, passing through Meryton, thought she might as well call on you. I suppose she had nothing particular to say to you, Lizzy?"

Elizabeth was forced to give into a little falsehood here; for to acknowledge the truth of what has passed between them was impossible.

CHAPTER 57

T HE DISCOMFITURE OF SPIRITS which this extraordinary visit threw Elizabeth into, could not be easily overcome; nor could she, after burying the ninjas, learn to think of it less than incessantly. Lady Catherine, it appeared, had actually taken the trouble of this journey from Rosings, for the sole purpose of breaking off her supposed engagement with Mr. Darcy. But from what the report of their engagement could originate, Elizabeth was at a loss to imagine; till she recollected that *his* being the intimate friend of Bingley, and *her* being the sister of Jane, was enough, at a time when the expectation of one wedding made everybody eager for another, to supply the idea. She had not herself forgotten to feel that the marriage of her sister must bring them more frequently together.

However, she could not help feeling some uneasiness as to the possible consequence of her duel with Lady Catherine. From what she had said of her resolution to prevent their marriage, it occurred to Elizabeth that she would relate the whole of their battle to her nephew; and how *he* might be swayed by her reasoning, and a natural admiration for his aunt.

If he had been wavering before as to what he should do, which had often seemed likely, the advice and entreaty of so near a relation might settle every doubt, and determine him at once to be as happy as dignity unblemished could make him. In that case he would return no more. Lady Catherine might see him in her way through town; and the sight of his aunt so freshly bloodied might provoke any number of feelings— not the least of which was resentment for the one who bore responsibility for the injuries.

The surprise of the rest of the family, on hearing who their visitor had been, was very great; but they obligingly satisfied it, with the same kind of supposition which had appeased Mrs. Bennet's curiosity; and Elizabeth was spared from much teasing on the subject.

The next morning, as she was going downstairs, she was met by her father, who came out of his library with a letter in his hand.

"Lizzy," said he, "I was going to look for you; come into my room."

She followed him thither; and her curiosity to know what he had to tell her was heightened by the supposition of its being in some manner connected with the letter he held. It suddenly struck her that it might be from Lady Catherine; and she anticipated with dismay all the consequent explanations.

She followed her father to the fire place, and they both sat down. He then said:

"I have received a letter this morning that has astonished me exceedingly. As it principally concerns yourself, you ought to know its contents. I did not know before, that I had two daughters on the brink of matrimony. Let me congratulate you on a very important conquest."

The colour now rushed into Elizabeth's cheeks in the instantaneous conviction of its being a letter from the nephew, instead of the aunt; and she was undetermined whether most to be pleased that he explained himself at all, or offended that his letter was not rather addressed to herself; when her father continued:

"You look conscious. Young ladies have great penetration in such matters as these; but I think I may defy even *your* sagacity, to discover the name of your admirer. This letter is from a Colonel Fitzwilliam—a man who, before receipt of this letter, I had never heard of in all my life."

"From Colonel Fitzwilliam! And what can he have to say?"

"Something very much to the purpose of course. He begins with congratulations on Jane's approaching nuptials, of which, it seems, he has been told by some good natured gentleman. I shall not sport with your impatience, by reading what he says on that point. What relates to yourself, is as follows:

> Having thus offered you the sincere congratulations on this happy event, let me now add a short hint on the subject of another; of which I have been advertised by the same authority. Your daughter Elizabeth, it is presumed, will not long bear the name of Bennet, after her elder sister has resigned it, and the chosen partner of her fate may be reasonably looked up to as one of the most illustrious personages in this land.

"Can you possibly guess, Lizzy, who is meant by this?"

> This young gentleman is blessed, in a peculiar way, with every thing the heart of mortal can most desire—splendid property, noble kindred, and extensive patronage. Yet in spite

of all these temptations, let me warn you of what evils you may incur by a precipitate closure with this gentleman's proposals, which, of course, you will be inclined to take immediate advantage of.

"Have you any idea, Lizzy, who this gentleman is? But now it comes out:"

My motive for cautioning you is as follows. We have reason to imagine that his aunt and mine, Lady Catherine de Bourgh, does not look on the match with a friendly eye.

"*Mr. Darcy*, you see, is the man! Now, Lizzy, I think I *have* surprised you. Could he have pitched on any man within the circle of our acquaintance, whose name would have given the lie more effectually to what they related? Mr. Darcy, who never looks at any woman but to see a blemish, and who probably never looked at *you* in his life! Imagine such a thing!"

Elizabeth tried to join in her father's pleasantry, but could only force one most reluctant smile. Never had his wit been directed in a manner so little agreeable to her.

"Are you not surprised?"

"Oh! Yes. Pray read on."

After mentioning the likelihood of this marriage to her last night, she immediately expressed what she felt on the occasion; when it became apparent, that on the score of some family objections on the part of your daughter, she would never give her consent to what she termed so disgraceful a match. I thought it my duty to give the speediest intelligence of this to you, that Elizabeth and her noble admirer may be aware of what they are about, and not run hastily into a marriage which has not been properly sanctioned.

"The rest of his letter is only about his sorrow upon hearing of Charlotte's beheading and Mr. Collins's suicide. But, Lizzy, you look as if you did not enjoy it. You are not, I hope, pretending to be affronted at an idle report."

"Oh!" cried Elizabeth, "I am excessively amused. But it is so strange!"

"Yes—*that* is what makes it amusing. Had they fixed on any other man it would have been nothing; but *his* perfect indifference, and your pointed dislike, make it so delightfully absurd! And pray, Lizzy, what said Lady Catherine about this report? Did she call to refuse her consent?"

To this question his daughter replied only with a laugh; and as it had been asked without the least suspicion. Elizabeth had never been more at a loss to make her feelings appear what they were not. It was necessary to laugh, when she would rather have cried. Her father had most cruelly mortified her, by what he said of Mr. Darcy's indifference, and she could do nothing but wonder at such a want of perception, or fear that perhaps, instead of his seeing too *little*, she might have fancied too *much*.

CHAPTER 58

T O ELIZABETH'S GREAT SURPRISE, Mr. Bingley brought Darcy with him to Longbourn before many days had passed after Lady Catherine's visit. The gentlemen arrived early; and, before Mrs. Bennet had time to tell him of their having seen his aunt, of which her daughter sat in momentary dread, Bingley, who wanted to be alone with Jane, proposed their all walking out. It was agreed to. Mrs. Bennet was not in the habit of walking; Mary could never spare time; but the remaining five set off together. Bingley and Jane, however, soon allowed the others to outstrip them. They lagged behind, while

Elizabeth, Kitty, and Darcy were to entertain each other. Very little was said by either; Kitty was too much afraid of him to talk; Elizabeth was secretly forming a desperate resolution; and perhaps he might be doing the same.

They walked towards the Lucases, because Kitty wished to call upon Maria; and as Elizabeth saw no occasion for joining her, when Kitty left them she went boldly on with him alone. Now was the moment for her resolution to be executed, and, while her courage was high, she immediately said:

"Mr. Darcy, I am a very selfish creature; and, for the sake of giving relief to my own feelings, care not how much I may be wounding yours. I can no longer help thanking you for your unexampled kindness to my poor sister. Ever since I have known it, I have been most anxious to acknowledge to you how gratefully I feel it. Were it known to the rest of my family, I should not have merely my own gratitude to express."

"I am sorry, exceedingly sorry," replied Darcy, in a tone of surprise and emotion, "that you have ever been informed of what may, in a mistaken light, have given you uneasiness. I did not think Mrs. Gardiner was so little to be trusted."

"You must not blame my aunt. Lydia's carelessness first betrayed to me that you had been concerned in the matter; and, of course, I could not rest till I knew the particulars. Let me thank you again and again, in the name of all my family, for that generous compassion which induced you to take so much trouble, and offer to kneel before you now and administer the seven cuts, that you might be honoured by trampling my blood."

"If you *will* thank me," he replied, "let it be for yourself alone. That the wish of giving happiness to you might add force to the other inducements which led me on, I shall not attempt to deny. But your *family* owe me nothing. Much as I respect them, I believe I thought only of *you*."

Elizabeth was too much embarrassed to say a word. After a short pause, her companion added, "You are too generous to trifle with me. If your feelings are still what they were last April, tell me so at once. *My affections and wishes are unchanged, but one word from you will silence me on this subject for ever."*

Elizabeth now forced herself to speak; and immediately, though not very fluently, gave him to understand that her sentiments had undergone so material a change, since the period to which he alluded, as to make her receive with gratitude and pleasure his present assurances. The happiness which this reply produced, was such as he had probably never felt before; and he expressed himself on the occasion as sensibly and as warmly as a man violently in love can be supposed to do. Had Elizabeth been able to encounter his eye, she might have seen how well the expression of heartfelt delight, diffused over his face, became him; but, though she could not look, she could listen, and he told her of feelings, which, in proving of what importance she was to him, made his affection every moment more valuable.

They walked on, without knowing in what direction. There was too much to be thought, and felt, and said, for attention to any other objects. She soon learnt that they were indebted for their present good understanding to the efforts of his aunt, who *did* call on him in her return through London, and there relate her journey to Longbourn, its motive, and the substance of her duel with Elizabeth; dwelling emphatically on the latter's failure to kill her when she had the chance, in the belief that such a show of weakness would forever turn Darcy's eye away. But, unluckily for her ladyship, its effect had been exactly contrariwise.

"It taught me to hope," said he, "as I had scarcely ever allowed myself to hope before. I knew enough of your disposition to be certain that, had you been absolutely, irrevocably decided against me, you would have beheaded Lady Catherine without a moment's hesitation."

Elizabeth coloured and laughed as she replied, "Yes, you know enough of my *temper* to believe me capable of *that*. After abusing you so abominably to your face, I could have no scruple in beheading any number of your relations."

"What did you say of me, that I did not deserve? For, though your accusations were ill-founded, formed on mistaken premises, my behaviour to you at the time had merited the severest reproof. It was unpardonable. I cannot think of it without abhorrence."

"We will not quarrel for the greater share of blame annexed to that evening," said Elizabeth. "The conduct of neither, if strictly examined, will be irreproachable; but since then, we have both, I hope, improved in civility."

"I cannot be so easily reconciled to myself. The recollection of what I then said, of my conduct, my manners, my expressions during the whole of it, is now, and has been many months, inexpressibly painful to me. Your reproof, so well applied, I shall never forget: 'had you behaved in a more gentlemanlike manner.' Those were your words. You know not, you can scarcely conceive, how they have tortured me— though it was some time, I confess, before I was reasonable enough to allow their justice."

"I was certainly very far from expecting them to make so strong an impression. I had not the smallest idea of their being ever felt in such a way."

Darcy mentioned his letter. "Did it make you think better of me?"

She explained what its effect on her had been, and how gradually all her former prejudices had been removed.

"I knew," said he, "that what I wrote must give you pain, but it was necessary. I hope you have destroyed the letter. There was one part especially, the opening of it, which I should dread your having the power of reading again. I can remember some expressions which might justly make you hate me."

"Think no more of the letter. The feelings of the person who wrote, and the person who received it, are now so widely different from what they were then, that every unpleasant circumstance attending it ought to be forgotten. You must learn some of my philosophy. Think only of the past as its remembrance gives you pleasure."

"With me, it is not so. Painful recollections will intrude which cannot, which ought not, to be repelled. I have been a selfish being all my life, in practice, though not in principle. As a child I was taught what was *right*, but I was not taught to correct my temper. I was given the best training, but left to use it in pride and conceit. Unfortunately an only son (for many years an only *child*), I was spoilt by my parents, who, though good themselves (my father, particularly, all that was benevolent and amiable), allowed, encouraged, almost taught me to be selfish and overbearing; to care for nothing beyond the defense of my estate; to think meanly of all the rest of the world. Such I was, from eight to eight-and-twenty; and such I might still have been but for you, dearest, loveliest Elizabeth! What do I not owe you! You taught me a lesson, hard indeed at first, but most advantageous. By you, I was properly humbled. I came to you without a doubt of my reception. You showed me how insufficient were all my pretensions to please a woman worthy of being pleased."

After walking several miles in a leisurely manner, and too busy to know anything about it, they found at last, on examining the precise position of the sun, that it was time to be at home.

"What could become of Mr. Bingley and Jane!" was a wonder which introduced the discussion of their affairs. Darcy was delighted with their engagement; his friend had given him the earliest information of it.

"I must ask whether you were surprised?" said Elizabeth.

"Not at all. When I went away, I felt that it would soon happen."

"That is to say, you had given your permission. I guessed as much." And though he exclaimed at the term, she found that it had been pretty much the case.

"On the evening before my going to London," said he, "I made a confession to him, which I believe I ought to have made long ago. I told him of all that had occurred to make my former interference in his affairs absurd and impertinent. His surprise was great. He had never had the slightest suspicion. I told him, moreover, that I believed myself mistaken in supposing, as I had done, that your sister was indifferent to him;

and as I could easily perceive that his attachment to her was unabated, I felt no doubt of their happiness together."

Elizabeth could not help smiling at his easy manner of directing his friend.

"Did you speak from your own observation," said she, "when you told him that my sister loved him, or merely from my information last spring?"

"From the former. I had narrowly observed her during the two visits which I had lately made here; and I was convinced of her affection."

"And your assurance of it, I suppose, carried immediate conviction to him."

"It did. Bingley is most unaffectedly modest. His timidity had prevented his depending on his own judgment in so anxious a case, but his reliance on mine made every thing easy. I was obliged to confess one thing, which for a time, and not unjustly, offended him. I could not allow myself to conceal that your sister had been in town three months last winter, that I had known it, and purposely kept it from him. He was angry. But his anger, I am persuaded, lasted no longer than he remained in any doubt of your sister's sentiments. He has heartily forgiven me now."

As they made for the house, Elizabeth and Darcy happened upon a herd of unmentionables, no more than a dozen in number, which had quartered itself in a garden not ten yards from the road. The creatures were crawling on their hands and knees, biting into ripe heads of cauliflower, which they had mistaken for stray brains. Elizabeth and Darcy laughed at the sight, and for a moment, resolved to keep walking—as the zombies had failed to take notice of them. But, sharing a glance and a smile, the pair realised they had stumbled onto their first opportunity to fight side by side.

And so they did.

"THE CREATURES WERE CRAWLING ON THEIR HANDS AND KNEES, BITING INTO RIPE HEADS OF CAULIFLOWER, WHICH THEY HAD MISTAKEN FOR STRAY BRAINS."

CHAPTER 59

"MY DEAR LIZZY, where can you have been walking to?" was a question which Elizabeth received from Jane as soon as she entered their room, and from all the others when they sat down to table. She had only to say in reply, that they had wandered about, till she was beyond her own knowledge. She coloured as she spoke; but neither that, nor anything else, awakened a suspicion of the truth.

The evening passed quietly. The acknowledged lovers talked and laughed, the unacknowledged were silent. Darcy was not of a disposition in which happiness overflows in mirth; and Elizabeth, agitated and confused, anticipated what would be felt in the family when her situation became known.

At night she opened her heart to Jane. Though suspicion was very far from Jane's general habits, she was absolutely incredulous here.

"You are joking, Lizzy. This cannot be! Engaged to Mr. Darcy! No, no, you shall not deceive me. I know it to be impossible."

"This is a wretched beginning indeed! My sole dependence was on you; and I am sure nobody else will believe me, if you do not. Yet, indeed, I am in earnest. I speak nothing but the truth. He still loves me, and we are engaged."

Jane looked at her doubtingly. "Oh, Lizzy! It cannot be. I know how much you dislike him."

"You know nothing of the matter. *That* is all to be forgot. Perhaps I did not always love him so well as I do now. But in such cases as these, a good memory is unpardonable. This is the last time I shall ever remember it myself."

Jane still looked all amazement. Elizabeth again, and more seriously assured her of its truth.

"Good Heaven! Can it be really so! Yet now I must believe you," cried Jane. "My dear, dear Lizzy, I would—I do congratulate you—but are you certain? Forgive the question—are you quite certain that you can be happy with him?"

"There can be no doubt of that. It is settled between us already, that we are to be the happiest couple in the world. But are you pleased, Jane? Shall you like to have such a brother?"

"Very, very much. Nothing could give either Bingley or myself more delight. But we considered it, we talked of it as impossible. And do you really love him quite well enough? Oh, Lizzy! Do anything rather than marry without affection. Are you quite sure that you feel what you ought to do?"

"Oh, yes! You will only think I feel *more* than I ought to do, when I tell you all."

"What do you mean?"

"Why, I must confess that I love him better than our games of Kiss Me Deer. I am afraid you will be angry."

"My dearest sister, now *be* serious. I want to talk very seriously. Let me know every thing that I am to know, without delay. Will you tell me how long you have loved him?"

"It has been coming on so gradually, that I hardly know when it began. But I believe I must date it from my first seeing the way his trousers clung to those most English parts."

Another entreaty that she would be serious, however, produced the desired effect; and she soon satisfied Jane by her solemn assurances of attachment. When convinced on that article, Miss Bennet had nothing further to wish.

"Now I am quite happy," said she, "for you will be as happy as myself. I always had a value for him. Were it for nothing but his love of you, I must always have esteemed him; but now, as Bingley's friend and your husband, there can be only Bingley and yourself more dear to me. But Lizzy, you have been very sly, very reserved with me. How little did you tell me of what passed at Pemberley and Lambton!"

Elizabeth told her the motives of her secrecy. But now she would no longer conceal from her Darcy's share in Lydia's marriage. All was acknowledged, and half the night spent in conversation.

"Good gracious!" cried Mrs. Bennet, as she stood at a window the next morning, "if that disagreeable Mr. Darcy is not coming here again with our dear Bingley! What can he mean by being so tiresome as to be always coming here? I had no notion but he would go a-shooting, or something or other, and not disturb us with his company. What shall we do with him? Lizzy, you must walk out with him again, that he may not be in Bingley's way."

Elizabeth could hardly help laughing at so convenient a proposal; yet was really vexed that her mother should be always giving him such an epithet.

As soon as they entered, Bingley looked at her so expressively, and shook hands with such warmth, as left no doubt of his good information; and he soon afterwards said aloud, "Mrs. Bennet, have you no more lanes hereabouts in which Lizzy may lose her way again to-day?"

"I advise Mr. Darcy, and Lizzy, and Kitty," said Mrs. Bennet, "to walk to the burning grounds of Oakham Mount this morning. It is a nice long walk, and Mr. Darcy has never seen the flames."

"It may do very well for the others," replied Mr. Bingley; "but I am sure it will be too much for Kitty. Won't it, Kitty?" Kitty owned that she had rather stay at home. Darcy professed a great curiosity to see the flames of the mount, and Elizabeth silently consented. As she went up stairs to get ready, Mrs. Bennet followed her, saying:

"I am quite sorry, Lizzy, that you should be forced to have that dis-agreeable man all to yourself. But I hope you will not mind it: it is all for Jane's sake, you know; and there is no occasion for talking to him, except just now and then. So, do not put yourself to inconvenience."

During their walk, it was resolved that Mr. Bennet's consent should be asked in the course of the evening. Elizabeth reserved to herself the application for her mother's. She could not determine how her mother would take it; sometimes doubting whether all his wealth and grandeur would be enough to overcome her abhorrence of the man.

In the evening, soon after Mr. Bennet withdrew to the library, she saw Mr. Darcy rise also and follow him, and her agitation on seeing it was extreme. She did not fear her father's opposition, but he was going to be made unhappy; and that it should be through her means—that *she*, his best warrior, should be distressing him by her choice, should be filling him with fears and regrets in disposing of her—was a wretched reflection, and she sat in misery till Mr. Darcy appeared again, when, looking at him, she was a little relieved by his smile. In a few minutes he approached the table where she was sitting with Kitty; and, while pretending to admire her work said in a whisper, "Go to your father, he wants you in the library." She was gone directly.

Her father was walking about the room, looking grave and anxious. "Lizzy," said he, "what are you doing? Are you out of your senses, to be accepting this man? Have not you always hated him?"

How earnestly did she then wish that her former opinions had been more reasonable, her expressions more moderate! It would have spared her from explanations and professions which it was exceedingly awkward to give; but they were now necessary, and she assured him, with some confusion, of her attachment to Mr. Darcy.

"He is rich, to be sure, and you may have more fine clothes and fine carriages than Jane. But will they make you happy?"

"Have you any other objection," said Elizabeth, "than your belief of my indifference, or the loss of my sword?"

"None at all. We all know him to be a proud, unpleasant sort of man; and Longbourn—indeed all of Hertfordshire would be the worse for losing you; but this would be nothing if you really liked him."

"I do, I do like him," she replied, with tears in her eyes, "I love him. Indeed he has no improper pride. He is perfectly amiable. You do not know what he really is; then pray do not pain me by speaking of him in such terms."

"Lizzy," said her father, "I have given him my consent. He is the kind of man, indeed, to whom I should never dare refuse anything, which he condescended to ask. I now give it to *you*, if you are resolved on having him. But let me advise you to think better of it. I know your disposition, Lizzy. I know that you could be neither happy nor respectable, unless you truly esteemed your husband; unless you looked up to him as a superior. Your extraordinary skill in the deadly arts would place you in the greatest danger in an unequal marriage. You could scarcely escape discredit and misery. My child, let me not have the grief of seeing you unable to respect your partner in life."

Elizabeth, still more affected, was earnest and solemn in her reply; and at length, by repeated assurances that Mr. Darcy was really the object of her choice, by explaining the gradual change which her estimation of him had undergone, relating her absolute certainty that his affection was not the work of a day, but had stood the test of many months' suspense, and enumerating with energy all his good qualities, she did conquer her father's incredulity, and reconcile him to the match.

"Well, my dear," said he, when she ceased speaking, "I have no more to say. If this be the case, he deserves you. I could not have parted with you, my Lizzy, to anyone less worthy."

To complete the favourable impression, she then told him what Mr. Darcy had voluntarily done for Lydia. He heard her with astonishment.

"This is an evening of wonders, indeed! And so, Darcy did every thing; gave the money, paid the fellow's debts, and rendered him lame! So much the better. It will save me a world of trouble and economy. Had it been your uncle's doing, I must and *would* have paid him; but these violent young lovers carry every thing their own way. I shall offer to pay him to-morrow; he will rant and storm about his love for you, and there will be an end of the matter."

He then recollected her embarrassment a few days before, on his reading Colonel Fitzwilliam's letter; and after laughing at her some time, allowed her at last to go—saying, as she quitted the room, "If any young men come for Mary or Kitty, send them in, for I am quite at leisure."

Elizabeth's mind was now relieved from a very heavy weight; and, after half an hour's meditation in her own room, she was able to join the others with tolerable composure. Every thing was too recent for gaiety, but the evening passed tranquilly away; there was no longer anything material to be dreaded, and the comfort of ease and familiarity would come in time.

When her mother went up to her dressing-room at night, she followed her, and made the important communication. Its effect was most extraordinary; for on first hearing it, Mrs. Bennet sat quite still, and unable to utter a syllable. Nor was it under many, many minutes that she could comprehend what she heard; she began at length to recover, to fidget about in her chair, get up, sit down again, wonder, and bless herself.

"Good gracious! Lord bless me! Only think! Dear me! Mr. Darcy! Who would have thought it! And is it really true? Oh! My sweetest Lizzy! How rich and how great you will be! What pin-money, what jewels, what carriages you will have! Jane's is nothing to it—nothing at all. I am so pleased—so happy. Such a charming man! So handsome! So tall! Oh, my dear Lizzy! Pray apologise for my having disliked him so much before. I hope he will overlook it. Dear, dear Lizzy. A house in town! Every thing that is charming! Three daughters married! Ten thousand a year, and very likely more! 'Tis as good as a Lord! And a special license. You must and shall be married by a special license. But my dearest love, tell me what dish Mr. Darcy is particularly fond of, that I may have it to-morrow."

This was a sad omen of what her mother's behaviour to the gentleman himself might be; and Elizabeth found that, though in the certain possession of his warmest affection, and secure of her relations' consent, there was still much to be wished for: peace in England, the approbation of Mr. Darcy's relatives, and a mother with whom she had anything whatsoever in common. But the morrow passed off much better than she expected; for Mrs. Bennet luckily stood in such awe of her intended son-in-law that she ventured not to speak to him, unless it was in her power to offer him more tea, or wipe crumbs from his trousers.

Elizabeth had the satisfaction of seeing her father taking pains to get acquainted with him; and Mr. Bennet soon assured her that he was rising every hour in his esteem.

"I admire all my three sons-in-law highly," said he. "Though Wickham," he said with a sly smile, "is perhaps my favourite, for he fidgets the least."

CHAPTER 60

ELIZABETH'S SPIRITS SOON rising to playfulness again, she wanted Mr. Darcy to account for his falling in love with her. "How could you begin?" said she. "I can comprehend your going on charmingly, when you had once made a beginning; but what could set you off in the first place?"

"I cannot fix on the hour, or the spot, or the look, or the words, which laid the foundation. It is too long ago. I was in the middle before I knew that I *had* begun."

"It could not have been my beauty, or my killing skills, for they are each quite equal to your own. As for my manners—my behaviour to *you* was at least always bordering on the uncivil, and I never spoke to you without wishing to give you pain. Now be sincere; did you admire me for my impertinence?"

"For the liveliness of your mind, I did."

"You may as well call it impertinence. It was very little else. The fact is, that you were sick of civility, of deference, of officious attention.

You were disgusted with the women who were always speaking, and looking, and thinking for *your* approbation alone. I roused, and interested you, because I was so unlike *them*. I knew the joy of standing over a vanquished foe; of painting my face and arms with their blood, yet warm, and screaming to the heavens—begging, nay daring, God to send me more enemies to kill. The gentle ladies who so assiduously courted you knew nothing of this joy, and therefore, could never offer you true happiness. There—I have saved you the trouble of accounting for it; and really, all things considered, I begin to think it perfectly reasonable. To be sure, you knew no actual good of me—but nobody thinks of *that* when they fall in love."

"Was there no good in your affectionate behaviour to Jane while she was ill at Netherfield?"

"Dearest Jane! Who could have done less for her? But make a virtue of it by all means. My good qualities are under your protection, and you are to exaggerate them as much as possible; and, in return, it belongs to me to find occasions for teasing and quarrelling with you as often as may be; and I shall begin directly by asking you what made you so unwilling to come to the point at last. What made you so shy of me, when you first called, and afterwards dined here? Why, especially, when you called, did you look as if you did not care about me?"

"Because you were grave and silent, and gave me no encouragement."

"But I was embarrassed."

"And so was I."

"You might have talked to me more when you came to dinner."

"A man who had felt less, might."

"How unlucky that you should have a reasonable answer to give, and that I should be so reasonable as to admit it! But I wonder how long you *would* have gone on, if you had been left to yourself. I wonder when you *would* have spoken, if I had not asked you!"

"Lady Catherine's unjustifiable endeavour to separate us, and your head from its perch, were the means of removing all my doubts. Your refusal to finish her had given me hope, and I was determined at once to know every thing."

"Lady Catherine has been of infinite use, which ought to make her happy, for she loves to be of use. But tell me, what did you come down to Netherfield for? Was it merely to ride to Longbourn and be embarrassed? Or had you intended any more serious consequence?"

"My real purpose was to see *you*, and to judge, if I could, whether I might ever hope to make you love me. My avowed one, or what I avowed to myself, was to see whether Jane was still partial to Bingley, and if she were, to make the confession to him which I have since made."

"Shall you ever have courage to announce to Lady Catherine what is to befall her?"

"Like you, I am not wanting courage; but I am wanting time, and if you will give me a sheet of paper, it shall be done directly."

"And if I had not a letter to write myself, I might sit by you and admire the evenness of your writing, as another young lady once did. But I have an aunt, too, who must not be longer neglected."

From an unwillingness to confess how her prospects with Mr. Darcy had been over-rated, Elizabeth had never answered Mrs. Gardiner's long letter; but now, having news which she knew would be most welcome, she was almost ashamed to find that her uncle and aunt had already lost three days of happiness, and immediately wrote as follows:

> I would have thanked you before, my dear aunt, as I ought to have done, for your long, kind, satisfactory, detail of particulars; but to say the truth, I was too cross to write. You supposed more than really existed. But now suppose as much as you choose; give a loose rein to your fancy, indulge your imagination in every possible flight which the subject will afford, and unless you believe me actually married, you cannot greatly err.

You must write again very soon, and praise him a great deal
more than you did in your last. I thank you, again and again, for
not going to the Lakes. How could I be so silly as to wish it!
Your idea of the phaeton and zombies is delightful. We will go
round the park every day, whipping them till their limbs fall off.
I am the happiest creature in the world. Perhaps other people
have said so before, but not one with such justice. I am happier
even than Jane; she only smiles, I laugh. Mr. Darcy sends you all
the love in the world that he can spare from me. You are all to
come to Pemberley at Christmas.

    YOURS, ETC.

The joy which Miss Darcy expressed on receiving similar information, was as sincere as her brother's in sending it. Four sides of paper were
insufficient to contain all her delight, and all her earnest desire of being
loved and trained by her sister.

CHAPTER 61

HAPPY FOR ALL HER MATERNAL feelings was the day on
which Mrs. Bennet got rid of her two most deserving daughters. With what delighted pride she afterwards visited the new Mrs.
Bingley, and talked of the new Mrs. Darcy, may be guessed. I wish I could
say, for the sake of her family, that the accomplishment of seeing so many
of her children happily settled made her a sensible, amiable, well-
informed woman for the rest of her life; though perhaps it was lucky for
her husband, who took such pleasure in teasing her, that she still was
occasionally nervous and invariably silly.

Mr. Bennet missed his second daughter exceedingly; his affection
for her drew him oftener from home than anything else could do. He

delighted in going to Pemberley, especially when he was least expected.

As Mr. Bennet had predicted, Hertfordshire also longed for the company of its two fiercest protectors. In the days and months proceeding, with only two of the younger Bennet sisters to ward them off, the zombies descended in ever greater numbers, until Colonel Forster returned with the militia and set the burning grounds afire once more.

Mr. Bingley and Jane remained at Netherfield only a twelvemonth. Jane could not bear to be so close to Longbourn as a married woman; for every unmentionable attack made her long for her sword. The darling wish of Mr. Bingley's sisters was then gratified; he bought an estate in a neighbouring county to Derbyshire, and Jane and Elizabeth, in addition to every other source of happiness, were within thirty miles of each other. Determined that they should keep their skills sharp, though His Majesty no longer required them to do so, their husbands built them a sparring cottage precisely between the two estates, in which the sisters met joyously and often.

Kitty, to her very material advantage, spent the chief of her time with her two elder sisters. In society so superior to what she had generally known, her improvement was great. She was not of so ungovernable a temper as Lydia; and, removed from the influence of Lydia's example, she became, by proper attention and management, less irritable, less ignorant, and less insipid. When she announced that she should like to return to Shaolin, for two or three years, in hopes of becoming as fine a warrior as Elizabeth, Mr. Darcy was only too happy to pay for the whole.

Mary was the only daughter who remained at home; both by the necessity of there being at least one warrior to protect Hertfordshire, and Mrs. Bennet's being quite unable to sit alone. As she was no longer mortified by comparisons between her sisters' beauty and her own, Mary began to mix more with the world, eventually taking up rather intimate, infrequent, friendships with several soldiers of the returned militia.

As for Wickham and Lydia, their characters suffered no revolution from the marriage of her sisters. In spite of every thing, they were not wholly without hope that Darcy might yet be prevailed on to make Wickham's fortune. The congratulatory letter which Elizabeth received from Lydia on her marriage, explained to her that, by his wife at least, if not by himself, such a hope was cherished. The letter was to this effect:

> MY DEAR LIZZY,
>
> I wish you joy. If you love Mr. Darcy half as well as I do my Dear, lame Wickham, you must be very happy. It is a great comfort to have you so rich, and when you have nothing else to do, I hope you will think of us. I am sure Wickham would like a parsonage very much when he is finished at seminary, and I do not think we shall have quite money enough to live upon without some help. Any parsonage would do, of about three or four hundred a year; but however, do not speak to Mr. Darcy about it, if you had rather not. I must be off, as my beloved has soiled himself anew.
>
> YOURS, ETC.

Elizabeth endeavoured in her answer to put an end to every entreaty and expectation of the kind. Such relief, however, as it was in her power to afford, in the form of fresh linens and salted beef, she frequently sent them. It had always been evident to her that such an income as theirs, under the direction of two persons so extravagant in their wants, and heedless of the future, must be very insufficient to their support; and whenever Wickham's studies required the purchase of a new hymnal for the lame, or lectern for the lame, or altar for the lame; either Jane or herself were sure of being applied to for some little assistance towards discharging their bills.

Though Darcy could never receive *him* at Pemberley, for Elizabeth's sake, he assisted him further in his profession. Lydia was occasionally a visitor there, when her husband was gone to minister in the asylums of London; and with the Bingleys they both of them frequently stayed so long, that even Bingley's good humour was overcome, and he proceeded so far as to *talk* of giving them a hint to be gone.

Miss Bingley was very deeply mortified by Darcy's marriage; but as she thought it advisable to retain the right of visiting at Pemberley, she dropt all her resentment; was fonder than ever of Georgiana, almost as attentive to Darcy as heretofore, and paid off every arrear of civility to Elizabeth.

Pemberley was now Georgiana's home; and the attachment of the sisters was exactly what Darcy had hoped to see. They were able to love each other even as well as they intended. Georgiana had the highest opinion in the world of Elizabeth; though at first she often listened with an astonishment bordering on alarm at her lively, sportive, manner of talking to her brother, and cringed at her tales of ripping the beating hearts from the chests of untold enemies. Through Elizabeth's instructions, Miss Darcy became a finer warrior than she ever dared hope—for beyond improving her musketry and bladesmanship, she also began to comprehend that a woman may take liberties with her husband which a brother will not always allow in a sister more than ten years younger than himself.

Lady Catherine was extremely indignant on the marriage of her nephew; and her reply to the letter which announced its arrangement came not in written form, but in the form of an attack on Pemberley by five-and-ten of her ladyship's ninjas. For some time after this was thwarted, all intercourse was at an end. But at length, by Elizabeth's persuasion, he was prevailed on to seek a reconciliation; and, after a little further resistance on the part of his aunt, her resentment gave way, either to her affection for him, or her curiosity to see how his wife conducted herself; and she condescended to wait on them at Pemberley, in spite of that pollution which its woods had received, not merely from the presence of such a mistress, but the visits of her uncle and aunt—with whom Darcy and Elizabeth were always on the most intimate terms.

Like so many before it, her ladyship's serum proved folly, for while it slowed some effects of the strange plague, it was helpless to stop them all. England remained in the shadow of Satan. The dead continued to claw their way through crypt and coffin alike, feasting on British brains. Victories were celebrated, defeats lamented. And the sisters Bennet—servants of His Majesty, protectors of Hertfordshire, beholders of the secrets of Shaolin, and brides of death—were now, three of them, brides of man, their swords quieted by that only force more powerful than any warrior.

THE END.

Pride and Prejudice and Zombies
A Reader's Discussion Guide

Pride and Prejudice and Zombies is a rich, multilayered study of love, war, and the supernatural. We hope these questions will deepen your appreciation and enjoyment of this towering work of classical zombie literature.

1. Many critics have addressed the dual nature of Elizabeth's personality. On one hand, she can be a savage, remorseless killer, as we see in her vanquishing of Lady Catherine's ninjas. On the other hand, she can be tender and merciful, as in her relationships with Jane, Charlotte, and the young bucks that roam her family's estate. In your opinion, which of these "halves" best represents the *real* Elizabeth at the beginning—and *end* of the novel?

2. Is Mr. Collins merely too fat and stupid to notice his wife's gradual transformation into a zombie, or could there be another explanation for his failure to acknowledge the problem? If so, what might that explanation be? How might his occupation (as a pastor) relate to his denial of the obvious, or his decision to hang himself?

3. The strange plague has been the scourge of England for "five-and-fifty years." Why do the English stay and fight, rather than retreat to the safety of eastern Europe or Africa?

4. Who receives the sorrier fate: Wickham, left paralyzed in a seminary for the lame, forever soiling himself and studying ankle-high books of scripture? Or Lydia, removed from her family, married to an invalid, and childless, yet forever changing filthy diapers?

5. Due to her fierce independence, devotion to exercise, and penchant for boots, some critics have called Elizabeth Bennet "the first literary lesbian." Do you think the authors intended her to be gay? And if so, how would this Sapphic twist serve to explain her relationships with Darcy, Jane, Charlotte, Lady Catherine, and Wickham?

6. Some critics have suggested that the zombies represent the authors' views toward marriage—an endless curse that sucks the life out of you and just won't die. Do you agree, or do you have another opinion about the symbolism of the unmentionables?

7. Does Mrs. Bennet have a single redeeming quality?

8. Vomit plays an important role in *Pride and Prejudice and Zombies*. Mrs. Bennet frequently vomits when she's nervous, coachmen vomit in disgust when they witness zombies feasting on corpses, even the steady Elizabeth can't help but vomit at the sight of Charlotte lapping up her own bloody pus. Do the authors mean for this regurgitation to symbolize something greater, or is it a cheap device to get laughs?

9. Is Lady Catherine's objection to Elizabeth (as a bride for her nephew) merely a matter of Elizabeth's inferior wealth and rank? Or could there be another explanation? Could she be intimidated by Elizabeth's fighting skills? Is she herself secretly in love with Darcy? Or is she bitter about the shortcomings of her own daughter?

10. Some scholars believe that the zombies were a last-minute addition to the novel, requested by the publisher in a shameless attempt to boost sales. Others argue that the hordes of living dead are integral to Jane Austen's plot and social commentary. What do you think? Can you imagine what this novel might be like without the violent zombie mayhem?